DISCARDED

# THE NEVER GAME

Nineteen-year-old Sophie is abducted one summer afternoon in Silicon Valley. She wakes up to find herself trapped inside a dark room, surrounded by five objects. If she uses them wisely, she will escape her prison. Otherwise she will die. Sophie's distraught father calls in the one man who can help find her: unique investigator Colter Shaw. Raised in the wilderness by survivalist parents, he's an expert tracker with a forensic mind trained to solve the most challenging cases. What seems at first like a straightforward operation quickly thrusts him into the dark heart of America's tech hub and cutthroat billion-dollar video gaming industry. And when more people go missing, the whole case gets turned on its head; because this killer isn't following the rules, he's changing them — one murder at a time . . .

JEFFERY DEAVER

# THE
# NEVER
# GAME

*Complete and Unabridged*

# CHARNWOOD
*Leicester*

First published in Great Britain in 2019 by
HarperCollins*Publishers*
London

First Charnwood Edition
published 2020
by arrangement with
HarperCollins*Publishers*
London

The moral right of the author has been asserted

*A catalogue record for this book is available from the British Library.*

ISBN 978-1-4448-4544-0

Published by
Ulverscroft Limited
Anstey, Leicestershire

Set by Words & Graphics Ltd.
Anstey, Leicestershire
Printed and bound in Great Britain by
T. J. International Ltd., Padstow, Cornwall

This book is printed on acid-free paper

To M and P

Gaming disorder is defined . . . as a pattern of gaming behavior ['digital-gaming' or 'video-gaming') characterized by impaired control over gaming, increasing priority given to gaming over other activities to the extent that gaming takes precedence over other interests and daily activities, and continuation or escalation of gaming despite the occurrence of negative consequences.

— THE WORLD HEALTH ORGANIZATION

Video games are bad for you? That's what they said about rock 'n' roll.

— NINTENDO GAME DESIGNER SHIGERU MIYAMOTO

# LEVEL THREE:

## THE
## SINKING
## SHIP

### Sunday, June 9

Sprinting toward the sea, Colter Shaw eyed the craft closely.

The forty-foot derelict fishing vessel, decades old, was going down by the stern, already three-fourths submerged.

Shaw saw no doors into the cabin; there would be only one and it was now underwater. In the aft part of the superstructure, still above sea level, was a window facing onto the bow. The opening was large enough to climb through but it appeared sealed. He'd dive for the door.

He paused, reflecting: Did he need to?

Shaw looked for the rope mooring the boat to the pier; maybe he could take up slack and keep the ship from going under.

There was no rope; the boat was anchored, which meant it was free to descend thirty feet to the floor of the Pacific Ocean.

And, if the woman was inside, take her with it to a cold, murky grave.

As he ran onto the slippery dock, avoiding the

most rotten pieces, he stripped off his blood-stained shirt, then his shoes and socks.

A powerful swell struck the ship and it shuddered and sank a few more inches into the gray, indifferent water.

He shouted, 'Elizabeth?'

No response.

Shaw assessed: there was a sixty percent chance she was on board. Fifty percent chance she was alive after hours in the waterlogged cabin.

Whatever the percentages, there was no debate about what came next. He stuck an arm beneath the surface and judged the temperature to be about forty degrees. He'd have thirty minutes until he passed out from hypothermia.

Let's start the clock, he thought.

And plunges in.

★ ★ ★

An ocean isn't liquid. It's flowing stone. Crushing.

Sly too.

Shaw's intention was to wrestle open the door to the cabin, then swim out with Elizabeth Chabelle. The water had a different idea. The minute he surfaced for breath he was tossed toward one of the oak pilings, from which danced lacy flora, delicate thin green hairs. He held up a hand to brace himself as he was flung toward the wood. His palm slid off the slimy surface and his head struck the post. A burst of yellow light filled his vision.

Another wave lifted and flung him toward the pier once more. This time he was just able to avoid a rusty spike. Rather than fighting the current to return to the boat — about eight feet away — he waited for the outflow that would carry him to the vessel. An upward swell took him and this time he gigged his shoulder on the spike. It stung sharply. There'd be blood.

Sharks here?

*Never borrow trouble . . .*

The water receded. He kicked into the flow, raised his head, filled his lungs and dove, swimming hard for the door. The salty water burned his eyes but he kept them wide; the sun was low and it was dark here. He spotted what he sought, gripped the metal handle and twisted. The handle moved back and forth yet the door wouldn't open.

To the surface, more air. Back under again, holding himself down with the latch in his left hand, and feeling for other locks or securing fixtures with his right.

The shock and pain of the initial plunge had worn off, but he was shivering hard.

Ashton Shaw had taught his children how to prepare for cold-water survival — dry suit, number one. Wet suit, second choice. Two caps — heat loss is greatest through the skull, even with hair as thick as Shaw's blond locks. Ignore extremities; you don't lose heat through fingers or toes. Without protective clothing, the only solution is to get the hell out as fast as you can before hypothermia confuses, numbs and kills.

Twenty-five minutes left.

Another attempt to wrench open the door to the cabin. Another failure.

He thought of the windshield overlooking the bow deck. The only way to get her out.

Shaw stroked toward the shore and dove, seizing a rock big enough to shatter glass but not so heavy it would pull him down.

Kicking hard, rhythmically, timing his efforts to the waves, he returned to the boat, whose name he noticed was *Seas the Day*.

Shaw managed to climb the forty-five-degree incline to the bow and perch on the upward-tilting front of the cabin, resting against the murky four-by-three-foot window.

He peered inside but spotted no sign of the thirty-two-year-old brunette. He noted that the forward part of the cabin was empty. There was a bulkhead halfway toward the stern, with a door in the middle of it and a window about head height, the glass missing. If she were here, she'd be on the other side — the one now largely filled with water.

He lifted the rock, sharp end forward, and swung it against the glass, again and again.

He learned that whoever had made the vessel had fortified the forward window against wind and wave and hail. The stone didn't even chip the surface.

And Colter Shaw learned something else too.

Elizabeth Chabelle was in fact alive.

She'd heard the banging and her pale, pretty face, ringed with stringy brown hair, appeared in the window of the doorway between the two sections of the cabin.

4

Chabelle screamed 'Help me!' so loudly that Shaw could hear her clearly through the thick glass separating them.

'Elizabeth!' he shouted. 'There's help coming. Stay out of the water.'

He knew the help he promised couldn't possibly arrive until after the ship was on the bottom. He was her only hope.

It might be possible for someone else to fit through the broken window inside and climb into the forward, and drier, half of the cabin.

But not Elizabeth Chabelle.

Her kidnapper had, by design or accident, chosen to abduct a woman who was seven and a half months pregnant; she couldn't possibly fit through the frame.

Chabelle disappeared to find a perch somewhere out of the freezing water and Colter Shaw lifted the rock to begin pounding on the windshield once more.

# LEVEL ONE:

# THE ABANDONED FACTORY

Friday, June 7, Two Days Earlier

# 1

He asked the woman to repeat herself.

'That thing they throw,' she said. 'With the burning rag in it?'

'They throw?'

'Like at riots? A bottle. You see 'em on TV.'

Colter Shaw said, 'A Molotov cocktail.'

'Yeah, yeah,' Carole was saying. 'I think he had one.'

'Was it burning? The rag part?'

'No. But, you know . . . '

Carole's voice was raspy, though she wasn't presently a smoker that Shaw had seen or smelled. She was draped with a green dress of limp cloth. Her natural expression seemed to be one of concern yet this morning it was more troubled than usual. 'He was over there.' She pointed.

The Oak View RV park, one of the scruffier that Shaw had stayed at, was ringed with trees, mostly scrub oak and pine, some dead, all dry. And thick. Hard to see 'over there.'

'You called the police?'

A pause. 'No, if it wasn't a . . . What again?'

'Molotov cocktail.'

'If he didn't have one, it'd be embarrassing. And I call the cops enough, for stuff here.'

Shaw knew dozens of RV park owners around the country. Mostly couples, as it's a good gig for middle-aged marrieds. If there's just a single manager, like Carole, it was usually a she, and she was usually a widow. They tend to dial 911 for camp disputes more than their late husbands, men who often went about armed.

'On the other hand,' she continued, 'fire. Here. You know.'

California was a tinderbox, as anybody who watched the news knew. You think of state parks and suburbs and agricultural fields; cities, though, weren't immune to nature's conflagrations. Shaw believed that one of the worst brush fires in the history of the state had been in Oakland, very near where they were now standing.

'Sometimes, I kick somebody out, they say they'll come back and get even.' She added with astonishment, 'Even when I caught them stealing forty amps when they paid for twenty. Some people. Really.'

He asked, 'And you want me to . . . ?'

'I don't know, Mr. Shaw. Just take a look. Could you take a look? Please?'

Shaw squinted through the flora and saw, maybe, motion that wasn't from the breeze. A person walking slowly? And if so did the pace mean that he was moving tactically — that is, with some mischief in mind?

Carole's eyes were on Shaw, regarding him in a particular way. This happened with some frequency. He was a civilian, never said he was anything else. But he had cop fiber.

Shaw circled to the front of the park and walked on the cracked and uneven sidewalk, then on the grassy shoulder of the unbusy road in this unbusy corner of the city.

Yes, there was a man, in dark jacket, blue jeans and black stocking cap, some twenty yards ahead. He wore boots that could be helpful on a hike through brush and equally helpful to stomp an opponent. And, yes, either he was armed with a gas bomb or he was holding a Corona and a napkin in the same hand. Early for a beer some places; not in this part of Oakland.

Shaw slipped off the shoulder into the foliage to his right and walked more quickly, though with care to stay silent. The needles that had pitched from branch to ground in droves over the past several seasons made stealth easy.

Whoever this might be, vengeful lodger or not, he was well past Carole's cabin. So she wasn't at personal risk. But Shaw wasn't giving the guy a pass just yet.

This felt wrong.

Now the fellow was approaching the part of the RV camp where Shaw's Winnebago was parked, among many other RVs.

Shaw had more than a passing interest in Molotov cocktails. Several years ago, he'd been searching for a fugitive on the lam for an oil scam in Oklahoma when somebody pitched a gas bomb through the windshield of his camper. The craft burned to the rims in twenty minutes, personal effects saved in the nick. Shaw still carried a distinct and unpleasant scent memory of the air surrounding the metal carcass.

The percentage likelihood that Shaw would be attacked by two Russian-inspired weapons in one lifetime, let alone within several years, had to be pretty small. Shaw put it at five percent. A figure made smaller yet by the fact that he had come to the Oakland/Berkeley area on personal business, not to ruin a fugitive's life. And while Shaw had committed a transgression yesterday, the remedy for that offense would've been a verbal lashing, a confrontation with a beefy security guard or, at worst, the police. Not a firebomb.

Shaw was now only ten yards behind the man, who was scanning the area — looking into the trailer park as well as up and down the road and at several abandoned buildings across it.

The man was trim, white, with a clean-shaven face. He was about five-eight, Shaw estimated. The man's facial skin was pocked. Under the cap, his brown hair seemed to be cut short. There was a rodent-like quality to his appearance and his movements. In the man's posture Shaw read ex-military. Shaw himself was not, though he had friends and acquaintances who were, and he had spent a portion of his youth in quasi-military training, quizzed regularly on the updated *U.S. Army Survival Manual FM 21-76*.

And the man was indeed holding a Molotov cocktail. The napkin was stuffed into the neck of the bottle and Shaw could smell gasoline.

Shaw was familiar with revolver, semiautomatic pistol, semiautomatic rifle, bolt-action rifle, shotgun, bow and arrow and slingshot. And he had more than a passing interest in blades. He now withdrew from his pocket the weapon he used most frequently: his mobile, presently an iPhone. He punched some keys and, when the police and fire emergency dispatcher answered, whispered his location and what he was looking at. Then he hung up. He typed a few more commands and slipped the cell into the breast pocket of his dark plaid sport coat. He thought, with chagrin, about his transgression yesterday and wondered if the call would somehow allow the authorities to identify and collar him. This seemed unlikely.

Shaw had decided to wait for the arrival of the pros. Which is when a cigarette lighter appeared in the man's hand with no cigarette to accompany it.

That settled the matter.

Shaw stepped from the bushes and closed the distance. 'Morning.'

The man turned quickly, crouching. Shaw noted that he didn't reach for his belt or inside pocket. This might have been because he didn't want to drop the gas bomb — or because he wasn't armed. Or because he was a pro and knew exactly where his gun was and how many seconds it would take to draw and aim and fire.

Narrow eyes, set in a narrow face, looked Shaw over for guns and then for less weaponly threats. He took in the black jeans, black Ecco shoes, gray-striped shirt and the jacket. Short-cut blond hair lying close to his head. Rodent would have thought 'cop,' yet the moment for a badge to appear and an official voice to ask for ID or some such had come and gone. He had concluded that Shaw was civilian. And not one to be taken lightly. Shaw was about one-eighty, just shy of six feet, and broad, with strappy muscle. A small scar on cheek, a larger one on neck. He didn't run as a hobby but he rock-climbed and had been a champion wrestler in college. He was in scrapping shape. His eyes held Rodent's, as if tethered.

'Hey there.' A tenor voice, taut like a stretched fence wire. Midwest, maybe from Minnesota.

Shaw glanced down at the bottle.

'Could be pee, not gas, don'tcha know.' The man's smile was as tight as the timbre of his voice. And it was a lie.

Wondering if this'd turn into a fight. Last thing Shaw wanted. He hadn't hit anybody for a long time. Didn't like it. Liked getting hit even less.

'What's that about?' Shaw nodded at the bottle in the man's hand.

'Who are you?'

'A tourist.'

'Tourist.' The man debated, eyes rising and falling. 'I live up the street. There's some rats in an abandoned lot next to me. I was going to burn them out.'

'California? The driest June in ten years?'

Shaw had made that up but who'd know?

Not that it mattered. There was no lot and there were no rats, though the fact that the man had brought it up suggested he might have burned rats alive in the past. This where dislike joined caution.

*Never let an animal suffer . . .*

Then Shaw was looking over the man's shoulder — toward the spot he'd been headed for. A vacant lot, true, though it was next to an old commercial building. Not the imaginary

14

vacant lot next to the man's imaginary home.

The man's eyes narrowed further, reacting to the bleat of the approaching police car.

'Really?' Rodent grimaced, meaning: You *had* to call it in? He muttered something else too.

Shaw said, 'Set it down. Now.'

The man didn't. He calmly lit the gasoline-soaked rag, which churned with fire, and like a pitcher aiming for a strike, eyed Shaw keenly and flung the bomb his way.

# 2

Molotov cocktails don't blow up — there's not enough oxygen inside a sealed bottle. The burning rag fuse ignites the spreading gas when the glass shatters.

Which this one did, efficiently and with modest spectacle.

A silent fireball rose about four feet in the air.

Shaw dodged the risk of singe and Carole ran, screaming, to her cabin. Shaw debated pursuit, but the crescent of grass on the shoulder was burning crisply and getting slowly closer to tall shrubs. He vaulted the chain-link, sprinted to his RV and retrieved one of the extinguishers. He returned, pulled the pin and blasted a whoosh of white chemical on the fire, taming it.

'Oh my God. Are you okay, Mr. Shaw?' Carole was plodding up, carrying an extinguisher of her own, a smaller, one-hand canister. Hers wasn't really necessary, yet she too pulled the grenade pin and let fly, because, of course, it's always fun. Especially when the blaze is nearly out.

After a minute or two, Shaw bent down and, with his palm, touched every square inch of the scorch, as he'd learned years ago.

*Never leave a campfire without patting the ash.*

A pointless glance after Rodent. He'd vanished.

A patrol car braked to a stop. Oakland PD. A

large black officer, with a glistening, shaved head, climbed out, holding a fire extinguisher of his own. Of the three, his was the smallest. He surveyed the embers and the char and replaced the red tank under his front passenger seat.

Officer L. Addison, according to the name badge, turned to Shaw. The six-foot-five cop might get confessions just by walking up to a suspect and leaning down.

'You were the one called?' Addison asked.

'I did.' Shaw explained that the person who'd thrown the cocktail had just run off. 'That way.' He gestured down the weedy street, handfuls of trash every few yards. 'He's probably not too far away.'

The cop asked what had happened.

Shaw told him. Carole supplemented, with the somewhat gratuitous addendum about the difficulty of being a widow running a business by herself. 'People take advantage. I push back. I have to. You would. Sometimes they threaten you.' Shaw noted she'd glanced at Addison's left hand, where no jewelry resided.

Addison cocked his head toward the Motorola mounted on his shoulder and gave Central a summary, with the description from Shaw. It had been quite detailed but he'd left out the rodent-like aspect, that being largely a matter of opinion.

Addison's eyes turned back to Shaw. 'Could I see some ID?'

There are conflicting theories about what to do when the law asks for ID and you're not a suspect. This was a question Shaw often confronted, since he frequently found himself at crime scenes and places where investigations were under way. You generally didn't have to show anybody anything. In that case, you'd have to be prepared to endure the consequences of your lack of cooperation. Time is one of the world's most valuable commodities, and being pissy with cops guarantees you're going to lose big chunks of it.

His hesitation at the moment, though, was not on principle but because he was worried that his motorbike's license had been spotted at the site of yesterday's transgression. His name might therefore be in the system.

Then he recalled that they'd know him already; he'd called 911 from his personal phone, not a burner. So Shaw handed over the license.

Addison took a picture of it with his phone and uploaded the details somewhere.

Shaw noted that he didn't do the same with Carole, even though it was her trailer court that had tangentially been involved. Some minor profiling there, Shaw reflected: stranger in town versus a local. This he kept to himself.

Addison looked at the results. He eyed Shaw closely.

A reckoning for yesterday's transgression? Shaw now chose to call it what it was: theft. There's no escape in euphemism.

Apparently the gods of justice were not a posse after him today. Addison handed the license back. 'Did you recognize him?' he asked Carole.

'No, sir, but it's hard to keep track. We get a

lot of people here. Lowest rates in the area.'

'Did he throw the bottle at you, Mr. Shaw?'

'Toward. A diversion, not assault. So he could get away.'

This gave the officer a moment's pause.

Carole blurted: 'I looked it up online. Molotov secretly worked for Putin.'

Both men looked at her quizzically. Then Shaw continued with the officer: 'And to burn the evidence. Prints and DNA on the glass.'

Addison remained thoughtful. He was the sort, common among police, whose lack of body language speaks volumes. He'd be processing why Shaw had considered forensics.

The officer said, 'If he wasn't here to cause you any problem, ma'am, what was he here about, you think?'

Before Carole answered, Shaw said, 'That.' He pointed across the street to the vacant lot he'd noted earlier.

The trio walked toward it.

The trailer camp was in a scruffy commercial neighborhood, off Route 24, where tourists could stage before a trip to steep Grizzly Peak or neighboring Berkeley. This trash-filled, weedy lot was separated from the property behind it by an old wooden fence about eight feet tall. Local artists had used it as a canvas for some very talented artwork: portraits of Martin Luther King, Jr., Malcolm X and two other men Shaw didn't recognize. As the three got closer, Shaw saw the names printed below the pictures: Bobby Seale and Huey P. Newton, who'd been connected with the Black Panther Party. Shaw remembered cold nights in his television-free childhood home. Ashton would read to Colter and his siblings, mostly American history. Much of it about alternative forms of governance. The Black Panthers had figured in several lectures.

'So,' Carole said, her mouth twisted in distaste. 'A hate crime. Terrible.' She added, with a nod to the paintings, 'I called the city, told them they should preserve it somehow. They never called back.'

Addison's radio crackled. Shaw could hear the transmission: a unit had cruised the streets nearby and seen no one fitting the description of the arsonist.

Shaw said, 'I got a video.'

'You did?'

'After I called nine-one-one I put the phone in my pocket.' He touched the breast pocket, on the left side of his jacket. 'It was recording the whole time.'

'Is it recording now?'

'It is.'

'Would you shut it off?' Addison asked this in a way that really meant: Shut it off. Without a question mark.

Shaw did. Then: 'I'll send you a screenshot.'

'Okay.'

Shaw clicked the shot, got Addison's mobile number and sent the image his way. The men were four feet apart but Shaw imagined the electrons' journey took them halfway around the world.

The officer's phone chimed; he didn't bother to look at the screenshot. He gave Carole his card, one to Shaw as well. Shaw had quite the collection of cops' cards; he thought it amusing that police had business cards like advertising executives and hedge fund managers.

After Addison left, Carole said, 'They're not going to do winkety, are they?'

'No.'

'Well, thanks for looking into it, Mr. Shaw. I'd've felt purely horrid you'd gotten burned.'

'Not a worry.'

Carole returned to the cabin and Shaw to his Winnebago. He was reflecting on one aspect of the encounter he hadn't shared with Officer Addison. After the exasperated 'Really?' in reference to the 911 call, Rodent's comment might have been 'Why'd you do that shit?'

It was also possible — more than fifty percent — that he'd said, 'Why'd you do that, Shaw?'

Which, if that had in fact happened, meant Rodent knew him or knew about him.

And that, of course, would put a whole new spin on the matter.

# 3

Inside the Winnebago, Shaw hung his sport coat on a hook and walked to a small cupboard in the kitchen. He opened it and removed two things. The first was his compact Glock .380 pistol, which he kept hidden behind a row of spices, largely McCormick brand. The weapon was in a gray plastic Blackhawk holster. This he clipped inside his belt.

The second thing he removed was a thick 11-by-14-inch envelope, secreted on the shelf below where he kept the gun, behind condiment bottles. Worcestershire, teriyaki and a half dozen vinegars ranging from Heinz to the exotic.

He glanced outside.

No sign of Rodent. As he'd expected. Still, sometimes being armed never hurt.

He walked to the stove and boiled water and brewed a ceramic mug of coffee with a single-cup filter cone. He'd selected one of his favorites. Daterra, from Brazil. He shocked the beverage with a splash of milk.

Sitting at the banquette, he looked at the envelope, on which were the words *Graded Exams 5/25*, in perfect, scripty handwriting, smaller even than Shaw's.

The flap was not sealed, just affixed with a flexible metal flange, which he bent open, and then he extracted from the envelope a rubber band-bound stack of sheets, close to four hundred of them.

Noting that his heart thudded from double time to triple as he stared at the pile.

These pages were the spoils of the theft Shaw had committed yesterday.

What he hoped they contained was the answer to the question that had dogged him for a decade and a half.

A sip of coffee. He began to flip through the contents.

The sheets seemed to be a random collection of musings historical, philosophical, medical and scientific, maps, photos, copies of receipts. The author's script was the same as on the front of the envelope: precise and perfectly even, as if a ruler had been used as a guide. The words were formed in a delicate combination of cursive and block printing.

Similar to how Colter Shaw wrote.

He opened to a page at random. Began to read.

*Fifteen miles northwest of Macon on Squirrel Level Road, Holy Brethren Church. Should have a talk with minister. Good man. Rev. Harley Combs. Smart and keeps quiet when he should.*

Shaw read more passages, then stopped. A couple sips of coffee, thoughts of breakfast. Then: Go on, he chided himself. You started this, prepared to accept where it would lead. So keep going.

His mobile hummed. He glanced at the caller ID, shamefully pleased that the distraction took him away from the stolen documents.

'Teddy.'

'Colt. Where am I finding you?' A baritone grumble.

'Still the Bay Area.'

'Any luck?'

'Some. Maybe. Everything okay at home?' The Bruins were watching his property in Florida, which abutted theirs.

'Peachy.' Not a word you hear often from a career Marine officer. Teddy Bruin and his wife, Velma, also a veteran, wore their contradictions proudly. He could picture them clearly, most likely sitting at that moment where they often sat, on the porch facing the hundred-acre lake in northern Florida. Teddy was six-two, two hundred and fifty pounds. His reddish hair was a darker version of his freckled, ruddy skin. He'd be in khaki slacks or shorts because he owned no other shade. The shirt would have flowers on it. Velma was less than half his weight, though tall herself. She'd be in jeans and work shirt, and of the two she had the cleverer tattoos.

A dog barked in the background. That would be Chase, their Rottweiler. Shaw had spent many afternoons on hikes with the solid, good-natured animal.

'We found a job close to you. Don't know if you're interested. Vel's got the details. She's coming. Ah, here.'

'Colter.' Unlike Teddy's, Velma's voice was softly pouring water. Shaw had told her she should record audiobooks for kids. Her voice would be like Ambien, send them right to sleep.

'Algo found a hit. That girl sniffs like a bluetick hound. What a nose.'

Velma had decided that the computer bot she used (Algo, as in 'algorithm') searching the internet for potential jobs for Shaw was a female. And canine as well, it seemed.

'Missing girl in Silicon Valley,' she added.

'Tipline?'

Phone numbers were often set up by law enforcement or by private groups, like Crime Stoppers, so that someone, usually with inside knowledge, could call anonymously with information that might lead to a suspect. Tiplines were also called dime lines, as in 'diming out the perp,' or snitch lines.

Shaw had pursued tipline jobs from time to time over the years — if the crime was particularly heinous or the victims' families particularly upset. He generally avoided them because of the bureaucracy and formalities involved. Tiplines also tended to attract the troublesome.

'No. Offeror's her father.' Velma added, 'Ten thousand. Not much. But his notice was . . . heartfelt. He's one desperate fellow.'

Teddy and Velma had been helping Shaw in his reward operation for years; they knew desperate by instinct.

'How old's the daughter?'

'Nineteen. Student.'

The phone in Florida was on SPEAKER, and Teddy's raspy voice said, 'We checked the news. No stories about police involvement. Her name didn't show up at all, except for the reward. So, no foul play.'

The term was right out of Sherlock Holmes yet law enforcement around the country used it frequently. The phrase was a necessary marker in deciding how police would approach a missing-person situation. With an older teen and no evidence of abduction, the cops wouldn't jump on board as they would with an obvious kidnapping. For the time being, they'd assume she was a runaway.

Her disappearance, of course, could be both. More than a few young people had been seduced away from home willingly only to find that the seducer wasn't exactly who they thought.

Or her fate might be purely accidental, her body floating in the cold, notoriously unpredictable waters of the Pacific Ocean or in a car at the bottom of a ravine a hundred feet below sidewinding Highway 1.

Shaw debated. His eyes were on the four hundred-odd sheets. 'I'll go meet with the father. What's her name?'

'Sophie Mulliner. He's Frank.'

'Mother?'

'No indication.' Velma added, 'I'll send you the particulars.'

He then asked, 'Any mail?'

She said, 'Bills. Which I paid. Buncha coupons. Victoria's Secret catalog.'

Shaw had bought Margot a present two years ago; Victoria had decided his address was no secret and delivered it unto her mailing-list minions. He hadn't thought about Margot for . . . Had it been a month? Maybe a couple of weeks. He said, 'Pitch it.'

'Can I keep it?' Teddy asked.

A thud, and laughter. Another thud.

Shaw thanked them and disconnected.

He rebanded the sheaf of pages. One more look outside. No Rodent.

Colter Shaw lifted open his laptop and read Velma's email. He pulled up a map to see how long it would take to get to Silicon Valley.

# 4

As it turned out, by the estimation of some, Colter Shaw was actually in Silicon Valley at that very moment.

He'd learned that a number of people considered North Oakland and Berkeley to be within the nebulous boundaries of the mythical place. To them, Silicon Valley — apparently, 'SV' to those in the know — embraced a wide swath from Berkeley on the east and San Francisco on the west all the way south to San Jose.

The definition was largely, Shaw gathered, dependent on whether a company or individual wanted to be in Silicon Valley. And most everyone did.

The loyalists, it seemed, defined the place as west of the Bay only, the epicenter being Stanford University in Palo Alto. The reward offeror's home was near the school, in Mountain View. Shaw secured the vehicle's interior for the drive, made sure his dirt bike was affixed to its frame on the rear and disconnected the hookups.

He stopped by the cabin to break the news to Carole and a half hour later was cruising along the wide 280 freeway, with glimpses of the suburbia of Silicon Valley through the trees to his left and the lush hills of the Rancho Corral de Tierra and the placid Crystal Springs Reservoir to the west.

This area was new to him. Shaw was born in

Berkeley — twenty miles away — but he retained only tatters of memories from back then. When Colter was four, Ashton had moved the family to a huge spread a hundred miles east of Fresno, in the Sierra Nevada foothills — Ashton dubbed the property the 'Compound' because he thought it sounded more forbidding than 'Ranch' or 'Farm.'

At the GPS guide's command, Shaw pulled off the freeway and made his way to the Westwinds RV Center, located in Los Altos Hills. He checked in. The soft-spoken manager was about sixty, trim, a former Navy man or Merchant Marine, if the tattoo of the anchor signified anything. He handed Shaw a map and, with a mechanical pencil, meticulously drew a line from the office to his hookup. Shaw's space would be on Google Way, accessed via Yahoo Lane and PARC Road. The name of the last avenue Shaw didn't get. He assumed it was computer-related.

He found the spot, plugged in and, with his black leather computer bag over his shoulder, returned to the office, where he summoned an Uber to take him to the small Avis rental outfit in downtown Mountain View. He picked up a sedan, requesting any full-sized that was black or navy blue, his preferred shades. In his decade of seeking rewards he'd never once misrepresented himself as a police officer, but occasionally he let the impression stand. Driving a vehicle that might be taken for a detective's undercover car occasionally loosened tongues.

On his mission over the past couple of days, Shaw had ridden his Yamaha dirt bike between

Carole's RV park and Berkeley. He would ride the bike any chance he got, though only on personal business or, of course, for the joy of it. On a job he always rented a sedan or, if the terrain required, an SUV. Driving a rattling motorbike when meeting offerors, witnesses or the police would raise concerns about how professional he was. And while a thirty-foot RV was fine for highways, it was too cumbersome for tooling about congested neighborhoods.

He set the GPS to the reward offeror's house in Mountain View and pulled into the busy suburban traffic.

So, this was the heart of SV, the Olympus of high technology. The place didn't glisten the way you might expect, at least along Shaw's route. No quirky glass offices, marble mansions or herds of slinky Mercedeses, Maseratis, Beemers, Porsches. Here was a diorama of the 1970s: pleasant single-family homes, mostly ranch-style, with minuscule yards, apartment buildings that were tidy but could use a coat of paint or re-siding, mile after mile of strip malls, two- and three-story office structures. No high-rises — perhaps out of fear of earthquakes? The San Andreas Fault was directly underneath.

Silicon Valley might have been Cary, North Carolina, or Plano, Texas, or Fairfax County, Virginia — or another California valley, San Fernando, three hundred miles south and tethered to SV by the utilitarian Highway 101. This was one thing about midwifing technology, Shaw supposed: it all happens inside. Driving through Hibbing, Minnesota, you'd see the mile-deep crimson-colored iron mine. Or Gary, Indiana, the fortresses of steel mills. There were no scars of geography, no unique superstructures to define Silicon Valley.

In ten minutes he was approaching Frank Mulliner's house on Alta Vista Drive. The ranch wasn't designed by cookie cutter, though it had the same feel as the other houses on this lengthy block. Inexpensive, with wood or vinyl siding, three concrete steps to the front door, wrought-iron railings. The fancier homes had bay windows. They were all bordered by a parking strip, sidewalk and front yard. Some grass was green, some the color of straw. A number of home-owners had given up on lawns and hardscaped with pebbles and sand and low succulents.

Shaw pulled up to the pale green house, noting the FORECLOSURE SALE sign on the adjoining property. Mulliner's house was also on the market.

Knocking on the door, Shaw waited only a moment before it opened, revealing a stocky, balding man of fifty or so, wearing gray slacks and an open-collar blue dress shirt. On his feet were loafers but no socks.

'Frank Mulliner?'

The man's red-rimmed eyes glanced quickly at Shaw's clothes, the short blond hair, the sober demeanor — he rarely smiled. The bereft father would be thinking this was a detective come to deliver bad news, so Shaw introduced himself quickly.

'Oh, you're . . . You called. The reward.'

31

'That's right.'

The man's hand was chill when the two gripped palms.

With a look around the neighborhood, he nodded Shaw in.

Shaw learned a lot about offerors — and the viability, and legitimacy, of the reward — by seeing their living spaces. He met with them in their homes if possible. Offices, if not. This gave him insights about the potential business relationship and how serious were the circumstances giving rise to the reward. Here, the smell of sour food was detectable. The tables and furniture were cluttered with bills and mail folders and tools and retail flyers. In the living room were piles of clothing. This suggested that even though Sophie had been missing for only a few days, the man was very distraught.

The shabbiness of the place was also of note. The walls and molding were scuffed, in need of painting and proper repair; the coffee table had a broken leg splinted with duct tape painted to mimic the oak color. Water stains speckled the ceiling and there was a hole above one window where a curtain rod had pulled away from the Sheetrock. This meant the ten thousand cash he was offering was hard to come by.

The two men took seats on saggy furniture encased in slack gold slipcovers. The lamps were mismatched. And the big-screen TV was not so big by today's standards.

Shaw asked, 'Have you heard anything more? From the police? Sophie's friends?'

'Nothing. And her mother hasn't heard

anything. She lives out of state.'

'Is she on her way?'

Mulliner was silent. 'She's not coming.' The man's round jaw tightened and he wiped at what remained of his brown hair. 'Not yet.' He scanned Shaw closely. 'You a private eye or something?'

'No. I earn rewards that citizens or the police've offered.'

He seemed to digest this. 'For a living.'

'Correct.'

'I've never heard of that.'

Shaw gave him the pitch. True, he didn't need to win Mulliner over, as a PI seeking a new client might. But if he were going to look for Sophie, he needed information. And that meant cooperation. 'I've got years of experience doing this. I've helped find dozens of missing persons. I'll investigate and try to get information that'll lead to Sophie. As soon as I do, I tell you and the police. I don't rescue people or talk them into coming home if they're runaways.'

While this last sentence was not entirely accurate, Shaw felt it important to make clear exactly what he was providing. He preferred to mention rules rather than exceptions.

'If that information leads to her you pay me the reward. Right now, we'll talk some. If you don't like what you hear or see, you tell me and I won't pursue it. If there's something I don't like, I walk away.'

'Far as I'm concerned, I'm sold.' The man's voice choked. 'You seem okay to me. You talk straight, you're calm. Not, I don't know, not like a bounty hunter on TV. Anything you can do to find Fee. Please.'

'Fee.'

'Her nickname. So-*fee*. What she called herself when she was a baby.' He controlled the tears, though just.

'Has anybody else approached you for the reward?'

'I got plenty of calls or emails. Most of 'em anonymous. They said they'd seen her or knew what had happened. All it took was a few questions and I could tell they didn't have anything. They just wanted the money. Somebody mentioned aliens in a spaceship. Somebody said a Russian sex-trafficking ring.'

'Most people who contact you'll be that way. Looking for a fast buck. Anybody who knows her'll help you out for free. There's an off chance that you'll be contacted by somebody connected with the kidnapper — if there is a kidnapper — or by somebody who spotted her on the street. So listen to all the calls and read all the emails. Might be something helpful.

'Now, finding her is our only goal. It might take a lot of people providing information to piece her whereabouts together. Five percent here. Ten there. How that reward gets split up is between me and the other parties. You won't be out more than the ten.

'One more thing: I don't take a reward for recovery, only rescue.'

The man didn't respond to this. He was kneading a bright orange golf ball. After a moment he said, 'They make these things so you can play in the winter. Somebody gave me a box of them.' He looked up at Shaw's unresponsive eyes. 'It never snows here. Do you golf? Do you want some?'

'Mr. Mulliner, we should move fast.'

'Frank.'

'Fast,' Shaw repeated.

The man inhaled. 'Please. Help her. Find Fee for me.'

'First: Are you sure she didn't run off?'

'Absolutely positive.'

'How do you know?'

'Luka. That's how.'

# 5

Shaw was sitting hunched over the wounded coffee table.

Before him was a thirty-two-page, 5-by-7-inch notebook of blank, unlined pages. In his hand was a Delta Titanio Galassia fountain pen, black with three orange rings toward the nib. Occasionally people gave him a look: Pretentious, aren't we? But Shaw was a relentless scribe and the Italian pen — not cheap, at two hundred and fifty dollars, yet hardly a luxury — was far easier on the muscles than a ballpoint or even a rollerball. It was the best tool for the job.

Shaw and Mulliner were not alone. Sitting beside Shaw and breathing heavily on his thigh was the reason that father was sure daughter had not run away: Luka.

A well-behaved white standard poodle.

'Fee wouldn't leave Luka. Impossible. If she'd run off, she would've taken him. Or at least called to see how he was.'

There'd been dogs on the Compound, pointers for pointing, retrievers for retrieving — and all of them for barking like mad if the uninvited arrived. Colter and Russell took their father's view that the animals were employees. Their younger sister, Dorion, on the other hand, would bewilder the animals by dressing them up in clothing she herself had stitched and she let them sleep in bed with her. Shaw now accepted

Luka's presence here as evidence, though not proof, that the young woman had not run off.

Colter Shaw asked about the details of Sophie's disappearance, what the police had said when Mulliner called, about family and friends.

Writing in tiny, elegant script, perfectly horizontal on the unlined paper, Shaw set down all that was potentially helpful, ignoring the extraneous. Then, having exhausted his questions, he let the man talk. He usually got his most important information this way, finding nuggets in the rambling.

Mulliner stepped into the kitchen and returned a moment later with a handful of scraps of paper and Post-it notes containing names and numbers and addresses — in two handwritings. His and Sophie's, he confirmed. Friends' numbers, appointments, work and class schedules. Shaw transcribed the information. If it came to the police, Mulliner should have the originals.

Sophie's father had done a good job looking for his daughter. He'd put up scores of MISSING flyers. He'd contacted Sophie's boss at the software company where she worked part-time, a half dozen of her professors at the college she attended and her sports coach. He spoke to a handful of her friends, though the list was short.

'Haven't been the best of fathers,' Mulliner admitted with a downcast gaze. 'Sophie's mother lives out of state, like I said. I'm working a couple of jobs. It's all on me. I don't get to her events or games — she plays lacrosse — like I should.' He waved a hand around the unkempt house. 'She doesn't have parties here. You can see why. I don't have time to clean. And paying for a service? Forget it.'

Shaw made a note of the lacrosse. The young woman could run and she'd have muscle. A competitive streak too.

Sophie'd fight — if she had the chance to fight.

'Does she often stay at friends' houses?'

'Not much now. That was a high school thing. Sometimes. But she always calls.' Mulliner blinked. 'I didn't offer you anything. I'm sorry. Coffee? Water?'

'No, I'm good.'

Mulliner, like most people, couldn't keep his eyes off the scripty words Shaw jotted quickly in navy-blue ink.

'Your teachers taught you that? In school?'

'Yes.'

In a way.

A search of her room revealed nothing helpful. It was filled with computer books, circuit boards, closetsful of outfits, makeup, concert posters, a tree for jewelry. Typical for her age. Shaw noted she was an artist, and a good one. Watercolor landscapes, bold and colorful, sat in a pile on a dresser, the paper curled from drying off the easel.

Mulliner had said she'd taken her laptop and phone with her, which Shaw had expected but was disappointed that she didn't have a second computer to browse through, though that was usually not particularly helpful. You rarely found an entry: *Brunch on Sunday, then I'm going to run away because I hate my effing parents.*

And you never have to search very hard to find the suicide note.

Shaw asked for some pictures of the young woman, in different outfits and taken from different angles. He produced ten good ones.

Mulliner sat but Shaw remained standing. Without looking through his notebook, he said, 'She left at four in the afternoon, on Wednesday, two days ago, after she got home from school. Then went out for the bike ride at five-thirty and never came home. You posted an announcement of the reward early Thursday morning.'

Mulliner acknowledged the timing with a tilt of his head.

'It's rare to offer a reward that soon after a disappearance — absent foul play.'

'I was just . . . you know. It was devastating. I was so worried.'

'I need to know everything, Frank.' Shaw's blue eyes were focused on the offeror's.

Mulliner's right thumb and forefinger were kneading the orange golf ball again. His eyes were on the Post-it notes on the coffee table. He gathered them, ordered them, then stopped. 'We had a fight, Fee and I. Wednesday. After she came home. A big fight.'

'Tell me.' Shaw spoke in a softer voice than a moment ago. He now sat.

'I did something stupid. I listed the house Wednesday and told the broker to hold off putting up the For Sale sign until I could tell Fee. The Realtor did anyway and a friend up the street saw it and called her. Fuck. I should've thought better.' His damp eyes looked up. 'I tried everything to avoid moving. I'm working those two jobs. I borrowed money from my ex's new husband. Think about that. I did everything I could but I just can't afford to stay. It was our family house! Fee grew up in it, and I'm going to lose it. The taxes here in the county? Jesus, crushing. I found a new place in Gilroy, south of here. A long way south. It's all I can afford. Sophie's commute to the college and her job'll be two hours. She won't see her friends much.'

His laugh was bitter. 'She said, 'Great, we're moving to the fucking Garlic Capital of the World.' Which it is. 'And you didn't even tell me.' I lost it. I screamed at her. How she didn't appreciate what I did. How my commute'll be even longer. She grabbed her backpack and stormed out.'

Mulliner's eyes slid away from Shaw's. 'I was afraid if I told you, you'd be sure she ran off, and wouldn't help.'

This answered the important question: Why the premature reward offer? Which had raised concerns in Shaw's mind. Yes, Mulliner seemed truly distraught. He'd let the house go to hell. This testified to his genuine concerns about his daughter. Yet murderous spouses, business partners, siblings and, yes, even parents some-times post a reward to give themselves the blush of innocence. And they tend to offer fast, the way Mulliner had done.

No, he wasn't completely absolved. Yet admitting the fight, coupled with Shaw's other conclusions about the man, suggested he had

40

nothing to do with his daughter's disappearance.

The reason for the early offer of a reward was legitimate: it would be unbearable to think that he'd been responsible for driving his daughter from the house and into the arms of a murderer or rapist or kidnapper.

Mulliner said now, his voice flat as Iowa and barely audible, 'If anything happens to her ... I'd just ... ' He stopped speaking and swallowed.

'I'll help you,' Shaw said.

'Thank you!' A whisper. He now broke into real tears, racking. 'I'm sorry, I'm sorry, I'm sorry ... '

'Not a worry.'

Mulliner looked at his watch. 'Hell, I have to get to work. Last thing I want to do. But I can't lose this job. Please call me. Whatever you find, call me right away.'

Shaw capped his pen and replaced it in his jacket pocket and rose, closing the notebook. He saw himself out.

# 6

In assessing how to proceed in pursuing a reward — or, for that matter, with most decisions in life — Colter Shaw followed his father's advice.

'Countering a threat, approaching a task, you assess the odds of each eventuality, look at the most likely one first and then come up with a suitable strategy.'

The likelihood that you can outrun a forest fire sweeping uphill on a windy day: ten percent. The likelihood you can survive by starting a firebreak and lying in the ashes while the fire burns past you: eighty percent.

Ashton Shaw: 'The odds of surviving a blizzard in the high mountains. If you hike out: thirty percent. If you shelter in a cave: eighty percent.'

'Unless,' eight-year-old Dorion, always the practical one, had pointed out, 'there's a momma grizzly bear with her cubs inside.'

'That's right, Button. Then your odds go down to really, really tiny. Though here it'd be a black bear. Grizzlies are extinct in California.'

Shaw was now sitting in his Chevy outside the Mulliners' residence, notebook on lap, computer open beside him. He was juggling percentages of Sophie's fate.

While he hadn't told Mulliner, he believed the highest percentage was that she was dead.

He gave it sixty percent. Most likely murdered

by a serial killer, rapist or a gang wannabe as part of an initiation (the Bay Area crews were among the most vicious in the nation). A slightly less likely cause of death was that she had been killed in an accident, her bike nudged off the road by a drunk or texting driver, who'd fled.

That number, of course, left a significant percentage likelihood that she was alive — taken at the hands of a kidnapper for ransom or sex, or pissed at Dad about the move and, the Luka poodle factor notwithstanding, was crashing on a friend's couch for a few days, to make him sweat.

Shaw turned to his computer — when on a job he subscribed to local news feeds and scanned for stories that might be helpful. Now he was looking for the discovery of unidentified bodies of women who might be Sophie (none) or reports over the past few weeks of serial kidnappers or killers (several incidents, but the perpetrator was preying on African American prostitutes in the Tenderloin of San Francisco). He expanded his search around the entire northern California area and found nothing relevant.

He skimmed his notes regarding what Frank Mulliner had told him, following his own search for the girl Wednesday night and yesterday. He'd called as many friends, fellow students and coworkers whose names he could find. Mulliner had told Shaw that his daughter had not been the target of a stalker that any of them knew of.

'There is someone you ought to know about, though.'

That someone was Sophie's former boyfriend.

Kyle Butler was twenty, also a student, though at a different college. Sophie and Kyle had broken up, Mulliner believed, about a month ago. They'd dated off and on for a year and it had become serious only in early spring. While he didn't know why they split he was pleased.

Shaw's note: *Mulliner: KB didn't treat Sophie the way she should be treated. Disrespectful, said mean things. No violence. KB did have a temper and was impulsive. Also, into drugs. Pot mostly.*

Mulliner had no picture of the boy — and Sophie had apparently purged her room of his image — but Shaw had found a number on Facebook. Kyle was a solidly built, tanned young man with a nest of curly blond hair atop his Greek god head. His social media profile was devoted to heavy metal music, surfing and legalizing drugs. Mulliner believed he worked part-time installing car stereos.

*Mulliner: No idea what Sophie saw in him. Believed maybe Sophie thought herself unattractive, a 'geek girl,' and he was a handsome, cool surfer dude.*

Her father reported that the boy hadn't taken the breakup well and his behavior grew inappropriate. One day he called thirty-two times. After she blocked his number, Sophie found him on their front yard, sobbing and begging to be taken back. Eventually he calmed down and they flopped into a truce. They'd meet for coffee occasionally. They went to a play 'as friends.' Kyle hadn't pushed hard for reconciliation, though Sophie told her father he wanted desperately to get back together.

Domestic kidnappings almost always are parental abductions. (Solving one such snatching, on a whim, in fact, had started Shaw on his career as a reward seeker.) Occasionally, though, a former husband or boyfriend would spirit away the woman of his passion.

Love, Colter Shaw had learned, could be an endlessly refillable prescription of madness.

Shaw put Kyle's guilt at ten percent. He might have been obsessed with Sophie, but he also seemed too normal and weepy to turn dark. However, the kid's drug use was a concern. Had Kyle inadvertently jeopardized her life by introducing her to a dealer who didn't want to be identified? Had she witnessed a hit or other crime, maybe not even knowing it?

He gave this hypothesis twenty percent.

Shaw called the boy's number. No answer. His message, in his best cop voice, was that he had just spoken to Frank Mulliner and wanted to talk to Kyle about Sophie. He left the number of one of his half dozen active burners, with the caller ID showing Washington, D.C. Kyle might be thinking FBI or, for all Shaw knew, the National Missing Ex-girlfriend Tactical Rescue Operation, or some such.

Shaw then cruised the three miles to Palo Alto, where he found the boy's beige-and-orange cinder-block apartment complex. The doors were, inexplicably, baby blue. At 3B, he pounded on the door, rather than using the ringer, which he doubted worked anyway, and called out, 'Kyle Butler. Open the door.'

45

Cop-like, yet not cop.

No response, and he didn't think the boy was dodging him, since a glance through the unevenly stained curtain showed not a flicker of movement inside.

He left one of his business cards in the door crack. It gave only his name and the burner number. He wrote: *I need to talk to you about Sophie. Call me.*

Shaw returned to his car and sent Kyle's picture, address and phone number to his private investigator, Mack, requesting background, criminal and weapons checks. Some information he wanted was not public but Mack rarely differentiated between what was public and what was not.

Shaw skimmed the notebook once more and fired up the engine, pulling into traffic. He'd decided where the next step of the investigation would take him.

Lunch.

# 7

Colter Shaw walked through the door of the Quick Byte Café in Mountain View.

This was where Sophie had been at about 6 p.m. on Wednesday — just before she disappeared.

On Thursday, Mulliner had stopped in here, asking about his daughter. He'd had no luck but had convinced the manager to put up a MISSING flyer on a corkboard, where it now was pinned beside cards for painters, guitar and yoga instruction and three other MISSING announcements — two dogs and a parrot.

Shaw was surveying the place and smelling the aroma of hot grease, wilty onions, bacon and batter (BREAKFAST SERVED ALL DAY).

The Quick Byte, EST. 1968, couldn't decide if it wanted to be a bar, a restaurant or a coffee shop, so it opted to be all three.

It might also function as a computer showroom, since most of the patrons were hunched over laptops.

The front was spattered plate glass, facing a busy commercial Silicon Valley street. The walls were of dark paneling and the floor uneven wood. In the rear, backless stools sat in front of the dim bar, which was presently unmanned. Not surprising, given the hour — 11:30 a.m. — though the patrons didn't seem the alcohol-drinking sort; they exuded geek. Lots of stocking caps, baggy sweats, Crocs. The majority were white, followed by East Asian and then South Asian. There were two black patrons, a couple. The median age in the place was about twenty-five.

The walls were lined with black-and-white and color photographs of computers and related artifacts from the early days of tech: vacuum tubes, six-foot-high metal racks of wires and square gray components, oscilloscopes, cumbersome keyboards. Display cards beneath the images gave the history of the devices. One was called Babbage's Analytical Engine — a computer powered by steam, one hundred and fifty years old.

Shaw approached the ORDER HERE station. He asked for green huevos rancheros and a coffee with cream. Cornbread instead of tortilla chips. The skinny young man behind the counter handed him the coffee and a wire metal stand with a numbered card, 97, stuck in the round spiral on top.

Shaw picked a table near the front door and sat, sipping coffee and scanning the place.

The unbusy kitchen served up the food quickly and the waitress, a pretty young woman, inked and studded, brought the order. Shaw ate quickly, half the dish. Though it was quite good and he was hungry, the eggs were really just a passport to give him legitimacy here.

On the table he spread out the pictures of Sophie that her father had given him. He took a shot of them with his iPhone, which he then emailed to himself. He logged on to his computer, through a secure jetpack, opened the messages and loaded the images onto the screen. He positioned the laptop so that anyone entering or leaving the café could see the screen with its montage of the young woman.

Coffee in hand, he wandered to the Wall of Fame and, like a curious tourist, began reading. Shaw used computers and the internet extensively in the reward business and, at another time, he would have found the history of high technology interesting. Now, though, he was concentrating on watching his computer in the reflection in the display case glass.

Since Shaw had no legal authority whatsoever, he was present here by the establishment's grace. Occasionally, if the circumstances were right and the situation urgent, he'd canvass patrons. Sometimes he got a lead or two. More frequently he was ignored or, occasionally, asked to leave.

So he often did what he was doing now: fishing.

The computer, with its bright pictures of Sophie, was bait. As people glanced at the photos, Shaw would watch them. Did anyone pay particular attention to the screen? Did their face register recognition? Concern? Curiosity? Panic? Did they look around to see whose computer it was?

He observed a few curious glances at the laptop screen but they weren't curious enough to raise suspicion.

Shaw could get away with studying the wall for about five minutes before it looked odd, so he bought time by pulling out his mobile and having an imaginary conversation. This was good for another four minutes. Then he ran out of fake and returned to his seat. Probably fifteen people had seen the pictures and the reactions were all blasé.

He sat at the table, sipping coffee and reading texts and emails on his phone. The computer was still open for all to see. There were no tugs on the fishing line. He returned to the ORDER HERE counter, now staffed by a woman in her thirties, a decade removed from the waitress who had served him but with similar facial bones. Sisters, he guessed.

She was barking orders and Shaw took her to be the manager or owner.

'Help you? Your eggs okay?' The voice was a pleasant alto.

'They were good. Question: That woman on the bulletin board?'

'Oh, yeah. Her father came in. Sad.'

'It is. I'm helping him out, looking for her.'

A statement as true as rain. He tended not to mention rewards unless the subject came up.

'That's good of you.'

'Any customers say anything about her?'

'Not to me. I can ask people who work here. Anybody knows anything, I'll call you. You have a card?'

He gave her one. 'Thanks. He's anxious to find her.'

The woman said, 'Sophie. Always liked that name. It says 'student.' The flyer does.'

Shaw said, 'She's at Concordia. Business. And codes part-time at GenSys. According to her father, she's good at it. I wouldn't know a software program if it bit me.'

Colter Shaw was quiet by nature, yet when working a job he intentionally rambled. He'd found that this put people at ease.

The woman added, 'And I like what you called her.'

'What was that?'

'*Woman*. Not *girl*. She looks young and most people would've called her girl.' She glanced toward the waitress, willowy and in baggy brown jeans and a cream-colored blouse. She nodded the server over.

'This's my daughter, Madge,' the manager said.

Oh. Not sister.

'And I'm Tiffany.' Mom read the card. 'Colter.' She extended a hand and they shook.

'That's a name?' Madge said.

'Says so right here.' Tiffany flicked the card. 'He's helping find that missing woman.'

Madge said, 'Oh, girl on the poster?'

Tiffany gave a wry glance toward Shaw.

*Girl* . . .

Madge said, 'I saw her pictures on your computer. I wondered if you were a policeman or something?'

'No. Just helping her dad. We think this is the last place she was at before she disappeared.'

The daughter's face tightened. 'God. What do you think happened?'

'We don't know yet.'

'I'll check inside,' said Tiffany, the mother — the generation-bending names of the women

51

were disorienting. He watched her collect the flyer from the corkboard and disappear into the kitchen, where, presumably, it was displayed to cooks and busboys.

She returned, pinning up the flyer once more. 'Nothing. There's a second shift. I'll make sure they see it.' She sounded as if she definitely would, Shaw thought. He was lucky to have found a mother, and one close to her child. She'd sympathize more with the parent of missing offspring.

Shaw thanked her. 'You mind if I ask your customers if they've seen her?'

The woman seemed troubled and Shaw suspected she wouldn't want to bother clientele with unpleasant news.

That wasn't the reason for the frown, however. Tiffany said, 'Don't you want to look at the security video first?'

# 8

Well. This was interesting news. Shaw had looked for cameras when he'd first walked in but had seen none. 'You've got one?'

Tiffany turned her bright blue eyes away from Shaw's face and pointed to a small round object in the liquor bottles behind the bar.

A hidden security camera in a commercial establishment was pointless, since the main purpose was deterrence. Maybe they were getting . . .

Tiffany said, 'We're getting a new system put in. I brought mine from home for the time being. Just so we'd have something.' She turned to Madge and asked the young woman to show Sophie's picture to customers. 'Sure, Mom.' The waitress took the flyer and started on her canvass.

Tiffany directed Shaw into the cluttered office. She said, 'I would've told her father about the tape but I wasn't here when he brought the poster in. Didn't think about it again. Not till you showed up. Have a seat.' With a hand on his shoulder, Tiffany guided Shaw into an unsteady desk chair in front of a fiberboard table, on which sat stacks of paper and an old desktop computer. Bending down, her arm against his, she began to type. 'When?'

'Wednesday. Start at five p.m. and go from there.'

Tiffany's fingers, tipped in lengthy black-polished nails, typed expertly. Within seconds a video appeared. It was clearer than most security cams, largely because it wasn't the more common wide-angle lens, which encompass a broader field of view yet distort the image. Shaw could see the order station, the cash register, the front portion of the Quick Byte and a bit of the street beyond.

Tiffany scrubbed the timeline from the moment Shaw had requested. On the screen patrons raced to and from the counter, like zipping flies.

Shaw said, 'Stop. Back up. Three minutes.'

Tiffany did. Then hit PLAY.

Shaw said, 'There.'

Outside the café Sophie's bike approached from the left. The rider had to be the young woman: the color of the bike, helmet, clothes and backpack were as Mulliner had described. Sophie did something Shaw had never seen a cyclist do. While still in motion she swung her left leg over the frame, leaving her right foot on the pedal. She glided forward, standing on that foot, perfectly balanced. Just before stopping, she hopped off. A choreographed dismount.

Sophie went through the ritual of affixing the bike to a lamppost with an impressive lock and a thick black wire. She pulled off her red almond-shell helmet and entered the Quick Byte and looked around. Shaw had hoped she might wave to somebody whom a staff member or patron could identify. She didn't. She stepped out of sight, to the left. She returned a moment later and ordered.

On the silent tape — older security systems

generally didn't waste storage space or transmission bandwidth with audio — the young woman took a mug of coffee and one of the chrome number-card holders. Shaw could see her long face was unsmiling, grim.

'Pause, please.'

Tiffany did.

'Did you serve her?'

'No, it would have been Aaron working then.'

'Is he here?'

'No, he's off today.'

Shaw asked Tiffany to take a shot of Sophie on her phone, send it to Aaron and see if he recalled anything about her, what she said, who she talked to.

She sent the shot to the employee, with the whooshing sound of an outgoing text.

Shaw was about to ask her to call him, when her phone chimed. She looked at the screen. 'No, he doesn't remember her.'

On the video Sophie vanished from sight again.

Shaw then noticed somebody come into view outside. He, or she, was of medium build and wearing baggy dark sweats, running shoes, a windbreaker and a gray stocking cap, pulled low. Sunglasses. Always damn sunglasses.

This person looked up and down the street and stepped closer to Sophie's bike and crouched quickly, maybe to tie a shoelace.

Or not.

The behavior earned Shaw's assessment that it was possibly the kidnapper. Male, female, he couldn't tell. So Shaw bestowed the gender-neutral nickname, Person X.

55

'What's he doing?' Tiffany asked in a whisper. Sabotage? Putting a tracking device on it?

Shaw thought: Come in, order something.

He knew that wouldn't happen.

X straightened, turned back in the direction he had come and walked quickly away.

'Should I fast-forward?' Tiffany asked.

'No. Let it run. Regular speed.'

Patrons came and went. Servers delivered and bused dishes.

As they watched the people and drivers stream past, Tiffany asked, 'You live here?'

'Florida, some of the time.'

'Disney?'

'Not all that close. And I'm not there very often.'

Florida, he meant. As for Disney, not at all.

She might have said something else but his attention was on the video. At 6:16:33, Sophie left the Quick Byte. She walked to her bike. Then remained standing, perfectly still, looking out across the street, toward a place where there was nothing to look at: a storefront with a sun-bleached FOR LEASE sign in the window. Shaw noted one hand absently tightening into a fist, then relaxing, then tightening again. Her helmet slipped from the other and bounced on the ground. She bent fast to collect and pull it over her head — angrily, it seemed.

Sophie freed her bike and, unlike the elegant dismount, now leapt into the seat and pedaled hard, to the right, out of sight.

Staring at the screen, Shaw was looking at passing cars, his eyes swiveling left to right — in the direction Sophie'd headed. It was, however, almost impossible to see inside the vehicles. If stocking-capped, sunglasses-wearing Person X was driving one, he couldn't see.

Shaw asked Tiffany to send this portion of the tape, depicting X, to his email. She did.

Together they walked from the office into the restaurant proper and made their way back to the table. Madge, the daughter with the mother name, told him that no one she'd showed the picture to had seen the girl. She added, 'And nobody looked weird when I asked.'

'Appreciate it.'

His phone sang quietly and he glanced at the screen. Mack's research into Kyle Butler, Sophie's ex-boyfriend, revealed two misdemeanor drug convictions. No history of violence. No warrants. He acknowledged the info, then signed off.

Shaw finished his coffee.

'Refill? Get you anything else? On the house.'

'I'm good.'

'Sorry we couldn't help you more.'

Shaw thanked her. And didn't add that the trip to the Quick Byte had told him exactly where he needed to go now.

# 9

Colter Shaw, fifteen, is making a lean-to in the northwest quadrant of the Compound, beside a dry creek bed, at the foot of a sheer cliff face, a hundred feet high.

The lean-to is in the style of a Finnish *laavu*. The Scandinavians are fond of these temporary structures, which are found commonly on hunting and fishing grounds. Colter knows this only because his father told him. The boy has never been outside California or Oregon or Washington State.

He's arranged pine boughs on the sloping roof and is now collecting moss to provide insulation. The campfire must remain outside.

A gunshot startles him. It's from a rifle, the sound being chestier than the crack of a pistol.

The weapon was fired on Shaw property because it could not have been fired anywhere else; Ashton and Mary Dove Shaw own nearly a thousand acres, and from here it's more than a mile's hike to the property line.

Colter pulls an orange hunting vest from his backpack, dons the garment and walks in the direction of the shot.

About a hundred yards along, he's startled when a buck, a small one, sprints past, blood on its rear leg. Colter's eyes follow it as it gallops north. Then the boy continues in the direction the animal came from. He soon finds the hunter, alone, hiking deeper into the Shaw property. He doesn't see or hear Colter approach. The boy studies him.

The broad man, of pale complexion, is wearing camouflage overalls and a brimmed cap, also camo, over what seems to be a crew-cut scalp. The outfit seems new and the boots are not scuffed. The man is not protected with an orange vest, which is a hugely bad idea in thick woods, where hunters themselves can be mistaken for game or, more likely, bush. The vests don't alert deer to your presence; the animals are sensitive to the color blue, not orange.

The man wears a small backpack and, on his canvas belt, a water bottle and extra magazines for his rifle. The gun is a curious choice for hunting: one of those black, stubby weapons considered assault rifles. They're illegal in California, with a few exceptions. His is a Bushmaster, chambered for a .223 bullet — a smaller round than is usually chosen for deer hunting and never used for bigger game. The shorter barrel also means it is less accurate at a distance. These guns are semiautomatics, firing each time the trigger is pulled; that aspect is perfectly legal for hunting, but Colter's mother, the marksman in the family, has taught the children to hunt only with bolt-action rifles. Mary Dove's thinking is that if you can't drop your target fast with a single shot you (a) haven't worked hard enough to get closer or (b) have no business hunting in the first place.

And, also odd, the Bushmaster isn't equipped

with a scope. Using iron sights to hunt? Either he's an amateur's amateur or one hell of a shot. Then Colter reflects: he only wounded the deer. There's the answer.

'Sir, excuse me.' Colter's voice — even then, a smooth baritone — startles the man.

He turns, his clean-shaven face contracting with suspicion. He scans the teenager. Colter is the same height then as now, though slimmer; he won't put on bulking muscle until college and the wrestling team. The jeans, sweatshirt, serious boots and gloves — the September day is cool — suggest the boy is just a hiker. Despite the vest, he can't be a hunter, as he has no weapon.

Colter is teased frequently by his sister for never smiling, yet his expression is usually affable, as it is now.

Still, the man keeps his hand on the pistol grip of the .223. His finger is extended, parallel to the barrel and not on the trigger. This tells Colter there is a bullet in the chamber and that the hunter is familiar with weapons, if not the fine art of hunting. Maybe he was a soldier at one time.

'How you doing?' Colter asks, looking the man straight in the eye.

'Okay.' A high voice. Crackly.

'This is our property, sir. There's no hunting. It's posted.' Always polite. Ashton has taught the children all aspects of survival, from how to tell poisoned berries from safe, to how to stymie bears, to how to defuse potential conflicts.

*Never antagonize beast or man . . .*

'Didn't see any signs.' Cold, cold dark eyes.

Colter says, 'Understood. It's a lot of land. But it is ours and there's no hunting.'

'Your dad around?'

'Not nearby.'

'What's your name?'

Ashton taught the children that adults have to earn your respect. Colter says nothing.

The man tilts his head. He's pissed off. He asks, 'Well, where *can* I hunt?'

'You're a mile onto our land. You would've parked off Wickham Road. Take it east five miles. That's all public forest.'

'You own all this?'

'We do.'

'You're kind of like a *Deliverance* family, aren't you? You play banjo?'

Colter doesn't understand; he would later.

'I'll head off then.'

'Wait.'

The man stops, turning back.

Colter's confused. 'You're going after that buck, aren't you?'

The man gives a look of surprise. 'What?'

'That buck. He's wounded.' Even if the man is inexperienced, everyone knows this.

The hunter says, 'Oh, I hit something? There was just a noise in the bushes. I thought it was a wolf.'

Colter doesn't know how to respond to this bizarre comment.

'Wolves hunt at dusk and night,' he says.

'Yeah? I didn't know that.'

And pulling a trigger without a sure target?

'Anyway, sir. There's a wounded buck. You've

got to find him. Put him down.'

He laughs. 'What is this? I mean, who're you to lecture me?'

The teenager guesses that this man, with his ignorance and the little-worn outfit, had been asked to go hunting with friends and, never having been, wanted to practice so he wouldn't be embarrassed.

'I'll help you,' Colter offers. 'But we can't let it go.'

'Why?'

'A wounded animal, you track it down. You don't let it suffer.'

'Suffer,' the man whispers. 'It's a deer. Who cares?'

*Never kill an animal but for three reasons: for food or hide, for defense, for mercy.*

Colter's father has given the children a lengthy list of rules, most of them commencing with the negative. Colter and his older brother, Russell, who call their father the King of Never, once asked why he didn't express his philosophy of life with 'always.' Ashton answered, 'Gets your attention better.'

'Come on,' Colter says. 'I'll help. I can cut sign pretty well.'

'Don't push me, kid.'

At that point the muzzle of the Bushmaster strays very slightly toward Colter.

The young man's belly tightens. Colter and his siblings practice self-defense frequently: grappling, wrestling, knives, firearms. But he's never been in a real fight. Homeschooling effectively eliminates the possibility of bullies.

He thinks, stupid gesture by a stupid man.

And stupid, Colter knows, can be a lot more dangerous than smart.

'So what kind of father you have that lets his son mouth off like you do?'

The muzzle swings a few degrees closer. The man certainly doesn't want to kill, but his pride has been thumped like a melon and that means he may shoot off a round in Shaw's direction to send him rabbit-scurrying. Bullets, though, have a habit of ending up in places where you don't intend them to go.

In one second, possibly less, Colter draws the old Colt Python revolver from a holster in his back waistband and points it downward, to the side.

*Never aim at your target until you're prepared to pull the trigger or release the arrow.*

The man's eyes grow wide. He freezes.

At this moment Colter Shaw is struck with a realization that should be shocking yet is more like flicking on a lamp, casting light on a previously dark place. He is looking at a human being in the same way he looks at an elk that will be that night's dinner or at a wolf pack leader who wishes to make Colter the main course.

He is considering the threat, assigning percentages and considering how to kill if the unfortunate ten percent option comes to pass. He is as calm and cold as the pseudo-hunter's dark brown eyes.

The man remains absolutely still. He'll know that the teenager is a fine shot — from the way he handles the .357 Magnum pistol — and that the boy can get a shot off first.

'Sir, could you please drop that magazine and unchamber the round inside.' His eyes never leave the intruder's because eyes signal next moves.

'Are you threatening me? I can call the police.'

'Roy Blanche up in White Sulphur Springs'd be happy to talk to you, sir. Both of us in fact.'

The man turns slightly, profile, a shooter's stance. The ten percent becomes twenty percent. Colter cocks the Python, muzzle still down. This changes the gun to single-action, which means that when he aims and fires, the trigger pull will be lighter and the shot more accurate. The man is thirty feet away. Colter has hit pie tins, center, at this distance.

A pause, then the man drops the magazine — with the push of a button, which means it is definitely an illegal weapon in California, where the law requires the use of a tool to change mags on semiauto rifles. He pulls the slide and a long, shiny bullet flies out. He scoops up the magazine but leaves the single.

'I'll take care of that deer,' Colter says, heart slamming hard now. 'If you could leave our property, sir.'

'Oh, you bet I'll leave, asshole. You can figure on me being back.'

'Yessir. We will figure on that.'

The man turns and stalks off.

Colter follows him — silently, the man never knows he's being tailed — for a mile and a half, until he gets to a parking lot beside a river popular with white-water rafters. He tosses his weapon into the back of a big black SUV and speeds away.

Then, intruder gone, Colter Shaw gets down to work.

*You're the best tracker of the family, Colter. You can find where a sparrow breathed on a blade of grass . . .*

He starts off in search of the wounded animal.

*For mercy . . .*

There isn't much blood trail and the ground on this part of the property is mostly pine-needle-covered, where it isn't rock; hoof tracks are nearly impossible to see. The classic tried-and-true techniques for sign cutting won't work. But the boy doesn't need them. You can also track with your mind, anticipating where your prey will go.

A wounded animal will seek one of two things: a place to die or a place to heal.

The latter means water.

Colter makes his way, silently again, toward a small pond named — by Dorion, when she was five — Egg Lake, because that's the shape. It's the only body of water nearby. Deer's noses — which have olfactory sensors on the outside as well as within — are ten thousand times more sensitive than humans'. The buck will know exactly where the lake is from the molecules off-gassed by minerals unique to pond water, the crap of amphibians and fish, the algae, the mud, the rotting leaves and branches, the remains of frogs left on the shore by owls and hawks.

Three hundred yards on, he locates the creature, blood on its leg, head down, sipping, sipping.

Colter draws the pistol and moves forward silently.

And Sophie Mulliner?

Like the buck, she too would want solace, comfort, after her wounding — her father's decision to move and the hard words fired at her through the smoke of anger. He recalled on the video: the young woman standing with shoulders arched, hand clenching and unclenching. The fury at the fallen helmet.

And her Egg Lake?

Cycling.

Her father had said as much when Shaw had interviewed him. Shaw recalled too the horseman's elegant dismount as Sophie pulled up to the Quick Byte, and the powerful, determined lunge as she sped away from the café, feet jamming down on the pedals in fury.

Taking comfort in the balance, the drive, the speed.

Shaw assessed that she'd gone for the damn hardest bike ride she could.

Sitting in the front seat of the Malibu, he opened his laptop bag and extracted a Rand McNally folding map of the San Francisco Bay Area. He carried with him in the Winnebago a hundred or so of these, covering most of the United States, Canada and Mexico. Maps, to Colter Shaw, were magic. He collected them — modern, old and ancient; the majority of the decorations in his house in Florida were framed maps. He preferred paper to digital, in the same way he'd choose a hardcover to an ebook; he was convinced the experience of paper was richer.

On a job, Shaw made maps himself — of the most important locations he'd been to during the investigation. These he studied, looking for clues that might not be obvious at first but that slowly rise to prominence. He had quite a collection of them.

He quickly oriented himself, outside the Quick Byte Café, in the middle of Mountain View.

Sophie's launch had been to the north. With a finger he followed a hypothetical route in that direction, past the 101 freeway and toward the Bay. Of course, she might have turned toward any compass point, at any time. Shaw saw, though, that if she continued more or less north she would have come to a large rectangle of green: San Miguel Park, two miles from the café. He reasoned that Sophie would pick a place like that because she could shred furiously up and down the trail, not having to worry about traffic.

Was the park, however, a place where one could bike? Paper had served its purpose; time for the twenty-first century. Shaw called up Google Earth (appropriately, since the park was only a few miles from the company's headquarters). He saw from the satellite images that San Miguel was interlaced with brown-dirt or sand trails and was hilly — perfect for cycling.

Shaw started the Malibu and headed for the place, wondering what he'd find.

Maybe nothing.

Maybe cyclist friends who'd say, 'Oh, Sophie? Yeah, she was here Wednesday. She left. Headed west on Alvarado. Don't know where she was going. Sorry.'

Or: 'Oh, Sophie? Yeah, she was here Wednesday. Pissed at her dad about something. She was going to her friend Jane's for a few days. Kind of sticking it to him for being a prick. She said she'd be home Sunday.'

After all, happy endings *do* occur.

As with the buck at Egg Lake.

It turned out that the fast but thin bullet had zipped into and out of the deer's haunch with no bone damage and had largely cauterized the wound.

Standing ten feet from the oblivious, drinking animal, Colter had replaced the pistol in his holster and withdrawn from his backpack the pint bottle of Betadine disinfectant he and his siblings kept with them. Holding his breath, he stepped in utter silence to within a yard of the deer and stopped. The creature's head jerked up, alerted by a few molecules of alien scent. The boy aimed the nozzle carefully and squirted a stream of the ruddy-brown antiseptic onto the buck's wound, sending the animal two feet into the air, straight up. Then it zipped out of sight like a cartoon creature. Colter had had to laugh.

And you, Sophie? Shaw now thought as he approached the park. Was this a place for you to heal? Or a place for you to die?

# 10

San Miguel Park was divided evenly, forest and field, and criss-crossed by dry culverts and stream-beds, as well as the paths that Shaw had seen thanks to the mappers of Google. In person, he observed they were packed dirt, not sand. Perfect for hard biking: both Sophie's muscular variety and his own preferred petrol.

Owing to the drought, the place was not the verdant green that Rand McNally had promised, but was largely brown and beige and dusty.

The main entrance was on the opposite side of the park but Sophie's route would have brought her here, to the bike paths off the broad shoulder of Tamyen Road. While not familiar with the area, he knew the avenue's name. Hundreds of years ago the Tamyen, a tribe of Ohlone native people, had lived in what was now Silicon Valley. Their lands had been lost in a familiar yet particularly shameful episode of genocide — not at the hands of the conquistadors but by local officials after California achieved statehood.

Shaw's mother, Mary Dove Shaw, believed an ancestor to be an Ohlone elder.

He killed the engine. Here were two openings in the line of brush and shrubbery that separated the shoulder from the park proper. The gaps led down a steep hill to trails, imprinted with many footprints and tire tread marks.

Climbing from the car, Shaw surveyed the

expansive park. He heard a sound he knew well. The whine of dirt bikes, a particular pitch that gets under the skin of some but to others — Shaw, for one — is a siren's song. Motorbiking was illegal here, a sign sternly warned. If he hadn't been on a job, though, Shaw'd have had his Yamaha off the rack in sixty seconds and on the trails in ninety.

So: One, assume kidnapping. Two, assume it was Person X, in the gray stocking cap and sunglasses. Three, assume X put a tracker on Sophie's bike and followed her.

How would it have gone down?

X would snatch her here, before she got too far into the park. He'd worry about witnesses, of course, though the area around Tamyen Road wasn't heavily populated. Shaw had passed a few companies, small fabricators or delivery services. But the buildings had no view of the shoulder. There was little traffic.

The scenario? X spots her. Then what? How would he have approached? Asking for directions?

No, a nineteen-year-old honors student and employee of a tech company wouldn't fall for that, not in the age of GPS. Exchanging pleasantries to get close to her? That too didn't seem likely. X would see she was strong and athletic and probably suspicious of a stranger's approach. And she could zip into the park, away from him, at twenty miles an hour. Shaw decided there'd be no ruse, nothing subtle. X would simply strike fast before Sophie sensed she was a target.

He began walking along the edge of the

shoulder nearest the park. He spotted a tiny bit of red. In the grass between the two trail entrances was a triangular shard of plastic — that could easily have come from the reflector on a bike. With a Kleenex he collected the triangle and put it in his pocket. On his phone he found the screenshot of Sophie's bike outside the Quick Byte — lifted from Tiffany's security camera video. Yes, it had a red disk reflector on the rear.

Made sense. X had followed Sophie here and — the moment the road was free of traffic — he'd slammed into the back of her bike. She'd have tumbled to the ground and he'd have been on her in an instant, taping her mouth and hands and feet. Into the trunk with her bike and backpack.

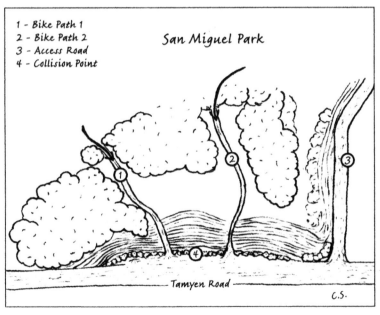

1 - Bike Path 1
2 - Bike Path 2
3 - Access Road
4 - Collision Point

San Miguel Park

Tamyen Road

C.S.

Some brush had been trampled near the plastic shard. He stepped off the shoulder and

71

peered down the hill. He could see a line of disturbed grass leading directly from where he was standing to the bottom of a small ravine. Maybe the plan hadn't gone quite as X had hoped. Maybe he'd struck Sophie's bike too hard, knocking her over the edge, and she'd tumbled down the forty-five-degree slope.

Shaw strode down one path to the place where she would have landed. He crouched. Broken and bent grass, and gouges in the dirt that might have come from a scuffle. Then he spotted a rock the size of a grapefruit. There with a smear on it: brown, the shade of dried blood.

Shaw pulled out his phone and dialed a number he'd programmed in several hours ago. He hit CALL. About ten feet up the hill came a soft sound, repeated every few seconds. It was the Samsung whistling ringtone.

The phone number he'd dialed was Sophie's.

# 11

Now, time for the experts.

Shaw called Frank Mulliner and told him what he'd found.

The man greeted the news with a gasp.

'Those sons of bitches!'

Shaw didn't understand at first. Then he realized Mulliner was referring to the police.

'If they'd gotten on board when they should have . . . I'm calling them now!'

Shaw foresaw disaster: a rampaging parent. He'd seen this before. 'Let me handle it.'

'But — '

'Let me handle it.'

Mulliner was silent for a moment. Shaw imagined the man's mobile was gripped in white, trembling fingers. 'All right,' Sophie's father said. 'I'm heading home.'

Shaw got the names of the detectives whom Mulliner had first spoken to about Sophie's disappearance: Wiley and Standish of the Joint Major Crimes Task Force, based in nearby Santa Clara.

After disconnecting with Mulliner, Shaw called the JMCTF's main number and asked for either of them. The prim-voiced desk officer, if that was her job title, said they were both out. Shaw said it was an emergency.

'You should call nine-one-one.'

'This is a development in a case Detectives

Standish and Wiley are involved in.'

'Which case?'

Of course, there was none.

'Can you give me your address?' Shaw asked.

Ten minutes later he was headed for the JMCTF headquarters.

There's no shortage of law enforcement in California. Growing up in the eastern wilderness of the state, the Shaw family had contact with park rangers — the Compound abutted tens of thousands of acres of state and federal forest. The family was no stranger to other agencies either: state police, the California Bureau of Investigation and, on rare occasion, the FBI. Not to mention Sheriff Roy Blanche.

The JMCTF was new to Colter Shaw. In a brief online search he'd found that it was charged with investigating homicides, kidnappings, sexual assaults and larcenies in which an injury occurred. It had a small drug enforcement group.

He was now approaching the headquarters: a large, low '50s-style building on West Hedding Street, not far from the Santa Clara County Sheriff's Office. He steered the Chevy into the lot and walked along the curving sidewalk bordered with succulents and red flowers, hearing the persistent rush of traffic on the Nimitz Freeway. At the front desk, he walked up to the window behind which a blond uniformed officer sat.

'Yessir?'

He knew the voice. It was the same young woman who'd fielded his earlier call. She was calm and stodgy. Her face was pert.

74

He asked again for either Detective Wiley or Detective Standish.

'Detective Standish is still out. I'll see if Detective Wiley is available.'

Shaw sat in an orange-vinyl-and-aluminum chair. The waiting room was like a doctor's office, without the magazines . . . and with bulletproof glass protecting the receptionist.

Shaw opened his computer bag, extracted his bound notebook and began to write. When he was done, he walked to the desk officer. The woman looked up.

'Could you please make me a copy of this? It's for an investigation Detective Wiley's running.'

Or, is soon to be running.

Another pause. She took the notebook, did as he'd requested and returned the notebook and copies to him.

'Many thanks.'

As soon as Shaw sat down, the door clicked open and a large man in his mid-forties stepped into the waiting area.

The plainclothes officer was an inverted pyramid: broad shoulders and a solid chest, testing the buttons of his shirt, tapering to narrow hips. Had to have played football in school. His salt-and-pepper hair was thick and swept back from a high forehead. The proportioned bulk, hair, along with the eagle's beak nose and solid jaw, could have landed him a role as a detective in a thriller movie. Not the lead but the dependable — and often expendable — sidekick. His weapon was a Glock and it rode high on the hip.

His eyes, muddy brown, looked Shaw up and down. 'You wanted to see me?'

'Detective Wiley?'

'Yes.'

'Colter Shaw.' He rose and extended his arm, forcing a hand-shake. 'You got a call from Frank Mulliner about his daughter, Sophie. She disappeared on Wednesday. I'm helping him find her. I've found some things that make it clear she was kidnapped.'

Another pause. ''Helping him find her.' You're a friend of the family?'

'Mulliner offered a reward. That's why I'm here.'

'Reward?'

Wiley was going to be a problem.

'You're a PI?' the detective asked.

'No.'

'BEA?'

'Not that either.' Bond enforcement agents are highly regulated. One reason not to go down that road. Also, Shaw had no desire to chase Failure to Appears in Piggly Wiggly parking lots, cuff them and haul their sweaty bodies to the grim receiving docks of sheriffs' departments.

Shaw continued: 'This is urgent, Detective.'

Another scan. Wiley waited a moment and said, 'You're not armed?'

'No.'

'Come on back to the office. We'll just have a look in that bag first.'

Shaw opened it. Wiley prodded and then turned and walked through the security doorway. Shaw followed him along the functional corridors, past offices and cubicles populated with about fifteen men and women — slightly more of the former than latter. Uniforms — all gray — prevailed. There were suits too, as well as the scruffy casual garb of those working undercover.

Wiley directed him into a large, austere office. Minimal décor. On the open door were two signs: DET. D. WILEY and DET. L. STANDISH. The desks were in the corners of the rooms, facing each other.

Wiley sat behind his, the chair creaking under his weight, and looked at phone message slips. Shaw sat across from him, on a gray metal chair whose seat was not molded for buttocks. It was extremely uncomfortable. He supposed Wiley perched suspects there while he conducted blunt interrogations.

The detective continued to adeptly ignore Shaw and studied the message slips intently. He turned away and typed on his computer.

Shaw grew tired of the pissing game. He took Sophie's cell phone, wrapped in Kleenex, from his pocket and set it on Wiley's desk. It thunked, as he'd intended. Shaw opened the tissue to reveal the cell.

Wiley's narrow eyes narrowed further.

'It's Sophie's mobile. I found it in San Miguel Park. Where she'd been cycling just before she disappeared.'

Wiley glanced at it, then back to Shaw, who explained about the video at the Quick Byte Café, the possibility of the kidnapper following her, the park, the car's collision with the bike.

'A tracker?' That was his only response.

'Maybe. I've got a copy of the video and you can see the original at the Quick Byte.'

'You know Mulliner or his daughter before this reward thing?'

'No.'

The detective leaned back. Wood and metal creaked. 'Just curious about your connection with all this. It's Shaw, right?' He was typing on his computer.

'Detective, we can talk all about my livelihood at some point. But right now we need to start looking for Sophie.'

Wiley's eyes were on the monitor. He'd probably found some articles in which Shaw was cited for helping police find a fugitive or locate a missing person. Or checking his record, more likely, and finding no warrants or convictions. Unless, of course, the powers that be at Cal had learned he was behind the theft of the four hundred pages yesterday from their hallowed academic halls, and he was now a wanted man.

No handcuffs were forthcoming. Wiley swung back. 'Maybe she dropped it. Didn't want to go home because Dad'd paid eight hundred bucks for it. She went to stay with a friend.'

'I found indications there'd been a scuffle. A rock that might have blood on it.'

'DNA is taking us twenty-four hours minimum.'

'It's not about confirming it's Sophie's. It suggests that she was attacked and kidnapped.'

'Were you ever law enforcement?'

'No. But I've assisted in missing-person cases for ten years.'

'For profit?'

'I make a living trying to save people's lives.'
Just like you.
'How much is the reward?'
'Ten thousand.'
'My. That's some chunk of change.'
Shaw extracted a second bundle of tissue. This contained the small triangular shard of red reflector, which he believed had come from Sophie's bike.

'I picked them both up with tissues, this and the phone. Though the odds of the perp's prints being on them are low. I think after she fell down the hill she was trying to call for help. When the kidnapper came after her, she pitched the phone away.'

'Why?' Wiley's eyes strayed to a file folder. He extracted a mechanical pencil and made a note.

'Hoping that when a friend or her father called, somebody'd find it and they could piece together that she'd been kidnapped.' He continued: 'I marked where I found it. I can help your crime scene team. Do you know San Miguel Park? The Tamyen Road side?'

'I do not.'

'It's near the Bay. There aren't a lot of places a witness might've been but I spotted some businesses on the way to the park. Maybe one of them has a CCTV. And there's a half dozen traffic cams on the route from the Quick Byte to San Miguel. You might be able to piece together a tag number.'

Wiley jotted another note. The case or a grocery list?

The detective asked, 'When do you collect your money?'

Shaw rose and picked up the phone and the bit of plastic, put them back in his bag. Wiley's face flashed with astonishment. 'Hey there — '

Shaw said evenly, 'Kidnapping's a federal offense too. The FBI has a field office here, in Palo Alto. I'll take it up with them.' He started for the door.

'Hold on, hold on, Chief. Take it easy. You gotta understand. You push the kidnap button, a lot of shit happens. From brass down to the swamp of the press. Take a bench there.'

Shaw paused, then turned and sat down. He opened his computer bag and extracted the copy of the notes he'd jotted while waiting for Wiley. He handed the sheets to the detective.

'The initials FM is Frank Mulliner. SM is Sophie. And the CS is me.'

Obvious, but in Wiley's case Shaw wasn't taking any chances.

- *Missing individual: Sophie Mulliner, 19*

- *Site of kidnapping: San Miguel Park, Mountain View, shoulder of Tamyen Road*

- *Possible scenarios:*

  - *Runaway: 3% (unlikely because of her phone, the reflector chip and evidence of struggle; none of her close friends — 8 interviewed by FM — give any indication she's done this).*

- *Hit-and-run: 5% (driver probably would not have taken her body with him).*

- *Suicide: 1% (no history of mental issues, no previous attempts, no suicidal communication, doesn't fit with scene in San Miguel Park).*

- *Kidnapping/murder: 80%.*

  - *Kidnapped by former boyfriend Kyle Butler: 10% (somewhat unstable, possibly abusive, drug history, didn't take breakup well; hasn't returned calls of CS).*

  - *Killed in gang initiation: 5% (MT-44 and several Latino gangs active in area, but crews generally leave corpses in public as proof of kill).*

  - *Kidnapped by FM's former wife, Sophie's mother: <1% (Sophie is no longer a minor, the divorce happened seven years ago, criminal records and other background check of mother make this unlikely).*

  - *For-profit kidnapping: 10% (no ransom demand, they usually occur within 24 hours of abduction; father isn't wealthy).*

  - *Kidnapped to force FM to divulge sensitive information from one of his two jobs: 5% (one, middle management in* automotive parts sales; the other, warehouse manager with no access to sensitive or valuable information or products). Would expect contact by now.

- Kidnapped to force Sophie to divulge information about her part-time job as coder at software development company, GenSys: 5% (does work not involving classified information or trade secrets).

- Killed because she witnessed a drug sale between boyfriend, Kyle Butler, and dealer who didn't want identity known: 20% (NOTE: Butler is missing too; related victim?).

- Kidnapped/killed by antisocial perpetrator, serial kidnapper or killer; SM raped and murdered or kept for torture and sex, eventual murder: 60%–70%.

- Unknown motive: 7%.


- Relevant details:

- SM's credit cards have not been used in two days; FM is on cards and has access.

- Quick Byte Café has video of possible suspect following her. Manager has preserved original and uploaded to cloud. Tiffany Monroe. CS has copy.

- *Under expectation-of-privacy laws, FM cannot access her phone log.*

- *Perpetrator possibly put tracking device on bike to follow her.*

- *Mulliner's house just on market, no prospective buyers yet to case the location for kidnapping potential.*

The detective's carefully shaved face wore a frown. 'The hell all this come from, Chief?'

The nickname rankled but Shaw ignored it; he was making headway. 'The information?' He shrugged. 'Facts from her father, some legwork of mine.'

Wiley muttered, 'What's with the percentages?'

'I rank things in priority. Tells me where to start. I look at the most likely first. That doesn't pan out, I move to the next.'

He read it again.

'They don't add up to a hundred.'

'There's always the unknown factor — that something I haven't thought of's the answer. Will you send a team to the park, Detective?'

'Alrightyroo. We'll look into it, Chief.' He smoothed the copy of Shaw's analysis and shook his head, amused. 'I can keep this?'

'It's yours.'

Shaw set the cell phone and the chip of reflector in front of Wiley.

His own phone was humming with a text. He glanced at the screen, noted the word *Important!*

Slipped the mobile away. 'You'll keep me posted, Detective?'

'Oh, you betcha, Chief. You betcha.'

# 12

At the Quick Byte Café, Tiffany greeted him with a troubled nod.

It was she who'd just texted, asking if he could stop by.

*Important!* . . .

'Colter. Come here.' They walked from the order station to the bulletin board on which Frank Mulliner had tacked up Sophie's picture.

The flyer was no longer there. In its place was a white sheet of computer paper, 8½ by 11 inches. On it was an odd black-and-white image, done in the style of stenciling. It depicted a face: two eyes, round orbs with a white glint in the upper-right-hand corner of each, open lips, a collar and tie. On the head was a businessman's hat from the 1950s.

'I texted as soon as I saw, but whoever it was might've taken it anytime. I asked everybody here, workers, customers. Nothing.'

The corkboard was next to the side door, out of view of the camera. No help there.

Tiffany gave a wan smile. 'Madge? My daughter? She's pissed at me. I sent her home. I don't want her here until they find him. I mean, she bikes to work three, four times a week too. And he was just here!'

'Not necessarily,' Shaw said. 'Sometimes people take Missing posters for souvenirs. Or, if they're after the reward themselves, they throw it out to narrow the field.'

'Really? Somebody'd do that?'

And worse. When the rewards hit six digits and up, reward seekers found all sorts of creative ways to discourage competition. Shaw had a scar on his thigh as proof.

This eerie image?

Was it an intentional replacement, tacked up by the kidnapper?

And if so, why?

A perverse joke? A statement?

A warning?

There were no words on it. Shaw took it down, using a napkin, and slipped it into his computer bag.

He looked over the clientele, nearly every one of them staring at screens large and screens small.

The front door opened and more customers entered, a businessman in a dark suit and white shirt, no tie, looking harried; a heavyset woman in blue scrubs; and a pretty redhead, mid-twenties, who looked his way quickly, then found an empty spot to sit. A laptop — what else? — appeared from her backpack.

Shaw said to Tiffany, 'I saw a printer in your office.'

'You need to use it?'

He nodded. 'What's your email?'

She gave it to him and he sent her Sophie's picture. 'Can you make a couple of printouts?'

'Sure.' Tiffany did so and soon returned with the sheets. Shaw printed the reward information at the bottom of one and tacked it back up.

'When I'm gone, can you move the camera so it's pointed this way?'

'You bet.'

'Be subtle about it.'

The woman nodded, clearly still troubled about the intrusion.

He said, 'I want to ask if anybody's seen her. That okay?'

'Sure.' Tiffany returned to the counter. Shaw detected a change in the woman; the thought that her kingdom here had been violated had turned her mood dark, her face suspicious.

Shaw took the second printout Tiffany had made and began his canvass. He was halfway through — with no success — when he heard a woman's voice from behind him. 'Oh, no. That's terrible.'

Shaw turned to see the redhead who'd walked into the café a few minutes ago. She was looking at the sheet of paper in his hand.

'Is that your niece? Sister?'

'I'm helping her father find her.'

'You're a relative?'

'No. He offered a reward.' Shaw nodded toward the flyer.

She thought about this for a moment, revealing nothing of her reaction to this news. 'He must be going crazy. God. And her mother?'

'I'm sure. But Sophie lives here with her father.'

The woman had a face that might be called heart-shaped, depending on how her hair framed her forehead. She was constantly tugging the strands, a nervous habit, he guessed. Her skin was the tan of someone who was outside frequently. She was in athletic shape. Her black leggings revealed exceptional thigh muscles. He guessed skiing and running and cycling. Her shoulders were broad in a way that suggested she'd made them broad by working out. Shaw's exercise was also exclusively out of doors; a treadmill or stair machine, or whatever they were called, would have driven a restless man like him crazy.

'You think something, you know, bad happened to her?' Her green eyes, damp and large, registered concern as they stared at the picture. Her voice was melodic.

'We don't know. Have you ever seen her?'

A squint at the sheet. 'No.'

She shot her eyes down toward his naked ring finger. Shaw had already noticed the same about hers. He made another observation: she was ten years younger than he was.

She sipped from a covered cup. 'Good luck. I really hope she's okay.'

Shaw watched her walk back to her table, where she booted up her PC, plugged in what he took to be serious headphones, not buds, and started typing. He continued canvassing, asking if the patrons had seen Sophie.

The answer was no.

That took care of all those present. He decided to get back to San Miguel Park and help the officers that Detective Dan Wiley had sent to run the crime scene. He thanked Tiffany and she gave him a furtive nod — meaning, he guessed, that she was going to start her surveillance.

Shaw was heading for the door when he was

aware of motion to his left, someone coming toward him.

'Hey.' It was the redhead. Her headset was around her neck and the cord dangled. She walked close. 'I'm Maddie. Is your phone open?'

'My — ?'

'Your phone. Is it locked? Do you need to put in a passcode?'

Doesn't everybody?

'Yes.'

'So. Open it and give it to me. I'll put my number in. That way I'll know it's there and you're not pretending to type it while you really enter five-five-five one-two-one-two.'

Shaw looked over her pretty face, her captivating eyes — the shade of green that Rand McNally had promised, deceptively, to be the color of the foliage in San Miguel Park.

'I could still delete it.'

'That's an extra step. I'm betting you won't go to the trouble. What's your name?'

'Colter.'

'That has to be real. In a bar? When a man's picking up a woman and gives her a fake name, it's always Bob or Fred.' She smiled. 'The thing is, I come on a little strong and that scares guys off. You don't look like the scare-able sort. So. Let me type my number in.'

Shaw said, 'Just give it to me and I'll call you now.'

An exaggerated frown. 'Oh-oh. That way I'll have captured you on incoming calls and stuck you in my address book. You willing to make that commitment?'

89

He lifted his phone. She gave him the number and he dialed. Her ringtone was some rock guitar riff Shaw didn't recognize. She frowned broadly and lifted the mobile to her ear. 'Hello? ... Hello? ... ' Then disconnected. 'Was a telemarketer, I guess.' Her laugh danced like her eyes.

Another hit of the coffee. Another tug of her hair. 'See you around, Colter. Good luck with what you're up to. Oh, and what's my name?'

'Maddie. You never told me your last.'

'One commitment at a time.' She slipped the headphones on and returned to the laptop, on whose screen a psychedelic screen saver paid tribute to the 1960s.

# 13

Shaw couldn't believe it.

Ten minutes after leaving the café he was pulling onto the shoulder of Tamyen Road, overlooking San Miguel Park. Not a single cop.

*Alrightyroo. We'll look into it, Chief . . .*

Guess not.

Shaw approached the only folks nearby — an elderly couple in identical baby-blue jogging outfits — and displayed the printout of Sophie. As he'd expected, they'd never seen her.

Well, if the police weren't going to search, he was. She'd — possibly — flung the phone, as a signal to alert passersby when someone called her.

Maybe she'd also scrawled something in the dirt, a name, part of a license plate number, before X got her. Or perhaps they'd grappled and she'd grabbed a tissue or pen or bit of cloth, rich with DNA or decorated with his finger-prints, tossing that too into the grass.

Shaw descended into the ravine. He walked on grass so he wouldn't disturb any tracks left by the kidnapper in sand and soil.

Using the brown-smeared stone as a hub, Shaw walked in an ever-widening spiral, staring at the ground ahead of him. No footprints, no bits of cloth or tissue, no litter from pockets.

But then a glint of light caught his eye.

It came from above him — a service road on

the crest of the hill. The flash now repeated. He thought: a car door opening and closing. If it was a door, it closed in compete silence.

Crouching, he moved closer. Through the breeze-waving trees, he could make out what might indeed have been a vehicle. With the glare it was impossible to tell. The light wavered — which might have been due to branches bending in the wind. Or because someone who'd exited the car had walked to the edge of the ridge and was looking down.

Was this a jogger stretching before a run, or someone pausing on a long drive home to pee?

Or was it X, spying on the man with a troubling interest in Sophie Mulliner's disappearance?

Shaw started through the brush, keeping low, moving toward the base of the ravine, above which the car sat — if it was a car. The hill was quite steep. This was nothing to Shaw, who regularly ascended vertical rock faces, but the terrain was such that a climb would be noisy.

Tricky. Without being seen, he'd have to get almost to the top to be able to push aside the flora and snap a cell phone picture of the tag number of the jogger. Or pee-er. Or kidnapper.

Shaw got about twenty feet toward the base of the hill before he lost sight of the ridge, due to the angle. And it was then, hearing a snap of branch behind him, that he realized his mistake. He'd been concentrating so much on finding the quietest path ahead of him that he'd been ignoring his flank and rear.

*Never forget there are three hundred and sixty*

*degrees of threat around you* . . .

Just as he turned, he saw the gun lifting toward the center of his chest and he heard a guttural growl from the hoodie-clad young man. 'Don't fucking move. Or you're dead.'

# 14

Colter Shaw glanced at the attacker with irritation and muttered, 'Quiet.'

His eyes returned to the access road above them.

'I'll shoot,' called the young man. 'I will!'

Shaw stepped forward fast and yanked the weapon away and tossed it into the grass.

'Ow, shit!'

Shaw whispered sternly, 'I told you: Quiet! I mean it.' He pushed through a knotty growth of forsythia, trying to get a view of the road. From above came the sound of a car door slamming, an engine starting and a gravel-scattering getaway.

Shaw scrabbled up the incline as fast as he could. At the top, breathing hard, he scanned the road. Nothing but dust. He climbed back down to the ravine, where the young man was on his knees, patting the grass for the weapon.

'Leave it, Kyle,' Shaw muttered.

The kid froze. 'You know me?'

He was Kyle Butler, Sophie's ex-boyfriend. Shaw recognized him from his Facebook page.

Shaw had noted the pistol was a cheap pellet gun, a one-shot model whose projectiles couldn't even break the skin. He picked up the toy and strode to a storm drain and pitched it in.

'Hey!'

'Kyle, somebody sees you with that and you get shot. Which entrance did you use to get into the park?'

The boy rose and stared, confused.

'Which entrance?' Shaw had learned that the quieter your voice, the more intimidating you were. He was very quiet now.

'Over there.' Nodding toward the sound of the motorbikes. The main entrance to the east. He swallowed. Butler's hands rose fast, as if Shaw presently had a gun on him.

'You can lower your arms.'

He did so. Slowly.

'Did you see that car parked on the ridge?'

'What ridge?'

Shaw pointed to the access road.

'No, man. I didn't. Really.'

Shaw looked him over, recalling: surfer dude. The boy had frothy blond hair, a navy-blue T-shirt under the black hoodie, black nylon workout pants. A handsome young man, though his eyes were a bit blank.

'Did Frank Mulliner tell you I was here?'

Another pause. What to say, what not to say? Finally: 'Yeah. I called him after I got your message. He said you said you found her phone in the park.'

The excess of verbs in the last sentence explained a lot to Shaw. So, the lovesick boy had conjured up the idea that Shaw had kidnapped his former girlfriend to get the reward. He remembered that Butler's job was bolting big speakers into Subarus and Civics and his passion was riding a piece of waxed wood on rollicking water. Shaw decided that the percentage likelihood of Kyle Butler being the kidnapper had dropped to nil.

95

But there was that related hypothesis. 'Was Sophie ever with you when you scored weed, or coke, or whatever you do?'

'What're you talking about?'

First things first.

'Kyle, does it make sense that I'd kidnap somebody hoping her father would post a reward? Wouldn't I just ask for a ransom?'

He looked away. 'I guess. Okay, man.'

The sound of the motorbikes rose and fell, buzz-sawing in the distance.

Butler continued: 'I'm just . . . It's all I can think about: Where is she? What's happening to her? Will I ever see her again?' His voice choked.

'At any time was she with you when you scored?'

'I don't know. Maybe. Why?'

He explained that a dealer might have been concerned that Sophie was a witness who could identify him.

'Oh God, no. The dudes I buy from? They're not players. Just, like, students or board heads. You know, surfers. Not bangers from East Palo or Oakland.'

This seemed credible.

Shaw asked, 'You have any idea who might've taken her? Her dad didn't think she had any stalkers.'

'No . . . ' The young man's voice faded. His head was down, slowly shaking now. Shaw saw a glistening in his eyes. 'It's all my fault. Fuck.'

'Your fault?'

'Yeah, man. See, Wednesdays we always did things together. They were like our weekend, 'cause I had to work Saturday and Sunday. I'd go out and new-school — you know, trick surf at Half Moon or Maverick. Then I'd pick her up and we'd hang with friends or do dinner, a movie. If I hadn't . . . If I hadn't fucked up so bad, that's what we would've done last Wednesday. And this never would've happened. All the weed. I got mean, I was a son of a bitch. I didn't want to; it just happened. She'd had enough. She didn't want to be with a loser.' He wiped his face angrily. 'But I'm clean. Thirty-four days. And I'm switching majors. Engineering. Computers.'

So Kyle Butler was the knight coming to San Miguel Park with a BB gun to confront the dragon and rescue the damsel. He'd win her back.

Shaw looked toward the shoulder of Tamyen Road. Still no cops. He called the Task Force. Wiley was out. Standish was out.

'Find me a bag,' Shaw said to Butler.

'Bag?'

'Paper, plastic, anything. Look on the shoulder. I'll look here.'

Butler climbed the hill to Tamyen Road and Shaw walked the trails, hoping for a trash can. He found none. Then he heard: 'Got one!' Butler trotted down the hill. 'By the side of the road.' He held up the white bag. 'From Walgreens. Is that okay?'

Colter Shaw was a man who smiled rarely. This drew a faint grin. 'Perfect.'

Sticking to the grass once more, he walked to the bloodstained rock and picked it up with the bag.

'What're you going to do with it?'

'Find a private lab to do a DNA test — I'm

sure it's Sophie's blood.'

'Oh, Jesus.'

'No, it's just from a scrape. Nothing serious.'

'Why're you doing that? Because the cops aren't?'

'That's right.'

Butler's eyes flashed wide. 'Yo, man, let's look for her together! If the cops aren't doing shit.'

'It's a good idea. But I need your help first.'

'Yeah, man. Anything.'

'Her father's on his way home from work.'

'His weekend job's over in the East Bay.' Butler's face showed pity. 'Two hours each way. Got another job during the week. And he still couldn't afford to keep their house, you know?'

'When he gets back, I need you to find out something.'

'Sure.'

'Sorry, Kyle. Might be kind of tough. I need to find out if she's been dating anybody. Go through her room, talk to friends.'

'You think that's who it is?'

'I don't know. We have to look at every possibility.'

Butler gave a wan smile. 'Sure. I'll do it. It's just a stupid dream I had anyway, us getting back together. It's not going to happen.' The young man turned and started up the hill. Then he stopped and returned. He shook Shaw's hand. 'I'm sorry, man. I didn't mean to go all *Narcos* on you. You know?'

'Not a worry.'

He watched Butler hike back toward the far entrance.

On his mission.

His futile mission.

From his interview with her father and examination of her room, Shaw didn't believe that Sophie was seeing anyone, not seriously, much less anyone who might have kidnapped her. But it was important for the poor kid to be elsewhere when Shaw discovered what he was now sure he'd find: Sophie Mulliner's body.

# 15

Shaw was driving along winding Tamyen Road, having left San Miguel Park behind.

A serial kidnapper stashing his victims in a dungeon for any length of time wasn't an impossible likelihood. It did seem rare enough, though, that he focused on a more realistic fate: that Sophie'd been the victim of a sexual sociopath. In Shaw's experience, the majority of rapists might be serial actors, but almost always with multiple victims. The rapist's inclination was to kill and move on.

This meant Sophie's corpse lay somewhere nearby. X was clearly not stupid — the tracker on her bike, the obscuring clothing, the selection of a good attack zone. He wouldn't drive any distance with a body in his trunk. There might be an accident or traffic violation or a checkpoint. He'd do what he wanted, near San Miguel Park, and flee. In this southwest portion of San Francisco Bay were acres and acres of wet, sandy earth soft enough to dig a quick, shallow grave. But the area was open, with good visibility for hundreds and hundreds of yards; X would want his privacy.

Shaw came to a large, abandoned self-storage operation of about a hundred compartments. The facility was in the middle of an expanse of weeds and sandy ground. He parked and noted that the gap in the chain-link gate was easily wide enough for two people to slip through. He did so himself and began walking up and down the aisles. It was an easy place to search because the paneled overhead doors to the units had been removed and lay in a rust-festering pile behind one of the buildings, like the wings of huge roaches. Maybe this was done for safety's sake, the way refrigerator doors are removed upon discarding so a child can't get trapped inside. Whatever the reason, this practice made it simple to see that Sophie's body wasn't here.

Soon the Malibu was cruising again.

He saw a feral dog tugging something from the ground about thirty feet away. Something red and white.

Blood and bone?

Shaw braked fast and climbed out of the Chevy. The dog wasn't a big creature, maybe forty or fifty pounds and rib-skinny. Shaw approached slowly, keeping a steady pace.

*Never, ever startle an animal . . .*

The creature moved toward him with its black eyes narrowed. One fang was missing, which gave it an ominous look. Shaw avoided eye contact and continued forward without hesitating.

Until he was able to see what the dog was tugging up.

A Kentucky Fried Chicken bucket.

He left the scrawny thing to its illusory dinner and returned to the car.

Tamyen Road made a long loop past more marshes and fields, and with San Francisco Bay to his left he continued south.

The cracked and bleached asphalt led him to a row of trees and brush, behind which was a large industrial facility, seemingly closed for decades.

An eight-foot-high chain-link fence encircled the weed-choked facility. There were three gates, about thirty yards apart. Shaw pulled up to what seemed to be the main one. He counted five — no, six — dilapidated structures, marred with peeling beige paint and rust, sprouting pipes and tubing and wires. Some walls bore uninspired graffiti. The outlying buildings were one-story. In the center was an ominous, towering box, with a footprint of about a hundred by two hundred feet; it was five stories high and above it soared a metal smokestack, twenty feet in diameter at the base, tapering slightly as it rose.

The grounds abutted the Bay and the skeleton of a wide pier jutted fifty yards into the gently rocking water. Maybe maritime equipment had been fabricated here.

Shaw edged the car off the driveway. There was nowhere to hide the vehicle completely, so he parked on the far side of a stand of foliage. Difficult to see from the road. Why risk a run-in with local cops for violating the old yet unambiguous NO TRESPASSING signs? Shaw was mindful too of the individual twenty minutes ago possibly surveilling him from the ridge above San Miguel Park. Person X, he might as well assume. He placed his computer bag and the bloody rock in the trunk. He scanned the road, the forest on the other side of it, the grounds here. He saw no one. He believed that a car had driven through the main gate at some point in the recent past. The grounds were tall grass and bent in a way that suggested a vehicle's transit.

Shaw walked to the gate, which was secured by a piece of chain and a lock. He wasn't looking forward to scaling the fence. It was topped with the upward-pointed snipped-off ends of the links, not as dangerous as razor wire but sharp enough to draw blood.

He wondered if there was any give to the two panels of this gate, as there had been at the self-storage operation. Shaw tugged. The two sides parted only a few inches. He took hold of the large padlock to get a better grip. He pulled hard and it opened.

The lock was one of those models without keys; instead they have numbered dials on the bottom. The shank had been pushed in. Whoever had done it had not spun the dials to relock the mechanism. Two things intrigued Shaw. First, the lock was new. Second, the code was not the default — usually 0-0-0-0 or 1-2-3-4 — but, he could see by looking at the dials, 7-4-9-9. Which meant someone had been using it to secure the gate and had neglected to lock it the most recent time he had been here.

Why? Maybe the laziness of a security guard?

Or because the visitor had entered recently, knowing he'd be leaving soon.

Which meant that perhaps he was still here.

Call Wiley?

Not yet.

He'd have to give the detective something concrete.

He opened the gate, stepped inside and

replaced the lock as it had been. He then walked quickly over the weed-filled driveway for twenty yards to the first building — a small guardhouse. He glanced in. Empty. He scanned two other nearby buildings, Warehouse 3 and Warehouse 4.

Keeping low, Shaw moved to the closest of these, eyes scanning the vista, noting the vantage points from which a shooter could aim. While he had no particular gut feeling that he was in fact in any cross-hairs, the lock that should have been locked and wasn't flipped a switch of caution within him.

*Bears'll come at you pushing brush. You'll hear. Mountain lions will growl. You'll hear. Wolf packs're silver. You'll see. You know where snakes'll be. But a man who wants to shoot you? You'll never hear, you'll never see, you'll never know what rock he's hiding under.*

Shaw looked into each of the warehouses, pungent with mold and completely empty. He then moved along the wide driveway between these buildings and the big manufacturing facility. Here he could see faded words painted on the brick, ten feet high, forty long, the final letters weathered to nothing.

AGW INDUSTRIES, INC. — FROM OUR
HANDS TO Y

Shaw stepped across the driveway and into the shadows of the big building.

*You're the best tracker in the family . . .*

Not his father's words, his mother's.

He was looking for a trail. In the wild, cutting

for sign is noting paw prints and claw marks, disturbed ground, broken branches, tufts of animal coat in brambles. Now, in suburbia, Colter Shaw was looking for tire treads or footprints. He saw only grass that might have been bent by a car a month ago — or thirty minutes.

Shaw continued to the main building — the loading dock in the back, where the vehicle might have stopped. He quietly climbed the stairs, four feet up, and walked to a door. He tried to open it. The knob turned yet the door held fast.

Someone had driven sharp, black Sheetrock screws into the jamb. He checked the door at the opposite end of the dock. The same. At the back of the dock was a window of mesh-impregnated glass and that too was sealed. The screws appeared new, just like the lock.

This gave Shaw a likely scenario: X had raped and killed Sophie and left the body inside, screwed the doors and windows shut to keep trespassers from finding her.

Now, time to call the police.

He was reaching for his phone when he was startled by a male voice: 'Mr. Shaw!'

He climbed off the loading dock and walked along the back of the building.

Kyle Butler was approaching. 'Mr. Shaw. There you are!'

What the hell was he doing here?

Shaw was thinking of the open gate, the likelihood that the kidnapper was still here. He held his finger to his lips and then gestured for the boy to crouch.

Kyle paused, confused. He said, 'There's

105

somebody else here. I saw his car in a parking lot back over there.'

He was pointing to the line of trees on the other side of which was one of the outlier structures.

'Kyle! Get down!'

'Do you think Sophie's — ' Before he finished his sentence, a pistol shot resounded. Butler's head jerked back and a mist of red popped into the air. He dropped straight to the ground, a bundle of dark clothing and limp flesh.

Two shots followed — make-sure bullets — striking Butler's leg and chest, tugging at his clothing.

Think. Fast. The shooter would've heard Butler calling him and would know basically where Shaw was. And to make the headshot, he would have been close.

But the shooter — most likely X — would also be cautious. He would have seen Shaw at San Miguel Park and suspected he wasn't the law but he couldn't be sure. And would be assuming Shaw was armed.

Shaw glanced at Kyle Butler.

Dead, glazed eyes and shattered temple. Much blood.

And then, for the moment, Shaw forced himself to forget about him entirely.

He backed away, crouching, heading for the drive where he'd spotted the bent grass. As he did, he punched in 911 and reported an 'active shooter' at the old AGW plant off Tamyen Road.

He whispered to the dispatcher, 'Do you know where that is?'

'Yessir, we'll have units responding. Stay on the line, please, and give me your — '

He disconnected.

All Shaw had to do now was find cover and avoid getting shot. He guessed that X would figure that he, whether civilian or cop, would have called for help. The kidnapper would flee.

Except, apparently, X hadn't done that at all.

Above Shaw came a crash of shattering glass and around him shards fell to the ground as he crouched and covered his head with his arm.

X wasn't finished yet. He'd gotten into the factory and climbed to an upper floor where he'd have a clearer shot at Shaw. He was now about to stick his head and arm out the window he'd just smashed and pepper Shaw with rounds.

There was no cover here, not for fifty feet.

Shaw turned and began sprinting toward the closest warehouse, waiting for the pop, then the slam of the slug in his back.

That didn't happen.

Instead, he heard from inside a woman's fierce scream. He stopped and looked back.

It was Sophie Mulliner who stood at the shattered window, her face turned toward the bloody body of Kyle Butler.

Then she looked at Shaw. A look of pure rage filled her face. 'What've you done? What've you done?'

She vanished inside.

# 16

Colter Shaw stood on a mesh catwalk inside the dim, cavernous manufacturing space. He crouched, listening.

Sounds, echoing from everywhere. Footsteps? Dripping water? The ancient structure settling? And then the roar of jet engines overhead. The factory was along the final approach path to San Francisco Airport. The gassy howl made it momentarily impossible to hear anything else.

Like someone coming up behind you.

Shaw had found one door that had not been secured with Sheetrock screws. He'd opened it and quickly stepped inside, closing it after him. He climbed to the third-floor catwalk so he could get an overview of the space below.

He saw no sign of Sophie or of X. Was the kidnapper still here? He would've guessed Shaw called for help. But he also might risk remaining for some minutes to find and murder Shaw, who might have some incriminating information, like his license tag number. Sophie Mulliner, of course, would die too.

He climbed down metal staircases to the ground floor, the labyrinth he'd surveyed from above, a network of offices, workstations, concrete slabs and machinery, presumably still here because technology had made the equipment obsolete, not even worth parts.

All surreal, in the gloom. Shaw was dizzy too;

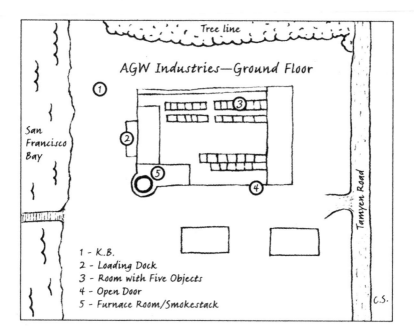

Tree line

AGW Industries—Ground Floor

San Francisco Bay

Tamyen Road

1 - K.B.
2 - Loading Dock
3 - Room with Five Objects
4 - Open Door
5 - Furnace Room/Smokestack

C.S.

this, he guessed, was from air infused with the astringent fumes of diesel oil, grease and vast colonies of mold.

He spotted the window Sophie had broken — beside another cat-walk on the fourth level — but there were no hiding spots there. She'd have gone to cover somewhere on the main floor. Shaw started through that level now, weaving around slabs and bins and machinery and workstations. He passed rows of rooms — ROTOR DESIGN II, ENGINEERING SUPERVISION, WAR DEPARTMENT LIAISON. Shaw paused beside each, listening — for breathing, for gritty scrapes underfoot, for that altered echo when a human takes up space in a room.

No, they were empty.

But one office was different from the others. Its door was closed and sealed with the same Sheetrock screws that held fast the outer doors.

Shaw stopped. On the wall nearby was a crude painting — an approximation of the eerie stenciled face on the flyer in the Quick Byte Café. Which answered the question of who had tacked it up.

He turned back to the office with the sealed door. A crude hole, about two by two feet, had been cut and punched through the wall, from the inside out; bits of the plasterboard and dust lay on the floor outside. Shaw crouched and noted footprints in the white powder, small — Sophie's? She hadn't been wearing shoes or socks or been barefoot. It looked like she'd wrapped her feet in rags.

Listening again, his ear near the jagged hole, which was big enough — just — for a person to fit through.

The kidnapper might have stashed Sophie here and, somehow, she'd managed to free herself from the duct tape — which he'd surely used — and found something inside to break through the wall with. She'd probably tried to get out of the building and hadn't found a door that wasn't screwed shut.

He was debating his next steps when he heard a faint click to his right, followed by what might have been a low muttering sound, as if someone were angry he'd accidentally given himself away. It came from the end of a nearby corridor, between long metal walls lined with pipes and conduit. A sign read DON'T 'BUCK' THE RULES: HARD HAT OR FINE. YOU CHOOSE!

At the end of the corridor were racks holding fifty-five-gallon oil drums and piles of lumber.

110

The muttering sound once more.

Sophie or X?

Then, his eyes growing yet more sensitive to the dimness, he could make out, at the end of the corridor, a shadow on the factory floor. It was moving slightly, cast by someone standing just out of sight, to the left at the T intersection of aisles.

Shaw couldn't pass up the advantage. He'd ease slowly to the corner and step around fast. If the shadow belonged to X he'd secure the gun hand and take him down. He knew a number of ways to get someone onto the floor such that they weren't inclined to get up anytime soon.

He moved closer. Twenty feet. Ten. Five.

The shadow shifted slightly, rocking back and forth.

Another step.

And Shaw walked right into the trap.

A tripwire. He went down fast and hard, getting his hands up just in time. The agonizing pushup saved his jaw from fracture. He rose, crouching, found himself looking at a sweatshirt hanging on a hook. To it was tied a piece of fishing line.

Which meant . . .

Before he could rise fully, an oil drum rolled from the rack and slammed into his shoulders. It was empty but the impact toppled him. He heard a voice, Sophie's, screaming, 'You son of a bitch! You killed him!'

The young woman was advancing on him, hair disheveled, eyes wide, her T-shirt stained. In her hand was what seemed to be a shiv, a homemade glass knife, the handle a strip of cloth wrapped around it.

Shaw muscled the drum off — it bounced loudly on the concrete. With that sound and the scream, X would know more or less where they were.

'Sophie!' Shaw whispered, climbing to his feet. 'It's okay! Don't say anything.'

Her courage broke and she turned and fled.

'Wait,' he called in a whisper.

She vanished into another room and swung a solid-metal door shut behind her. Shaw followed, thirty feet away. He stuck to her path, where there'd be no more traps. He pushed open the door and found himself in a boiler or smelting room. Coal bins lined the walls, some still half filled. There was dust, ash and soot everywhere.

And light at the far end of a long row of furnaces.

Shaw followed her footsteps, toward the cool illumination, whose source filtered down from a hundred feet above him; Shaw stood at the base of the smokestack. With less concern about the environment in the factory's working days, the furnaces would have spewed fumes into the air throughout the south Bay Area. In the middle of the base was a pit, fifteen feet across, filled with a gray-brown muck, presumably ancient ash and coal dust mixed with rainwater.

Shaw was looking for Sophie's footprints.

Which had simply vanished.

And then he saw why. Mounted into the inside of the smokestack's wall were rectangular rungs, like large staples, protruding about eight inches from the brick: a ladder for daredevil workers climbing to the top to replace aircraft warning lightbulbs, he guessed.

She was thirty feet up and climbing. A fall from there would kill or paralyze her.

'Sophie, I'm a friend of your father's. I've been looking for you.' Shaw saw a glint and jumped back fast as something she'd flung fell toward him.

It was what he'd guessed — the shiv — and it just missed him, shattering at his feet. He glanced toward the entrance to the furnace room. No sign of the kidnapper. Yet.

Her voice was unsteady and she was crying. 'You killed him! I saw you!'

'I was there. But the shot came from whoever kidnapped you.'

'You're lying!'

'We have to be quiet! He could still be here.' Shaw was speaking in a harsh whisper. He remembered her father's nickname for her. 'Fee! Please.'

She stopped.

Shaw added, 'Luka. Luka's your poodle. A white standard.'

'How do you know . . . ?' Her voice fading.

'You named yourself Fee when you were a baby. Your father offered a reward to find you. That's what I'm doing.'

'He did?'

'I went to your house. Alta Vista Drive. Luka sat next to me on the couch with the gold slipcover. The ugly gold slipcover. In front of the coffee table with the broken leg.'

113

'What color is Luka's collar?'

'Blue with white rhinestones,' Shaw said, then added, 'Or maybe diamonds.'

Her face went still. Then a faint smile. 'He offered a reward?'

'Come on down, Fee. We've got to hide.'

She debated for a moment.

Sophie began the climb to the floor. Shaw saw that her legs were trembling. Heights could do that to you.

More rungs. When she was about fifteen feet above the brick floor, Sophie released the grip with her right hand and wiped her palm on her thigh, drying the sweat.

Before she could take the rung again, though, her left hand slipped off the one she was gripping. Screaming, she made a desperate lunge for the rung but missed. She pitched backward, headfirst, tumbling exactly toward the spot on the brick where the glass knife had shattered into razor-sharp splinters.

# 17

Unlike at San Miguel Park, the law had arrived fast and en masse. Ten official cars, a carnival of flashing lights.

The medical examiner technician had just finished with Kyle Butler; that team had been the first to get to work. This always seemed odd to Shaw. You'd think corpses could wait — once you'd confirmed they were indeed corpses, of course — while evidence might dry up or blow away or change in composition. But they were the experts.

The heart and brain of the investigation seemed to be the Task Force, specifically Dan Wiley. The imposing man was conferring with others, some local, some Santa Clara County, and a few plainclothes who, Shaw overheard, were from the Bureau of Investigation — California, not federal. Shaw was mildly surprised the FBI was not present. As he'd reminded Wiley, kidnapping is a federal crime as well as state.

Shaw was standing near the loading dock, where he'd been directed to wait by Wiley. He had told the detective about Kyle Butler's words and suggested that X — though using the preferred police term *unsub*, for 'unknown subject' — had fled south on Tamyen Road.

'At Highway 42 and Tamyen, there might be CCTVs. I don't know the make or color of the car. He'll be driving carefully. Stopping for red lights, not speeding.'

Wiley had grunted and wandered off to deliver this information to minions — or not.

He was now barking to a young woman officer, her hair in a constricted blond bun, 'I said to search it. I meant to search it. Why would I not mean for you to search it?'

The woman reluctantly deflated her defiant gaze. She walked away to search it, whatever *it* was.

Shaw glanced at the pair of ambulances, forty feet in front of him. One of the boxy vehicles held the deceased Kyle Butler, the other Sophie Mulliner, whose condition he didn't yet know. He'd managed to avert her landing on the glass-strewn floor by leveraging her into the ash pit — disgusting but softer than brick. He'd felt a bone pop with this maneuver — hers, not his — and she'd veered into the unpleasant soup. He pulled her out immediately as she moaned in pain and retched. The cleanest water he could find was standing rainwater, more or less clear, and he scooped up handfuls, draining it into her mouth and telling her, like a dentist, to rinse and spit. The chemicals in the pit could not be good. The fracture was bad, both radius and ulna, though not a through-the-skin fracture.

Shaw had not heard her account of the kidnapping; their time together in the smokestack had been devoted to first aid. He now saw the medical technician who'd been attending to Sophie walk away, speaking on his cell phone.

Shaw pushed off the loading dock wall and

started toward the ambulance to speak to the young woman.

Wiley saw him. 'Don't wander too far, Chief. We need to talk.'

Shaw ignored him and continued toward the ambulances. To his right, on the far side of the chain-link, he could see a gaggle of news vans and maybe thirty reporters and camera operators. Some spectators.

He found Sophie, sitting up, groggy, eyes glazed. Her right arm, the broken one, was in a temporary cast. She'd be on the way to the hospital soon. Shaw was familiar with breaks; surgery would be involved. The medics had apparently used an emergency wash to clean off what chemicals they could.

She blinked in Shaw's direction. 'Is he really . . .' Her voice was harsh and she coughed. 'Kyle?'

'He's gone. I'm sorry.'

She lowered her head and cried, covering her eyes. Catching her breath, she asked, 'Did they . . . Have they found him?'

'No.'

'Jesus.' She tugged a tissue from a box and used that to wipe her eyes and nose.

'Why Kyle?'

'He saw the kidnapper's car. He could identify it.'

'Did he come with you?'

'No. I told him to go to your house, to see your father. But he was worried about you. He wanted to help me search.'

More sobbing. 'He just . . . He was so sweet. Oh, his mom. Somebody'll have to tell her. And

117

his brother.' Eyes easing into and out of focus. 'How did you . . . How did you find me?'

'Checked places near San Miguel Park you might've been.'

'That's where this is?' She looked up at the towering building.

'Did you get a look at him, recognize him?' Shaw asked.

'No. He had a mask on, like a ski mask, and sunglasses.'

'Gray? The mask?'

'I think. Yes.'

The stocking cap.

Shaw's phone hummed. He looked at the screen. He hit ANSWER and handed the unit to her.

'Your father.'

'Daddy! . . . No, I'm okay. My arm. I broke my arm . . . Kyle's gone. Daddy, he killed Kyle. He shot him . . . I don't know . . . That man . . . Mr . . . '

She looked his way.

'Shaw.'

'Mr. Shaw. Daddy, he found me. He saved me . . . Okay . . . Where are you? . . . I love you too. Call Mom. Can you call her? . . . Love you.'

She disconnected and handed the phone back. 'He's on his way.'

Her eyes looked past Shaw to the building where she'd been held captive. She whispered, 'He just left me there.' Her voice revealed bewilderment. 'I woke up in this dark room. Alone. That was almost scarier than if he'd tried to rape me. I would've fought him. I would've fucking killed him. But he just left me there. Two days. I had to drink rainwater. Disgusting.'

'You found that glass and cut your way out with it?'

'There was a bottle inside. I broke it and made a knife.'

Another voice, from behind him: 'Mr. Shaw?'

He turned to the blond officer who'd been dressed down by the detective earlier.

'Detective Wiley asked me to bring you to see him.'

Sophie reached out with her good arm and gripped Shaw's shoulder. 'Thank you,' she whispered. And her eyes began to well with tears.

The officer said, 'Please, Mr. Shaw. Detective Wiley said *now*.'

# 18

Shaw followed the officer to where Wiley stood, by the loading dock, lording over the crime scene, snapping at yet another young deputy.

Shaw wished Detective Standish had drawn the case. However obnoxious, he couldn't be as insufferable as his partner.

As they approached, Wiley gave a nod and said to the officer who'd brought Shaw to him, 'Kathy, dear, do me a solid. I sent Suzie out front. See if she's got anything for me. Hop hop.'

'Suzie? Oh, you mean Deputy Harrison.'

Wiley was oblivious to the snap of the correction whip. He simply added, ominously, 'And don't talk to a single reporter. Am I clear on that?'

The blond officer's face grew dark as she too reined in her anger. She disappeared down the broad driveway between the manufacturing building and the warehouses.

The detective turned to him now and patted one of the stairs on the loading dock. 'Take a pew, Chief.'

Remaining standing, Shaw crossed his arms — Wiley lifted an eyebrow, as if to say, *Whatever* — and Shaw asked, 'Did they find any CCTV at that intersection, Tamyen and Forty-two?'

'It's being looked into.' Wiley pulled out a pen and pad. 'Now, whole ball of wax. Tell me from when you left my office.'

'I went back to the Quick Byte. Somebody'd taken the Missing poster Sophie's father'd put up.'

'Why'd they do that?'

'And replaced it with this.' He patted his pocket.

'Whatcha got there, Chief? Tobacco chaw? A fidget stick?'

'You have a latex glove?'

Wiley hesitated, as Shaw knew he would. But — also as Shaw anticipated — handed him one. Shaw pulled it on and fished in his pocket. He extracted the sheet of paper from the Quick Byte. The eerie stenciled image of the man's face. He displayed it.

'So?' Wiley asked.

'This image?'

'I see it.' A frown.

'In the room where he put Sophie? The same thing — or close to it — was graffitied on the wall.'

Wiley pulled on his own gloves. He took the sheet and gestured a crime scene tech over. He gave her the paper and asked her to run an analysis. 'And check in the databases if it means anything.'

'Sure, Detective.'

Bullying and talent, Shaw reminded himself, are not mutually exclusive.

'You were in the café. And after that?'

'I went back to San Miguel Park. I thought you were going to send a team there.'

Wiley set the pad and pen down on the chest-high loading dock. For a moment Shaw

121

actually believed Wiley was planning to deck him. The detective removed a metal container, like a pill bottle, from his front slacks pocket. He unscrewed the top and extracted a tooth-pick. Shaw smelled mint.

'Better if you stay on message here, Chief.' He pointed the toothpick at Shaw and then slipped it between his teeth. He wore a thick, engraved wedding ring. He reversed the ritual of the container and picked up his writing implement once more.

Shaw continued with his chronology: Kyle approaching him and the car on the ridge.

'Was it you?' Shaw asked. 'In the car?'

Wiley blinked. 'Why'd I do that?'

'Was it?'

No answer. 'You see that vehicle?'

'I didn't.'

'Lot of invisible cars around here,' Wiley muttered. 'Go on.'

Shaw explained his conclusion that Sophie had been raped and killed and the body disposed of. He went looking for the most logical places where that might have been and ended up here. 'I told Kyle to go to Sophie's house. He didn't.'

'Why do you think the kidnapper didn't come after you?'

'Thought I was armed, I'm guessing. Detective, all the doors on the ground level were screwed shut, except one. Why would he leave it open?'

'The whole point, Chief. He came back to rape her.'

'Then why not put a lock on that too, like he did the gate?'

122

'This's one sick pup, Chief. Can't hardly expect people like that to behave like you and me, can we now?' The toothpick moved from one side of his mouth to the other, via tongue only. It was a clever trick. 'I suppose you'll be getting that reward.'

'That's between me and Mr. Mulliner, a business arrangement.'

'Arrangement,' the officer said. His voice was as impressive as his bulk. Shaw could smell a fragrance and thought it was probably from the ample hairspray with which he froze his black-and-white mane in place.

'At least tell me how you heard about it, Chief.'

'My name's Colter.'

'Aw, that's just an endearment. Everybody uses endearments. Bet you do too.'

Shaw said nothing.

The toothpick wiggled. 'This reward. How'd you hear about it?'

'I'm not inclined to talk about my business anymore,' Shaw said. Then added, 'You might want to get security video from the Quick Byte and go through the past month. You could find a clearer image of the perp — if he was staking it out.'

Wiley jotted something, though whether it was Shaw's suggestion or something else, Shaw had no idea.

The young woman officer Wiley'd sent to search for 'it' returned.

Wiley raised a bushy eyebrow. 'What'd you find, sweetheart?'

She held up an evidence bag. Inside was the Walgreens plastic bag containing the rock stained with what Shaw now knew was Sophie's blood.

'It was in his car, Detective.'

Wiley clicked his tongue. 'Hmm, stealing material evidence from a scene? That's obstruction of justice. Do the honors, sweetheart. Read him his rights. So, turn around, Mr. Shaw, and put your hands behind your back.'

Shaw courteously complied, reflecting: at least Wiley'd dropped the 'Chief.'

# 19

In the sprawling cabin on the Compound, where the Shaws lived, several rooms, *large* rooms, were devoted to books. The collection came from the days when Ashton and Mary Dove were academics — he taught history, the humanities and political science. She was a professor in the medical school and was also a PI — principal investigator, overseeing how corporate and government money was spent at universities. Then there was Ashton's flint-hard devotion to survivalism, which meant yet more books — hard copies, of course.

*Never trust the internet.*

This one too was so obvious Ashton didn't bother to codify it in his Never rulebook.

Colter, Dorion and Russell read constantly, and Colter was drawn to the legal books in particular, of which there were hundreds. For some reason, on the exodus from Berkeley to the wilderness east of Fresno, Ashton had brought along enough jurisprudential texts to open a law firm. Colter was fascinated with the casebooks — collections of court decisions on topics like contracts, constitutional law, torts, criminal law and domestic relations. He liked the stories behind each of the cases, what had led the parties to court, who would prevail and why. His father taught his children the rules for physical survival; law provided the rules for social survival.

After college — he graduated cum laude from

the University of Michigan — Shaw returned to California and interned in a public defender's office. This taught him two things. First, he would never, ever work in an office again, thus ending any thoughts of law school and a legal career. Second, he'd been right about the law: it was a brilliant weapon for offense and defense, like an over-under shotgun or a bow or a slingshot.

Now, sitting in an interview room in the sterile lockup attached to the Joint Major Crimes Task Force, Colter Shaw was summoning up what criminal law he knew. He'd been arrested more than a few times in his career. Though he'd never been convicted of any crime, the nature of his work meant he occasionally butted heads with the police, who, depending on their mood and the circumstances, might haul him in front of a booking desk.

He massaged his right arm, which had taken the brunt of deflecting the tumbling Sophie Mulliner, and calmly, in an orderly way, prepared his defense. This didn't take long.

The door opened and a balding man, slim, in his fifties, walked inside. His scalp was shiny, as if it had been waxed, and Shaw had to force himself not to look at it. The man wore a light gray suit, with a badge on his belt. His tie was a bold floral, the knot perfectly symmetrical. Colter Shaw had last worn a tie . . . Well, he couldn't exactly remember. Margot had said he looked 'distinguished.'

'Mr. Shaw.'

A nod.

The man introduced himself as 'Joint Task Force Senior Supervisor Cummings,' a mouthful that spoke more about the man's nature than about the job description. 'Fred' or 'Stan' would have painted him better.

Cummings sat across the table from Shaw. The table, like the benches, was bolted down and made of sturdy metal. Cummings had a notebook and a pen. Shaw couldn't spot the cameras, but they'd be here.

'The detention officer said you wanted to talk to me. So you've changed your mind about waiving your right to speak to us without an attorney.'

'I didn't change my mind. I wouldn't speak to Detective Wiley, with or without an attorney. I'll speak to you.'

The lean man digested this, tapping the end of the Bic against a notepad. 'I'm at a disadvantage here. This happened pretty fast and I don't have all the facts. There's something about a reward that the victim's father was offering? You're trying to get that?'

While Shaw preferred 'earn,' he nodded.

'That's your job?'

'It is. And it's not relevant to our conversation.'

Cummings processed once more. 'Dan Wiley can be a difficult person to deal with. But he's a good officer.'

'Have there ever been complaints against him? Women officers, for instance?'

Cummings gave no response. 'He tells me that you stole evidence from a crime scene. With the evidence missing, it would have looked like you were the only one who found the girl. And that meant you'd be entitled to the reward.'

Shaw had to give Wiley credit. Clever.

'Now, what we'll do — and Detective Wiley's on board with this — is knock down the obstruction to tampering. Misdemeanor. You forget about that reward and leave the area — you live in the Sierra Nevadas, right?'

'That's my residence.'

'We'll do recognizance. And you can walk now. The prosecutor's got the paperwork ready.'

Shaw was tired. A long day — from Molotov cocktail to murder — and it was only 6 p.m.

'Supervisor Cummings, Detective Wiley arrested me because he needs to steer this whole ship in a different direction. If I don't pursue the reward and I leave town, it doesn't look like Wiley screwed up and a civilian solved his case.'

'Hold on, Mr. Shaw.'

But Shaw didn't hold on. 'Wiley had all the information he needed to realize this was an active kidnapping. He should've had twenty-five uniforms in and around San Miguel Park to search for Sophie Mulliner. And if he had, they would've found her — because I found her by myself in a half hour — and Kyle Butler'd be alive right now and, likely, you'd have your unsub in custody.'

'Mr. Shaw, the fact is you removed evidence from a crime scene. That's an offense. The law is black-and-white on that.'

Cummings had helpfully walked right into Shaw's trap.

Shaw leaned forward ever so slightly. 'One, I took that rock to have a DNA test done, at my own expense, to prove that Sophie'd been kidnapped — because none of you believed it. Two' — Shaw held up a hand to silence Cummings's impending sputter — 'San Miguel Park wasn't a crime scene. Dan Wiley never declared it one. I picked up a piece of granite in a county park. Now, Supervisor Cummings, I'm ending our conversation. You can discuss all this with your DA or I'll call my attorney and she'll take it from there.'

# 20

Shaw opted for one of those packets of peanut butter crackers.

All the other snacks in the Joint Major Crimes Task Force lobby were of the sweet variety, other than some unpopped cheddar popcorn, though how a visitor might prepare it was a mystery, there being no microwave that he could see.

He bought a bottled water too. The coffee, he figured, would be undrinkable.

He'd just finished the delicacy when Cummings's assistant, a sharp-eyed young man, entered the lobby through the submarine-quality security door and said that, unfortunately, Shaw's car had been towed to the pound.

Shaw didn't bother to ask why. So while he'd been released, his wheels were still in detention.

'I'm not being charged.'

'I know that, sir.'

'But I can't get my car?'

'No, sir. Some evidence was found in the car. I need a detective to sign off on it.'

'Supervisor Cummings will.'

'Well, he's gone home. We're looking for a supervising detective who can authorize the release.'

'How long do you think it will take?'

'There's paperwork. Usually four, five hours.'

It was a rental; maybe he'd just leave it and get a new one. Then he decided there might be some penalty. He always bought the collision damage waiver option. On the other hand, rental contracts had a lot of fine print. There was possibly a provision that voided the protection if a customer intentionally abandoned the car at the police pound.

'We have your phone number. We'll call when it's ready to be released.'

'Do you know if the suspect has been identified?'

'Suspect?' The tone: *Which one?*

'The Sophie Mulliner abduction.'

'I wouldn't know.' The assistant was swallowed up through the doomsday door, which clicked shut with reverberation.

Shaw looked out the front of the Task Force headquarters. Four news station vans were there. Reporters and camera operators jockeyed. Shaw had been cleared as a suspect in the heinous crime of putting evidence in a Walgreens bag and there would be no indictment or arraignment details in public records featuring his name. But he was a participant and had been spotted, surely, by a keen-eyed reporter or two at the crime scene. With his gunslinger kind of job and his resemblance to a movie star, even if a generic one, Colter Shaw could be media fodder.

He returned to the officer behind the bulletproof glass — not the one who'd made the copy for him — and said to her, 'You have a side entrance here?'

She debated, eyeing the reporters outside and assuming he'd been booked for something and didn't want his wife to see him on the eleven o'clock news. She pointed to a windowless door not far from the vending machines.

'Thanks.'

Shaw left via this side corridor. A flash of brilliant early-evening sunlight fired into his eyes as he stepped out. He walked up the street, passing bail bond storefronts and the small offices of hardscrabble lawyers. He was about to summon an Uber to hitch a ride to the Winnebago when he found a bar. Mexican-themed, which appealed to him.

A few minutes later a freezing can of Tecate was in his hand. He worked a lime wedge through the opening. He never squeezed the fruit juice in; Shaw thought a float in the can was enough.

A long swallow. Another, as he looked over the menu.

His phone hummed and he recognized the number. 'Mr. Mulliner?'

'Make it Frank. Please.'

'Okay, Frank.'

'I don't know where to begin.' Breathless.

'How's Sophie?'

'She's home. Really shaken up, you can imagine. The break's bad. But the cast doesn't cover her fingers, so she can still use a keyboard. And text her friends.' The laugh went quiet quickly. He would be deciding how to control the sudden urge to cry. 'They checked her out at the hospital. Everything else is okay.'

A euphemism, 'everything else.' There'd been no sexual assault, words a father would find so ver difficult to utter.

'But . . . you? How are you?'

'Fine.'

'The police said somebody helped them find her. Sophie said you were the only one.'

'The cops played cavalry.'

'She said they took you away, they arrested you!'

'Not a worry. It got worked out. Is her mother coming?'

A pause. 'She'll be here in a couple of days. She had a meeting — a board meeting. She said it was important.' Which told Shaw all about the former Mrs. Mulliner. 'Mr . . . Colter, I owe you everything . . . I just can't describe it. Well, you've probably heard that before.'

He had.

'But . . . Kyle.' Frank's voice had lowered and Shaw supposed Sophie was nearby. 'Jesus.'

'That was a shame.'

'Listen, Colter. I have your reward. I want to give it to you in person.'

'I'll come over tomorrow. The police must've debriefed Sophie?'

'A detective was here, yes. Detective Standish.'

The elusive partner had surfaced — now that the case had proved to be real.

'Do they have any leads?'

'No.'

Shaw said, 'Did the Task Force leave a car out front of your house, Frank?'

'A squad car? Yes.'

'Good.'

'Do you think he'll come back?'

'No. But better to be safe.'

They arranged a time to meet tomorrow and disconnected.

Shaw was about to order the *came asada* when his iPhone buzzed once more. He recognized this number too. He hit ACCEPT. 'Hello.'

'It's me. Pushy Girl.'

The redhead from the café. 'Maddie?'

'You remembered! I saw the news. They found that girl you were looking for. The police saved her. They said a 'concerned citizen' helped. That was you, right?'

'It was me.'

'Somebody was killed. Are you all right?'

'Fine.'

'They didn't catch him, I heard.'

'Not yet, no.'

A pause. 'So. You're wondering, what's up with stalker chick?'

He said nothing.

'Do you like Colter or Colt?'

'Either.'

'It's Poole, by the way. Last name.'

*Commitment* . . .

'Did you get the reward?'

'Not yet.'

'They pay in cash? I'm just wondering.' Maddie's mind seemed to dance like a water droplet on a hot skillet. 'Okay, I'm getting a feel for you. You don't like to answer pointless questions. Noted and absorbed. What've you been up to since you saved her?'

Jail. And Tecate with lime.

'Nothing much.'

'So you're not doing anything now? This

minute? Immediately?'

'No.'

'There's something I want to show you. You game?'

Shaw pictured her angelic face, the wispy hair, the athletic figure.

'Sure. I don't have wheels.'

'That's cool. I'll pick you up.'

He asked the bartender for a card and gave Maddie the address of the restaurant.

'Where are we going?' he asked.

'I just gave you a clue,' she said breezily. 'You can figure it out.' The line went dead.

# 21

Colter Shaw had never seen anything like it in his life.

He stood at the entrance to an endless convention center — easily a half mile square — and was being assaulted by a million electronically generated sounds, from ray guns to automatic weapons to explosions to chest-drumming music to the actorly voices of demons and superheroes — not to mention the occasional dinosaur roar. And the visuals: theatrical spotlights, LEDs, backlit banners, epilepsy-inducing flashers, lasers and high-definition displays the size of school buses.

*You game?*

Maddie Poole's clue: Not as in 'Are you game?' but '*Do* you game?'

Clever.

For this, apparently, was ground zero of the video gaming world, the international C3 Conference at the San Jose Convention Center. Tens of thousands of attendees moved like slow fish in a densely inhabited aquarium. The light here was eerily dim, presumably to make the images on the screens pop.

Beside him Maddie was a kid in a candy store, gazing around in delight. She wore a black stocking cap, a purple hoodie with UCLA on the chest, jeans and boots. She had a small tat of three Asian-language characters on her neck; he hadn't noticed them earlier. As at the café, she tugged at her lush hair — those strands that escaped the cap. Her unpolished nails were short, the flesh of her fingertips was wrinkled and red — he wondered what profession or hobby had done that. She wore no makeup. On her cheeks and the bridge of her nose was a dusting of freckles that some women would have covered up. Shaw was glad she didn't.

Maddie had given him the rundown on the drive here. Video gaming companies from around the world came to exhibit their wares at elaborate booths, where attendees could try out the latest products. There'd be tournaments between teams for purses of a million dollars, and cosplay competition among fans dressing up as their favorite characters. Film crews would roam the aisles for live streaming broadcasts. A highlight would be press conferences where company executives would announce new products — and field questions from journalists and fans about the minutiae of the games.

They eased past the booths, filled with players at gaming stations. He saw signs above some of them. TEN-MINUTE LIMIT. THERE'S A LOT OF OTHER SHIT TO SEE. And: MATURE 17+ ESRB. Presumably a rating board designation for games.

'What're we doing here?' he shouted. He foresaw a raspy throat by the end of the evening.

'You'll see.' She was being coy.

Shaw was not a big fan of surprises. But he decided to play along.

He paused at a huge overhead monitor, which glowed white with blue type:

WELCOME TO C3

WHERE TODAY MEETS THE FUTURE . . .

Below that, stats scrolled:

DID YOU KNOW . . .

THE VIDEO GAMING INDUSTRY REVENUES WERE $142 BILLION LAST YEAR, UP 15% FROM THE YEAR BEFORE.

THE INDUSTRY IS BIGGER THAN HOLLYWOOD.

180 MILLION AMERICANS REGULARLY PLAY VIDEO GAMES.

135 MILLION AMERICANS OVER 18 REGULARLY PLAY.

40 MILLION AMERICANS OVER 50 REGULARLY PLAY.

FOUR OUT OF FIVE HOUSEHOLDS IN AMERICA OWN A DEVICE THAT WILL PLAY GAMES.

THE MOST POPULAR CATEGORIES ARE:

— ACTION/ADVENTURE: 30%
— SHOOTERS: 22%
— SPORTS: 14%
— SOCIAL: 10%

THE MOST POPULAR PLATFORMS ARE:

— TABLETS AND SMARTPHONES: 45%

— CONSOLES: 26%
— COMPUTERS: 25%

SMARTPHONE GAMING IS THE FASTEST-GROWING
SEGMENT.

Shaw'd had no idea about the industry's size and popularity.

They made their way through a crowd clustering around the booth for *Fortnite*, which seemed to attract the most attention in this portion of the hall. Some attendees within the cordoned-off portion of the booth were at computers, playing the game, in which avatars ran around the landscape and homemade structures — forts, he assumed. The characters would blast away at creatures and occasionally break into a bizarre dance.

'This way,' Maddie said. 'Come on.' She clearly had a mission. She called, 'What was your favorite game growing up?'

His turn to be wry. He said, 'Venison.'

A brief moment passed. Maddie laughed, a light, high voice, as she got the joke. Then she eyed him. 'Serious? You hunt too?'

Too? One of those something-in-common moments? He nodded.

'My father and I'd go out every fall for duck and pheasant,' she said. 'Kind of a tradition.' They dodged a pair of Asian women in bobbed wigs, one of which was bright green, one yellow. They wore snakeskin bodysuits.

Maddie asked, 'You didn't play games?'

'No computers in our house.'

'So you played on consoles?'

'None of the above,' he said.

'Hmm,' she said. 'Never met anybody who grew up on Mars.'

On the Compound, in the rugged Sierra Nevadas, the Shaw family had two basic cell phones — prepaid, of course, and for use in emergencies only. There was a shortwave radio, which the children could listen to, but like the phones it could be used for transmission only in dire straits. Ashton warned that 'fox hunters' — people with devices to locate the source of radio signals — might be roaming the area to find him. When the family made the trip to the nearest town, White Sulphur Springs, twenty-five miles away, Ashton and Mary Dove had no problem with the children's logging on to the antiquated computers in the town library, or using them at their aunts' and uncles' homes during their summer visits to 'civilization' — Portland and Seattle. But when your daily routine might find you rappelling down cliffs or confronting a rattlesnake or moose, vaporizing fictional aliens was a bit frivolous.

'Oh, oh, oh! . . . Come on.' Maddie charged off toward a large monitor on which a gamer — a young man in stocking cap and sweats and an attempt at a beard — was firing away at bulky monsters, blowing most of them up.

'He's good. The game's *Doom*,' she said, shaking her head, sentimental. 'A classic. Like *Paradise Lost* or *Hamlet* . . . Caught you almost looking surprised there, Colter. I have a B.A. in English lit and a master's in information science.'

She picked up a controller. She offered it to him. 'Try your hand?'

'I'll pass.'

'You mind if I do?'

'Go right ahead.'

Maddie dropped into a seat and began to play. Her eyes were focused and her lips slightly parted. She sat forward and her body swayed and jerked, as if the world of the game were the only reality.

Her movement was balletic, and it was sensuous.

Speakers behind Shaw roared with the sound of a rocket and he turned, looking across the jammed aisle. He gazed up at the monitor, on which a preview of this company's game was displayed. In *Galaxy VII* the player guided an astronaut piloting a flying ship over a distant planet. The craft set down and the gamer directed the character to leave the vehicle and walk into a cave, where he explored tunnels and collected items like maps, weapons and 'Power Plus wafers.' Which sounded to Colter like a marathon runner's food supplement.

The game was calmer and subtler than the shoot-'em-up carnage of *Doom*.

Maddie appeared beside him. 'I saved the world. We're good.' She gripped his arm and leaned close, calling over the noise, 'The gaming world in a nutshell.' She pointed back to *Doom*. 'One, where it's all from your perspective and you mow down the bad guys before they mow you down. They're called first-person shooters.' Then she turned to the game he'd been looking

141

at. 'Two, action-adventure. They're third-person role playing, where you direct your character — avatar — you know *avatar*?' He nodded. 'Direct your avatar around the set, overcoming challenges, collecting things that might help you. You try to stay alive. Not to worry, you can still use a pulse laser to fry Orc butt.'

'*Lord of the Rings.*'

'Hey.' She laughed and squeezed his arm. 'Hope for you after all.'

When there's no TV, you gravitate toward books.

'One last lesson.' She pointed up to the *Galaxy VII* screen. 'See the other avatars walking around? Those are players somewhere else in the world. It's not just a role-playing game but a 'multi-player online role-playing game,' a MORPG. The other gamers might be on your side or you might be fighting them. At any given moment in the popular games — like *World of Warcraft* — there could be a quarter million people online playing.'

'You game a lot?'

She blinked. 'Oh, I never told you: it's my job.' She dug into her pocket and handed him a business card. 'I'll introduce myself proper. My real name is GrindrGirl88.' And she shook his hand with charming formality.

# 22

Maddie Poole didn't design games, didn't create their graphics, didn't write their ad campaigns.

She played them professionally.

Grinding — as in her online nickname — was when one played hour after hour after hour for streaming sites like Twitch. 'I'm going to give up asking if you know any of this, okay? Just go with it. So what happens is people log on to the site and watch their favorite gamers play.'

It was a huge business, she explained. Gamers had agents just like sports figures and actors.

'You have one?'

'I'm thinking about it. When that happens, you end up committed to a gig. You're not as free to play where you want, when you want. You know what I mean?'

Colter Shaw said nothing in response. He asked, 'The people who log on? They play along?'

'No. Just watch. They see my screen while I'm gaming, like they're looking over my shoulder. There's also a camera on me so they see my cute face. I have a headset and mic and I explain my gameplay, what I'm doing, why I'm doing it, and crack jokes, and chat. A lot of guys — and some girls — have crushes on me. A few stalkers, nothing I can't handle. We gaming girls gotta be tough. Almost as many women play games as men, but grinding and tournaments're a guys' world, and the guys give us a lot of crap.'

Her face screwed up with disgust. 'A gamer I know — she's a kid, eighteen — she beat two assholes playing in their loser basement in Bakersfield. They got her real name and address and SWAT'd her. You know it? Capital S-W-A-T.'

Shaw didn't.

'When somebody calls the police and says there's a shooter in your house, they described her. The cops, they've gotta follow the rules. They kicked in the door and took her down. Happens more than you'd think. Of course, they let her go right away and she traced the guys who did it, even with their proxies, and they ended up in jail.'

'What's your tat?' A glance toward her neck.

'I'll tell you later. Maybe. So. Here's your answer, Colt.'

'To what question?'

'What we're doing here. Ta-da!'

They were in front of a booth in the corner of the convention center. It was as big as the others yet much more subdued — no lasers, no loud music. A modest electronic billboard reported:

HSE PRESENTS
*IMMERSION*
THE NEW MOVEMENT IN VIDEO GAMING

This booth featured no play stations; the action, whatever it might be, was taking place inside a huge black-and-purple tent. A line of attendees waited to get inside.

144

Maddie walked up to a check-in desk, behind which sat two Asian women in their thirties, older than most employees at the other booths. They were dressed in identical conservative navy-blue business suits. Maddie showed her ID badge, then a driver's license. A screen was consulted and she was given a pair of white goggles and a wireless controller. She signed a document on a screen and nodded toward Shaw.

'Me?'

'You. You're my guest.'

After the ID routine, Shaw received his set of the toys too. The document he'd signed was a liability release.

They walked toward the curtained opening to the tent, lining up in a queue of other people, mostly young men, holding their own controllers and goggles.

Maddie explained, 'I'm also a game reviewer. All the studios hire us to give them feedback about the beta version of new games. *Immersion*'s one I've been waiting for for a long time. We'll just try it out here for the fun of it, then I'll take it home for a serious test drive.'

He studied the complicated goggles, which had a row of buttons on each side and earpieces.

The line moved slowly. Shaw noted that a pair of employees — large, unsmiling men dressed in the male version of the women's somber suits — stood at the entryway, admitting a few people at a time, only after the same number had left by a nearby exit, handing back their goggles to yet another employee. Shaw noted the expressions on the faces of those leaving. Some seemed dumbfounded, shaking their heads. Some were awestruck. One or two looked troubled.

Maddie was explaining, 'HSE is 'Hong-Sung Enterprises.' A Chinese company. Video gaming's always been international — the U.S., England, France and Spain all developed games early. Asia's where it really took off. Japan, in particular. Nintendo. You know Nintendo?'

'Mario, the plumber.' Once off the Compound for college, then work, Shaw's education in modern culture took off exponentially.

'It was a playing card company in the eighteen hundreds and eventually pioneered console gaming — those're like arcade games for the home. The name's interesting. Most people say it means 'leave luck to Heaven.' Sort of a literal translation. But I was playing with some Japanese gamers. They think it has a deeper meaning. *Nin* means 'chivalrous way,' *ten* refers to 'Tengu,' a mythical spirit who teaches martial arts to those who've suffered loss, and *do* is 'a shrine.' So, to me, Nintendo means a shrine to the chivalrous who protect the weak. I like that one better.

'Now, back to history class. Japan soared in the video gaming world. China missed the party entirely — that's a joke. Because the Communist Party didn't approve of gaming. Subversive or something. Until, natch, they realized what they were missing out on: money. Two hundred million Americans play video games. *Seven* hundred million play in China.

'The government got involved and Beijing had a problem: players sit on their asses all day long.

They get fat; they're out of shape. They're in their thirties and they have heart attacks. So HSE, Hong-Sung Enterprises, did something about it.' Maddie waved her hand at the *Immersion* sign. 'When you play, you actually move — everywhere, not just standing in front of your TV, swinging a fake tennis racket. You walk around, you run, you jump. Your basement, your living room, your backyard. The beach, a field. There's a version you can play on a trampoline and they're working on one you can use in a pool.'

She held up the goggles and pointed. 'See, cameras in the front and on the sides? You put it on, get a cellular or Wi-Fi connection and go out into your backyard, but it's not your backyard anymore. The game's algorithms change what you see. The tricycle, the barbecue, the cat — everything's been turned into something else. Zombies, monsters, rocks, volcanoes.

'I'm pretty into sports and exercise, which is why it's totally my kind of game. *Immersion's* going to be the NBT — the next big thing. The company's already donating thousands of the units to schools, to hospitals to help with rehab, to the Army. There's software to replicate battlefields, so soldiers can train anytime. In the barracks, at home, wherever.'

They were next to go in. 'Okay, this's it, Colter. Put the goggles on.' He did. It was like looking through lightly tinted gray sunglasses.

'The controller's your weapon.' She smiled. 'Umm, you've got it backward. You fire that way, you'll shoot yourself in the groin.'

He turned the thing around. It was like a remote control and felt comfortable in his hand.

'Just press that button to shoot.'

Then Maddie took his left hand and lifted it to that side of the goggles. 'This is the on switch. Press it for a second or so after we get inside. And this button. Feel it?'

He did.

'If you die, hit it. It resets you back to life.'

'Why do you think I'm going to die?'

She only smiled.

# 23

When they walked inside the tent, an employee directed them down a corridor to Room 3.

The thirty-by-thirty-foot space looked like a theater's backstage: walkways, stairs, platforms, furniture, a fake rubber tree, a large sprawl of tarp, a table on which sat bags of potato chips and cans of food, a grandfather clock. He and Maddie had the room to themselves.

Just a game, of course, but Shaw felt himself go into set mode. Just like before rappelling off a cliff, or streaking up a hill on the Yamaha fast enough to go airborne, you have to ready yourself.

*Never be unprepared physically or mentally . . .*

A voice from on high said: 'Prepare for combat. On one, engage your goggles. Three . . . two . . . one!'

Shaw pressed the button Maddie had indicated.

And the world changed.

Astonishing.

The grandfather clock was some sort of bearded wizard, the platforms were icy ledges, the rubber plant a campfire burning with green flame. The tarp was now a rocky coast overlooking a turbulent ocean in which whirlpools swirled and sucked ships into dark spirals. There were two suns in the sky, one yellow and

149

one blue, and they cast a faint green haze over the world. The walls were no longer black curtains but instead distant vistas of snowcapped peaks and a towering volcano, which was erupting. All in stunning 3-D.

He glanced to his right and saw Maddie, now dressed in black armor. He then looked at his own legs and found he was wearing the same. His hands were in black metallic gloves, and in his right the controller had become a ray gun.

A consuming experience.

*Immersion* was aptly named.

'Colt,' Maddie called, though it wasn't her voice. The tone was husky.

'I'm here,' he said. His voice too had changed from its easy baritone to a rugged bass.

He noted her climbing up a rocky ledge, which had been a simple scaffolding before putting on the goggles. She was crouched low, head sweeping back and forth. 'They're coming. Get ready.'

'Who's — '

He gasped. A creature pounced on the ledge beside her. The glistening blue thing had a human face — with the minor addition of saber teeth and an extra eye, glowing red. The creature swung a sword at Maddie. She blasted it. It didn't die right away but kept coming after her, taking the sparking hits from her weapon. It swung a second glowing sword. She had to dodge, leaping off the rocks onto a grassy field. Here too there was an elegance to her moves.

*Sensuous . . .*

Which is when a flying pterodactyl dropped

150

from the sky and ripped Shaw's heart out of his chest.

YOU'VE JUST DIED! a sign in the goggle screen announced.

He remembered which button to hit.

*RESET* . . .

He was alive once more. And, now, his survival upbringing returned.

*Never lose sight of your surroundings* . . .

He spun around — just in time to dodge a squat creature attacking with a fiery hammer. It took five shots of the laser to kill it and he had to leap back from a final swing of its weapon before it died.

The goggle message was YOU'VE JUST EARNED A LAVA HAMMER. A small picture of one popped up in the lower-right-hand corner of the screen. The window was called WEAPONS STASH.

A shadow appeared on the grassy field in front of him.

Shaw's heart thudded and he looked up fast, just in time to kill one of those damn flying things. It too had a human face.

He found himself sweating, tense. He felt an urge to be trigger-happy, blasting creatures through weeds and trees, shooting when he had no clear line of sight.

He thought of the hunter, all those years ago, shooting the buck through a stand of brush.

*I hit something? There was just a noise in the bushes. I thought it was a wolf* . . .

Shaw calmed and took control of his tactics. He zapped a slew of running, flying and

151

slithering things — until an alien unsportingly dropped a boulder off a hilltop and crushed him.

*RESET.*

He saw Maddie Poole taking on three creatures at once, ducking for cover behind a downed tree trunk, laden with bags of corn and peasant bread — it was the table on which sat the chips and soup cans. Shaw had a good shot at one and killed it. She didn't acknowledge the aid. Like a real soldier, she wouldn't let her attention waver.

An Asian-inflected voice came through the speakers: 'Your *Immersion* experience will end in five minutes.'

After Maddie killed her other two assailants, she hit a button on her goggles and walked up to Shaw and pressed the same on his. While the fantasy world remained, the aliens had vanished. It was suddenly quiet, aside from the make-believe sound of the ocean and the wind. There were no laser guns in their hands any longer.

'Hell of an experience,' he told her.

She nodded. 'Totally. Notice how all the creatures had variations on human faces.'

He said he had.

'Hong Wei, the CEO of the company, ordered focus groups to help select villains. Gamers are much more comfortable killing anything that resembles people than animals. We're fodder; Bambi's safe.'

Shaw looked around. 'Where's the exit?'

She said coyly, 'We've got a few minutes left. Let's fight some more.'

He was tired, after the eventful day. But he

152

was enjoying the time with her. 'I'm game.'

She smiled, then took his hand and put it on yet another button on his goggles.

'On three, press this one.'

'Got it.'

'One . . . two . . . three!'

He pushed where instructed and, from the controller, a red-hot glowing sword blade emerged. One appeared in her hand too. This time there were no other creatures, just the two of them.

Maddie Poole didn't waste a second. She leapt at him, swinging the sword overhead, bringing it down fast. While Shaw knew knives well, he'd never held a sword. Still, combat with the weapon was instinctual. He effectively parried her blow and, finding himself irritated that she'd withheld what this portion of the game would entail, he charged forward. She deflected each of his thrusts and swings or dodged out of the way. As soon as he missed her, she was back, coming at him. His advantages were longer legs and strength, hers were speed and being a smaller target.

He was breathing hard . . . and only partly from the effort of climbing on the ledges and rocks.

They received a two-minute warning from the heavens. The deadline seemed to energize Maddie. She charged forward repeatedly. He took a cut on his leg, and she one on the upper arm. Blood appeared in the wound, an eerie sight. A meter on his goggles reported that he had ninety per-cent life left.

He feinted and Maddie fell for it. She dodged too late to miss a slash on her upper thigh, a shallow wound, and he could hear her low, murky voice: 'Son of a bitch.'

Shaw pressed forward and Maddie backed up. She tried to make a leap onto a low ledge — a platform about eighteen inches off the ground — misjudged and fell hard. Though the floor was padded with foam, her side had collided with the edge of the platform. She dropped to her knees and gripped her ribs. He heard her grunt in pain.

Standing straight, he lowered the sword and walked forward to help her up. 'You all right?'

He was about three feet away when she sprang to her feet and plunged her blade into his gut.

YOU'VE JUST DIED!

It had all been a trick. She'd fallen on purpose, landing in a particular way — with her feet under her so she could leverage herself up and lunge.

The overlord in the ceiling announced that their time was up. The fantasy world became a backstage once more. He and Maddie pulled their goggles off. He started to give her a nod and say, 'That was a low blow' — not a bad joke — but he didn't. She wiped sweat from her forehead and temple with the back of her sleeve and looked about with an expression that wasn't a lot different from that of the creatures that had killed him. Not triumph, not joy in victory. Nothing. Just ice.

He recalled what she'd said before they stepped inside the booth.

*We'll just try it out here for the fun of it . . .*

As they walked to the exit, it was as if she grew aware suddenly that she wasn't alone. 'Hey, you're not mad, are you?' she said.

'All's fair.'

The awkward atmosphere leveled but didn't exactly vanish as they walked outside. What did disappear was his intention to ask her to dinner. He would — might — later. Not tonight.

They handed their goggles to the HSE employee, who put them in a bin for sanitizing. At the desk, Maddie was given a canvas bag, which he assumed contained a new game for her to take home and review.

His phone hummed.

A local area code.

Berkeley police, to arrest him for the transgressing larceny? Dan Wiley and Supervisor Cummings deciding to arrest him anew after changing their minds about the Great Evidence Robbery?

It was from JMCTF, though just the desk officer, telling him his car was available to be picked up at the pound.

Exhausted and having died three times in ten minutes — or was it four? — Shaw thought: Give it a shot. 'Can somebody deliver it to me?'

The silence — which he imagined was accompanied by a look of bewilderment on the officer's face — lasted a good three seconds. 'I'm afraid we can't do that, sir. You'll have to go to the pound to pick it up.'

She gave him the address, which he memorized.

He eased a glance Maddie's way. 'My car's ready.'

'I can drive you.'

It was obvious that her preference was to stay. Which was fine with him.

'No, I'll get an Uber.'

He hugged her and she kissed his cheek.

'It was fun — ' he started.

''Night!' Maddie called. Then she was off, tugging at her hair and striding toward another booth — with the marauding aliens, the swords and Shaw himself completely erased, like data dumped from a hard drive's random access memory.

# 24

No logical reason in the world to pay one hundred and fifty dollars to retrieve a car that should never have been held hostage in the first place.

But there you have it.

Adding insult, the charge was five percent more if you used a credit card. Colter checked his cash: one hundred and eighty-seven dollars. He handed over the Amex, paid and walked to the front gate to wait.

The pound was a sprawling yard in a seedy part of the Valley, on the east side of the 101. Some of the cars had been there for months, to judge from the grime. He counted airliners on final approach to San Francisco Airport, thinking of how the sound of the planes had unsettlingly masked the noise of any attackers when he was searching for Sophie at that old factory. Now he gave up at sixteen jets. The vehicle arrived five minutes later. Shaw examined it. No scratches or dents. His computer bag was still in the trunk and had probably been searched, yet nothing had been damaged or taken.

The crisp voice of the GPS guided him back into a tamer part of Silicon Valley, quieted in the late evening. He was headed toward his RV park in Los Altos Hills. Colter Shaw had, however, chosen a circuitous route, ignoring the electronic lady's directives — and her patient recalculating corrections.

Because someone was following him.

When he'd left the pound, he'd been aware of car lights flicking on and the vehicle to which they were attached making a U-turn and proceeding in his direction. Maybe a coincidence? When Shaw stopped abruptly at a yellow light that he could easily have rolled through without a ticket, the car or truck behind him swerved quickly to the curb. He couldn't tell the make, model or color.

A random carjacker or mugger? Two percent. A Chevy Malibu wasn't worth the jail time.

Detective Dan Wiley, planning to beat the crap out of him? Four percent. Satisfying but a career ender. The man was a narcissist, not a fool.

Detective Dan Wiley, hoping to catch him score some street pot or coke? Fifteen percent. He seemed like a vindictive prick.

A felon Shaw had helped put inside or a hitman or leg breaker hired by said felon? Ten percent. No shortage of those. It would have been hard for someone to have traced him to the police pound yet not impossible. Shaw gave it double digits because he tended to skew the number higher when the consequences of what might occur were particularly painful. Or fatal.

The more likely possibility, Person X — whose plans for Sophie Mulliner had been spoiled and who'd come for revenge: sixty percent.

He muted the GPS lass, turned off the automatic braking system and steered down a quiet street. He hit the gas hard, as if trying to run, spinning tires. The pursuer sped up too. At fifty mph he crunched the brake pedal and turned into a left-hand skid. Almost lost it — the asphalt was dew-damp — then steered in the direction of the car's veering rear end. He controlled the flamboyant maneuver just in time and the Malibu zipped neatly into the entrance of a darkened parking garage. Twenty feet inside he made a U-turn, the sound a teeth-setting squeal due to the concrete acoustics. He goosed the accelerator and sped back to the entrance.

Shaw's phone was up, camera videoing, car lights on high beam. Ready to capture an image of the tail.

His prey never appeared. A minute later he gunned the engine and exited, turning right, expecting his pursuer to be waiting.

The street was empty.

He continued to the RV park, this time obeying Ms. GPS to the letter. He paused at the entrance to the trailer park and looked around. Traffic, but the vehicles streamed by, their drivers uninterested in him. He continued into the park, turned on Google Way and parked.

He climbed out, locked the car and walked quickly to the Winnebago door. Inside, leaving the lights off, he retrieved his Glock from the spice cabinet. For five minutes he peered through the blinds. No cars.

Shaw went into the small bathroom, where he took a hot, then ice-cold, shower. He dressed in jeans and a sweatshirt, and made dinner of scrambled eggs with some of the gun-cabinet herbs (tarragon, sage), buttered toast and a piece of salty country ham, along with an Anchor Steam. Eleven p.m. was often his dinnertime.

He sat at the banquette to dine and perform his nightly check of the local news feeds. Another woman had been attacked — in Daly City — the perp arrested before Shaw had rescued Sophie. Some irrelevant stories: a popular labor organizer denying corruption claims, a terrorist plot thwarted on the Oakland docks, a surge in voter registration as Californians prepared to go to the polls on some special referenda.

As for the Sophie Mulliner kidnapping, the anchors and commentators didn't provide any news that Shaw wasn't aware of, while still doing what they did best: ramping up the paranoia. 'That's right, Candy, my experience has been that kidnappers like this — 'thrill kidnappers,' we call them — often go after multiple victims.'

Shaw had made the news as well.

Detective Dan Wiley said that a concerned citizen, Colter Shaw, pursuing the reward offered by Mr. Mulliner — making him sound particularly mercenary — had provided information that proved helpful in the rescue.

He logged off and shut down computer and router.

*Proved helpful . . .*

Nearly midnight.

Shaw was ready for sleep but sleep was not on the immediate horizon. He returned to the kitchen cabinet and once more removed the envelope he'd stolen from the Cal archives, the one with the elegant penmanship emblazoned on the front: *Graded Exams 5/25*. Inside were the documents

160

he'd skimmed earlier. He opened a blank note-book and uncapped his fountain pen.

A sip of beer and he began to read in earnest, wondering if in fact he'd find an answer to the question: What had actually happened in the early-morning hours of October 5, fifteen years ago, on bleak Echo Ridge?

# LEVEL THREE:

## THE SINKING SHIP

### Sunday, June 9

The rock had had no effect on the windshield of the foundering *Seas the Day*.

Shaw tossed it back into the grim, turbulent Pacific and pulled the locking-blade knife from his pocket. He'd use it to try to remove the screws securing the window frame to the front of the cabin.

He heard, over the gutsy roar of waves colliding with rock and sand, Elizabeth Chabelle shouting something.

Probably: 'Get me the fuck out of here!'

Or a variation.

Gripping a scabby railing with his left hand, he began on the screws. There were four — standard heads, not Phillips. He fitted the blade in sideways and rotated counterclockwise. Nothing for a moment. Then, with all his strength, he twisted and the hardware moved. A few minutes later the screw was out. Then the second. The third.

He was halfway through the fourth screw

162

when a large swell smacked the side of the boat and sent Shaw over the railing backward, between the ship and a pylon.

Instinctively grabbing for a handhold, he let go of the knife and saw it vanish in a graceful spiral on its way to the ocean floor. He kicked to the surface and muscled his way once more onto the forward deck.

Back to the window, loosened but not free.

Okay. Enough. Angrily Shaw gripped it with both hands, planted his feet on the exterior side wall of the cabin and pulled — arm muscles, leg muscles, back muscles.

The frame broke away.

Shaw and the window went over the side.

Oh, hell, he thought, grabbing a breath just before he hit.

Kicking to the surface again. The shivering was less intense now and he felt a wave of euphoria, hypothermia's way of telling you that death can be fun.

Scrabbling back onto the foredeck, he dropped into the front portion of the cabin and slid to the bulkhead separating this part from the aft. The vessel was now down by the stern at a forty-five-degree angle. Below him, exhausted Elizabeth Chabelle had left her bunk bed perch in the half-flooded aft section of the cabin. She gripped the frame of the small window in the door. He saw wounds on her hands; she would have shattered the glass and reached through to find the knob.

Which had been removed.

She sobbed, 'Why? Who did this?'

'You'll be fine, Elizabeth.'

Running his hands around the perimeter of the interior door, Shaw felt the sharp points. It had been sealed from the other side with Sheetrock screws, just like at the factory where Sophie had been stashed.

'Do you have any tools?'

'No! I l-looked for f-fucking tools.' Stuttering in the cold.

Where was the hypothermia clock now? Probably ten minutes and counting down.

Another wave crashed into the boat. Chabelle muttered something Shaw couldn't understand, her shivering was so bad. She repeated it: 'Wh-who . . . ?'

'He left things for you. Five things.'

'It's so f-fucking c-cold.'

'What did he leave you?'

'A kite . . . th-there was a kite. A power bar. I ate it. A f-flashlight. Matches. They're all wet. A p-p-pot. F-flowerpot. A f-fucking f-flowerpot.'

'Give it to me.'

'Give — ?'

'The pot.'

She bent down, feeling under the surface, and a moment later handed him the brown-clay pot. He shattered it against the wall and, picking the sharpest shard, began digging at the wood around the hinges.

'Get back on the bunk,' Shaw told her. 'Out of the water.'

'There's n-no . . . '

'As best you can.'

She turned and climbed to the top of the bed.

164

She managed to keep most of her body, from ample belly up, above the surface.

Shaw said, 'Tell me about George.'

'Y-you know m-my boyfriend?'

'I saw a picture of you two. You ballroom dance.'

A faint laugh. 'He's t-terrible. But he t-tries. Okay with f-fox-trot. Do you . . . '

Shaw gave a laugh too. 'I don't dance, no.'

The wood was teak. Hard as stone. Still he kept at it. He said, 'You get to Miami much, see your folks?'

'I — I . . . '

'I've got a place in Florida. Farther north. You ever get to the 'Glades?'

'One of those b-boats, with the airplane p-propellers. I'm going to d-die, aren't I?'

'No you're not.'

While the glass knife might have cut through plaster to free Sophie, the pottery shard was next to useless. 'You like stone crabs?'

'Broke my t-tooth on a . . . on a shell one time.' She began sobbing. 'I d-don't know who you are. Thank you. Get out. Get out now. S-save yourself . . . It's t-too late.'

Shaw looked into the dim portion of the cabin where she clung to the post of the bunk.

'P-please,' she said. 'Save yourself.'

The ship settled further.

# LEVEL TWO:

# THE
# DARK
# FOREST

Saturday, June 8, One Day Earlier

# 25

At 9 a.m. Colter Shaw was in one of the twenty-five million strip malls that dotted Silicon Valley, this one boasting a nail salon, a Hair Cuttery, a FedEx operation and a Salvadoran restaurant — the establishment he was now sitting in. It was a cheerful place, decorated with festive red-and-white paper flowers and rosettes and photos of mountains, presumably of the country back home. The restaurant also offered among the best Latin American coffee he'd ever had: Santa Maria from the 'microregion' of Potrero Grande. He wanted to buy a pound or two. It wasn't for sale by the bag.

He sipped the aromatic beverage and glanced across the street. On his drive to the mall he'd passed imposing mansions just minutes away, but here were tiny bungalows. One was in foreclosure — he thought of Frank Mulliner's neighbor — and another for sale by owner. Two signs sat in the parking strips of houses. VOTE YES PROPOSITION 457. NO PROPERTY TAX HIKES!!! And a similar message with the addition of a skull and crossbones and the words SILICON VALLEY REAL ESTATE — YOU'RE *killing* US!!

Shaw turned back to the stack of documents he'd removed from the university the other day. Stolen, true, though on reflection he supposed an argument might be made that the burglary was justified.

After all, they had been written or assembled by his father, Ashton Shaw.

Two of whose rules he thought of now:

*Never adopt a strategy or approach a task without assigning percentages.*

*Never assign a percentage until you have as many facts as possible . . .*

That, of course, was the key.

Colter Shaw couldn't make any assessment of what had happened on October 5, fifteen years ago, until he gathered those facts . . . What in these pages addressed that? There were three hundred and seventy-four of them. Shaw wondered if the number itself were a message; after all, his father had been given to codes and cryptic references.

Ashton had been an expert in political science, law, government, American history, as well as — an odd hobby — physics. The pages contained snippets of all those topics. Essays started but never completed and essays completed but making no sense whatsoever to Shaw. Odd theories, quotations from people he'd never heard of. Maps of neighborhoods in the Midwest, in Washington, D.C., in Chicago, of small towns in Virginia and Pennsylvania. Population charts from the 1800s. Newspaper clippings. Photographs of old buildings.

Some medical records too, which turned out to be from his mother's research into psychosis for East Coast drug companies.

Too much information is as useless as too little.

Four pages were turned down at the corner, suggesting that his father, or someone, wished to return to those pages and review them carefully. Shaw made a note of these and examined each briefly. Page 37 was a map of a town in Alabama; page 63, an article about a particle accelerator; page 118 was a photocopy of an article in *The New York Times* about a new computer system for the New York Stock Exchange; page 255 was a rambling essay by Ashton on the woeful state of the country's infrastructure.

And Shaw reminded himself that it was possible these documents had no relevance whatsoever. They'd been compiled not long before October 5, yes, yet look by whom they'd been compiled: a man whose relationship with reality had, by that time, grown thread-thin.

As Shaw stretched, looking up from examining a picture of an old New England courthouse, he happened to see a car moving slowly along the street, pausing at his Malibu. It was a Nissan Altima, gray, a few years old, its hide dinged and scraped. He couldn't see the driver — too much glare — though he did notice that he or she didn't sit tall in the seat. Just as Shaw was rising, phone ready for a picture of the tag, the vehicle sped up and vanished around the corner. He hadn't seen the tag number.

The person from last night? The person spying on him from above San Miguel Park? Which begged the all-important question: Was it X?

He sat down once again. Call the Task Force?

And, then, what would he tell Wiley?

His phone hummed. He looked at the screen: Frank Mulliner. They weren't scheduled to meet for an hour.

'Frank.'

'Colter.' The man's voice was grim. Shaw wondered if the young woman's health had taken a bad turn; maybe the fall had been worse than it seemed originally. 'There's something I have to talk to you about. I'm . . . I'm not supposed to but it's important.'

Shaw set down the cup of superb coffee. 'Go ahead.'

After a pause the man said, 'I'd rather meet in person. Can you come over now?'

# 26

A white-and-green Task Force police cruiser sat like a lighthouse in front of the Mulliners'. The uniformed deputy behind the wheel was young and wore aviator sunglasses. Like many of the officers Shaw had spotted in the HQ, his head was shaved.

The deputy had apparently been told that Shaw was soon to arrive, along with a description. A glance Shaw's way and he turned back to his radio or computer or — after Shaw's indoctrination into the video gaming world yesterday — maybe *Candy Crush*, which Maddie Poole had told him was considered a 'casual' game, the sort played to waste time on your phone.

Mulliner let him in and they walked into the kitchen, where the man fussed over coffee. Shaw declined.

The two men were alone. Sophie was still sleeping. Shaw saw motion at his feet and looked down to see Luka, Fee's standard poodle, stroll in, sip some water and flop down on the floor. The two men sat and Mulliner cupped his mug and said, 'There's been another kidnapping. I'm not supposed to tell anybody.'

'What're the details?'

The second victim was named Henry Thompson. He and his marriage partner lived south of Mountain View, in Sunnyvale, not far

173

away. Thompson, fifty-two, had gone missing late last night, after a presentation at Stanford University, where he was speaking on a panel. A rock or a brick had crashed into his windshield. When he stopped, he'd been jumped and kidnapped.

'Detective Standish said there weren't any witnesses.'

'Not Wiley?'

'No, it was just Detective Standish.'

'Ransom demand?'

'I don't think so. That's one of the reasons they think it's the same man who kidnapped Fee,' he said, then continued: 'Now, Henry Thompson's partner got my name and number and called. He sounded just like I did when Fee was missing. Half crazy . . . Well, you remember. He'd heard about you helping and asked me to get in touch with you. He said he'd hire you to find him.'

'I'm not for hire. But I'll talk to him.'

Mulliner wrote the name and number on a Post-it: Brian Byrd.

Shaw bent down and scratched the poodle on the head. While the dog wouldn't, of course, understand that Shaw had saved his mistress, you might very well think so from its expression: bright eyes and a knowing grin.

'Henry Thompson.' Shaw was typing into Google on his phone. 'Which one?' There were several in Sunnyvale.

'He's a blogger and LGBT activist.'

Shaw clicked on the correct one. Thompson was round and had a pleasant face, which was depicted smiling in almost every picture Google had of him. He wrote two blogs: one was about the computer industry, the other about LGBT rights. Shaw sent the man's web page to Mack, asking for details on him.

The reply was typical Mack: ''K.'

Shaw said to Mulliner, 'Can I see Fee?'

He left and returned a moment later with his daughter. She wore a thick burgundy robe and fuzzy pink slippers. Her right arm was embraced by quite the cast, pale blue. And there were bandages on the back of her other hand.

Her eyes were hollow, red-rimmed.

Sophie leaned into a gentle hug from her father.

'Mr. Shaw.'

'How does it feel? The break?'

Expressionless, she looked at her arm. 'Okay. Itches under the cast. That's the worst.' She walked to the refrigerator and poured some orange juice, then returned to the stool and sat. 'They put you in a police car. I told them you saved me.'

'Not a worry. All good now.'

'Did you hear? He kidnapped somebody else?'

'I did. I'm going to help the police again.'

A fact the police did not yet know.

Shaw told her, 'I know it might be tough but would you tell me what happened?'

She sipped the orange juice, then drank half the glass down. Shaw guessed she was on painkillers that made her mouth dry. 'Like, sure.'

Shaw had brought one of his notebooks and opened it. Sophie looked at the fountain pen, again without expression.

'Wednesday. You got home.'

In halting words, Sophie explained that she'd been angry. 'About stuff.'

Frank Mulliner's mouth tightened but he said nothing.

She'd biked to Quick Byte Café for a latte and some food — she couldn't remember what now — and called some friends to check on lacrosse practice. Then to San Miguel Park. 'Whenever I get pissed or sad, at anything, I go there to bike. To shred, rage. You know what I mean 'rage'?'

Shaw knew.

Her voice caught. 'What Kyle used to do on his board. Half Moon Bay and Maverick.' Her teeth set and she wiped a tear.

'I pulled onto the shoulder of Tamyen to tighten my helmet. Then this car slammed into me.'

The police would have asked and he did as well: 'Did you see it?' Shaw thinking gray Nissan, though he'd never lead a witness.

'No. It was, like, *boom*, the fucker slammed me.'

She'd lain stunned at the bottom of the hill and heard footsteps coming closer. 'I knew it wasn't an accident,' she said. 'The shoulder was really wide — there was no reason to hit me unless he wanted to. And I heard the car spin its wheels just before it hit, so he was, like, aiming. I got my phone to call nine-one-one but it was too late. I just threw it, so they could track it maybe and find me. Then I tried to get up but he tackled me. And kicked me or hit me in the

176

back, the kidney — so I was, like, paralyzed. I couldn't get up or roll over.'

'Smart, tossing your phone. It's how I found out what happened to you.'

She nodded. 'Then I got stabbed in the neck, a hypodermic needle. And I went out.'

'Did the doctors or police say what kind of drug?'

'I asked. They just said a prescription painkiller, dissolved in water.'

'Any more thoughts about their appearance?'

'Did I tell you . . . ? I was telling somebody. Gray ski mask, sunglasses.'

He showed her the screenshot from the security video at the Quick Byte.

'Detective Standish showed it to me. No, I never saw anybody like that before.' She rose, found a chopstick in a drawer and worked it under the cast, rubbing it up and down.

'If you had to guess, a man or a woman?'

'Assumed a man. Not tall. It could've been a woman but if it was she was strong, strong enough to carry me or drag me to the car. And, I mean, kicking me in the back when I was down? You wouldn't think a woman would do that to another woman.' She shrugged. 'I guess we can be as messed up as a man.'

'Did they say anything?'

'No. Next thing, I woke up in that room.'

'Describe it.'

'There was a little light but I couldn't see much.' Her eyes now flared. 'It was just so fucking weird. I thought, in the movies, somebody's kidnapped and there's a bed and a blanket and a bucket to pee in, or whatever. There *was* a bottle of water. But no food. Just a big empty glass bottle, this wad of cloth, a spool of fishing line and matches. The room was really old. Moldy and everything. The bottle, the rag — that stuff was new.'

Shaw told her again how smart she was, breaking the bottle to make a glass blade and cutting through the Sheetrock.

'I started looking for a way out. The only windows that weren't boarded up were on the top floor. I couldn't just break one and climb out. I started looking for a door. They were locked or nailed shut.'

Screwed shut, actually, Shaw recalled. Recently. He told them that he too had looked and found only one open — in the front.

'Didn't get that far.' She swallowed. 'I heard the gunshots and . . . Kyle . . . ' She sobbed quietly. Her father approached and put his arm around her and she cried against his chest for a moment.

Shaw explained to him how Sophie had made a trap from the fishing line and had used another piece to tie it to her jacket and made it move back and forth so there'd be a shadow on the floor. To lure the kidnapper closer. And nail him with an oil drum.

Mulliner was wide-eyed. 'Really?'

In a soft voice she said, 'I was going to kill you . . . him. Stab him. But I just panicked and ran. I'm sorry if you got hurt.'

'I should've figured it out,' Shaw said. 'I knew you'd be a fighter.'

At this she smiled.

Shaw asked, 'Did he touch you?'

Her father stirred, but this was a question that needed to be asked.

'I don't think so. All he took off was my shoes and socks. My windbreaker was still zipped up. Your handwriting's really small. Why don't you just write on a computer or tablet? It'd be faster.'

Shaw answered the young woman. 'When you write something by hand, slowly, you own the words. You type them, less so. You read them, even less. And you listen, hardly at all.'

The idea seemed to intrigue her.

'Anybody at the Quick Byte try to pick you up recently?'

'Guys flirt, you know. Ask, 'Oh, what're you reading?' Or 'How're the tamales?' What guys always do. Nobody weird.'

'This was in the Quick Byte.' On his phone Shaw displayed a photo of the sheet that had been left in place of her MISSING poster. The stenciled image of the eerie face, the hat, the tie. 'There was also a version on the outside wall of the room where you were held.'

'I don't remember it. The place was so dark. It's creepy.'

'Does it mean anything to either of you?'

They both said it did not. Mulliner asked, 'What's it supposed to be?'

'I don't know.' He'd searched for images of men's faces in hats and ties. Nothing close to this showed up.

'Detective Standish didn't ask you about it?'

'No,' Sophie said. 'I would have remembered.'

179

A ringtone sounded from inside her robe pocket. It was the default. She hadn't had time to change it on her new phone. The old was in Evidence and would probably die a silent death there. She looked at the screen and answered. 'Mom?'

She glanced toward Shaw, who said, 'I have enough for now, Fee.'

Sophie embraced him and whispered, 'Thank you, thank you . . . ' The young woman shivered briefly and, with a deep inhalation, walked away, lifting the phone. 'Mom.' She picked up the glass of orange juice in her other hand and walked back to her room, Luka following. 'I'm fine, really . . . He's being great . . . '

The corner of Mulliner's mouth twitched. He glanced at Shaw's naked ring finger. 'You married?'

'No. Never.' And, as happened occasionally when the topic was tapped, images of Margot Keller's long, Greek goddess face appeared, framed by soft dark blond curls. In this particular slideshow she was looking up from a map of an archaeological dig. A map that Shaw himself had drawn.

Then Mulliner was offering an envelope to him. 'Here.'

Shaw didn't take it. 'Sometimes I work out payment arrangements. No interest.'

'Well . . . ' Mulliner looked down at the envelope. His face was red.

Shaw said, 'A thousand a month for ten months. Can you swing that?'

'I will. Whatever it takes. I will.'

Shaw made this arrangement with some frequency and it drove business manager Velma Bruin to distraction. She'd delivered many variations on the theme: 'You do the job, Colt. You deserve the money when it's due.'

Velma was right, but there was nothing wrong with flexibility. And that was particularly true on this job. He'd gotten the lesson about the financial stresses of Silicon Valley.

The Land of Promise, where so very many people struggled.

# 27

Halfway to Henry Thompson's address, Colter Shaw noted that his pursuer was back. Maybe.

He'd twice seen a car behind him making the same turns he'd made. A gray sedan, like the one outside Salvadoran coffee heaven. The grille logo was indiscernible six or seven car lengths back. Nissan? Maybe, maybe not.

He believed, to his surprise, that the driver was a woman.

Shaw had been keeping an eye on the car when the driver blew through a red light to make a turn in his direction. He caught a glimpse of a silhouette through the driver's-side window. He saw again the short stature and frizzy hair tied in a ponytail. Not exclusive to women, of course, but more likely F than M.

*You wouldn't think a woman would do that to another woman. I guess we can be as messed up as a man . . .*

Shaw made two unnecessary turns and the gray car followed.

Eyeing the street, the asphalt surface, measuring angles, distances, turning radii.

Now . . .

He slammed on the brake and skidded one hundred and eighty degrees, to face the pursuer. He earned a middle finger or two and at least a half dozen horns blared.

A new sound joined the salute.

The bleep of a siren. Shaw hadn't noticed that he'd U-turned directly in front of an unmarked Chrysler.

A sigh. He pulled over and readied license and rental contract.

A stocky Latino in a green uniform walked up to him.

'Sir.'

'Officer.' Handing over the paperwork.

'That was a very unsafe thing you did.'

'I know. I'm sorry.'

The cop — his name was P. ALVAREZ — wandered back to his car and dropped into the front seat to run the info. Shaw was looking at the space where the gray car had been and was no longer. At least he'd confirmed that it was the same vehicle as at the Salvadoran restaurant — a Nissan Altima, the same year, with the same dings and scrapes. He hadn't caught the license tag.

The man returned to the driver's window and gave Shaw back the documents.

'Why'd you do that, sir?'

'I thought somebody was following me. Was worried about a carjacker. I heard they go after rental cars.'

Alvarez said slowly, 'Which is why rental cars don't have any markings to indicate they're rental cars.'

'That right?'

'You troubled by something, call nine-one-one. That's what we're here for. You're from out of town. You have business here?'

A nod. 'Yep.'

Alvarez seemed to ponder. 'All right. You're lucky. It's my court day and I don't have time to write this up. But let's not do anything stupid again.'

'I won't, Officer.'

'Be on your way.'

Shaw restowed the papers and started the engine, driving to the intersection where he'd last seen the Nissan. He turned left, in the direction where she would logically have escaped. And, of course, found no trace.

He returned to the GPS route and in fifteen minutes was at the complex where Henry Thompson shared a condo with his partner, Brian Byrd. A police car, unmarked, sat in front of the building. Unlike with Sophie's kidnapping, the Task Force, or whoever was running the disappearance, would know for certain that Henry Thompson had been kidnapped, having found the man's damaged car. The officer — maybe the elusive Detective Standish — would be with Byrd, waiting for the ransom demand that Shaw knew would never come.

His phone hummed with a text. He parked and read it. Mack had discovered no criminal history in the lives of Thompson or Byrd. No weapons registrations. No security clearances or sensitive employment that might suggest motive — Thompson was the blogger and gay rights activist that Wikipedia assured Shaw he was. Byrd worked as a financial officer for a small venture capital firm. No domestic abuse complaints. Thompson had been married for a year to a woman, but a decade ago. There

184

seemed to be no bad blood between them. Like Sophie, he appeared to have been picked at random.

Very wrong time, very wrong place.

After leaving the Mulliners, Shaw had texted Byrd to make sure he was home, asking if they could meet. He immediately replied yes.

Shaw now called the number.

'Hello?'

'Mr. Byrd?'

'Yes.'

'Colter Shaw.'

Byrd was then speaking to someone else in the room: 'It's a friend. It's okay.'

Then back to Shaw: 'Can we talk? Downstairs? There's a garden outside the lobby.'

Neither of them wanted the police to know that Shaw was involved.

'I'll be there.' Shaw disconnected, climbed from the Malibu and strolled through manicured grounds to a bench near the front door. A fountain shot mist into the air, the rainbow within waving like a flag.

He scanned the roads beyond the lovely landscaping looking for gray Nissans.

Byrd appeared a moment later. He was in his fifties, wearing a white dress shirt and dark slacks, belly hanging two inches over the belt. His thinning white hair was mussed and he hadn't shaved. The men shook hands and Byrd sat on the bench, hunched forward, fingers interlaced. He arranged and rearranged the digits constantly, the way Frank Mulliner had toyed with the orange golf ball.

'They're waiting for a ransom call.' He spoke in a weak voice. 'Ransom? Henry's a blogger and I'm a CFO, but the company's nothing by SV standards. We don't even do tech start-ups.' His voice broke. 'I don't have any money. If they want some, I don't know what I'm going to do.'

'I don't think it's about money. There might not even be a motive. It could be he's just deranged.' Shaw was going with *he*; no need to muddy the conversation with talk about gender.

Byrd turned his red eyes to Shaw. 'You found that girl. I want to hire you to find Henry. Detective Standish seems smart . . . Well, I want you. Name your price. Anything. I may have to borrow but I'm good for it.'

Shaw said, 'I don't work for a fee.'

'Her father . . . He paid something.'

'That was a reward.'

'Then I'll offer a reward. How much do you want?'

'I don't want any money. I have an interest in the case now. Let me ask you some questions. Then I'll see what I can do.'

'God . . . Thank you, Mr. Shaw.'

'Colter's fine.' He withdrew his notebook and uncapped the pen. 'With Sophie, the kidnapper spotted her ahead of time and followed her. It's logical that he'd have done the same with Henry.'

'You mean, staking him out?'

'Probably. He was very organized. I want to check all of the places Henry was, say, thirty-six hours before he was kidnapped.'

Byrd's fingers knitted once more and the

knuckles grew white. 'He was here, of course, at night. And we had dinner at Julio's.' A nod up the street. 'Two nights ago. The lecture at Stanford last night. Other than that, I have no idea. He drives all over the Valley. San Francisco, Oakland too. He must drive fifty miles a day for research. That's why the blogs are so popular.'

'Do you know about any meetings in the past few days?'

'Just the lecture he was driving home from when he was kidnapped. Other than that, no. I'm sorry.'

'What articles was he working on? We can try to piece together where he was.'

Byrd looked down at the sidewalk at their feet. 'The one he was most passionate about was an exposé about the high cost of real estate in SV — Silicon Valley, you know?'

Shaw nodded.

'Then there was an article about game companies data-mining players' personal information and selling it. The third was about revenue streams in the software industry.

'For the real estate blog, he drove everywhere. He talked to the tax authorities, zoning board brokers, homeowners, renters, landlords, builders . . . For the data-mining and revenue-stream stories, he went to Google and Apple, Facebook, a bunch of other companies; I don't remember which.' He tapped his knee. 'Oh, Walmart.'

'Walmart?'

'On El Camino Real. He mentioned he was going there and I said we'd just been shopping. He said no, it was for work.'

'The panel at Stanford last night? What facility?'

'Gates Computer Science Building.'

'Did he go to any LBGT rights meetings lately?'

'No, not recently.'

Shaw asked him to look over Thompson's notes and any appointment calendars he could find to see where else Thompson might have gone. Byrd said he would.

'Would Henry have gone to the Quick Byte Café in Mountain View recently?'

'We've been there, but not for months.' Byrd couldn't sit still. He rose and looked at a jacaranda tree, vibrantly purple. 'What was it like for the girl? Sophie. The police wouldn't tell me much.'

Shaw explained about her being locked in a room, abandoned. 'There were some things he left. She used them to escape and rigged a trap to attack him.'

'She did that?'

Shaw nodded.

'Henry would hate that. Just hate it. He's claustrophobic.' Byrd began to cry. Finally he controlled himself. 'It's so quiet in the condo. I mean, when Henry's away and I'm home, it's quiet. Now, I don't know, it's a different kind of quiet. You know what I mean?'

Shaw knew exactly what the man meant but there was nothing he could say to make it better.

# 28

Shaw was making the rounds of places Henry Thompson had been prior to his kidnapping.

Apple and Google were big and formidable institutions and without the name of an employee Thompson had contacted there, Shaw had no entrée to start the search. And there'd be no chance to reprise any Quick Byte scenario in which a Tiffany would help him play spy and give him access to security videos.

Stanford University was a more logical choice. The kidnapper was likely to have followed Thompson from the lecture, then passed him on a deserted stretch of road, stopped a hundred or so yards ahead and, when Thompson caught up, flung the brick or rock into his windshield.

But the Gates Computer Center, the site of the panel, was in a congested part of the Stanford campus. There was no parking nearby and Thompson might have walked as far as two hundred yards in any direction to collect his car. He shared Thompson's picture with a handful of employees, guards and shopkeepers; no one recognized him.

Shaw knew the road where Thompson had been taken. He drove past it. The car had been towed but a portion of the shoulder was encircled by yellow tape. It was a grassy area; probably picked by X to avoid leaving tire prints, like at the factory. There were no houses or other buildings nearby.

Then there was the Walmart that Byrd had said Thompson had driven to. Why had the blogger's research taken him to a superstore?

He set the GPS for the place and piloted the Malibu in that direction. Over the wide streets of sun-grayed asphalt. Past perfectly trimmed hedges, tall grass, sidewalks as white as copier paper, blankets of radiant lawns, vines and shaggy palms. He noted the stylish and clever buildings that architects might put on page one of their portfolios, with mirrored windows like the eyes of predatory fish, uninterested in you . . . though only at the moment.

Then, just as had happened on his drive from his camper to the Salvadoran restaurant, Shaw left behind the mansions and glitzy corporations and suddenly entered a very different Silicon Valley. Small residences, stoic and worn, reminiscent of Frank Mulliner's house. The owners had made the choice between food and fresh paint.

He now pulled into the parking lot of Walmart, a chain with which he was quite familiar. A dependable source of clothing, food, medical supplies and hunting and fishing and other survival gear — and, just as important, last-minute presents for the nieces — his sister's children, whom he saw several times a year.

What could have brought Henry Thompson here?

Then he understood the blogger's likely mission. In a far corner of the parking lot were a number of cars, SUVs and pickups. Sitting in and around the vehicles — front seats and lawn chairs — were men in clean, if wrinkled, clothing. Jeans, chinos, polo shirts. Even a few sport coats. Everyone, it seemed, had a laptop. Ninety years ago, during the Great Depression, they would have gathered around a campfire; now they sat before the cold white light of a computer screen.

A new breed of hobo.

Shaw parked the Malibu and climbed out. He made the rounds, displaying Thompson's picture on his phone screen and explaining simply that the man had gone missing and he was helping find him.

Shaw learned to his surprise that none of these men — and it was men exclusively — was in fact homeless or unemployed. They had jobs here in the Valley, some with prestigious internet companies, and they had residences. Yet they lived miles and miles away, too far to commute daily, and they couldn't spare the money for hotel or motel rooms. They'd stay here for two, three or four days a week, then drive back to their families. At night, Shaw learned, the camp was more crowded; this group worked evening or graveyard shifts.

This would be why Henry Thompson had come here: to interview these men for his blog about the hardship of owning or renting property in the Valley.

A lean, wiry Latino living out of his Buick crossover told Shaw, 'This is a step up for me. I used to spend all night riding the bus to Marin, then back. Six hours. The drivers, they didn't care, you buy a ticket, you can sleep all night.

191

But I got mugged twice. This's better.'

Some were janitorial, some maintenance. Others were coders and middle management. Shaw saw one young man with an elaborate hipster mustache and filigree gold earrings drawing on a large artist's pad, sketching out what seemed to be a trade ad for a piece of hardware. He was talented.

Only one man remembered Henry Thompson. 'A couple days ago, yessir. Asked me questions about where I lived, the commute, had I tried to find someplace closer? He was interested if I'd been pressured out of my house. Had somebody tried to bribe me or threaten me? Especially government workers or developers.' He shook his head. 'Henry was nice. He cared about us.'

'Was anybody with him or did you see anybody watching him?'

'Watching?'

'We think he might've been kidnapped.'

'Kidnapped? Are you serious? Oh, man. I'm sorry.' He gazed around. 'People come and go here. I can't help you.'

Shaw surveyed the lot. There was a security camera on the Walmart building itself but too distant to pick up anything here. And there was the No Tiffany factor.

He climbed back into the Malibu. Just as he did, his phone hummed and he answered.

'Hello?'

'Oh, Colter. It's Brian Byrd.'

'Have you heard anything?'

'No. I did want to tell you I looked everywhere and couldn't find any more notes of Henry's. You

192

know, where he might've been if that guy was watching him. Henry must've had everything with him. You had any luck, anything at all?'

'No.'

'Who does something like this?' Byrd whispered. 'Why? What's the point? There's no ransom demand. Henry never hurt anybody. I mean, Jesus. It's like this guy's playing some goddamn sick game . . . ' Shaw heard a deep sigh. 'Why the hell's he doing this? You have any idea?'

After a moment Colter Shaw said, 'I might, Brian. I just might.'

# 29

Shaw sped back toward the Winnebago. He kept an eye out for cops but at the moment he didn't care about a ticket.

Once in the camper he went online and began his search. He was surprised that it didn't take very long to find what he hoped he might. And the results were far better than he'd expected. He called the Joint Major Crimes Task Force and asked for Dan Wiley.

'I'm sorry. Detective Wiley's not available.'

'His partner?'

'Detective Standish's not available either.'

The message of the woman at the JMCTF desk was getting as familiar as her voice.

Shaw hung up. He'd do what he did before: go to the Task Force in person and insist on seeing Wiley or Standish, if either of the men was in the office. Or Supervisor Cummings, if not. Better in person anyway, he decided. Getting the police to accept his new hypothesis of the case would take some persuasion.

He printed out a stack of documents, the fruits of his research, and slipped them into his computer bag. He stepped outside, locked the door and turned to the right, where he'd parked the Malibu. He got as far as the electrical and water hookups and froze.

The gray Nissan Altima had blocked in his rental. Its driver's seat was empty, the door open.

Back to the camper, get your weapon.

Dropping his computer bag, he pivoted and strode to the door, keys out.

Three locks. Fastest way to get them undone: slowly.

*Never rush, however urgent . . .*

He never got to the last lock. Twenty feet in front of him, a figure holding a Glock pistol stepped from the shadows between his Winnebago and the neighboring Mercedes Renegade. It was the driver of the Nissan — yes, a woman, African American, her hair in the ragged ponytail he'd seen in silhouette. She wore an olive-drab combat jacket — of the sort favored by gangbangers — and cargo pants. Her eyes were fierce. She raised the weapon his way.

Shaw assessed: nothing to do against a gun that's eight paces distant and in the hand of somebody who clearly knows what to do with a weapon.

Odds of fighting: two percent.

Odds of negotiating your way out: no clue, but better.

Still, sometimes you have to make what seem like inane decisions. The wrestler in him lowered his center of gravity and debated how close he could get before he passed out after a gunshot to the torso. After all, lethal shots are notoriously difficult to make with pistols. Then he recalled: if this was the kidnapper, she'd killed Kyle Butler with a headshot from much farther away than this.

The grim-faced woman squinted and moved in, snapping with irritation, 'Get down! Now!'

It wasn't get down or I'm going to shoot you.

195

It was get down, you're in my goddamn way.

Shaw got down.

She jogged past him, her eyes on a line of trees that separated the trailer camp from a quiet road, the gun aimed in that direction. At the end of the drive, she stopped and peered through a dense growth of shrubs.

Shaw rose and quietly started for the Winnebago's door again, pulling the keys from his pocket.

Eyes still on the trees, both hands on the gun, ready to shoot, the woman said in a blunt voice, 'I told you. Stay down.'

Shaw knelt once more.

She pushed farther into the brush. A whisper: 'Damn.' She turned around, holstering her weapon.

'Safe now,' she said. 'You can get up.'

She walked to him, fishing in her pocket. Shaw wasn't surprised when she displayed a gold badge. What he didn't expect, though, was what came next: 'Mr. Shaw, I'm Detective LaDonna Standish. I'd like to have a talk.'

# 30

Shaw collected his computer bag from the clump of grass where he'd dropped it.

As he and Standish approached the Winnebago door, an unmarked police car squealed to a stop in front of the camper. Shaw recognized it. It was the same vehicle that had lit him up after the dramatic U-turn on his way to Henry Thompson's condo. Officer P. Alvarez.

Shaw looked from the detective to the cop. 'You were both following me?'

Standish said, 'Double team tailing. The only way it works. Ought to be triple, but who can afford tying up three cars these days?' She continued: 'Budget, budget, budget. Had to follow you myself last night. Peter here was free this morning.'

Alvarez said, 'I didn't want to have to pull you over but it'd been more suspicious if I didn't. Was an impressive turn, Mr. Shaw. Stupid, like I said, but impressive.'

'I hope I don't need to do it again.' He cast a dark glance toward Standish, who snickered. Shaw nodded to the bushes. 'So, who'd you spot?'

'Don't know,' she said with some irritation in her voice. 'Had a report of somebody near your camper, possible trespasser. Smelled funky to me, all things considered.'

Her radio clattered. Another officer, apparently also cruising the area, had not spotted the suspect. Then came one more transmission, from a different patrolman. She told them to continue to search. She told Alvarez to do the same. When he drove off, she nodded toward the Winnebago. After Shaw unlocked the last lock, she preceded him inside.

The word *warrant* glanced off his thoughts. He let it go. He closed and locked the door behind them.

'You've got a California conceal carry,' she said. 'Where's your weapon? Or weapons?' She walked to his coffeepot and poked through the half dozen bags of ground beans in a basket bolted to the counter.

'The spice cabinet,' he said. 'My carry weapon.'

'Spice cabinet. Hmm. And it's a . . . ?'

'Glock 42.'

'Just leave it there.'

'And under the bed, a Colt Python .357.'

She lifted an eyebrow. 'Must be doing well in the reward business to afford one of those.'

'Was a present.'

'Other CCPs?'

A concealed carry permit in California is available only to residents. The California ticket doesn't let you carry in many other states. He had a nonresidence permit issued by Florida and that was good in a number of jurisdictions. Shaw, though, rarely went around armed; it was a pain to constantly pay attention to where you could and couldn't carry — schools and hospitals, for instance, were often no-gun zones. The laws varied radically from state to state.

Shaw said, 'You thought I might be the kidnapper.'

'Crossed my mind at first. I confirmed your alibi, what you told Dan Wiley. Didn't mean you weren't working with somebody, of course. But snatching some soul and hoping her daddy'll hand over a reward? Well, there's stupid and then there's stupid. I checked you out. You're not either variety.'

He then understood why she'd been tailing him. 'You were using me as bait.'

A shrug. 'You went and ruined a play date for the perp. Got Sophie home safe. Pissed that boy off in a large way, I'm thinking. Pissed him off enough that he went out and did it again — with Henry Thompson.'

'That was the kidnapper following me?' A nod outside.

'Big mug of coincidence if it wasn't. And if it's like Sophie's case he'd just leave Thompson on his own. Have himself plenty of free time to come visit you. If he was so inclined. As maybe he was. Unless you have other folks might want to have a few words with you? As I suspect might be the case, given your career.'

'Some. I've got people who keep an eye on that. And no reports of anything.'

Shaw's friend and fellow rock climber Tom Pepper, former FBI, ran a security company in Chicago. He and Mack kept track of those felonious alumni of Shaw's successful rewards jobs who'd threatened him.

He continued: 'Description of the perp here?'

'Dark clothing. Nothing else. Nothing on the vehicle.'

'You said *him*.'

'Ah. Him or her.'

'Is Detective Wiley at Brian Byrd's condo?'

She paused. 'Detective Wiley is no longer with the Criminal Investigations Division of the Task Force.'

'He's not?'

'I rotated him to Liaison.'

'You rotated him?'

Standish angled her head slightly. 'Oh, you thought he was the boss and that I worked for him? Why would that be, Mr. Shaw? Because I'm' — there was a fat pause — 'shorter?'

It was because she was younger but he said, 'Because you're so bad at surveillance.'

The touché moment landed and her mouth curved into a brief smile.

Shaw continued: 'Wiley's gone because he arrested me?'

'No. I would've done that. Oh, his grounds for the collar were wrong — like you told Cummings. Tampering with evidence we missed and you secured? My oh my, the JMCTF would look mighty bad if you mentioned that to the press. Which you would have done.'

'Maybe.'

'I would've taken you in as a material witness and not behind Plexiglas, thank you very much. Just till we checked you out properly. No, Dan got kicked down 'cause he didn't follow up on that memo of yours. You've got good handwriting. Bet you've heard that before. He should've jumped on the case with both feet. You ever work in law enforcement?'

'No. What's Liaison? That you sent him to?'

'We're a Task Force, right? We come from eight different agencies and there's a lot of back-and-forth. Dan'll get reports to where they belong.'

A messenger. Shaw thought, Tough break, Chief.

Standish said, 'Dan's not a bad guy. Had a bad spell recently. He was admin for years. Good at it, real good. Then his wife passed away. It was sudden. Thirty-three days from diagnosis to the end. He wanted to try something new. Get out, away from the desk. He thought the field would help. Man sure looks like a cop, doesn't he?'

'Central casting.'

'He was out of his league on the street. Insecurity and authority — bad combo. There were other complaints too.'

*What'd you find, sweetheart? . . .*

Standish was looking over a map of a trail in the Compound. 'That's . . . ?'

'My family home. Not far from Sierra National Forest.'

'You grew up there?'

'I did. My mother still lives on the family place. I was heading there for a visit until this happened.'

Her finger followed a red marker line on the map.

He said, 'Was going for a rock climb there.'

Standish exhaled a brief laugh. 'You do that for the fun of it?'

He gave a nod.

'Your mom? Lives there? Middle of nowhere?'

Shaw didn't give Standish too much history,

just explained that Mary Dove Shaw had become a sort of Georgia O'Keeffe — both in spirit and, with her lean sinewy figure and long hair, in appearance. With her background as a psychiatrist, med school professor and principal investigator, she had turned the Compound into a retreat for fellow doctors and scientists. Women's health was a popular theme of the get-togethers. Hunting parties too. One needs to eat, after all.

Shaw added that he made it a point to visit several times a year.

'That's the way,' Standish said, and his impression was that she was devoted to her parents too.

Shaw asked, 'Anything new about Henry?'

'Henry Thompson? No.'

He asked, 'Forensics?'

Shaw guessed she wouldn't share with a civie. Standish instead spoke without hesitation. 'Not good. No touch DNA on Sophie's clothes. Too early to tell with Thompson's car and the rock that got pitched into his windshield, but why would the unsub turn careless now? No prints anywhere. Wore cloth gloves. Can't source anything — the screws he sealed the door with, the water, the matches and the other stuff he left. Tire treads're useless, thanks to the grass, which I guess you knew. Oh, and I did have a team look over that access road where you said somebody was watching you.'

When he met Kyle Butler. Shaw nodded.

'That was gravel. So: useless encore. And I ran the traffic cams on Tamyen en route to the park from the Quick Byte . . . ' She furrowed her brow, staring at his face. 'You told Dan to check them out too?'

'I did.'

'Hmm. Well, nothing, sorry to report. No cars parked near the café were tagged on Tamyen.'

A good job, Shaw was thinking.

'With Thompson, he picked another place with a grassy field — no tire tracks there. Now, our unsub's shoes're men's size nine and a half Nikes. That means he — or she — was wearing men's size nine and a half Nikes. Doesn't mean they have size nine and a half feet. No security camera footage except for what you found at the Quick Byte Café. Had an unfortunate rookie spend hours scrubbing through the tape. Nobody seemed interested in Sophie, going back for two weeks. Other stores, bars and restaurants? Nothing. Was it you or Dan thought of the CCTV at Tamyen and Forty-two?'

'Did it show anything?'

Standish seemed amused Shaw wouldn't say. 'There wasn't one. Weapon was a Glock nine. And he took the brass with him. While he *was* a ways from Kyle Butler, he made a clean headshot. He's done some range time in his day. I'd say he was a pro, but pros don't do weird things like lock people in rooms. They shoot them or promise *not* to shoot them if the family coughs up the bucks.'

'You?' Shaw said.

'Me what?'

'Combat.' Shaw nodded at the OD jacket.

'No. It's cozy. I chill easy.'

'You canvassed for the gray stocking cap?'

'From the Quick Byte tape? Yep. Nothing yet. I've got another rookie looking at about ten hours of security video from the parking lots at Stanford.'

Shaw said, 'The lots on Quarry Road would be best. The ones closer to the Gates Center are small and they fill up fast.'

'What I was thinking too.'

He added that he had canvassed stores and security guards on the campus. She smiled when he used the cop term.

'Anybody talk to you?'

'Most of them did. Nobody saw Thompson.'

'And what about the poster?' Shaw asked.

She frowned quizzically.

'That I gave to Wiley. Of the face.'

She flipped through her notebook. 'Something about a sheet of paper left at a café. The lab ran it and it was negative DNA and prints. I didn't see it.'

Explained why she hadn't shown it to Sophie.

Shaw opened his computer bag and withdrew the sheets he'd printed earlier. On top was the image of the stenciled face, which he turned her way.

'What's this?'

'It's the Whispering Man.'

'Why's it important?' she asked.

'Because it might be the key to the whole case.'

# 31

Shaw was explaining. 'I was looking into some leads that Brian Byrd gave me. Places that Henry had been over the past day or so. I wanted a witness who'd seen somebody following him, maybe find another security video. Nothing panned out. I told that to Brian. And he said it made no sense to kidnap Henry. It was somebody playing a sick game.'

Standish grunted, though it was a benign grunt. She looked up from the printout.

Shaw continued: 'You know the C3 Conference in town?'

'Computers. Gamers, right? Screwing up traffic. But that's in San Jose, so I don't care in particular. What's that got to do with the unsub?'

'He could've raped or killed Sophie anytime. He didn't. He left her in that room in the factory with things she could use to survive. Five things: fishing line, matches, water, a glass bottle and a strip of cloth.'

'Okay.'

He sensed she was guessing where this was going and the skeptic's flag was starting to go up.

'I was at the conference yesterday.'

'You were? You into games?'

'No. I went with a friend.'

*I had time to kill after your people hijacked my car . . .*

He said, 'And I saw a game where you collect

objects you can use to play. Like weapons, clothes, food, magic power things.'

'Magic.'

'What if Byrd was right? This *is* a sick game? I went online and looked for video games where players are given five things and have to use them to survive. I found one. *The Whispering Man.*'

She fanned out the top few sheets. While the stenciled image of the Whispering Man was crudely done, Shaw had downloaded a number of pictures that were professionally drawn or painted, most from promotions or ads for the game. Some from rabid fans.

'Is he a ghost?' she asked. 'Or what?'

'Supernatural, who knows? In the game he knocks you out. You wake up barefoot — like Sophie — and all you have are the five things. You can trade them, use them as weapons to kill other players and steal what they have. Or players can work together — you've got a hammer and somebody else has nails. You play online. At any given time, there're a hundred thousand people playing, all over the world.'

'Mr. Shaw,' she began, the cynic's flag wholly unfurled now.

He continued: 'There're ten levels of play, going from easier to harder. The first is called The Abandoned Factory.'

Standish remained silent.

'Look at this.' He turned to his Dell and loaded YouTube. They leaned close to the screen. He typed into the search block and scores of videos depicting scenes from *The Whispering Man* came up. He clicked one. The video began with a first-person view, strolling down a sidewalk in pleasant suburbia. The music soundtrack was soft, under which you could hear what might be footsteps behind you. The player stopped and looked back. Nothing except the sidewalk. When he turned to continue, the Whispering Man was blocking the way, a faint smile on his face. A pause, then the creature lunged forward. The screen went black. A man's voice, high-pitched and giddy, whispered, 'You've been abandoned. Escape if you can. Or die with dignity.'

The screen slowly lightened, as if the player were growing conscious. Looking around, you could see it was an old factory, with five objects sitting in view — a hammer, a blowtorch, a spool of thread, a gold medallion and a bottle of some kind of blue liquid.

As they watched, the point-of-view character looked up to see a woman avatar walking stealthily closer, about to reach for his gold medallion; he picked up the hammer and beat her to death.

'Lord.' This from Standish.

A line of text appeared: *You have just earned water purification tablets, a silk ribbon, and what appears to be a clock but might not be.*

'At the factory? The unsub gave Sophie enough tools to escape, if she could figure out how. He screwed all the doors shut except for one. He was giving her a chance to win.'

She said nothing for a moment. 'So your theory is he's basing the kidnappings on the game.'

'It's a hypothesis,' Shaw corrected. 'A theory is a hypothesis that's been verified.'

Standish glanced at him, then turned back to the screen. 'I don't know, Mr. Shaw. Most crime's simple. This's complicated.'

'It's happened before. With the same game.' He handed Standish another sheet, an article from a Dayton newspaper. 'Eight years ago, two boys in high school got obsessed with the game.'

'This game? *The Whispering Man?*'

'Right. They played it in real life and kidnapped a girl classmate. A seventeen-year-old. They hid her in a barn, tied up. She was badly injured trying to escape. Then they decided they'd better kill her. They tried to but she got away. One of the boys went to a mental hospital, the other was sentenced to twenty-five years in prison.'

This got her attention. She asked, 'And are they . . . ?'

'They're both still in the system.'

She looked at the printouts and folded them.

'Worth looking into. 'Preciate it. And I appreciate what you did for Sophie Mulliner, Mr. Shaw. You saved her life. Dan Wiley didn't. I didn't. My experience is, though, that civilians can . . . muddy an investigation. So, with all respect, I'll ask you to fire up this nifty camper of yours and get on with that visit to your mother. Or see the sequoias, see Yosemite. Go anywhere else you want. As long as it isn't here.'

# 32

Colter Shaw was not on his way to the Compound to see his mother, nor en route to marvel at millennia-old trees nor planning a climb up towering El Capitan in Yosemite.

Nor anywhere else.

He was still smack in the middle of Silicon Valley — at the Quick Byte Café, to be specific. He was sipping coffee that was perfectly fine, though it didn't approach the Salvadoran beans from Potrero Grande, wherever that was.

He glanced at the bulletin board; the picture of Sophie he had pinned up yesterday was still there. Shaw wondered if that was because of the video camera now aimed at the board. He returned to yet more printouts — material that private eye Mack had just sent him in response to his request. He looked for Tiffany to thank her for the help, but she and her daughter were not in at the moment.

A woman's sultry voice from nearby: 'I rarely get calls from men after I kill them. I'm glad you don't wear grudges, son.'

Maddie Poole was approaching. Her pretty, appealing face, sprinkled with those charming freckles, was smiling. She dropped into the chair opposite him. The green eyes sparkled.

*Son . . .*

Shaw thought of Dan Wiley's reference to him as 'Chief' and reflected that one's tolerance for endearments depends largely on the person doing the endearing.

'Get you something?' he asked.

She glanced at a neighboring table. Two young men in baggy sweats and jackets were sitting with Red Bulls and coffees. They were bleary-eyed. Shaw remembered that this was a hub of the computing and gaming world. The hour — 10:30 a.m. — was probably savagely early for them. Maddie's eyes too were red-rimmed. 'That,' Maddie said. 'RB and coffee. Not mixed together, of course. That would be strange. And no milk or anything that might upset the caffeine. Oh, and something sweet maybe? You mind?'

'Not a worry.'

'You like sweet stuff, Colt?'

'No.'

'Pity poor.'

At the counter he perused the pastries, under plastic domes. He called, 'Cinnamon roll?'

'You read my mind.'

These choices didn't require a numbered card. The kid heated the half-pound roll, dripping with icing, for thirty seconds, then placed it and the beverages on a tray. A second cup of coffee for Shaw too.

He carried the tray to the table.

Maddie thanked him and drank down the entire Red Bull and took a fast slug of coffee. The giddiness vanished. 'Look. Yesterday — at the Hong-Sung game, *Immersion?* It's hard to explain. The thing is, I get sort of possessed when I play. Any game. I can't control myself. Or sports. I used to downhill-ski, and race mountain bikes too. You ever race?'

'Motocross. AMA. Too much work to pedal. I've got a gas engine.'

'Then maybe you know: you just *have* to win. No other option.'

He did know. No further explanation necessary.

'Thanks,' she said. Now the tense, troubled mood was jettisoned. 'Sure you don't want a bite?'

'No.'

She tore off a hunk of the excessive roll with a fork. It sped to her mouth and, as she chewed, she closed her eyes and exhaled extravagantly.

'Do I look like a commercial? Those restaurant ads where somebody takes a bite of steak or shrimp and they get all orgasmic.'

Shaw didn't see many commercials. And he'd definitely seen no commercials like that.

'You've been back to the conference?' he asked.

'I go back and forth. There, then my rental, where my rig's set up. GrindrGirl's gotta make a living.' She took another bite and on its heels another slug of coffee. 'Sugar rush. I've never done coke. No need when you've got icing. You agree?'

Was she asking about his interest in drugs? He had none, never had. Other than the occasional painkiller when there was a need. This was a question on the road to Relationship. Now was not the time.

'There's been another kidnapping.'

Her fork went to the plate. The smile vanished.

211

'Shit. By the same guy?'

'Probably.'

'Have they found this victim?'

'No. He's still missing.'

'He? So it's not a pervert?' Maddie asked.

'Nobody knows.'

'There a reward again?'

'No, I'm just helping the police. And I could use some help from you.'

'Nancy Drew.'

'Who?'

'You have a sister, Colt?'

'Three years younger.'

'She didn't read Nancy Drew?'

'A kid's book?'

'A series, yeah. Girl detective.'

'I don't think so.' The Shaw children had read a great deal yet children's fiction was not to be found in the substantial library in the cabin at the Compound.

'I read them all growing up . . . We'll save the date talk for another time . . . You don't smile much, do you?'

'No, but I don't mind date talk.'

She liked that. 'Ask away.'

'The kidnapper might've based the crimes on a video game. *The Whispering Man*. Do you know it?'

Another bite of roll. She chewed, thoughtful. 'Heard of it. Been around for a long time.'

'You ever played it?'

'No. It's an action-adventure. NMS.' She noted his blank reaction. 'Sorry. 'Not my style.' I'm a first-person shooter, remember? I think the gameplay for that one is you're trapped somewhere and you have to escape. Something like that. It's the Survival subcategory of action-adventures. You think some psycho dude's acting out the game in real life for kicks?'

'One possibility. He's smart, calculating, plans everything out ahead of time. He knows forensics and how not to leave evidence. My mother's a psychiatrist. I've talked to her about some of the jobs I've worked. She told me that sociopaths — serial killers — are very rare and even the organized ones aren't usually this organized. Sure, he could be one. I'm guessing that's only a ten percent option. Somebody this smart might be acting crazy, to cover up what he's really doing.'

'Which is what?'

Shaw sipped coffee. 'Not many ideas there. One possibility? Drive the manufacturer of *The Whispering Man* out of business.'

He went on to explain about the incident of the schoolgirl in Ohio, the classmates who played the game in real life. Maddie said she hadn't heard of it.

He continued: 'Maybe those crimes gave the perp the idea. When word gets out that for the second time somebody's been inspired to re-create the game, the publicity might ruin the company.' He tapped some of the printouts. 'You probably know this, but there's a lot of concern about violence in video games. Maybe the perp's harnessing that.'

'The debates've been going on forever. Back to the seventies. There was an early arcade game

213

called *Death Race*, published by a company right here, I think, in Mountain View. It was cheesy: monochrome, two-D, stick figures. And it caused an uproar. You drove a car around the screen and ran over these characters. When you did, they died and a tombstone popped up. Congress, I mean everybody, freaked out. Now there's *Grand Theft Auto* . . . One of the most popular games ever. You get points for killing cops or just walking around and shooting people at random.' She touched his arm and looked into his eyes. 'I kill zombies for a living. Do I look disturbed?'

'The question is: Who'd have a motive to ruin the company?'

'Ex-wife of the CEO?'

'Thought of that. His name's Marty Avon and he's been happily married for twenty-five years. Well, I'm adding the *happily*. Let's just say there's no ex in the picture.'

'Disgruntled employee,' Maddie suggested. 'Plenty of those in the tech world.'

'Could be. Worth checking out . . . There's another thought too. What's the competition like in the gaming world? I mean, competing companies, not players.'

Maddie gave a sardonic laugh. 'More combat than competition.' Her eyes seemed wistful. 'Didn't used to be that way. In the old days. Your days, Colter.'

'Funny.'

'Everybody worked together. They'd write code for you for free, no bullshit about copyright. They'd donate computer time, give away games for nothing. The one that got me started was *Doom* — remember from C3 yesterday? Ground zero for first-person shooters. It was originally shareware. Free to anybody who wanted it. That didn't last long. Once the companies figured out they could make money in this business . . . Well, it was every shooter for himself.'

Maddie told him about the famous 'Console Wars,' the battle between Nintendo and Sega, Mario the plumber versus Sonic the hedgehog. 'Nintendo won.'

*A shrine to the chivalrous who protect the weak . . .*

'Nowadays, you can't look at the news out of SV without seeing stories about theft of trade secrets, ripping off copyrights, spies, insider trading, piracy, sabotage. Buying up companies, then firing everybody and burying their software because it might compete with yours.' She glanced at the remnants of the roll and pushed it away. 'But murdering somebody, Colter?'

Shaw had pursued rewards for fugitives who'd killed for less than the value of a businessman's second Mercedes. He recalled the welcome screen at the conference.

*THE VIDEO GAMING INDUSTRY REVENUES WERE $142 BILLION LAST YEAR, UP 15% FROM THE YEAR BEFORE . . .*

Plenty of motive with that kind of money.
'*The Whispering Man*'s made by — '
'Oh, Colt. We say *published*. A game's

published, like a book or a comic. By a studio, like Hollywood. Games actually are just like movies now: the avatars and creatures are real actors shot against green screens. There are directors, cinematographers, sound designers, writers, CG people, of course.'

Shaw continued: 'Published by Destiny Entertainment. Marty Avon and Destiny have been sued a dozen times. All the suits were settled or dismissed. Some complaints alleged that Avon stole source code. I'm not sure what that is but it seems important.'

'Just the way your heart and nervous system are important.'

'Maybe one of the plaintiffs got kicked out of court and wanted to get revenge against Destiny his own way.' Shaw slid a stack of sheets toward her. 'This's a list of lawsuits against Destiny for the past ten years. My private eye pulled them together.'

'You've got a private eye?'

'Can you see if there are any plaintiffs that publish games like *The Whispering Man* and were around ten years ago?'

Reading, Maddie said, 'It'd have to be an independent company. None of the big public companies — Activision Blizzard, Electronic Arts, id — are going to hurt anybody. That'd be crazy.'

Shaw didn't necessarily agree — thanks for the paranoia about corporate America, Ashton — but he decided to stick to private companies for the moment.

Maddie read for no more than two minutes

before stopping. 'Well. Think I just earned my Cinnabon,' she said, and brought her index finger down hard on a name.

# 33

Tony Knight was the founder and CEO of Knight Time Gaming Software.

He'd been creating video games and other programs for years. He'd been hugely successful, hobnobbing with politicians and venture capitalists and Hollywood. He'd also been down-and-out, bankrupt three times. Once, like the Walmart residents Shaw had spoken to, he'd lived out of his car in an abandoned lot in Palo Alto and written code on a borrowed laptop.

Maddie had ID'd Knight as a possible suspect because his company published a survival action-adventure game in the same vein as *The Whispering Man*. Knight's product was called *Prime Mission*.

'Let's see if it came first. If it did, maybe Knight believes Marty Avon stole his source code. He tried to sue and lost and now he's getting even.'

It took only a few minutes to find that, yes, *Prime Mission* preceded *The Whispering Man* by a year.

Maddie reminded Shaw that she wasn't particularly familiar with either game — they were action-adventures, which were too slow for her — but she did know that Tony Knight was known in the industry to have a raging ego, a ruthless nature and a short fuse . . . and a long memory for slights.

'How close are the games?' Shaw asked.

'Let's find out.' She nodded to his computer and scooted her chair close to his.

Lavender? Yes, he smelled lavender. Freckles and lavender seemed like a good combination.

And what was that tattoo?

She logged on to a website and an image of a labyrinth appeared — the Knight Time logo — then the words *Tony Knight's Prime Mission*.

A window appeared. Shaw expected ads for insurance or discount hotels. It was an actual news broadcast. Two attractive anchors — a man and a woman, both with fastidious hair and wearing sharp outfits — were reporting on the news of the day: a trade meeting of the G8 in Europe, a CEO of a Portland, Oregon, company under fire for suggesting the government was justified in interring U.S. citizens of Japanese descent during World War II, a shooting at a school in Florida, a Washington congressman under investigation for texting a gay teenage prostitute, an 'alarming' study about the cancer risks of a brand of soft drinks . . .

Cable news at its finest . . .

She nodded at the screen. 'Most video games're cheap to buy but you can't really play without the add-ons — things to help you win or just be cool — power-ups, costumes for your avatars, armor, weapons, spaceships, advanced levels . . . You can spend a ton of money.'

'The razor's free,' he said, 'but the razor blades . . . '

'Exactly. Knight Time never charges for any- thing — the game, the extras. You've just got to sit through this.' The newscast faded to a public service announcement encouraging voter registration. Maddie then pointed. 'See?' The announcer said players could get five hundred 'Knight points,' to be used to buy accessories for any Knight Time game, if they did in fact register.

Whether or not Tony Knight was in some way behind the kidnappings, Shaw had to give him credit for the public service. As a professor of politics, Ashton Shaw believed it was a travesty that the U.S. didn't have mandatory voting like many other countries.

★　★　★

And, finally, the logo for the game *Prime Mission* appeared.

'Watch,' Maddie said, nodding as type scrolled onto the screen.

YOU ARE THE PILOT OF A UNITED TERRITORIES XR5 FIGHTER SHIP. YOU HAVE CRASH-LANDED ON THE PLANET PRIME 4, WHERE UT FORCES HAVE BEEN BATTLING THE OTHERS. YOU HAVE LIMITED AIR AND FOOD AND WATER. YOU MUST REACH SAFE STATION ZULU, TWO HUNDRED KILOMETERS TO THE WEST.

The rest of the crawl revealed, in effect, that the character must take three items from the spaceship to use to survive on the trek. It ended with the admonition:

*You're on your own. Choose wisely. Your life depends upon it.*

'It's *The Whispering Man* in space,' Shaw said. 'Even those lines at the end are similar. In *The Whispering Man*, it's 'You've been abandoned. Escape if you can. Or die with dignity.' I want to see more about Knight.'

He logged out of the game and called up more articles about the CEO and the company.

Shaw learned that Knight Time fell into the mold of several big tech companies — cofounded by two men in a garage. Like Bill Gates and Paul Allen, Steve Jobs and Steve Wozniak, and Bill Hewlett and Dave Packard. Knight's partner was Jimmy Foyle, both from Portland, Oregon. Knight handled the business side of the company; Foyle designed the games.

The press accounts of the company revealed details that echoed what Maddie had told him about Knight's nature.

The stories pointed to Jimmy Foyle as the model of a professional tech industry expert, who'd spend eighty-hour weeks perfecting the code for the company's gaming engines. He was described as a 'gaming guru.'

This was in sharp contrast to Tony Knight. The handsome, dark-haired CEO had a legendary temper. He was paranoid, petty. Twice, police were called to the company headquarters in Palo Alto when employees claimed Knight had physically hurt them — shoving one to the floor and flinging a keyboard into the face of another. No charges were filed and 'generous' settlements were offered. Knight would sue for what he thought was a breach of a nondisclosure or noncompete, even if there was little reason to do so. He had also been arrested outside of the company for incidents like a pushing match over a parking space and a lawn worker whom he believed had stolen a shovel from his garage.

The industry was always anticipating a breakup between the partners because of their differing personalities. One inspired profile writer described the two as the 'Black Knight' and the 'White Knight' because Foyle had once been a well-known white hat hacker — someone hired by companies and the government to try to break into their IT systems and expose vulnerabilities.

Knight's lawsuit against Destiny had been dismissed and both parties moved to have the records sealed, claiming that the court documents connected to the case contained trade secrets. A Freedom of Information Act request could be made, but that would take months. Shaw would proceed on the assumption that Destiny Entertainment had in fact stolen Knight's code. And he'd make the assumption that Knight was egotistical and vindictive enough to exact revenge.

He said to Maddie, 'Still, it's a big risk for a man who's already rich.'

She replied, 'There's another piece. Knight Time's flagship game is *Conundrum*. It's an alternative reality game. Spectacular to watch. Too brainy for me, I'm not fast enough. The new installment is six months late. That's a no-no in the gaming world.'

Shaw added, 'And Knight waited until tens of thousands of gamers descend into the Valley. He hired somebody to be a psychotic player. Police wouldn't look past that. Great smoke screen.'

'You going to tell the police?'

'The detective wasn't impressed with my idea in the first place. When I suggest a famous CEO might be the perp, it'll make her even more skeptical. I need facts.'

Maddie was looking over his face. She said, 'I'd go hunting with my father sometimes, remember?'

He did, an interest they shared — though it was a sport for her while something else entirely for him.

'And there was this look he'd get. He wasn't really himself. He was in a different place. All that mattered was getting that deer or goose or whatever. That's what you're looking like now.'

Shaw knew what she was talking about — he'd seen the same expression in her face while she was stabbing him to death yesterday.

'Knight Time Gaming would have a booth at the C3 Conference?' he asked.

'Oh, yeah. One of the biggest.'

Shaw started assembling the printouts. 'I'm going to go pay a visit.'

'You want some company? Always more fun to hunt with somebody else.'

Shaw couldn't argue with that, thinking of the times he'd go out with his father or his brother into the forests and fields of the Compound. His mother too, who was the best shot in the family.

This, however, was different.

*Most crime's simple. This's complicated . . .*

'Think it's better for me to go on my own.' Shaw took one last hit of coffee and headed out the door, pulling out his phone to make a call.

# 34

Truth is a curious thing.

Often helpful, sometimes not.

Colter Shaw had learned in pursuing rewards that there usually was nothing to be gained by lying. It might get you a few quick answers, but if you were found out, as often happened, sources would dry up.

Which didn't mean that there weren't times when it was helpful to let the impression settle that you were someone other than who you were.

Shaw was once again strolling the chaotic aisles of the C3 Conference, wandering through the mostly young, mostly male audience.

He passed Nintendo, Microsoft, Bethesda, Sony and Sega. The same carnage as before yet also bloodless games, like soccer, football, race cars, dance, puzzle solving and, well, the just plain bizarre. One featured green squirrels wearing toreador outfits and armed with nets as they chased worried bananas.

Shaw thought, People actually spent their time this way?

Then: Was obsessively cruising the country in a battered camper any worthier?

You disregard others' passions at your peril.

The Knight Time booth was larger but more austere and somber than the others. The walls and curtains were black, the music eerie, not thumping in your chest. No flashing lights or spots. Of course, the booth boasted ten-foot-long high-def screens — those seemed to be requisite at C3. The displays showed trailers for the delayed installment *Conundrum VI*. The text promised *Coming Soon!*

Shaw watched the action on the big screen for a while. Planets, rockets, lasers, explosions. In the booth fifty or so young people sat at stations and tried their hand at Knight Time games. In front of him a young woman wearing stylish red glasses, her hair in a ponytail, was intently playing *Prime Mission*.

'Well, that sucks.' A teenager was talking to his friend. Waiting for a Knight Time game to start, he was gazing at the ad and news broadcast window Shaw remembered. On-screen was a pair of anchors, two young, geeky men. They were reporting on the fact that a congressman had supported a proposal to tax users' internet traffic over a certain number of gigabytes per day.

The gamer's friend lifted a middle finger to the screen.

They both relaxed when the game loaded and they could start to shoot aliens.

Shaw wandered up to an employee.

'Got a question,' Shaw said to the man, who was in black jeans and a gray T-shirt, which had KNIGHT TIME GAMING across the chest. The letters began at the left in solid black, then dissolved into pixels, graying so that the final ING was hard to see. He noted that all Knight Time employees wore the same outfit.

'Yessir?'

The man was six or seven years younger than Shaw. About Maddie Poole's age, he thought.

'I get games for my nieces — you know, birthdays and Christmas. I'm checking some out here.'

'Great,' said the man. 'What're they into?'

'*Doom. Assassin's Creed. Soldier of Fortune.*' Maddie Poole had briefed him.

'Classic. Hmm, girls? How old are they?'

'Five and eight.'

This gave the man pause.

'I've heard about *Conundrum.*' He nodded at the screen.

'I was going to say, it's a bit old for them. But if they play *Doom* . . . '

'The eight-year-old's favorite. What about your game *Prime Mission?* They like *The Whispering Man.*'

'I've heard of that one. Never played it. Sorry.'

'*Prime Mission*'s good, right?'

'Oh, a big winner at The Game Awards.'

'I'll take them both. *Conundrum* and *Prime Mission.*' Shaw looked around. 'Where do I buy the discs?'

The employee said, 'Discs? Well, we're download only. And it's free.'

'Free?'

'All our software is.'

'Well, that's a deal.' He glanced at the impressive monitor overhead. 'I've heard that the head of the company's a genius.'

Reverence dusted the kid's face. 'Oh, there's nobody in the business like Mr. Knight. He's one of a kind.'

Shaw looked up at the screen. 'That's the new installment? *Conundrum VI?*'

'That's it.'

'Looks good. How's it different from the current one?'

'The basic structure is the same, ARG.'

'ARG?'

'Alternative reality game. In Installment 6 we're upping the galaxies to explore to five quadrillion and the total planets to fifteen quadrillion.'

'*Quadrillion?* You mean, a player can visit that many planets?'

With geek pride, the man said, 'Theoretically, if you spent just one minute per planet, it would take you — I'm rounding — twenty-eight billion years to finish the game. So . . . '

'Pick your planet carefully.'

The employee nodded.

'It's been delayed, right? The new installment?'

He grew defensive. 'Just a little. Mr. Knight has to make sure it's perfect. He won't release anything before its time.'

'Should I wait for that one, for *VI?*' Another nod at the screen.

'No, I'd get *V.* Here.' He handed Shaw a card:

CONUNDRUM
KNIGHT TIME GAMING
EVER FREE . . .

On the back was a link for downloads. Into Shaw's back jeans pocket.

228

He thanked the employee and walked slowly past the players. He posed similar questions to a couple of other employees in the booth and got many of the same answers. Nobody seemed to know anything about *The Whispering Man*. He tried too to find out where Knight was presently and some things about his personal life. Nobody answered the specific questions, though the same message was often repeated: Tony Knight was a visionary, the paternal god atop the Olympus of high technology.

Smacked of cult, to Shaw.

He'd done all he could do here, so he headed to the booth's exit, walking past a curtained wall. He was halfway along it when he startled as a hundred lasers and spotlights positioned around the twenty-foot monitors towering over the booth shot fiery beams toward the ceiling. Amid a deafening blare of electronic music, a booming voice crid, '*Conundrum VI*, the future of gaming . . . Ever free . . . ' And on the screen, a death beam blew to pieces one of the fifteen quadrillion planets.

Everyone nearby turned to the display and the light show.

Which is why not a single person noticed when a flap in the curtains opened and two fiercely strong men yanked Colter Shaw into the darkness on the other side.

# 35

As he stood in a dim alcove, being expertly frisked in silence, he reflected on the flaw in his plan. Which had otherwise been a good one, he believed.

After a half hour of playing the role of naïve attendee, asking seemingly pointless yet probing questions, he'd assumed the Knight Time employees would realize he surely had to be here for some purpose other than buying children video games that were utterly inappropriate.

And so he would head outside the convention center to see if Knight's minders would take the bait: Shaw himself. As soon as he was in the parking lot, headed for the deserted corner where he'd left the Malibu, he would hit Mack's phone number and open a line. His PI would hear who and how many, if any, of Knight's men had come after him. If that happened and it sounded like he was endangered, the PI would call the JMCTF and the Santa Clara County Sheriff's Office. Shaw had also slipped his Glock into the glove compartment of the Malibu, just in case.

A good plan on paper, flushing Knight or his people as potential suspects.

But a plan based on the assumption that they wouldn't dare move on him at the convention center itself.

Got that one wrong.

He was now quick-marched a good thirty feet into the black heart of the Knight Time booth, through more shrouds of soundproof cloth. He'd heard the distant bass of the *Conundrum VI* ad. Then, once it had served its distractive purpose, the speaker volume dropped.

Shaw didn't bother to say anything. His bald minders wouldn't have answered anyway. He knew they were pros. Was the shorter one Person X? Sophie had said her kidnapper was not tall.

*Size nine and a half shoes . . .*

When they arrived at a proper door — not a fabric flap — they halted, then put everything Shaw had in his pockets into a plastic box, including, of course, the phone on which Mack's number was front and center but as yet undialed.

The box was handed off to someone else and the two men holding his arms escorted Shaw through the door and dropped him into a comfortable black chair, one of eight surrounding an ebony table. The walls had been constructed with baffles, the ceiling acoustical tile. All these surfaces were painted black or made from matte-black substances. The space was deathly silent. The only illumination came from a tiny dot at the bottom of one wall, like a night-light. Just enough to make out a few details: the chamber — the word came to mind automatically — was about twenty feet square, the ceiling about eight feet high. No telephones, no screens, no laptops. Just a room and furniture. Private, and secure from the outside world.

His father would have appreciated it.

The shorter guard left, the other remaining at the door. Shaw could see some features of his captor. No jewelry. The earpiece of the Secret Service and TV commentators. Dark suit, white shirt, striped tie that seemed to be clip-on — an old trick — so that it couldn't be used as a garrote in a fight. His face in the shadows so Shaw couldn't see any expressions. He guessed there'd be none. He knew men like this.

Shaw debated next steps.

Ninety percent odds that he'd come to no harm here because of the inconvenience of dealing with the aftermath — smuggling his damaged or dead body out of the convention center. He supposed that logic didn't mean much to abusive and temperamental Tony Knight, who, if he was behind the kidnappings, was risking everything over a vindictive whim to destroy a competitor who'd wronged him.

Suddenly a ceiling light came on, a downward-pointing spot. Cold. The door opened. Shaw squinted against the flare of illumination.

Tony Knight entered. The CEO was leaner and shorter than he'd appeared in the pictures Shaw had found online, though he was still a substantial man. And it occurred to Shaw: Why assume he'd farmed out the kidnapping job, if he was in fact behind it? With his temper and vengeful nature, he might very well have enjoyed snatching Sophie Mulliner and Henry Thompson himself.

The man's dark eyes were fixed and didn't waver as they met Shaw's blue. The shadows from the light above made his gaze all the more sinister. The executive wore expensive-looking black slacks and a white dress shirt, two buttons undone at the top revealing thick chest hair, which added to his animal intensity. His hands were large and kept flexing in and out of fists. Shaw was gauging where to roll to minimize the damage from the first blow.

Knight sat at the head of the table. Shaw, at the opposite end, noted that the chair he himself had been deposited in, and six of the others, were about two inches shorter than the eighth, Knight's. This room would be used for sensitive negotiations and the short CEO would want to be at eye level with, not looking up at, the others.

Knight withdrew his phone, plugged a bud into his ear and stared at the screen.

Survival, Ashton Shaw taught Russell, Colter and Dorion, is about planning.

*Never be caught off guard.*

Plan how you're going to avoid or eliminate a threat. Shaw'd assume the guard was armed and that Knight was not. While Shaw knew little about boxing or martial arts, his father had taught all the children grappling skills . . . And there *were* all those wrestling trophies from his Ann Arbor days.

Taking down the minder by the door would be relatively easy. Knight — and his ego — would have instructed the muscle to expect threats to their boss's life, not their own.

Shaw planted his feet on the floor and casually put a hand on the edge of the table. From the corner of his eye, he saw that the minder had missed the maneuver. Shaw's legs — strong from hiking and rock climbing — tensed and he adjusted his balance. Ten feet to the guard. Lunge and, at the same time, shove the table toward Knight. Body-slam the minder, maybe a palm to the jaw, an elbow to the solar plexus. Get the weapon, pull the slide to make sure a round was chambered, even if it meant ejecting one. Control the two men in the room. Get a phone, go out the way he came in, call LaDonna Standish.

Grim-faced, Knight now rose angrily.

Revise slightly. When he got close, grab his lapels and drive him back into the guard, get the weapon.

One . . .

The CEO strode to Shaw and leaned down, close, hands continuing to flex and unflex.

Two . . .

Shaw readied himself, judging distances. Apparently no video cameras here. Good.

It was then that Tony Knight, at an ear-ringing decibel, raged, '*Conundrum VI* is not vaporware. Can't you get that through your fucking skulls?'

He returned to his chair and sat down, crossing his arms and fixing Shaw with a petulant glare.

# 36

Colter Shaw had been accused of committing any number of offenses in his life, real and imagined.

The word *vaporware* had never figured in any of them.

There were many arrows of reply available in Shaw's quiver. He chose the most accurate: 'I don't know what you're talking about.'

Knight licked his lip, just the tip of his tongue. The flick wasn't exactly serpentine but wasn't far off.

'I heard it all.' The accent placed his roots in Ontario. He tapped his phone. 'The questions you were asking my people . . . You're not a gamer. We tagged your face and went back to the video, checked you out from the minute you entered the convention center. No interest in any other booths but mine. And asking bullshit questions, playing dumb, just to get information. You think this hasn't happened before? Trying to get somebody to turn? An employee? Turning against *me*? Do you really think that would ever fucking happen?'

Knight gestured in the general direction of the front of the booth. 'You saw the promo outside. Did it look like vaporware to you? Did it?'

The door opened again and the other minder, the bigger one, stepped inside. He bent down to Knight and whispered. Knight's eyes remained on Shaw. When the guard stood up, his boss asked, 'Verified?'

The muscle nodded. When Knight waved his hand, the man left. The other remained where he'd been, in Tower of London Beefeater mode.

Knight's anger had morphed to confusion. 'You're like a private eye?'

'No. Not a PI. I make my living collecting rewards.'

'You were the one who found that girl'd been kidnapped?'

A nod.

'You don't have any tech background.'

'No.'

'So nobody hired you to play corporate spy.'

'I don't even know what vaporware is.'

It would be dawning on Knight that Shaw wasn't a threat. It was dawning on Shaw that his hypothesis about Knight plotting to destroy a competitor might have a few holes.

'Vaporware's when a software company announces a new product that's either fake or won't be ready for a while. It's a tactic to gin up excitement, get some press. And keep the hordes at bay when you need more time to tweak the install. Because your fans can also be your biggest enemies if you don't deliver what you promised when you first promised it.'

Shaw said, 'That's the rumor about *Conundrum VI*? Vaporware?'

'Yeah.' Knight's voice was sardonic. 'It's just taken a little longer than I'd planned.'

Fifteen quadrillion planets would understandably require some time.

Knight gazed at Shaw closely. 'So, what's going on here?'

Sometimes you don't play the odds. Sometimes your gut gives you direction.

'Can we get out of here?' Shaw asked.

Knight debated. He nodded and the guard opened the door. The three of them stepped into a larger, brighter room, the inner sanctum of the booth. Two young women and a young man, wearing the corporate T-shirt and jeans uniform, labored away furiously at computer terminals. They shot wary looks toward their boss when he emerged and then their attention snapped back to their clattering tasks.

Shaw and Knight sat at the only table that didn't have an impressive computer perched upon it. A young woman with a crew cut brought Shaw the box containing his personal effects. He slipped them where they belonged.

Knight barked, 'So?'

'You sued Marty Avon a few years ago.'

Knight digested this with a frown. 'Avon? Oh, Destiny Entertainment? Did I? Probably. When somebody tries to fuck me over, I sue them. You're not answering my question.'

'That young woman who was kidnapped the other day, Sophie Mulliner? The kidnapper was re-creating *The Whispering Man*.'

Not a flicker of reaction, other than the appropriate confusion. Which effectively deflated Shaw's hypothesis about Knight to low single digits. 'Destiny's flagship game . . . What do you mean 'recreating'?'

Shaw explained about the room in the factory,

the five objects, the chance to survive.

'That's one sick fuck. Why?'

'Maybe a disturbed gamer . . . I have another idea.' He explained that the crime was intended to get even with Marty Avon or bring down Destiny. 'When word gets out that a kidnapper was inspired by the game, the company would be sued and boycotted by the anti-violent video game crowd. It goes out of business. Destiny's already been through this before.'

Shaw told him about the two teenagers who'd kidnapped their classmate and nearly killed her.

'I remember that. Sad story.' Then he scoffed. 'And you thought I was behind it? Because I had some grudge against Marty Avon for stealing code? Or I wanted him closed down because *The Whispering Man* competes against *Prime Mission?*'

'We need to explore every option. There's been another kidnapping.'

'Another one? Shit.' Knight asked, 'When was that first incident? The boys who hurt that girl?'

Shaw told him.

Knight stood and walked to a terminal where one of the uniformed employees sat. She glanced up with wide eyes and, when Knight lifted his palm abruptly, leapt up and held the chair for him. He sat and spent a few minutes keyboarding. Behind Shaw came humming and *ca-shhh* from a printer. Knight rose and collected several sheets of paper, which he placed before Shaw. Knight withdrew a pen from his pocket. It was a ballpoint, but an extremely expensive one — made from platinum, Shaw believed.

'We subscribe to a marketing data service that tracks the sales of products and services all over the world. Did Cheerios outsell Frosted Flakes in March of last year? In what regions? In the places where Cheerios won, what was the average household income? What are the ages of the schoolchildren in those homes? On and on and on. You get the idea.' He tapped the top sheet before Shaw with the pen. 'This chart tracks Destiny Entertainment's sales of *The Whispering Man.*'

Knight circled a flat line. 'That period was the two months following the Ohio girl's attack, when, we can assume, the protests were the loudest, the press was the worst. Somebody tries to murder a girl because of the game and what happens? No effect on sales whatsoever. People don't care. If there's a game they like, they'll buy it, and they don't give a shit if it inspires psychos or terrorists.'

Shaw noted that the data confirmed what Knight was telling him. He didn't ask if he could keep the sales stats; he folded the pages and slipped them in his pocket to verify them later, though he didn't doubt the figures were accurate.

The CEO said, 'What happened with Destiny is, the suit? I think they might've tried to poach some retailers I had an exclusive with. Penny-ante stuff. But I had to come down hard. You can't let people get away with anything. And Marty Avon? He's no threat. He's the mom-and-pop corner store of the gaming world.' Knight looked him over. 'So. We cool with everything?

239

My guys got too rough?'

'Not a worry.' Shaw rose and looked for the door.

'There.' Knight was pointing.

Shaw was almost to the exit when Knight said, 'Hold up.'

Shaw turned.

'There's somebody you should talk to.' He sent a text and then nodded to the table and the two men sat once more. 'I want some coffee. You want coffee? I fly the beans in directly from Central America.'

'El Salvador?'

'No way. It's my own farm in Costa Rica. Better than Salvadoran, hands down.'

Shaw said, 'Why not?'

# 37

Jimmy Foyle, the cofounder of Knight Time, was in his mid-thirties.

Shaw recalled that he was also the chief game designer, the 'gaming guru.' Whatever that meant.

The compact man had straight black hair in need of a trim. His face was boyish and chin dusted with faint stubble. His blue jeans were new, his black T-shirt ancient and the short-sleeved plaid over-shirt, faded orange and black, was wrinkled. No corporate uniform for him, presumably because, as the creator of fifteen quadrillion planets, he could wear whatever the hell he wanted to.

Shaw decided the look was Zuckerberg-inspired, though more formal, owing to the overshirt.

Foyle was fidgety, not in an insecure way but in the manner of those who are intensely smart and whose fingers and limbs move in time to their spiraling minds. He had joined Knight and Shaw at the table in the workstation room, and the three were alone. Knight had cleared the room of the keyboarding employees by shouting, 'Everyone, get out!'

Shaw sipped the coffee, which was a fine brew, yet the Costa Rican beans didn't live up to their claim of overshadowing the Salvadoran.

Foyle was listening to Shaw's explanation

about the kidnappings, sitting forward at an acute angle. The man seemed shy and had made no pleasantries, offered no greetings; he had not shaken Shaw's hand. A bit of Asperger's, maybe. Or perhaps because software code looped through his thoughts constantly and the idea of social interaction emerged briefly, if at all. He wore no wedding ring or other jewelry. His loafers needed replacement. Shaw recalled the article about the game designer and assumed if you spent eighty hours a week in a dark room, it was because you enjoyed spending eighty hours a week in a dark room.

When Shaw finished, Foyle said, 'Yes, I heard about the girl. And on the news this morning the other kidnapping. The journalists said it was likely the same man but they weren't sure.' A Bostonian lilt to his voice; Shaw supposed he'd acquired his computer chops at MIT.

'We think probably.'

'There was nothing about *The Whispering Man*.'

'That's my thought. I told the investigators but I'm not sure how seriously they took it.'

'Do the police have any hope of finding the new victim?' His language was stiff, formal in the way that Shaw supposed computer codes were formal.

'They didn't have any leads as of an hour ago.'

'And your thought is that either he's some troubled kid who's taken the game to heart, like those boys a few years ago, or — alternatively — someone has hired him to pretend he's a troubled kid to cover up something else.'

'That's right.'

Knight asked, 'What do you think, Jimmy?' Unlike his dictatorial attitude toward the other minions, with Foyle the CEO was deferential, almost obsequious.

Foyle drummed his fingers silently on his thigh while his eyes darted about. 'Masquerading as a troubled gamer to cover up another reason for a kidnapping? I don't know. It seems too complicated, too much work. There'd be too many chances to get found out.'

Shaw didn't disagree.

'A troubled player, though, stepping over the line.' The man nodded thoughtfully. 'Do you know Bartle's categorization of video game players?'

Knight offered a gutsy laugh. 'With all respect, he doesn't know shit about games.'

Which wasn't exactly true but Shaw remained silent.

Foyle went into academic mode. His eyes widened briefly — his first display of emotion, such as it was. 'This is significant. There are four personality profiles of gamers, according to Bartle. One: Achievers. Their motivation is accumulating points in games and reaching preset goals. Two: Explorers. They want to spend time prowling through the unknown and discovering places and people and creatures that haven't been seen before. Three: Socializers. They build networks and create communities.'

He paused for a moment. 'Then, fourth: Killers. They come to games to compete, to win. That's the sole purpose of gaming to them.

Winning. Not necessarily to take lives; they enjoy race car and sports games too. First-person shooters are their favorites, though.'

*Killers* . . .

Foyle continued: 'We spend a lot of time profiling who we're creating games for. The profile of Killers is mostly male, fourteen to twenty-three, who play for at least three hours a day, often up to eight or ten. They frequently have troubled family lives, probably bullied at school, loners.

'But the key element of Killers is they need someone to compete against. And where do they find them? Online.'

Foyle fell silent and his face revealed a subtle glow of satisfaction.

Shaw didn't understand why. 'How does that profile help us?'

Both Knight and Foyle seemed surprised at the question. 'Well,' the game designer said, 'because it might just lead you straight to his front door.'

# 38

Detective LaDonna Standish was saying, 'Don't mind admitting when I'm wrong.'

She was referring to her advice that Shaw leave Silicon Valley for home or to do some sightseeing.

They were in her office at the Task Force, only one half of which showed any signs of occupancy. The other hemisphere was completely vacant. There'd been no replacement found for Dan Wiley, who'd now be shuffling files to and from the various law enforcement agencies throughout Santa Clara County, a job that, to Shaw, would be a level of hell unto itself.

When Standish had stepped into the JMCTF reception area twenty minutes ago, Shaw had been amused to see her stages of reaction when he told her what he'd found: (1) confusion, (2) irritation and (3) after he'd shared what Jimmy Foyle had told him, interest.

Gratitude — reaction 3½? — had followed. She'd invited him to the office. Her desk was covered with documents and files. On the credenza pictures of friends and family, as well as several commendation plaques, were daunted by more files.

Jimmy Foyle's idea was that if the suspect were a Killer he would be online almost constantly.

'His online presence defines him,' the designer had said. 'Oh, he probably goes to school or a job, sleeps — though probably not much of that. He'll be obsessed with the game and play it constantly.' Foyle had then sat forward with a slight smile. 'But when do you know for certain the times he *wasn't* playing?'

A brilliant question, Shaw had realized. And the answer: he wasn't playing when he was kidnapping Sophie Mulliner and Henry Thompson and when he was shooting Kyle Butler.

He now told Standish, '*The Whispering Man* is a MORPG, a multiplayer online role-playing game. Players have to pay a monthly fee, which means Destiny, the publisher of the game, keeps credit cards on file.'

Standish's thinking gesture was to touch an earring, a stud in the shape of a heart, an accessory in stark contrast to her outfit of cargo pants, black T and combat jacket. Not to mention the big-game Glock .45 on her hip.

'Foyle said we could use the credit card information to get a list of all the subscribers in the Silicon Valley area. Then we find out from the company who, among those, play obsessively but who weren't online at the times of the kidnappings and Kyle's murder.'

'That'll work. I like it.'

'We need to talk to the head of Destiny, Marty Avon. Can you get a warrant?'

She chuckled. 'Paper? Based on a video game? I'd be laughed out of the magistrate's office.' She then turned her eyes his way. They were olive in color, and very dark, two tones deeper than her skin. Hard too. She added, 'One thing I'm hearing, Mr. Shaw.'

'How about we do 'Colter' and 'LaDonna.''

A nod. 'One thing I'm hearing: 'we.' The Task Force doesn't deputize.'

'I'm helpful. You know it.'

'Rules, rules, rules.'

Shaw pursed his lips. 'Upstate New York one time, I was visiting my sister. A boy'd gone missing, lost in the woods near his house, it looked like. Five hundred acres. The police were desperate, blizzard coming on. They hired a local consultant to help.'

'Consultant?'

'A psychic.'

'For real?'

'I went to the sheriff too. I told him I had experience sign cutting — you know, tracking. I said I'd help them for free. The psychic was charging. They agreed.' He lifted his palms. 'Don't deputize me, LaDonna. Consultize me. Won't cost the state a penny.'

A finger to the earlobe. 'Out of harm's way. No weapon.'

'No weapon,' he agreed, and could see, from the tightening of her lips, that she was aware he'd offered only half agreement.

They walked out of the Task Force building and into the parking lot, heading for her gray Altima. Standish asked, 'How'd it turn out, that missing boy? Did she help?'

'Who?'

'The psychic.'

'How'd you know it was a woman?' Shaw asked.

'I'm psychic,' Standish said.

247

'She said she had a vision of the boy near a lake, making shelter under the trunk of a fallen walnut tree, four miles from the family house. A milk carton was nearby. And there was an old robin's nest in a maple tree next to him.'

'Damn. That was one particular vision. Was she in the ballpark?'

'No. Took me ten minutes to find him. He was in the loft of the family's garage. He'd been hiding there the whole time. He didn't want to take his math test.'

# 39

'Your first name?' Standish asked Shaw. They were driving through Silicon Valley in her rickety car. Something was loose in the rear. 'Never heard of it.'

'I'm one of three children,' Shaw told her. 'Our father was a student of the Old West. I was named after the mountain man John Colter, with the Lewis and Clark Expedition. My kid sister's Dorion, after Marie Aioe Dorion, one of the first mountain women in North America. She and her two kids survived for two months in the dead of winter in hostile territory — Marie Aioe, not my sister. My older brother, Russell, he was named after Osborne Russell, a frontiersman in Oregon.'

'They do this reward stuff too?'

'No.'

Though the apples didn't fall far, at least in Dorion's case. She worked for an emergency preparedness consulting company. Maybe in Russell's too. But no one in the family knew where he was or what he was up to. Shaw had been trying to find him for years. Both hoping to and worried that he might succeed.

*October 5, fifteen years ago . . .*

Sometimes Shaw thought he should simply let it go.

He knew he wouldn't.

*Never abandon a task you know you must complete . . .*

They were cruising along the 101, south-bound, and had left the posh Neiman Marcus Silicon Valley behind, as well as the more modest yet tidy neighborhoods where the Quick Byte Café squatted and Frank Mulliner lived. Here, on either side of the freeway, badly in need of resurfacing, was hard urban turf, banger turf, city projects housing, abandoned buildings and overpasses dolled up with gang-sign graffiti.

According to GPS, the Destiny Entertainment Inc. offices were not far away. Shaw recalled Foyle telling him that *The Whispering Man* was the company's main game. Maybe they hadn't had any other big hits and the failures had kept the company on the wrong side of the tracks.

Shaw mentioned this to Standish as she pulled off the highway onto surface streets. 'But it's my wrong side of the tracks.'

He glanced her way.

'Home sweet home. EPA. East Palo Alto. Grew up here.'

'Sorry.'

She scoffed. 'No offense taken. EPA . . . Doesn't that confuse everybody? It's really north of the other Palo Alto. Place so far on the wrong side you couldn't even hear any train whistle. Your father liked his cowboys. Well, this was Tombstone back in the day. Highest murder rate in the country.'

'In Silicon Valley?'

'Yessir. It was mostly black then, thank you, because of the redlining and racial deed restrictions in SV.' She chuckled. 'When I was growing up here, there was gunfire every night. We kids

— I have three brothers — we'd hang out in Whiskey Gulch. Stanford was dry and didn't allow any liquor within a mile of campus. And what was one mile and one block away? Yep, a strip mall in EPA, with package stores and bars galore. That's where we'd play. Until Daddy came looking and dragged us home.

"Course, the Gulch all got torn down and replaced with University Circle. Lord, there's a Four Seasons Hotel there now! Just imagine that sacrilege, Colter. Last year, the murder rate was one — and that was a murder/suicide, some computer geek and his roommate. My daddy'd roll over in his grave.'

'You lose him recently?'

'Oh, years ago. Daddy, he didn't benefit from the new and improved statistics. He was shot and killed. Right in front of our apartment.'

'That why you went into policing?'

'One hundred percent. High school, college in three years and into the academy at twenty-one, the minimum age. Then signed on with EPA police. I worked street while I got my master's in criminal justice at night. Then moved to CID. Criminal investigation. Loved the job. But . . . ' A wan smile.

'What happened?'

'Didn't work out.' She added, 'I didn't blend. So I asked for a transfer to the Task Force.'

Shaw was confused. The population he was looking at was mostly black.

She noted his expression. 'Oh, not that way. I'm talking 'bout my father. I didn't explain. Yes, I went into policing because of him. But not because he was some poor innocent got gunned down in front of Momma and me. He was an OG.'

Shaw could imagine how her fellow cops would respond to working with the daughter of an original gangster whose crew might've shot at or even killed their friends.

'He was a captain in the Pulgas Avenue 13s. Warrant team from Santa Clara Narcotics came after him and it went south. After I was in, I snuck his file. My oh my, Daddy was a bad one. Drugs and guns, guns and drugs. Suspect in three hits. They couldn't make two of the cases. The one where they had a good chance, the witness disappeared. Probably in the Bay off Ravenswood.'

A click of her tongue. 'Wouldn't you know it, my brothers and I would come home from school and, damn, if Momma was sick he'd have dinner ready and be reading us *Harry Potter*. He'd take us to the A's games. Half my girlfriends didn't have a father. Daddy was there. Until, yeah, he wasn't.'

They continued in silence for five minutes, driving over dusty surface streets, wads of trash and soda and beer cans on the sidewalks and curbside. 'It's over there.' She nodded at a three-story building that seemed to be about fifty, sixty years old. This structure, along with several others nearby, wasn't as shabby as the approach suggested they'd be. Destiny Entertainment's headquarters was freshly painted, bright white. Shaw could see some smart storefront offices: graphic design and advertising agencies, a catering company, consulting.

Tombstone as reimagined by Silicon Valley developers.

They parked in the company's lot. The other cars here were modest. Not the Teslas, Maseratis and Beemers of the nearby Google and Apple dimension. The lobby was small and decorated with what seemed to be artists' renditions of the Whispering Man, ranging from stick drawings to professional-quality oils and acrylics. They'd have been done, he supposed, by subscribers. Shaw looked for the stenciled image that the kidnapper was fond of but didn't see it. Standish seemed to be doing the same.

The receptionist told them Marty Avon would be free in a few minutes. A display caught Shaw's eye and they walked to a waist-high table, six by six feet, that held a model of a suburban village. A sign overhead read WELCOME TO SILICON-VILLE.

A placard explained that the model was a mock-up of a proposed residential development that would be built on property in unincorpo-rated Santa Clara and San Jose counties. Marty Avon had conceived of the idea in reaction to the 'excruciatingly expensive' cost of finding a home in the area.

Shaw thought of Frank and Sophie Mulliner's exodus to Gilroy, the Garlic Capital of the World. And the Walmart hoboes whom Henry Thompson was writing about in his blog.

Eyes on the sign, Standish said, 'Have a couple open cases in the Task Force. Some of the big tech companies, they run their own employee

253

buses from San Francisco or towns way south or east. They've been attacked on the road. People're pissed, thinking it's those companies that're responsible for everything being so expensive. There've been injuries. I told them, 'Take the damn name off the side of the bus.' Which they did. Finally.' Standish added with a wry smile, 'Wasn't rocket science.'

Avon had created a consortium of local corporations, Shaw read, who would offer the reasonably priced housing to employees.

A generous gesture. Clever too: Shaw suspected that the investors were worried about a brain drain — coders moving to the Silicon Cornfields of Kansas or Silicon Forests in Colorado.

He wondered if because Destiny Entertainment wasn't in the same stratosphere as Knight Time and the other big gaming studios, Avon had chosen to expand into a new field — one with a guaranteed stream of revenue: real estate.

The receptionist then said that Avon would see them. They showed IDs and were given badges and directed to the top floor. Once off the elevator they noted a sign: THE BIG KAHUNA THATAWAY →.

'Hmm.' From Standish.

As they proceeded thataway, they passed thirty workstations. The equipment was old, nothing approaching the slick gadgets at Knight Time Gaming's booth; Shaw could only imagine what that company's headquarters was like.

Standish knocked on the door on which a modest sign read B. KAHUNA.

'Come on in!'

# 40

Gangly Marty Avon rose from his chair and strode across the room. He was tall, probably six foot five. Thin, though a healthy thin that probably came from a racehorse metabolism. Avon strode forward, hands dangling, feet flopping. His mass of curly blond hair — very '60s — jiggled. Shaw had expected the creator of *The Whispering Man* to be dressed gothic, in black and funereal purple. Nope. A too-large beige linen shirt, untucked, and, of all things, bell-bottoms in a rich shade of rust. His feet were in sandals because what else could they be in?

Shaw looked around the office, as did Standish. Their eyes met and he raised a brow. While the reception area may have featured pictures of the crazy psychopath, the Whispering Man, here the décor was kids' toy store: Lionel trains, plastic soldiers, dolls, building blocks, stuffed animals, cowboy guns, board games. Everything was from before the computer era. Most of the toys didn't even seem to need batteries.

Standish and Shaw shook his hand, and he directed them to sit on a couch in front of a coffee table on which sat a trio of plastic dinosaurs.

'You like my collection?' His high voice was dusted with a rolling Midwestern accent.

'Very nice,' Standish said noncommittally.

Shaw was silent.

'Did you both have a favorite toy growing up? I always ask my visitors that.'

'No,' they both answered simultaneously.

'You know why I love my collection? It reminds me of my philosophy of business.' He looked fondly at the shelves. 'There's one reason and one reason only that video games fail. Do you want to know why that is?'

He picked up a wooden soldier, an old one, resembling the nut-cracker from the ballet. The CEO looked from the toy to his visitors. 'The reason games fail is very simple. Because they aren't fun to play. If they're too complicated or too boring, too fast, too slow . . . gamers will walk away.'

Setting down the toy, he sat back. 'Nineteen eighty-three. Atari is stuck with nearly a million cartridges of games that nobody wanted, including the worst video game in history: *E.T.* Good movie, bad game. Supposedly, the games and consoles were buried in a secret landfill in New Mexico. Not long after that the entire industry collapsed. The stock market had the Great Crash of '29. Video gaming had '83.'

Standish steered the meeting back on track. She asked if Avon knew about the recent kidnapping.

'The girl from Mountain View? Yes.' Behind him was a huge poster for Siliconville. His desk was littered with maps, many official-looking documents, some photocopies and some with seals and original signatures. The real estate project seemed to be taking more time than his gaming business.

'There was another one too, late last night.'

'Oh, I heard about that! It's the same kidnapper?'

'We think so.'

'My God . . . ' Avon looked genuinely distraught. Though, understandably, his was probably a double-duty frown, the second meaning being: What does this have to do with me?

'And he appears,' Standish said, 'to be modeling the crimes after *The Whispering Man*.'

'No, no, no . . . ' Avon closed his eyes briefly.

She continued: 'We know about the incident in Ohio a few years ago.'

His head was hanging. 'Not again . . . '

Shaw explained what Sophie Mulliner had found in the room she'd been sealed into.

'Five objects.' Avon's voice was hollow. 'I came up with five because my daughter was learning to count. She used her fingers. She'd do the right hand and then, when she went to the left, she started over again.'

Shaw explained, 'One possibility is that the kidnapper's a player who's obsessed with the game and is acting it out. Like the boys in Ohio. If so, we want to try to trace him.'

The detective said, 'Mr. Shaw here had a conversation with Tony Knight and . . . ' A glance Shaw's way.

'Jimmy Foyle.'

'*Conundrum*. It's a real phenomenon. Supposedly the longest source code ever written for a game.'

257

*Fifteen quadrillion planets . . .*

Avon added, 'Alternative reality. I've thought about publishing one but you really need supercomputers for them to work right. You should see their servers. Well, what can I help with?'

Shaw explained what Foyle had suggested. How they wanted to locate local gamers who were online frequently — obsessed with the game — as well as offline at three specific times: when Sophie was kidnapped, when she was rescued and when Henry Thompson was taken.

Now would come the battle. Avon would say, Sure. And you don't get user logs without a warrant.

And he was indeed shaking his head.

'Look,' Standish said, 'I know you'll want a warrant. We're hoping you'll cooperate.'

Avon scoffed. 'Warrant. I don't care about that.'

Standish and Shaw regarded each other.

'You don't?'

The CEO chuckled. 'Do you know what an EUA is?'

Shaw said he didn't. The detective shook her head.

''End user agreement.' Whenever anybody subscribes to *The Whispering Man*, they have to agree to the EUA. Every software and hardware company makes you agree or you don't get the goods. Nobody reads 'em, of course. Ours has got a clause that gives us permission to use their data any way we want — even give it to the police without a warrant.

258

'No, we have other problems. We'll have to track the user — your suspect — through his IP address. We get hacked all the time — all game companies do — so we separate online presence from personal information. All our gaming servers know is that User XYZ has paid, but we don't know who he is. That might not be a problem, tracking IP to the user's computer. But most of our subscribers — at least the younger ones — use proxies.'

'Masks that hide their real location when they're online,' Shaw said. He did too in all of his online activity.

'Exactly. ID'ing somebody using a proxy is time consuming and sometimes impossible. But let's give it a shot. When was he offline?'

Shaw displayed his notebook.

'Now, we'll want subscribers who play for, let's say, twenty-five hours a week or more but were offline then.' Nodding at the notebook. 'Quite some handwriting.' Avon hunted and pecked and, as he did, he mused, 'Did you know that in China they're considering legislation to limit the hours you can play? And the World Health Organization just listed video gaming addiction as a disease. Ridiculous. That's like saying lawyers who work more than forty hours a week are dysfunctional. Nurses, surgeons.' He fiddled with a pencil that had a clown's head topper. He glanced at the screen. 'Okay. Here we go.'

Standish sat forward. 'You have results already?'

Shaw, familiar with the speed of Velma Bruin's rewards-finding algorithm, Algo, wasn't surprised.

259

Reading the screen, Avon said, 'The answer is a yes, with a caveat. There are about two hundred and fifty-five people who play the game at least twenty-five hours a week and they meet the offline timing criteria. Of those, sixty-four aren't anonymous — no proxies. But none of them are within a hundred miles of here. The others? They're behind proxies. So we have no idea where they are — maybe next door, maybe Uzbekistan.' He gazed at the list. 'Most of them are off-the-shelf proxies, not very righteous. They can be cracked but it'll take some time.'

He tapped out another request. Hit RETURN. 'There,' he said, 'I've got somebody on it.'

And then Marty Avon went into a different place mentally. Finally he asked, 'Where was the girl hidden?'

Shaw said, 'The Abandoned Factory. Level 1.'

'You know the game? You play it?'

'No. You're thinking he put Henry Thompson — that's the new victim — at a different level?'

Avon said, 'The kidnapper's a gamer, obviously, and it'd be a fail to repeat a level and a cheat to play out of order.'

Shaw, who embraced technology in his work, had been amused to learn that geeks often swapped verbs for nouns: A *fail* was 'a loss,' an *ask* was 'a question.'

'The second level's called The Dark Forest.'

'So Henry Thompson's being held in the woods somewhere.'

Standish grimaced. 'Got a few acres of those around here.'

Shaw's eyes fell on the set of toy soldiers. They

260

were about three inches high, dark green, in various combat poses. Troops from the Second World War, probably. Nowadays, what would the manufacturer produce? Men or women sitting at drone command stations? A cybersecurity expert at a desk, hacking into Russian defenses?

The CEO leaned back, lost in thought, eyes closed. They popped open. 'What were the five objects he left with the girl?'

Shaw told him: 'Water, glass bottle, a book of matches, fishing line, a strip of cloth.'

Avon said, 'Good.'

# 41

For all his traveling, the restless man had never been in a helicopter.

Now that he was, he wasn't enjoying it.

The altitude wasn't the problem, not even with the open door. Canvas and steel, in the proper configuration, are substances that you can depend on, and the harness in the Bell was intimately snug. Shaw and his siblings had gotten over any fear of heights early — Ashton again — by learning to climb before they were thirteen. When no challenging jobs beckoned, Shaw would find a nice vertical face and ascend (always free-climbing — using ropes to prevent falls, not to aid in the climb). Earlier in the day he'd looked fondly over Standish's shoulder at the trail map leading to the site of the climb he'd been planning while visiting his mother at the Compound.

No, the five hundred feet between him and the tree line was not a problem. Shaw simply didn't want to puke. That, he hated more than pain. Well, most pain.

Maybe inevitable, maybe not. Teeter-totter. He inhaled deeply. Bad idea; exhaust and fuel fumes were coconspirators.

LaDonna Standish was strapped in beside him. They were riding backward, facing two tactical officers, dressed in black, with matching body armor. POLICE was printed in white on their chests — their backs too, Shaw had seen, in larger type. They were holding Heckler & Koch machine guns. Standish was not enjoying the trip either. She refused to look out the open door, and she kept swallowing. She clutched an air-sickness bag and Shaw hoped she didn't start in with that. He *really* hoped she didn't. The power of suggestion is formidable.

She wore body armor and had only her sidearm. Shaw too was in a Kevlar vest, without weapon, per the rules. The out-of-harm's-way dictate had obviously gone to hell.

How they happened to be here was thanks to the creator of *The Whispering Man*, Marty Avon. The CEO had explained that the game's algorithm randomly assigned three of the five items that players were abandoned with, like Sophie's fishing line, scarf and glass bottle. The other two items might vary but fell into two categories: sustenance and communication. Food or water — Sophie had been given the latter — and some way to signal for help, to let an ally know where you were, or to warn about danger. Matches, in her case. Players sometimes got a flashlight or signal mirror. More often, they received a way to start a fire. If not matches, a cigarette lighter or a flint-and-steel kit. This could also help players stay alive in some of the colder game settings, like mountaintops and caves.

'If the victim's in a forest and he has matches or a cigarette lighter, he might try to start a fire,' Avon had suggested.

Shaw had said, 'A brush fire in northern

California? That's one thing that'd be sure to get somebody's attention.'

Drought, heat and winds had helped fires ravage part of central and northern California lately. Shaw and his family had battled one on the Compound years ago and nearly lost the cabin.

'He won't be a fool,' Standish had said. 'He'll control it. Probably set a small bonfire in a clearing or on rock, where it'll be noticed but won't spread.'

Standish had called the Park Service, which used drones and satellites mounted with thermal sensors to see if any of the systems had registered flames. She learned that, yes, the service had monitored a small blaze on a rocky hilltop in Big Basin Redwoods State Park. It had flared up about midnight, burned for a brief time and then went out. Infrared scans showed that by 1 a.m. the ground was fire- and ember-free once more. They'd marked the site to check it out later but sent no crews at that time.

Shaw had looked up the location on the map. It was a forty-minute drive from where Henry Thompson had been kidnapped.

Via speakerphone, the ranger had explained that it was curious there'd been a fire at that location at that time of the morning, since it wasn't near any hiking trails, and the only road nearby, an old logging way, was chained off. Odd too that there was a fire at all, since there'd been no lightning strikes and the blaze was limited to a rocky shelf that didn't seem to have any natural brush growing from the cracks in the stone. 'Best we could figure, some campers went off road.'

Standish had then asked, 'Satellite images of the site?'

The ranger had sent some and she, Shaw and Avon huddled over the game maker's high-def monitor.

They were looking at what might have been a configuration of rocks or shadows but also might have been a human form, standing near the fire.

'Good enough for me,' Standish had said and grabbed her phone, pressing a single button to make a call.

Standish and Shaw had sped to Moffett Field, an old military air base north of Sunnyvale and Mountain View — only ten minutes from Destiny Entertainment. At least, ten minutes the way Standish had been driving. Shaw had held on to the armrest and enjoyed the NASCAR ride.

The military air functions of the field, Standish had explained, were shrinking, though an air-rescue operation remained. Google leased much of the field and the internet company was involved in the restoration of Hangar 1, which was one of the largest wooden structures in the world, built in the '30s to house dirigibles and other lighter-than-air craft.

There they had climbed into the Task Force's Bell chopper, which was now — after only a twenty-minute flight — closing in on the spot where the fire had been tagged. Four other tac officers were in an Air National Guard Huey, old and olive-drab, presently thumping away fifty yards to the starboard.

265

Through his headphone, Shaw heard Standish's throat making tiny retching sounds and he pulled the unit off. It helped.

The hazy suburban sprawl of the valley became hills and trees, then the landscape turned tough, with lush, spiky redwoods giving way to rocky terrain, skeletal trees, dry riverbeds. This was the heart of Big Basin. Shaw had thought the rugged land would send updrafts skyward, making the ride worse. Oddly, though, the air was smooth; the bumpiness had been severe when they were over suburbia.

Standish's head tilted slightly. She must have heard the pilot say something. Shaw put his headset back on and entered the conversation.

'Negative,' Standish called.

The pilot: 'Copy. I'll find an LZ.'

Shaw looked at Standish, who said, 'Pilot asked if I wanted a flyby of the site. I told him no. Don't imagine the perp's here after all these hours, but he came back to the first site with a weapon. He'll hear us land, but I don't want him to see us.'

The odds he was back at this particular time? Shaw figured them to be low. Yet still vivid in his memory was the horrible collapse of Kyle Butler as the bullet struck him.

Two craft hovered over a clearing atop a plateau, two hundred feet from the valley floor, then touched down in tandem. Shaw was out fast, ducking his head unnecessarily — even though the rotors were high, you did it anyway. Almost immediately his gut felt better. And he didn't react when Standish jumped out the other

266

side and bent over, vomiting. She then stood up, spitting. She rinsed her mouth with water from a bottle the pilot handed her, as if he kept them on hand for that very purpose.

She joined Shaw. 'At least there's nothing left for the ride home.'

They and the two officers with them jogged to the edge of the clearing, where they were joined by the four-man team from the Huey, also in tactical gear. They nodded to Standish and Shaw, who was examined with glancing side looks. The detective didn't introduce him. The Bell pilot joined them and unfurled a map of the area. He'd been given the coordinates of the site of the fire and had marked it in red pen. He looked around, trying to judge where exactly they were in relation to it. Shaw glanced at the map, then the surrounding hills. He'd done orienteering on the Compound and, in college, had competed in the sport, a timed trek through the wilderness, following a route using only a compass and a map.

Shaw pointed. 'The fire was there, about five hundred yards. Over that ridge. Straight line.'

Everyone was staring at him. He in turn looked to Standish. This was, after all, her hunt.

'Your supervisors brief you?' She was talking to the four men from the other helicopter. They weren't Task Force, Shaw could see, different uniforms. Maybe county, maybe state. Their equipment was shiny, their boots polished, their guns hardly dinged.

One of these officers, a man with bulbous, dumbbell-lifting arms, said, 'No, ma'am. Other than a hostage sit, possible HT on the scene.'

'At the last taking — the Mulliner girl — the unsub came back to the scene with a weapon. That ended up a homicide.' Two of the men nodded, recalling. 'Weapon's a nine-millimeter handgun. Glock. Long barrel probably — the accuracy. He knows how to shoot. It's not likely he's here — we've done sat and drone surveillance and didn't see any vehicles — but, well, you can see the canopy. Lots of places to hide. Watch for shooters.'

Standish turned to Shaw. 'Best routes?'

He borrowed the pilot's red pen and drew lines, like parentheses, from where they stood to the ridge where the fire had been. 'The north one? You'll have to be careful.'

A SWAT officer asked, 'Umm, which one's north?'

Shaw touched it. 'When you get to the cedar, there'll be a drop-off.'

A pause. 'What's a cedar look like?'

Shaw pointed one out.

'A drop-off you won't see until you're almost on it. And once you crest the ridge, you'll have exposure to shooters from the high ground here and here. The sun's in a good spot. It'll be in his eyes. And if he's got binoculars or a scope, there'll be lens flare.'

Standish took over. 'The hostage won't have shoes. He may've made covering for his feet, but I don't think he's gone very far.'

Shaw added, 'And he was brought here unconscious, so, for all he knows, he's in the midst of Yosemite or the Sierra Madres. He's not an outdoorsman, so I don't think he'll try to hike out. I was him, I'd look for water and shelter in place.'

Standish: 'Secure the scene first and then we look for him. You probably gathered Mr. Shaw here's done some tracking work. He'll help us. He's a consultant with the Task Force.'

She then asked Shaw where the logging road was. He glanced at the map and turned and pointed.

'He and I'll go this way,' Standish said, nodding. 'The unsub wouldn't've dragged the vic that far — the ridge where the fire was. He would've left him near the road. Mr. Shaw and I'll look for that scene and secure it.' She looked at them all in turn. 'You good with that?'

Nods all around.

'Questions?'

'No, Detective.'

Standish started in the direction of the logging road while Shaw reviewed the map, deciding where would be the most logical place for the Whispering Man, playing Level 2 of the game, to have abandoned Henry Thompson.

*The Dark Forest . . .*

The officers clustered, talking among themselves, presumably selecting who wanted to go with whom. Someone barked a brief laugh. Shaw folded the map carefully and walked over to them. As he hadn't known who'd spoken the words he'd just heard, he let his eyes tap them all. He nodded.

They nodded back. Discomfort settled like fog.

'I don't know if Detective Standish's a lesbian or not,' he whispered, having heard their infantile comment. 'I'm pretty sure if you're not part of the team you don't say 'dyke.' I know for a fact that 'nappy-headed' is just plain wrong.'

They looked back, their eyes various degrees subzero. Two then examined the ground carefully.

He'd thought it would be the big one who'd push back; he had 'bully' written in his furrowed brow and bulky arms. It was the slightest of the officers who said, 'Come on, man. Doesn't mean anything. The way it is in Tactical. You know, combat. You joke. We live on the edge. Burn off steam.'

Shaw glanced down at the man's pristine weapon, which they both knew had been fired on the range only. The officer looked away.

Shaw scanned the rest of them. 'And I do have a little Native American blood in me, my mother's side. Great-great-grandmother. But you know my name. And it's not Geronimo.'

The look of disgust on several officers' faces was meant to convey that this untidy incident was Shaw's fault for not playing along. Shaw turned to follow Standish, to look for the nest where the unsub had left Henry Thompson to escape if he could.

Or to die with dignity.

# 42

By the time he'd caught up with her, he glanced back. The teams were deploying along the routes he had set out.

Beside him, Standish said, 'I get it some.'

'You heard?'

'No, but I saw you turn back. Was it about being gay or about being black?'

'A bit of both. Wondering if you're gay. And your hair.'

She laughed. 'Oh, not 'nappy' again. Seriously? Those boys.'

'Struck me as odd, them saying it. It was about something else?'

Standish, still smiling. 'You got that right.'

Shaw was silent.

'I moved in from EPA police direct to the Task Force, I was telling you. Moved up to gold shield fast. And I mean months.'

'How'd that happen?' Shaw was surprised.

She shrugged. 'Ran some ops that ended okay.'

The modesty told Shaw that they were big, critical operations and they ended much better than okay. He remembered the commendations on the credenza behind her desk, including some actual medals, on ribbons, still in their plastic cases.

'Got me twenty K more salary.' She nodded toward the other officers. 'You probably figured,

Shaw, there're two Silicon Valleys.'

'You're from north of the 101. They're from the south.'

'That's it. They're soccer dads who play golf when they're not out at an air-conditioned gun range. Barbecues and boats. God bless 'em. Never the twain shall meet. They don't want to take orders from somebody like me. And it doesn't help I'm younger than the youngest.' She glanced at Shaw; he could feel her eyes. 'I don't need protecting.'

'I know. Just can't help myself sometimes.'

A nod. He believed it meant she was exactly the same.

'Was that your partner? The picture on your desk?' Shaw had seen a photo in her office of Standish with a pretty white woman, their heads together, smiling.

'Karen.'

Shaw asked, 'How long you been together?'

'Six years, married four. You were probably wondering about the name. Standish.'

Shaw shrugged.

'I took her name. She and I have something in common, you know? The rumors are that Karen's family came over on the *Mayflower*. You know, Myles Standish?'

'*That* Standish? What do you have in common?'

'My ancestors came over on a boat too.' Standish couldn't restrain her laugh. Shaw had to smile.

'Kids?'

'Two-year-old. Gem's her name. Karen's the

birth mother. We're going to — '

Suddenly, Shaw lifted a hand and they stopped. He scanned the dense forest. Where they stood was particularly congested, a soupy tangle of pine, oak, vines. A good place for a shooter to hide.

Standish's hand dropped to her holster. 'You see something?'

'Heard something. Gone now.' He scanned the trees and shrubbery, the rocks. Motion everywhere but no threat. You learn the difference early.

They continued toward the logging road, looking for where Henry Thompson had been abandoned. Had to be here somewhere. Shaw was searching for marks left by shoes, either walking or being dragged.

She asked, 'You married?'

'No.'

'Sounds like you prefer I don't ask if there's anybody you're with.'

'No preference. But there isn't. Not at the moment.'

Another image of Margot began to form. It remained silent and opaque. Then, fortunately, disappeared.

'How 'bout kids?'

'No.'

They continued on for another fifty yards. Standish cocked her head — she'd gotten a transmission and was listening through her ear-bud. She lifted the Motorola mic and said, 'Roger. Join up with the other teams.'

She hooked the radio back on her belt.

'They're at the clearing where the fire was. No sign of the unsub. Or Thompson.'

He crouched. Crushed grass. Caused by animal hooves and paws, not leather soles. Rising, he scanned the terrain. His head dipped and he said, 'There. He walked that way.'

It was a faint trail that led toward the logging road. They started along it.

Standish said, 'You know, we need a name for him.'

'Who?'

'The unsub. We sometimes do that. We get a lot of unsubs and it helps keep 'em separate. A nickname. Any ideas?'

With a reward, you usually knew the name of the missing person or fugitive you were after. Even if you didn't, you didn't give them a nickname. At least, Shaw didn't. He told her, 'No.'

Standish said, 'The Gamer. How's that?'

It seemed self-conscious. Then again, it wasn't his case and he wasn't a cop with a lot of unsubs that needed telling apart. 'Why not?'

Ten feet farther along the logging road, Standish stopped. 'There,' she said.

Shaw looked down at a circular indentation in the pine needles, right beside the old logging road. Within the circle were a plastic bag of marbles like children play with, a coil of laundry line, a box of double-edged razor blades and a large package of beef jerky.

'Look.' Shaw was pointing at a flat surface of rock a few feet above where the Gamer had left the five items. Those, and the matches or lighter

274

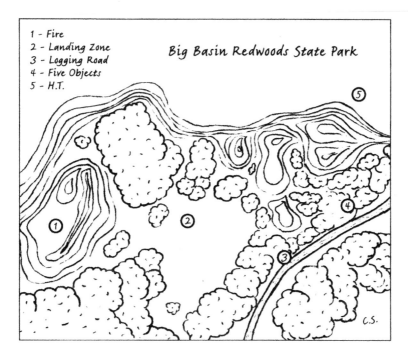

Big Basin Redwoods State Park

he'd used to start the fire, were this victim's infamous five items from *The Whispering Man*.

'Is that . . . ?'

It was. A version of the face on the sheet at the Quick Byte and graffitied on the wall near the room where Sophie Mulliner had been left.

The stark image of the Whispering Man.

She took a step forward, when Shaw stopped and closed his hand around her muscular biceps. 'Don't move. And quiet.'

Standish had good training. Or instinct. She didn't look at Shaw. But as she crouched to make herself a smaller target, she scanned for a threat.

It wasn't the kidnapper that Shaw had heard. The slow crackling of branches and a low vibration — a sound unlike any other on Earth — told him exactly who the visitor was.

Thirty feet away, a mountain lion — a big male, one hundred and thirty pounds — stepped into view and looked them over with fastidious eyes.

# 43

'Oh, man,' LaDonna Standish whispered. She stood straight and reached for her weapon.

'No,' Shaw said.

'We got a protocol in Santa Clara. They're not endangered. We can shoot.'

'We don't know if the Gamer's nearby. Do you really want to tell him where we are?'

She hadn't thought about this and withdrew her hand. Then said, 'It *is* a fucking mountain lion.'

The creature's muzzle was red with blood. Was it Henry Thompson's?

'Look him in the eyes. And stand as tall as you can.'

'This's as tall as I get,' she whispered.

'Don't bend over. The more you look four-legged, the more you seem like prey to him.'

'It's a boy?'

'Male, yeah. And open your jacket.'

'Showing him my weapon's not going to make him go away, Colter. I'm just saying.'

'Makes you look bigger.'

'I shouldn't have to be worried about this shit.' She opened the windbreaker slowly and held the zipper ends outward. She resembled one of those young folks Shaw occasionally saw when rock-climbing, wearing wingsuits, leaping into the void and arcing through the air like diving falcons.

He added, 'And don't run. Whatever happens, even if he approaches, don't run.'

The animal, with perfect muscles and a rich tan coat, sniffed the air. His ears were low — a bad sign — and his long fangs, yellow and bloody and three times the length of his other teeth, were prominently displayed. Another mean growl emanated from his throat.

'What exactly does that purr mean?'

'He's getting information. He wants to know our story. Are we strong or weak? Are *we* predators?'

'Who the hell'd mess with him?'

'Bear. Wolves. Humans with guns.'

She gave her own mean growl. '*I'm* a human with a gun.'

Keeping his eyes locked onto the animal's, Shaw slowly crouched and, after a brief glance down, picked up a rock about the size of a grapefruit. He rose, an inch at a time. Confident, calm. Not aggressive.

*Never display fear.*

'You can fight. Just have to keep them away from your face and neck. That's what they go for.'

'You're not going to . . . ?' Her voice sounded astonished.

'Rather not, but . . . ' Then Shaw said, 'Open your mouth.'

'You want me to . . . ?'

'You're breathing fast and loud. Open mouths're quieter. You sound scared.'

'That can't come as a surprise.' She did as he'd instructed.

Shaw continued: 'They're not used to anything fighting back. He's debating now. Is this dinner going to be worth it? He sees two. The size difference — he might be thinking you're my young. You'd be vulnerable and tasty, yet he'd have to go through me and he knows that I'd fight till the end to save you. He's already eaten so he's not driven by hunger. And we're not running, we're defiant, so he's uneasy.'

'*He's* uneasy?' She scoffed. 'Is my jacket big enough?'

'You're doing fine. By the way, if he does come after us and I can't stop him, then you can shoot him.'

The creature's head lowered.

Shaw gripped the rock, kept his eyes on the predator, and arched his shoulders. The black feline pupils surrounded by yellow remained fixed on Shaw. He really was a magnificent creature. His legs were like flexing metal. The face gave off what seemed to be an evil glare; of course, it was nothing of the kind. It was no more evil than Shaw's when he was about to tuck into a bowl of stew for dinner.

Assessing. Odds that he'd attack: fifty percent.

He really hoped it wouldn't come to shooting. He didn't want the beautiful creature to die.

*For food or the hide, for defense, for mercy* . . .

Gripping the stone.

Decision made. The animal backed away, then turned and vanished. Shaw was aware of the faint crackling of underbrush once more, like the sound of distant fire, muted in humid air. It lasted only a second or two. For all their size, mountain lions had perfected the art of entering and leaving the stage quietly.

'Jesus.' Standish slumped, eyes closed. Her hands were shaking. 'He going to come back?'

'Not likely.'

'But that doesn't mean no.'

'Correct,' he said.

'Shot at by punks and junkies, Shaw.' She paused. 'Sorry, *Colter*.'

'Know what? 'Shaw' and 'Standish' are fine. I think we've graduated. Mountain lions can do that.'

Margot had called him by his last name. He'd always liked it.

She continued: 'Had an informant turn, halfway through a set, and come at me with a razor. That was a day's work, I'm saying. Mountain lions're not a day's work.'

Depends on the day and depends on the work, Shaw supposed.

Standish had brought a roll of yellow tape and now spent a few minutes running it from tree to tree, encircling the crime scene.

'So, the blood?' she asked.

'Thompson's?' Shaw replied. 'A possibility.' He walked in the general direction the animal had vanished — cautiously. He climbed a rock formation and examined the tableau before him.

He returned.

Standish glanced his way. 'You found something?'

'A deer carcass. He'd eaten most of it. That's why he wasn't so interested in us.'

She finished stringing the tape. Then rose.

Shaw studied the ground. 'I can't tell if Henry walked that way or not. I think so.' He was looking at a limestone shelf that led to a line of trees. On the other side there seemed to be a deep valley.

Shaw climbed onto the rock and helped Standish up. Together they walked toward the edge of the cliff.

There, they paused.

A hundred feet below lay Henry Thompson's crumpled, bloody body.

# 44

Ten minutes later two tactical officers were on the floor of the canyon, having rappelled down the sheer face — and doing a smart job of it.

'Detective?' one of them radioed.

'Go ahead, K,' Standish said.

'Have to tell you. Cause of death wasn't the fall. He's been shot.'

She paused. 'Roger.'

Shaw was not surprised. He muttered, 'Explains it.'

'What?'

'Why the Gamer comes back to the scenes. *The Whispering Man* — the game — it isn't only about escaping. It's also about fighting.' He reminded Standish about the gameplay: the players might form alliances or they might try to kill one another. And the Whispering Man himself, in his funereal suit and dapper hat, roams the game, ready to murder for the fun of it.

Shaw remembered that the character would come up behind you and whisper advice — which might be real or might be a trick. He might also attack, shooting you with an old-time flintlock pistol or slicing your throat or plunging a blade into your heart, whispering a poem as your screen went black and eerie music played.

*Say good-bye to the life you've known,*
*to your friends and lovers and family home.*

282

*Run and hide as best you can.*
*There's no escaping the Whispering Man.*
*Now, die with dignity . . .*

The Gamer was simply following the storyline as written. He'd returned to the scene of Sophie Mulliner's captivity to pursue her. He'd done the same here. He'd left Henry Thompson alone for a time, let him build the signal fire — the way he'd given Sophie a chance to escape. Then it was time to return and finish the game.

Standish said nothing but walked along the rocky ground to the clutch of tactical officers who'd joined them here. Shaw sat on a rocky ledge. He received a text from Maddie Poole.

So, you de-looped me?? Is Knight in jail? Are you still alive?

Shaw's inclination was not to reply. But he did, texting that he was with the police. He'd be in touch.

The forensic officers weren't here yet. There was no such thing as a Crime Scene Unit helicopter, so the vans would be driving up the logging trail the long way around to avoid contaminating the shorter way to the highway on the assumption that the kidnapper had taken that route. Yet finding helpful tire tracks seemed an impossible task; the trail was largely covered with a thick carpet of leaves and where it was bare it was baked dry. Why would the Gamer turn careless now?

Standish and the tactical officers were staying

clear of the immediate scenes — here and in the nest of pine needles where the Gamer had originally left Thompson. They were visually perusing the site and gauging where the kidnapper might have stalked Thompson. Everyone was a pro now; whatever resentments lingered, they weren't interfering with the mission of solving this crime to prevent others.

'This boy's enjoying himself,' one of the officers muttered grimly. 'He ain't going to stop.'

A SWAT cop suggested Shaw go back to the chopper, not wanting a civilian on the scene. But Standish pointed out that he wasn't armed and that there was at least one hostile in the vicinity — the mountain lion. It also wasn't absolutely certain that the killer was gone. There was some logic to this, though scant; a tac cop, armed for big game, could have accompanied him. Shaw sensed that Standish wanted him here, perhaps to offer insights. Unfortunately, at the moment, he had none.

He gazed down at Thompson's body. There was no blessing in it but at least the man had died quickly, not thanks to the ripping teeth and claws of a wild animal. The shot was to his forehead. Thompson would have returned from setting the fire and made his way back to the nest, for the beef jerky and to rest, awaiting rescue. There, the Gamer would have been waiting. Thompson would have run. His bare feet would have slowed his escape.

Shaw stepped away from the crime scene and walked farther along the stone ridge. He stopped a few feet from the edge. Eyeing the rock face, he noted that it would be a good climb. Lots of cracks and out-croppings. Challenging, with its nearly ninety-degree surfaces, but doable. An overhang that would take quite some strategy to surmount.

Looking down, he didn't plot out, as usual, a route to the bottom.

Nor did he think about poor Henry Thompson.

No, seeing the cliff and the creek bed below, he thought of one thing only.

Echo Ridge.

# 45

Colter's eyes instantly open when the cabin floor creaks.

He sometimes thinks his father has taught him to sleep light, though that doesn't seem possible. Must've been born with the skill.

The sixteen-year-old's hand dips to the box beneath the bed where his revolver rests. Hand around the grip. Thumb on the trigger to cock it to single action.

Then he sees his mother's silhouette. Mary Dove Shaw, a lean woman, hair always braided, standing in his doorway. No religion in the Shaw household. When he's older, Colter will come to think of his mother in saintly terms, a woman taking comfort in her husband's good moments and sheltering her children from the bad. Protecting Ashton for himself too.

Her nature was clothed in kindness. Underneath was iron.

'Colter. Ash is missing. I need you.'

Everyone awakes early on the Compound, but this hour is closer to night. Not quite 5 a.m. That it's his mother in the doorway doesn't stay his hand from touching the cold steel and rough grip of the .357 Python. Intruders?

Then, swimming closer to wakefulness, he sees in her face concern, not alarm. He rises, leaving the weapon under the bed.

'Ash went out after I fell asleep, about ten. He

hasn't come back. The Benelli's gone.'

His father's favorite shotgun.

Camping and expeditions in the Compound are always planned and, in any event, there is no reason for Ashton to go out at that hour, much less to stay out all night.

*Never hike anywhere without telling at least one person where you'll be.*

The way his mind had been sputtering recently, Mary Dove had made sure she or one of the children accompanied him on the longer forays within the Compound. Chaperoning was especially essential when he went into White Sulphur Springs because on those outings he'd taken to carrying a weapon. Two in fact: in the car and on his person. There'd been no incidents but Mary Dove thought it best to have a family member with him. Even thirteen-year-old Dorion has the grit and intelligence to defuse what might become a confrontation.

Only three people in the Compound tonight, apart from Ashton: Dorion, Colter and Mary Dove. Colter's older brother, Russell, is in Los Angeles. He is starting to become a recluse, a role he will perfect in later years. Even if he had been here, though, Mary Dove would have come to her middle child for help.

'You're the best tracker of the family, Colter. You can find where a sparrow breathed on a blade of grass. I need you to find him. I'll stay here with your sister.'

'He take anything else?'

'Nothing that I could tell.'

In five minutes Colter is dressed for the

predawn wilderness. October in eastern California can be fickle, so he wears thermals and two shirts under his canvas jacket. Jeans, thick socks and boots he broke in when he stopped growing two years ago; they feel like cotton on his feet. He has a night bag with him: clothes, flashlights, flares, food, water, sleeping bag, first aid, two hundred feet of rope, rappelling hardware, ammunition. For weapons: the Ka-Bar Army knife, ten-inch, and the Python. Ashton, who carries a .44 Magnum revolver, says that mud and water and tumbles won't affect a revolver's action the way they might a semiautomatic like a Glock, despite the gun manufacturer's assertions to the contrary.

'Wait,' Mary Dove says. She goes to the mantel and opens a box, from which wires sprout, connected to the wall outlet. She removes one of the mobile phones inside, powers it on and gives it to Colter. He hasn't held the phone in two years and he's never used it.

In his hand the unit feels alien. Taboo. He places it in the bag as well.

Colter slips on gloves and a stocking cap that can pull down to a ski mask. He steps out into the bracing, damp chill, feeling the sting of cold in his nose. As soon as he steps off the porch he catches a break. A handful of trails lead from the cabin into the fields and woods on the property and beyond. One of these paths is rarely hiked and it's on this one that the boy sees fresh boot prints — his father's, which he knows well. The stride is curious. It's longer than that of a man leisurely strolling into the woods. There is urgency in it. There's purpose in it.

Colter continues cutting for sign in the direction his father took about five or six hours previously, to judge from the snapped grasses. It's an easy track, since there are no forks or cross-paths. He can move quickly, stopping only sporadically to confirm that Ash came this way.

A mile from the cabin he spots another boot print in soft earth, paralleling his father's route. He can't tell its age. It might have been made months ago, by one of his father's friends who'd come to visit — friends from the old days before he fled the Bay Area. They would frequently trek out together, just the two or three of them, for the day. His mother too has colleagues from her teaching days who visit.

But this is not a likely route for a leisurely walk with acquaintances. Being in a valley, there's nothing to see. And here it's a chore to hike — the angle, the rocks and pits and gravelly slopes. He continues along the trail, confirming again that his father came this way. Confirming too that the Second Person did as well.

Onward. Until he comes to a fork and sees that his father has turned left and that means only one destination: Crescent Lake, a large body of water that resembles either a smile or a frown, depending.

In twenty minutes Colter comes to the mucky shore. He looks across, a half mile at the widest. The water is black now, though the sky is going to a soft glow. The surface is mirror-still. The distant shore rises in forest to ragged peaks. He assumes his father has gone there because the family's canoe is missing.

Why would he cross? It's a warren of thickets and rocks on the other side.

He looks for signs of the Second Person's prints and can find none. Widening his search circle, he finally does locate the sign. The man stood on the shore, perhaps looking around for Ashton. He then started up the steep trail to Echo Ridge, from which he can gaze over the whole terrain and possibly spot the man.

The ground is soft here, so Colter can see the Second Person's prints clearly.

And something else.

His father's prints. On top of the other man's.

Ashton knew he was being followed. He probably hid in the canoe until the man started up the trail and then followed.

The pursuer became prey.

The trail isn't so very fresh — the men were here some hours ago — yet an urgency ignites within Colter and he muscles up the trail, quickly, after the two men, a thirty-degree incline through rocks and over small, sandy ledges. He has never been to Echo Ridge, a craggy rise in the foothills of the Sierra Nevadas. The terrain is unforgiving. Echo Ridge was one place on the Compound that the children were not allowed to go.

Yet it was to Echo Ridge that Ashton Shaw followed someone who had been pursuing him. And Echo Ridge is the place to which his son is climbing now.

Ten minutes later a breathless Colter crests the summit and stands against a rock face, sucking in air. In his hand is the Colt Python.

He's looking over the tree- and brush-covered plateau of the ridge. To his left — west — is a pelt of forest and a layered maze of rock formations and caves, where your assumption is: bears in the big ones, snakes in the small.

To Colter's right — east — is a cliff face, ninety degrees, a hundred feet or more straight down to a dry creek bed on the valley floor.

The same creek bed where last year Colter had the confrontation with the hunter, who'd blindly shot into a bush and wounded the buck.

He now looks east again, at the brightening morning sky, and sees the sharp black silhouette of the Sierra Nevada peaks, a massive jaw of broken teeth.

As for his father's footsteps? The other man's? He can't see either. The plateau is rock and gravel. No cutting for sign here.

Now the sun rises over the mountains and pastes orangey light on the rock and the forest of Echo Ridge.

The light also pings off a shiny object fifty yards away.

Glass or metal? It's not too early for ice, but the glint is coming from the floor of pine needles, where there would be no standing water to freeze.

Colter cocks the pistol and lifts it as he walks forward. The gun is a heavy one, weighing two and a half pounds, but he hardly notices the weight. He proceeds toward the flash, eyeing the forest to his left; no threat could come from the cliff edge on his right, except from that hundred-foot drop to the creek bed below.

When he's still about twenty feet from the light source, he sees what it is. He stops, gazing around him. He doesn't move for a moment, then slowly he walks in a circle, which ends at the cliff's edge.

Colter swaps the gun for the cell phone. He flips it open and takes a moment to remember how it works. Then he dials a number he memorized years ago.

★　★　★

Now, fifteen years later, Colter Shaw was looking at a configuration of rock so very similar to Echo Ridge.

He gazed at the crime scene tape around the place where Henry Thompson lay.

Shaw thought about the button on the Hong-Sung goggles — the one you pushed to be resurrected.

*RESET . . .*

Over the crest of the rise, four newcomers walked slowly, carrying and wheeling large cases — like professional carpenters' toolboxes. The Joint Major Crimes Task Force crime scene team wore blue jumpsuits, the hoods pulled low around their necks. The day was not particularly hot but the sun was relentless and wearing the contamination-proof coveralls would be unbearable after any length of time.

Standish approached and offered Shaw a bottle of water. He took it and drank down half, surprised at how thirsty he was. 'We'll leave it to

Crime Scene and the ME. No hurry to get back. I'm going to hitch a ride in the vans. Not in an airborne mood at the moment.'

Shaw agreed.

The detective was staring over the cliff. After a moment she asked, 'You see that big cat again?'

'No.'

Absently she said, 'You know, there were a couple of them in Palo Alto the other day. I read the story in the *Examiner*. Safeway parking lot. Roughhousing like kittens. Then they ran off into the woods and disappeared. They interviewed somebody. He said, 'The mountain lion you can't see is worse than the one you can.' Is that the truth about life or what, Shaw?'

His phone vibrated. He read the text.

A moment of debate as he stared down the rock face. He typed and sent a reply.

He slipped the phone away and said to Standish that he'd changed his mind and would take the chopper back after all.

# 46

Six p.m., and Colter Shaw was back in the Quick Byte Café.

He tilted the beer bottle back, drank long. It was a custom of his to drink locally brewed beer whenever he traveled. In Chicago, Goose Island. In South Africa, Umqombothi, which smelled and looked daunting but tricked you with a three percent alcohol content. In Boston, Harpoon — not that other stuff.

And in the San Francisco Bay Area: Anchor Steam, of course. Tiffany, back on duty, had given it to him on the house, delivered with a wink.

He set down the bottle and closed his eyes briefly, seeing Henry Thompson's body, the gradient colors of his blood on the rock, as white and flat as that creek bed below Echo Ridge.

In ten years of seeking rewards Shaw had been successful the majority of the time. Not a landslide but respectable nonetheless.

He might have given his success rate a percentage number. He never did. It seemed flippant, disrespectful.

He could remember some of the victories — the tricky ones, the dangerous ones, the ones occasioned by desperation and despair on the part of loved ones whose lives crashed when their child or spouse went missing and that Shaw pieced back together — like the final scenes in time travel movies when disaster is miraculously reversed.

Other than those, though, most jobs were just that: assignments, assignments like a plumber or an accountant might take on. They drifted down into the recesses of the brain, some lost forever, some filed away to be recalled if needed, which was rarely.

The losses? They stayed forever.

This one would. That there'd been no reward offered to find Henry Thompson was irrelevant. Because the truth was, for Colter Shaw it was never about the money. The reward was important mostly because it was a spotlight illuminating a challenge that no one else had yet been able to meet. What mattered was finding the child, the elderly parent addled by dementia, the fugitive. What mattered was saving the life.

Sophie Mulliner was safe, but that was no solace at all. Kyle Butler was dead. Henry Thompson was dead. And at times like this the restlessness grew and became a person itself, following Shaw, close behind. Like the Whispering Man.

He sipped more of the ripe, rich beer. The cold was more of a comfort than the alcohol. Neither was much of a balm.

He walked back to the counter and asked Tiffany for the remote. He wanted to change the station on the set above the bar. She handed it to him. They had a brief conversation about TV programs, to which he couldn't contribute much. She would have liked to continue talking to him, Shaw could tell, but an order was ready. He was relieved when she went to deliver it and he sat down at his table once more. Shaw changed the channel from a sports game no one was watching — not a lot of jocks in the Quick Byte Café — to a local news channel.

A minor earthquake had troubled Santa Cruz; a labor organizer was fighting cries for removal, claiming the rumors that he'd paid money under the table for a green card were false; a whale had been saved at Half Moon Bay; a Green Party congressman in L.A., running for reelection, had withdrawn after stories surfaced he'd been allied with ecoterrorists who'd burned down a ski resort at Tahoe a few years before. He vehemently denied his involvement. 'A man's career can be ruined based on lies. That's what it's come to . . .'

His attention waned until finally: 'And in local news, a Sunnyvale blogger and gay rights activist was found murdered today in Big Basin Redwoods State Park. Police reported that Henry Thompson, fifty-two, was kidnapped on the way home from a lecture at Stanford last night, taken to the park and murdered. No motive has been established. A spokesperson for the Joint Major Crimes Task Force in Santa Clara said that the crime may be related to the kidnapping of a Mountain View woman on June fifth. Sophie Mulliner, nineteen, was rescued unharmed by the Task Force two days later.'

The story ended with a scroll at the bottom of the screen of the hotline to call if anyone was on the block when Thompson was kidnapped or was hiking in Big Basin today.

Behind him, in the Quick Byte, a woman's strident voice interrupted Shaw's thoughts.

'Well, I didn't message you. I don't know you.'

Shaw and other patrons looked toward the

296

source of the shrill words. An attractive woman of about twenty was sitting in front of her Mac and holding a mug of coffee. Her long chestnut hair was tinted purple near the tips. She was dressed like a model or an actress: studied casual. The blue jeans were close-fitting and intentionally torn in places. The white T-shirt was baggy and off the shoulder, revealing purple undergarment straps. The nails were oceanic blue, the eye shadow autumnal shades.

Standing over her was a young man about her age, on the other end of the style spectrum. The baggy cargo pants were well worn, and the loose red-and-black-checked shirt too large; this made him seem smaller than his frame, which was probably five-eight or -nine, slim. He had straight hair that was none too clean and was self-cut or clipped by a mother or sister. His dark brows nudged close over his fleshy nose. A big gray laptop, twice as thick as Shaw's, was clutched in his hands. His face was bright red with embarrassment. Anger was in his eyes too. 'You're Sherry 38.' He shook his head. 'We instant-messaged in *Call to Arms IV*. You said you'd be here. I'm Brad H 66.'

'I'm not Sherry anybody. And I don't know who the hell you are.'

The man lowered his voice. 'You said you wanted to hook up. You said it!' He muttered. 'Then here I show up and you don't like what you see. Right?'

'Oh, excuse me. You really think I'm the sort of loser plays *Call to Arms*? Fuck off, okay?'

Once more a scan of the room. The young man

297

surrendered and walked to the order station.

The perils of the internet. Had the poor kid been set up by bullies? Shaw recalled what Maddie Poole had told him about SWAT'ing. And what Marty Avon had told him about the ease of hacking gaming servers.

Or was the kid right, that the description he'd sent the woman online didn't match the in-person geek version, so she'd bailed on him?

The kid placed an order, paid and took the number on the wire metal stand to a table in the back, dropped into a chair and opened his computer. He plugged in a bulky headset and began pounding away on the keys. His face was still red and he was muttering to himself.

Shaw pulled out a notebook and opened his fountain pen. From memory he sketched a map of where Hank Thompson had been killed. His sure hand completed the drawing in five minutes. He signed it with his initials in the lower-right-hand corner, as he always did. He was waiting for the ink to dry when he looked up. Maddie Poole was walking in. Their eyes met. She smiled; he nodded.

'Lookit you,' she said, possibly meaning his posture. He was leaning back in his chair, his feet stretched out in front of him, the Ecco tips pointed ceilingward.

Then the smile faded. She'd scanned his face. The eyes, in particular.

She sat down, took the bottle of beer from him and lifted it to her own lips. Drank a large mouthful.

'I'll buy you another one.'

'Not a worry,' he said.

'What is it? And you'd better not say 'Nothing.''

He hadn't texted or spoken about Thompson's murder.

'We lost the second victim.'

'Colt. Jesus. Wait. Was it that murder in the state park? The guy who was shot?'

A nod.

'*The Whispering Man* thing again?'

'The police still aren't talking about that in the news — they don't want the Gamer to know how much they know.'

'Gamer?'

'That's what they're calling him.' He sipped the beer. 'He took Thompson into the mountains and left him with the five objects. Thompson came to and started a signal fire. That's how we got onto him. But the Gamer came back to hunt him. That's part of the game too.'

She looked over the map, then up at his eyes, a frown of curiosity on her face. He explained about his custom of drawing the maps.

'You're good.'

Shaw happened to be looking at the spot on the map that represented the foot of the cliff where Henry Thompson had died. He closed the notebook and put it away.

Maddie touched his forearm firmly. 'I'm sorry. What about Tony Knight? You didn't tell me what happened. I was worried until I got your text.'

'Things got busy. And Knight? I was wrong. It wasn't him. He's been helpful.'

'Do the police have any ideas who it is?'

'No. If I had to guess, a sociopath. Nothing I've ever seen before — this elaborate modeling on the game. My mother might have known people like that.'

'You said she was a psychiatrist.'

He nodded.

Mary Dove Shaw had done a lot of research into medications for treating the criminally insane and as a principal investigator had funneled a lot of grant money to Cal and other schools.

That was earlier in her career — before the migration east, of course. In the later years her practice was limited to family medicine and midwifing in and around White Sulphur Springs and the management of paranoid personality and schizophrenia, though the latter practice involved only one patient: Ashton Shaw.

Shaw had yet to share with Maddie much about his father.

She asked, 'Are the police offering a reward?'

'Maybe, I don't know. I'm not interested in that. I just want to get him. I — '

The rest of the sentence was never uttered. Maddie had lunged forward and kissed him, her strong hands gripping his jacket, her tongue probing.

He tasted her, a hint of lipstick, though he hadn't seen any color. Mint. He kissed back, hard.

Shaw's hand slipped to the back of her head, fingers splayed, entwined in her sumptuous hair. Pulling her closer, closer. Maddie leaned in and he felt her breasts against his chest.

They began to speak simultaneously.

300

She touched his lips with a finger. 'Let me go first. I live three blocks from here. Now what were you going to say?'

'I forgot.'

# 47

Shaw led a nomadic life and didn't have a large inventory of possessions. But the Winnebago was downright cluttered compared with Maddie Poole's rental.

True, it was temporary; she was only in town for C3, had driven up from her home outside L.A. Still . . .

One aspect exaggerated the emptiness: the ancient place was huge, five bedrooms, possibly more. A cavernous dining room. A living room that could be a wedding venue.

It was occupied by few possessions; her big desktop computer — a twenty-something-inch monitor dominating the table it sat on. On either side of the big Dell were cardboard cartons serving as end tables; they held books and magazines, DVDs and boxes of video game cartridges. An office chair rested before it. Surrounding the workstation were shopping bags from computer companies — giveaways, he guessed, from the conference.

A mountain bike, well-used, sat in the corner. The brand was SANTA CRUZ. Shaw didn't bike but when hiking or climbing he came across bikers often. He knew this make could go for nine thousand dollars. Also, there were free weights — twenty-five-pounders — and some elastic exercise contraption.

In the bedroom, to the right, was a

double-sized mattress and box spring, sitting on the floor. The sheets were atop it, untucked and swirled like a lazy hurricane.

In the living room an unfortunate beige couch rested before a coffee table that made Frank Mulliner's limb-fractured model look classy. The laminated dark wood top of Maddie's was curling upward at the ends.

The kitchen was empty of furniture and appliances other than those built in: a range, a fridge, an oven and a microwave. On the counter was a box of cornflakes and two bottles of white wine, a six-pack of Corona beer.

Shaw dated the huge house around the 1930s. It was sorely in need of paint and repair. Water damage was prevalent and the plaster walls cracked in a dozen places.

'Out of *The Addams Family*, right?' Maddie said, laughing.

'True.'

Last Halloween, Shaw had taken his nieces to an amusement park; it had featured a haunted house that looked a lot like this.

She went on to explain that she'd found it through an Airbnb kind of service. It was available only because its days were numbered; next month it was being demolished, thanks to Siliconville. The stained wallpaper was of tiny, dark flowers on a pale blue background. The dotted effect was oddly disconcerting.

'Wine?'

'Corona.'

She got a cold bottle from the refrigerator and poured herself a tall glass of wine, returned to the couch, handed him the beer and curled up. He sat too; their shoulders touched.

'So . . . ?' From her.

'This is where you ask if there's anybody in my life.'

'Good-looking *and* a mind reader.'

'Wouldn't be here if there was.'

Clinking glasses. 'Lot of men say that but I believe you.'

He kissed her hard, his hand around the back of her neck once more, surprised that the tangles of her rust-shaded hair were so soft. He thought they'd be more fibrous. She leaned in and kissed back, her lips playful.

She took a large sip of wine. A splash hit the couch.

'Oops. Good-bye, security deposit.'

He started to take the glass from her. She had one more hit and then relinquished it. The glass and his beer ended up on the wavy coffee table. They were kissing harder yet. Her legs straightened from their near-lotus fold and she eased back onto the cushions. His right hand descended from her hair to her ear to her cheek to her neck.

'Bedroom?' Shaw whispered.

A nod, a smile.

They rose and walked inside. Just past the threshold Shaw kicked off his shoes. Maddie lagged, diverting momentarily, shutting out the living room and kitchen lights. He sat on the bed and tugged his socks off.

'Got something that might be fun,' her voice whispered seductively from the dark space on the other side of the doorway.

'Sure,' he said.

When Maddie appeared in the doorway, she was wearing the Hong-Sung *Immersion* goggles.

'Lord, Colter, I got what I think is the first smile out of you in two days.'

She pulled them off and set them on the floor.

Shaw reached out a hand and tugged her to him. He kissed her lips, the tattoo, her throat, her breasts. He started to pull her into the bed. She said in a soft voice, 'I'm a lights-out girl. You okay with that?'

Not his preference but under the circumstances perfectly fine.

He rolled across the bed and clicked the cheap lamp off and, when he turned back, she was on him and their hands began undoing buttons and zippers.

Naturally, it was played as a competitive game.

This one ended in a tie.

# 48

Nearly midnight.

Colter Shaw rose and walked into the bathroom. He turned the light on and in his peripheral vision he saw Maddie scrambling, urgently, to pull a sheet up to her neck.

Which explained the lights out. And explained the cover-up clothing of sweats and hoodies; many of the women at C3 wore tank tops and short-sleeved T's.

He'd gotten a glimpse of three or four scars on Maddie's body.

He recalled now that, earlier, as his hands and mouth roamed, she would subtly direct him away from certain places on her belly and shoulder and thigh.

He guessed an accident.

As they'd driven from the Quick Byte Café, she'd done so carelessly, speeding sometimes twenty over the limit, then slowed to let him catch up. Maybe she'd been in a car crash or biking mishap.

Making sure to shut out the bathroom light before he opened the door, Shaw returned to bed, a towel wrapped around his waist. He passed her by and went into the kitchen, fetched two bottles of water from the fridge and returned. He handed her one, which she took and set on the floor.

He drank a few sips, then lay back on the lumpy mattress. The room was not completely dark and he could see that she'd pulled a sweatshirt on while he was in the kitchen. The shirt had some writing on the front. He couldn't read the words. She was sitting up, checking texts. Shaw could see the light from her phone on her face — a ghostly image. The only other illumination was the faint glow from her monitor's screen saver bleeding through the door to the living room.

He moved closer to her, sitting up too. His fingers lightly brushed her tattoo.

*I'll tell you later. Maybe . . .*

Maddie stiffened. It was very subtle, almost imperceptible.

Yet not quite.

He put distance between them, propping the pillow up and sitting against it. He'd been here often enough — on both sides of the bed, so to speak — to know not to ask what was wrong. Words that came too fast were usually worse than no words at all.

Head on the pillow, he stared at the ceiling.

A moment later Maddie said, 'Damn air conditioner. Makes a racket. Wake you up?'

'Wasn't asleep.' He hadn't noticed. Now he did. And it was noisy.

'I'd complain but I'll be gone in a few days. And this place'll be in a scrapyard by next week. That Siliconville thing.'

Silence between them, though the groaning AC was now like a third person in the room.

'Look, Colt, the thing is . . . ' She was examining words, discarding them. She found some: 'I'm pretty good with the before part. And

I think I'm pretty good with the during part.'

That was true. But the rules absolutely required him to not respond.

'The after part? I'm not so good with that.'

Was she wiping away tears? No, just tugging at the tangle of hair in front of her face.

'Not a big deal. It's not, like, get the hell out of my life. Just, it happens. Not always. Usually.' She cleared her throat. 'You're lucky. I got pissed at you for bringing me water. Imagine what would've happened, you'd asked to meet the family. I can really be a bitch.'

'It's good water. You're missing out.'

Her shoulders slumped and she twined hair around her right index finger.

He said, 'Here's where I say we're a lot alike and that pisses you off more.'

'Fuck you. Quit being so nice. I want to throw you out.'

'See? Told you. We're a lot alike. I'm not so good with the after part either. Never have been.'

Her hand squeezed his knee, then retreated.

Shaw told her, 'Had two siblings, growing up. We fell out in three different ways. Russell, oldest, was the reclusive one. Dorie, our kid sister, was the clever one. I was the restless one. Was then, still am.'

The laugh from Maddie's mouth was barely perceptible but it was a laugh. 'You know, Colter, we should start a club.'

'A club.'

'Yeah. Both of us, good with before and during, not after. We'll call it the Never After Club.'

308

This struck home.

*The King of Never* . . .

Which he didn't share with her.

'I'll go,' he said.

'No way. You've gotta be beat. This's a hiccup, is all. Only don't plan on spooning till noon tomorrow and then make plans to take BART to an art museum and a waffle brunch.'

'The likelihood of that happening I'd put at, let's see, zero percent.'

Maddie gave a smile. A whatever happens, it's been good smile. 'Curl up or stretch out. Or whatever you do.'

'You going to . . . '

'Kill some aliens. What else?'

# LEVEL THREE:

# THE
# SINKING
# SHIP

Sunday, June 9

# 49

'We're calling it an accident. No other thing fits.'

Colter Shaw awoke, lying in Maddie Poole's disheveled bed, his eyes on the overhead fan, a palm frond design, one blade sagging, and though the room was hot he didn't think it was a good idea to flick the unit on.

*Accident . . .*

Maddie was not in bed nor was she in the living room, killing or maiming aliens. The big house creaked, the sounds from its infrastructure, not inhabitants.

Apparently the woman took the 'never after' part seriously.

The hour was close to 4 a.m.

Sleep was an illusion. He wondered if he'd had a nightmare. Maybe. *Probably.* Because he kept hearing the voice of White Sulfur Springs sheriff Roy Blanche.

'We're calling it an accident. No other thing fits.'

This was the opinion too of the county coroner, regarding the death of Ashton Shaw. He'd lost his footing and tumbled off the eastern side of Echo Ridge, a hundred-foot-plus plummet to the dry creek bed where Colter spotted him, that rosy-dawn morning, October 5, fifteen years ago. The boy had rappelled as fast as he'd ever descended in the hope that he might save his father. While he didn't know it at the time, a person falling from that height will reach a speed of about sixty-five miles per hour. Anything over forty-five or fifty is fatal.

The death occurred around six hours earlier — 1 a.m. Sheriff Blanche found a patch of wet leaves that might have been slick with an early frost. One step on them, with the incline, and Ashton would have gone over.

The glint that Colter had seen was the sun striking the chrome receiver of the Benelli Pacific Flyway shotgun. It was lying on the ground, ten feet from the edge, where it had flown after Ashton made a frantic grab for nearby branches to arrest his tumble.

Another possibility was in everyone's mind but on no one's tongue: suicide.

To Colter, though, both theories were flawed. Accident? Twenty percent. Suicide? One percent.

Ashton was a survivalist and outdoorsman and conditions like slippery foliage would have been just one more factor he'd have tucked into the equation on a trek, like gauging the dependability of ice on a pond or how fresh a bear paw print was and how big the creature that had left it.

As for suicide, Ashton Shaw's essence was survival and Colter couldn't envision any universe in which his father would have taken his own life. Mental issues? Sure. Yet as mad as he could be, his affliction was paranoia — which is, of course, all about protecting yourself from threats. He was also carrying a 12-gauge shotgun. If you want to end your life, why not just use a beloved weapon, like Papa Hemingway? Why tumble over and hope the fall will kill you? Colter and his mother had discussed it. She was as sure as her son that the death was not self-inflicted.

So, an accident.

To the world.

But not to Colter Shaw, who believed — around eighty percent — his father had been murdered. The killer was the Second Person, who had followed Ashton from the cabin and who had then become the pursued — after Ashton's clever canoe trick at Crescent Lake. The two had met atop Echo Ridge. There'd been a fight. And the killer had pushed Ashton over the edge to his death.

Yet Colter had said nothing to the police, to anyone, much less to his mother.

The reason? Simple. Because he believed that the Second Person was Colter's older brother, Russell.

Ashton would have been following the shadowy figure along the rocky ground of the ridge, the bead sight of his weapon on his back. He'd have demanded to know who he was. Russell would have turned and a shocked Ashton Shaw would have seen his eldest son. Dumbfounded, he would have lowered the gun.

Which is when Russell would have grabbed it, flung it away and pushed his father over the cliff.

Unthinkable. Why would a son do that?

Colter Shaw had an answer.

A month before his father died, Mary Dove was away; her sister was ill and she'd traveled to Seattle to help her brother-in-law and nieces and nephews while Emilia was in the hospital. So

315

very aware of her husband's troubles, she had asked Russell to drive up to the Compound from L.A., where he was in grad school at UCLA and working, to look out for her younger children in her absence. Colter was sixteen, Dorion thirteen.

Colter's brother, then twenty-two, sported a full beard and long dark hair — just like the mountain man he was named after — but wore city slicker clothes: slacks, dress shirt and sport coat. When he'd arrived, he and Colter had embraced awkwardly. Quiet as always, Russell deflected questions about his life.

One evening, Ashton looked out the window and said to his daughter, 'Graduation night, Dorion. Crow Valley. Suit up.'

The girl had frozen.

Colter thought: She was no longer 'Button.' Ashton's daughter was, in his mind, an adult now.

'Ash, I've decided. I don't want to,' Dorion said in an even voice.

'You can do it,' Ashton said calmly.

'No,' Russell said.

'Shh,' their father had whispered, waving his hand to silence his son. 'Mark my words. When they come, it's not going to do any good to say, 'I don't want to.' You'll have to swim, you'll have to run, you'll have to fight. You'll have to climb.'

Graduation was a rite of passage Ashton had decided upon: an ascent, at night, up a sheer cliff face, rising a hundred and fifty feet above the floor of Crow Valley.

Ashton said, 'The boys did it.'

That wasn't the point. When they were

thirteen, Colter and Russell had wanted to make the climb. Their sister didn't. Colter was aware too that Ashton had only proposed this when Mary Dove was away. She supported her husband, she sheltered him. But in addition to being his wife, she was his psychiatrist too. Which meant there were things he couldn't get away with when she was present.

'There's a full moon. No wind, no ice. She's as tough as you.' He started to pull Dorion to her feet. 'Get your ropes and gear. Change.'

Russell had then stood, removed his father's arm from his sister's and said in a low voice, 'No.'

What happened next seared itself into Colter's memory.

Their father pushed Russell aside and grabbed Dorion's arm once more. The older son had learned well and, in a flash, he slammed his open palm into their father's chest. The man stumbled back, shocked. And as he did, he reached for a carving knife on the table.

Everyone froze. A moment later Ashton took his hand off the knife. He muttered, 'All right. No climb. For now. For now.' And walked to his study, lecturing an invisible audience. He closed the door behind him.

A burning silence ensued.

'He's a stranger.' Dorion looked toward the study. Her eyes were as steady as her hands. The incident appeared to have affected her far less than it had her brothers.

Russell muttered, 'He's taught us how to survive. Now we have to survive him.'

It was two weeks later that Mary Dove awakened her middle child in the predawn hours.

*Colter. Ash is missing. I need you . . .*

Yes, Colter suspected Russell had killed their father. That was only circumstantial speculation. The hypothesis would move closer to theory, if not certainty, at their father's funeral.

Mary Dove arranged for a modest ceremony three days after her husband's death, attended by close family and colleagues from their former lives as academics at Berkeley.

Russell had flown back to L.A. after his mother returned from her sister's hospital stay. He then returned to the Compound for the funeral. And it was when the family had gathered for breakfast before the memorial that Colter heard a brief exchange.

A relative asked Russell if he'd flown in from L.A. and he said no, he'd driven. And then he mentioned the route.

Colter actually gasped, a reaction nobody else heard. Because the route Russell had described had been closed recently because of a rockslide; it had been clear on the day of Ashton's murder. This meant that Russell had been in the area for several days. He'd driven up earlier, hiding out nearby, maybe because his reclusive nature kept him from seeing family. Maybe to murder their father in the chill morning hours of October 5, for the purpose of saving his younger sister from any mad and dangerous 'graduations.'

And for another reason too: to put his father out of his misery.

*For food or hide, for defense, for mercy.*

Colter resolved at the funeral to wait and confront his brother later. Later never came, because Russell had left abruptly after the service and then went off the grid entirely.

The thought of patricide haunted Colter for years, a constant wound to the soul. But then, a month ago, some hope emerged that perhaps his older brother might not have been the killer after all.

He was at his house in Florida, sorting through a box of old pictures his mother had sent. He found a letter addressed to Ashton with no return address. The postmark was Berkeley and the date three days before he died. This caught Shaw's attention.

*Ash:*

*I'm afraid I have to tell you Braxton is alive! Maybe headed north. Be CAREFUL. I've explained to everybody that inside the envelope is the key to where you've hidden everything.*

*I put it in 22-R, 3rd floor.*

*We'll make this work, Ash. God bless.*

*— Eugene*

What could he make of this?

One conclusion was that Ashton — indeed 'everybody' in Eugene's note — was at risk.

And who was Braxton?

319

First things first. Find Eugene. Colter's mother said Ashton had a friend at Cal by that name, a fellow professor, but she couldn't remember his last name. And she'd never heard of a Braxton.

Shaw's search of staff at UC Berkeley fifteen years ago uncovered a professor Eugene Young, a physicist, who'd died, in a car crash, two years after Ashton had. The death itself seemed suspicious: driving off a cliff near Yosemite on a safe stretch of road. Shaw tracked down Young's widow, who had remarried. Shaw had called her, explaining who he was and adding that he was compiling material about his father. Did she have anything — correspondence or other documents — relating to Ashton? She said she'd disposed of all her late husband's personal documents over the years. Shaw gave her his number and told her he'd be in an RV park in Oakland for the next few days if she thought of anything.

Then Colter Shaw did what he was good at: tracking. Eugene Young was a professor on the Cal campus and he'd hidden something at a place designated as 22-R. It took Shaw two days to learn that only the Cal Sociology Department archives, located on the third floor, had a Room 22, with a stack *R*.

Which was where, three days ago, he found — and stole — the magic envelope.

*Graded Exams 5/25 . . .*

If there was any proof that someone other than Russell Shaw had killed Ashton — this Braxton or possibly an associate — it would be that

320

cryptic stack of documents the envelope contained.

Now, in Maddie's bed, he heard Sheriff Roy Blanche's words.

*We're calling it an accident. No other thing fits . . .*

Except, to his great relief, Colter Shaw had realized that perhaps something else did.

Braxton is alive!

The AC unit outside Maddie's window grew more temperamental yet. Returning to sleep was not an option, Shaw realized, so he rose and dressed. Opened another bottle of water and walked outside, extending the deadbolt so that the door wouldn't lock behind him. He sat down on an orange plastic deck chair, the sole bit of furniture in a porch space that could accommodate twenty times that. He sipped. On his phone, he found the local news to see if there'd been any more developments in the Henry Thompson case. As he waited for the story to appear, he saw another story that sounded familiar . . . Oh, right. It was about the congressman accused of texting young interns; he'd first heard the story on the broadcast within Tony Knight's game, *Prime Mission.* The politician, a representative named Richard Boyd, from Utah, had committed suicide, his note proclaiming innocence and citing a life in tatters due to the rumors. The story was more than just a tragic death. His seat in Congress could tip the party balance in the next election.

Shaw's father had been fascinated with politics, but this was a paternal gene that had not

321

been passed down to Colter.

Nothing in the news about Henry Thompson, so he shut the channel off and slipped his phone away.

The street was quiet, no insects, no owls. He heard the shush of traffic from a freeway, a few horns. While there were a half dozen airports nearby, this would be a no-fly time.

He looked over the avenue and saw one house in the process of being torn down and, next to it, a vacant lot recently bulldozed. Signs in both front yards read FUTURE HOME OF SILICON-VILLE!

Shaw was amused that spacey, frizzy-haired Marty Avon, the man who loved toys, was engaged in such a serious project as real estate development. Shaw guessed he'd had more fun designing and building the mock-up of Silicon-ville in the Destiny lobby than he would watching construction of the real thing.

Shaw finished the water and wandered back inside. He stepped to Maddie's thirty-inch computer monitor, on which a three-dimensional ball bounced slowly over the screen, its colors changing from purple to red to yellow to green, all rich shades.

He glanced at her desk — everything Maddie Poole owned was devoted to the art and science of video gaming: CD and DVD jewel cases, the circuit boards, RAM cards, drives, mouses and consoles. Game cartridges were everywhere. And cables, cables, cables. He picked up a few of her books, flipped through them. The word *Gameplay* figured in most of the titles. And, in some,

*Cheats* and *Work-arounds*. He skimmed *The Ultimate Guide to Fortnite*, recalling the company's booth at the C3 Conference. The complexity of the instructions was overwhelming. He started to set it back and he froze.

There was a booklet beneath the *Fortnite* guide. With a pounding heart, he picked it up and thumbed through the pages. Passages were circled and starred. And there were margin notes, references to knives, guns, torches, arrows. The title was:

## GAMEPLAY GUIDES. VOL. 12
### THE WHISPERING MAN

The game Maddie Poole had claimed she'd never played and knew virtually nothing about.

# 50

She'd lied to him.

Why?

Certainly, there might be innocent explanations. Maybe she'd played a long time ago and forgotten.

Were the notes even hers?

He found some Post-its with her handwriting on the small pink squares.

Yes, she'd made the notes in *The Whispering Man* book.

The implications: Maddie knew the Gamer. They'd learned Shaw was involved and the Gamer told her to pick him up at the Quick Byte and stay close to find out what the investigators knew.

*Do the police have any ideas who it is?*

Then he decided there was a problem with this hypothesis: the lack of evidence that a Second Person was involved in the Gamer's crimes.

Which left him with the heart-wrenching possibility: Maddie Poole was herself the Gamer.

Shaw stepped outside to his car and retrieved his computer bag. He returned to the house and extracted one of his notebooks and his fountain pen. Writing down the facts not only let him analyze the situation more clearly, it was a comfort. Which he needed at the moment.

Was this idea even feasible?

His first thought was that she perfectly fit the Killer category of gamer that Jimmy Foyle had told him about — supercompetitive, playing to win, to survive, to defeat, at all costs.

As he read through the facts and chronology, the percentage of her guilt edged upward. Maddie had come into the Quick Byte just after he had, on the day they'd met. She could have followed him from his meeting with Frank Mulliner. Then, after he'd left her at the café, he'd seen somebody spying on him at San Miguel Park. Had she followed him there, and to the old factory afterward?

She'd certainly come on to him, charming and flirtatious, called him to congratulate him on saving Sophie and invite him to the conference. To work her way into his life.

He reflected: the two victims had been taken by surprise, slammed to the ground and injected with the drug, then dragged to a car. Maddie was strong enough for that — he knew this for a fact from their time in bed a few hours ago. He thought of the ruthlessness he'd seen on her face when they'd played *Immersion* in the Hong-Sung booth. Her wolf eyes, triumphant in the act of killing him. And as a hunter, she'd know firearms.

This hypothesis he put at twenty-five percent.

That number didn't last long. It rose to thirty, then more, when he thought of a motive. He'd recalled her scars and how she'd tried to hide them from him. Was this from modesty or because she didn't want Shaw to suspect who she really was?

The high school girl kidnapped eight years ago by those teens who'd grown obsessed with *The Whispering Man* and tried to kill her. The news stories hadn't said how. It was possible they'd used knives — another of the Whispering Man's weapons.

Perhaps Maddie had come here to destroy the company that had published the game, drive it out of business. Of course, she wouldn't have known what Tony Knight had told him: that the attack had had no effect on sales.

He went online and searched for the earlier incident once more; the first time had been a cursory examination. There were many references to the crime. Because the girl was then seventeen, though, her name and photo had been redacted. He doubted that even Mack could get juvie reports. LaDonna Standish could, of course, and he'd have to tell her as soon as possible.

Shaw told himself to slow down.

Thirty-five percent isn't one hundred.

*Never move faster than the facts . . .*

He'd spent time with Maddie — in and out of bed. She simply didn't seem to be a murderer.

Then, scanning one article, Shaw learned that the teenager — Jane Doe — had suffered serious PTSD as a result of the attack. There'd been breaks with reality, a condition Shaw was more than familiar with thanks to his father. She'd been committed to a mental hospital. Maybe Maddie decided that the victims, Sophie Mulliner and Henry Thompson, were no more than avatars, easily sacrificed on her mission to destroy the Whispering Man himself, Marty Avon.

He swiped her mouse and the screen saver vanished. The password window came up. Shaw didn't bother to try. He rose and conducted a fast search of the house, looking for the gun, bloody knives, any maps or references to the locations where the victims had been taken. None. Maddie was smart. She'd have them hidden somewhere nearby.

*If* she was the perp.

Now the number edged up to sixty percent. Because Shaw was in Maddie's bathroom and looking at the bottles of opioid painkillers. Possibly the sort that had been used to knock out the Whispering Man's victims. Forensics would tell. He took a picture of the labels with his phone.

Just as he was slipping his phone away, it hummed.

Standish.

He answered and said, 'I was about to call you.'

Silence. But only for a brief moment. 'Shaw, where are you?'

He paused. 'Out. I'm not at my camper.'

'I know. I'm standing next to it. There's been a shooting. Could you get over here as soon as possible?'

# 51

A full-fledged crime scene.

Shaw accelerated fast along Google Way within the West-winds RV park, aiming for the yellow tape, noting two uniformed officers turning toward him. One lowered her hand toward her service weapon. Braking, he kept his hands on the steering wheel, statue-still, until Standish called to the cops nearby, 'His camper. It's okay.'

The JMCTF forensic van was parked within the yellow tape and robed and masked technicians were paying attention to the wall of a small shower/restroom in the middle of the park. They were digging at a black dot — extracting a slug, he guessed. Others were packing up evidence bags, concluding the search.

One uniform was rolling up the yellow tape. No press, Shaw noted. Maybe a shot or two didn't warrant a cam crew. Residents of the park, though, were present, standing well back from the scene as instructed.

The detective, in her ubiquitous combat jacket and cargo pants, gestured him to where she stood by the door to the Winnebago. She was wearing latex gloves.

'Camper and the ground here've been released. They're still mining for slugs.' A nod to the restrooms and tree. Shaw noticed that another team of gowned officers was at a maple, cutting into the trunk with a wicked-looking saw. How had they found the slug there? Metal detectors, he supposed. Or a really sharp eye.

'So. Here's what we've put together,' Standish said. Her eyes were red and her posture slumped. He wondered if she'd gotten any sleep last night. At least he'd had a few hours' worth. 'About an hour ago one of your neighbors saw somebody come through those bushes there.' She pointed to a sloppy hedge separating the camp from a side street. 'Look familiar?'

'Where you saw that visitor the other day.'

'Exactly the place. Yeah. The wit — means 'witness,' which I guess you know — didn't see more than dark clothes and a dark hat. Well, look at the lights. Which there aren't many of. He walked toward your camper. The wit lost sight and when she looked again he was gone. And, frankly, playing stupid, she went up close to the window and saw a flashlight inside. Your car wasn't here and where your locks used to be was shambles.'

Shaw looked over the remnants.

'Local uniforms from Traffic took the call, but' — she grimaced — 'wonderful, they kept their lovely illumination on, all red, white and blue and flashy.' She lowered her voice. 'Because what they're really good at is traffic and only traffic. Anyways, the perp saw the lights and opened up with his weapon. Took out a headlight and let fly another half dozen rounds.

'Our boys and gals hit the deck — did I mention the Traffic detail? — and by the time backup and SWAT got here, he was gone. No

329

description. Even the wit called nine-one-one didn't see anything useful. We need you to spot if he took anything.'

Shaw said nothing yet about the gender she'd assigned. He'd tell her about Maddie Poole in a moment.

He was looking at the wrecked door.

'Dent puller,' she said.

A tool with a screw at one end and a sliding weight on a shaft. It's used, yes, for pulling dents out of car bodies, but you can also screw the tip into a lock, nice and tight, then slam the weight back. Pops the whole cylinder out. Shaw had one lock that couldn't be pulled that way. The intruder had come equipped and used a pry bar to bend the tempered-steel flanges on the body of the camper. Winnebago makes a fine vehicle but titanium doesn't figure in the construction.

'There's something else you should know,' Standish said. She was pulling her phone from one of the pockets in her cargo pants. She called up an image. It was the stenciled drawing of the Whispering Man's face.

'That the one I gave to Dan Wiley?'

'No. It was left for me.' She paused, her face again a grimace. 'Actually, left for Karen, on her car. She was going to take Gem for ice cream and found it on the windshield. I sent them to my mother's. Maybe it was just to spook me. I wasn't going to take a chance, though.'

Shaw asked, 'Any forensics?'

'No. Like everything else.'

The black eyes, the slightly open mouth, the jaunty hat . . .

The RV park manager came by to see if Shaw was all right. Shaw told the old salt he was fine and asked if he'd be so kind as to get an emergency locksmith to take care of the Winnebago. He gave the manager one of his credit cards and a hundred dollars.

Then he and Standish stepped inside to survey the damage, which, on the surface, didn't seem too bad. First, of course, pantry and bed. His weapons were where he'd left them: spice cabinet for the Glock, the Colt Python under the bed.

Standish nodded to a small gun safe beside the bed, bolted to the floor. This couldn't be opened with a dent puller or much else, other than a diamond saw or a two-thousand-degree cutting stick. 'Anything in there?'

He explained that it contained only a rattrap. If he was ever forced to open the safe, the intruder would be rewarded with one or, ideally, two broken fingers. Shaw would then have time to reach under the bed and pull out his revolver.

'Hmm.'

For twenty minutes, Shaw conducted a step-by-step examination of the camper. Drawers had been opened and notebooks and clothes and toiletries disturbed. They were mostly about other jobs and some personal materials. All his notes on the kidnappings and on the Gamer were in his computer bag in the rental car, hidden under the passenger seat.

Some coins were on the floor, as were Post-it notes and pens, phone chargers and cables. The detritus from the junk drawer, identical to the

331

one that every household has: batteries, tools, wire, aspirin bottles, hotel key cards, loose nuts and bolts and screws.

Shaw also kept petty cash here. A few hundred dollars, U.S. and Canadian, was gone.

He told Standish this and added, 'Tossing the junk drawer was a cover. This wasn't a random break-in.' He pointed to the front of the vehicle. In the storage sleeve beside the driver's seat were two GPS units — a TomTom and a Garmin. He'd found that some brands worked better than others in different areas of the country. Any thief would have seen them while rifling the glove compartment.

Standish said, 'Wasn't really thinking a methhead anyway.'

'No. It's the Gamer. Wanted to take a look at my notes. And anything else on the case.'

'Taking a chance that you'd be out?'

Shaw picked up the Post-its and coins. 'No risk at all, Standish. She knew exactly where I'd be.'

'She?' Then the curiosity on Standish's face faded as she fielded his meaning.

# 52

Shaw walked to a drawer in the kitchenette and took out a plastic storage bag. He wrapped it around his hand as Standish looked on with curiosity. With this improvised glove, he extracted from his pocket the business card that Maddie Poole had given him.

*GrindrGirl88* . . .

'Here. In case there's a print on the brass or slug. Or maybe she got careless. See if there's a match.'

'Explain, Shaw.'

'Ohio. Eight years ago. The teenager attacked by her classmates playing *The Whispering Man*. Maddie could be that girl. Trying to close down Marty Avon and the game that ruined her life.'

'And this insight, which is a bizarre one, is based on what?'

He offered the analysis he'd hammered out just forty minutes before, including finding *The Whispering Man* book hidden in her house, a game she claimed she'd never played. 'And she left me in her house, knowing I'd stay — exactly when the break-in happened.' He nodded around the camper. 'To see what I'd found on the case.' He chose not to mention her edginess, her ruthless gaze when she'd stabbed him to death in the game. Stick with the objective.

'And here.' Shaw lifted his phone and displayed the pictures of the opioids and other drugs in Maddie's medicine cabinet.

'Powerful stuff. Send them to me. We'll check them against what was in Sophie Mulliner's and Henry Thompson's blood.'

Shaw uploaded the pictures to her phone and she in turn forwarded them onward.

'I'll check out that Ohio case.' She Googled it, read, then tucked her phone away. 'I'm going to call the sheriff in Cincinnati and the OSP. They get me the girl's name and picture. Might take a while. Juvie records usually need a magistrate's okay.'

He noted the time from the microwave. 'I'm going back.'

'Back . . . ?'

'To her place. I know some law. Maddie invited me in. I've got permission to be there. I only did a fast search before you called. There're suitcases, a couple of gym bags.'

'You'd be pushing the line there, Shaw. Permission to be in someone's residence . . . for one thing, that doesn't mean permission for others.'

'I'm not Crime Scene, Standish. I just want to know.'

Shaw's gut clenched again at Maddie's possible betrayal. Seeing her come up to him at the Quick Byte, taking his arm at the C3 Conference, her body against his. The flirt. And then tonight . . . In bed. Was that only to give herself a chance to go through his camper?

'I need to be back now. If I don't, she'll suspect something and vanish.'

Standish pointed to the woman's business

card in the plastic bag. 'We can find her.'

'That's an email address and a post office box.'

Colter Shaw knew very well that if you want not to be found, you can make sure you're not found.

Standish wasn't pleased. She debated. ''K. But with a team outside, I don't have time to wire you. Open up curtains, if you need to, so we can get eyes in.' She then summoned to the door of the camper the woman officer who'd accompanied him here and a male detective, plainclothes, and told them to go with Shaw and stage nearby.

To Shaw she said, 'You thinking odds on this one? Maddie?'

'Probably over fifty somewhere. I'm leaning toward less than that but that's because I want to lean toward less.'

*Never rely on your heart when it comes to survival . . .*

For good or bad, thank you, Ash.

He walked to the spice cabinet and removed the gray plastic inside-the-waistband holster for the Glock, which he mounted on his right hip. Dropping the gun's magazine, he checked to make sure it was loaded with the full six rounds, plus one in the chamber. He slipped the gun away.

LaDonna Standish watched him. She said nothing about the Glock. Now both the out-of-harm's-way rule and the no-weapons rule were history. As he walked to the door with a grim face she offered, 'I hope it's not her, Shaw.'

He stepped outside and climbed into the

Malibu. He was thinking that if Maddie had returned while he was away she might wonder about his absence.

So he stopped and bought breakfast at an all-night deli.

This confused the cops driving behind him but it was a logical thing for a man to do when he'd awakened to find his lover no longer in bed beside him. Making breakfast would have been too domestic and would have irritated a card-carrying member of the Never After Club. Buying it was a fine balance. He got scrambled eggs and bacon on rolls, fruit cups and two coffees. And a Red Bull for her, the selecting of which troubled him, recalling their meeting at the Quick Byte.

*Think I just earned my Cinnabon . . .*

Though the king of percentages reminded himself: a hypothesis is just a hypothesis until it's proven true.

Back in the car he sped to Maddie's house, with dawn tempering the sky. The air was rich with dew and pine-fragrant.

She had not yet returned.

Shaw parked quickly and walked to the officers' sedan.

'Her car's not here. If she comes back, text me.' He gave the woman officer his number and she put it into her mobile.

He then took the tray of aromatic food and coffee and walked into the house. Setting the tray on the counter in the kitchen, he turned to the basement door. It was unusual for houses to have cellars in California but this was an old structure — dating back to early in the prior century, he estimated. Shaw had decided that if Maddie Poole had any secrets she didn't wish to be discovered — the murder weapon, for instance — the basement was as good a place as any to hide them.

He paused at the door, glancing back at her fancy computer setup.

Could it really be her?

*You've been killed . . .*

Well, don't waste any more time. Find out yes, find out no.

He pulled open the basement door and was greeted with a complex scent of old and something sweet, something familiar — cleanser, he guessed.

He left the lights off — maybe there were windows to the outside and she might see the overhead basement lights when — or if — she returned. He chanced using the flashlight on his iPhone, shining it downward, to make his way along the rickety stairs.

Standing on the damp concrete slab floor, he swung the beam around him to see if there were any windows. No, he spotted none. He flicked the only light switch he could see, then noted there were no bulbs in the sockets.

The phone would have to do. He scanned the basement. There was nothing at all in the main room here, a roughly square twenty-by-twenty-foot area. But to his left was a corridor that led to what seemed to be storerooms. He searched them one by one; they were all empty.

Well, what had he been expecting to find?

A map of Basin Redwoods Park? Sophie Mulliner's bike and backpack?

On the one hand, this was absurd.

On the other, Sophie had admitted the kidnapper might have been a woman. And the forensics were inconclusive.

He turned the flashlight off and climbed the stairs.

He was turning from the kitchen into the living room when he stopped, inhaling a fast breath.

Maddie Poole was standing in front of him. She held a long kitchen knife in her hand. Her eyes looked him up and down, as if at a deer she was preparing to gut.

# 53

'Find anything interesting?'

There was no point in lying. There was no point in reaching for his weapon. The Glock was far more efficient than her blade but she could plant the Henckels between his ribs or in his throat before he could pull the trigger.

'Lose something? Get lost after going out to buy breakfast? Which would have been a charming gesture after sleeping with somebody — except it's pretty clear you had a different agenda.'

Her hand tightened its grip on the handle of the knife. In her eyes was a glaze of hysteria and he wondered how close he was to being stabbed.

The Maddie Poole of the *Immersion* game was back, with a very real blade, not one made up of a hundred thousand bytes of data. The tip now turned closer to him. Killing with a knife is hard work, and lengthy. Blinding or slashing tendons, though, can be done in an instant.

'Relax,' he said in a soft voice.

'Shut the hell up!' she raged. 'Who are you really?'

'Who I said I was.'

With her free hand, she tugged her hair, hard, fidgeting. The knife hand's digits continued to clench and unclench. She shook her head, hair whipping back and forth. 'Then why spy on me? Go through all of my things?'

'Because I thought there was a chance you might be the kidnapper. Or, if not, be working with him. Keeping an eye on me to see where the investigation was.'

*No point in lying . . .*

'Me?'

'The facts suggested it was a possibility. I had to check it out. I was looking for any evidence that connected you to the crimes.'

Her face twisted into a dark, unbelieving smile. 'You can't be serious.'

'I didn't think it was likely. But — '

'You had to check it out.' Bitter sarcasm. 'How long've you been spying on me? From the beginning, from our night at the conference?'

'You have the gameplay guide for *The Whispering Man*. You told me you'd never played, didn't know anything about it. I found it this morning.'

He told her his thought: that she was that girl in Ohio who was attacked by classmates who took the game to heart.

'Ah, the scars,' she said. 'You saw them.'

He added that she'd come up to him at the Quick Byte Café. 'After I'd started looking for Sophie. You might've followed me there.'

She held the knife up closer to him. Shaw tensed, judging angles.

Maddie spat out, 'Fuck.' And flung the blade across the room.

Her expression alone was evidence enough of her innocence — along with the fact that she hadn't hidden behind the door when he ascended the stairs and slashed him to death.

340

She was breathing hard. And, it seemed, trying to keep tears at bay. 'You're wondering how I knew. Well, take a look.' Her voice choked yet she had a sardonic smile on her face, just the lips. The eyes were a blend of sorrow and ice. She walked to her computer and sat down heavily in the seat. 'I've got a new video game, Colt. A hard one. I don't mean difficult. I mean it makes you feel shitty. I call it the *Judas Game*. Take a look.'

Onto the screen came not a game but a video, a wide-angle view, like that taken by a security cam. It was of this very living room and had been filmed within the past couple of hours. Colter Shaw was rifling through her books, opening drawers, reaching onto the tops of bookcases. He'd been looking for the gun. You couldn't see him photograph the medicine bottles — that was in the bathroom — but you could see the flash from his phone.

She shut off the clip. 'I told you about Twitch and the other streaming game sites where your fans want to see you playing? I was online earlier and forgot to shut the camera off. It wasn't broadcasting, just recording. I don't use a webcam. It's a wide-angle security camera. Better night vision. There's no red record light on it.'

Same thing he'd done at the Quick Byte, the first time there, to record anyone who was particularly interested in Sophie Mulliner's pictures.

Maddie reached for her backpack. She rummaged for a moment, then withdrew a small slip of paper. She handed it to him. It was a purchase receipt.

'A used-book store near Stanford. Specializes

in gaming books. Check the date on the receipt. I bought it for you today and made some notes in it about the game, things I thought might be helpful. I didn't have a chance to give it to you.' She looked to the bedroom.

'As for hitting on you? No, I wasn't following you, I didn't track you into the Quick Byte. Believe it or not, Colter, I saw a handsome dude, kind of a cowboy, tough, quiet, on a mission, looking for this missing girl. My sort of guy.' She swallowed. 'No motives, no agendas. It's a lonely life. Don't we all try to make it less lonely?

'And the scars . . . Sure, the scars . . . May as well have everything out. You've bought yourself the lurid details. I got married when I was nineteen. Love of my life. Joe and I lived outside of L.A., owned an athletic outfit store, ran day trips — you know, biking, hiking, rafting, skiing. It was heaven. Then a customer turned into a stalker. Totally psychotic. One night when my sister and her boyfriend were visiting he broke in and shot my husband and sister. Killed them both. I ran into the kitchen and got a knife. He took it away and stabbed me fourteen times before my sister's boyfriend tackled him.

'I almost died. A couple of times. Had nine surgeries. In the hospital and housebound for a year and two weeks. Video games were the only things that kept me from killing myself. See, for me, Colter, the Never After Club is real. It's not a commitment thing. There is no 'after' for me. Literally. I died four years ago.

'Look me up. It was all over the press in southern California. Maddie Gibson was my name then. I changed back to my maiden name because that asshole kept sending me love letters from prison.' She shook her head. 'I got back a half hour ago and saw the video. What the hell were you up to? I was thinking, maybe doing this reward stuff, the people you go after — like the kidnapper here — maybe that pushed *you* over the edge. Maybe *you* were a killer, a thief. It wasn't logical. But you go through what I did, it makes you a little paranoid, Colt.

'So. I had to find out. I moved my car around the corner and grabbed that' — she glanced to the floor where the knife lay — 'and waited for you to come back.' Some tears now.

'Look . . . ' Shaw began. He stopped when she lifted a brow. Now her eyes were the cold green of a dull emerald.

He fell silent. What was there to say?

That his restless mind sometimes took over and drove him to find the answers no matter what the cost?

That fragments of his father's paranoia and suspicion were lodged in his genes?

That he couldn't quite eradicate the images of Kyle Butler's and Henry Thompson's bodies, still and bloody?

Those were all true. They were also excuses.

He offered a faint nod — a flag signifying both his crime and the utter inadequacy of any remedies.

Colter Shaw walked to the door and, without a look back, let himself out.

At his car, he was startled by the squeal of tires coming his way. His hand dropping toward his weapon, he glanced to his left. It was the unmarked car that had accompanied him, speeding forward, now with its blue-and-white grille lights flashing. It skidded to a stop abruptly, directly beside him, the passenger window coming down.

The uniformed woman officer said, 'Mr. Shaw, Detective Standish just radioed. There's been another kidnapping. Can you follow us to the Task Force?'

# 54

The conference room was populated with fifteen or so men and women from various law enforcement agencies. Shaw saw the uniforms of deputies and police and the plainclothes suits and ensembles of agents and detectives. They stood in clusters, looking at a whiteboard on which were written details of the recent kidnapping.

Shaw walked up to LaDonna Standish, who said, 'What'd you find? About Maddie?'

Without expression Shaw said, 'I was wrong.'

As soon as he arrived at the Task Force headquarters he'd confirmed Maddie's story. The picture accompanying one article was an image of the woman, younger, on top of a mountain with her husband, both in ski gear, both smiling, taken a few months before the murders.

He nodded at the new bodies present. 'FBI?'

'California Bureau. Not the feds.'

Heading the show was a tall, chiseled B of I agent, dark-haired and wearing a gray suit a shade darker than his partner's — a man who was not tall, not thin, not good-looking. The name of the tall one was Anthony Prescott. Shaw had missed the other's.

Prescott said, 'Detective Standish, could you brief us on the latest taking?'

She explained how the vic was kidnapped in a

parking lot in Mountain View about an hour ago on her way to work. 'Municipal lot. No video. We canvassed and a wit saw a person in gray sweats and a gray stocking cap. Like on the Quick Byte Café security cam.'

Standish had created a file and made copies for everyone on the case. She handed Shaw one. Inside was a bio of the victim, which Shaw read through. There were pictures too.

The detective fired off other facts — the absence of fingerprints, the lack of DNA for tracing through the CODIS database, every piece of physical evidence the Gamer'd left behind being untraceable, the homemade knock-out potion, his weapons, the inability to identify his vehicle because he drove on grass or other ground cover and left no tread marks.

'In the files I gave you are security webcam shots of the suspect that Mr. Shaw here obtained at the Quick Byte. It doesn't show much but it might be helpful.'

Prescott asked, 'And who are you?' Then to Standish, 'And who is he?'

'A consultant.'

'Consultant?' the shorter CBI agent asked.

'Hmm,' Standish confirmed.

'Wait. The bounty hunter?' Prescott asked.

Shaw said, 'Frank Mulliner offered a reward to find his missing daughter.'

'Which he did,' Standish offered.

'Is there a fee to us involved?' Prescott's partner asked Shaw.

Shaw said, 'No.'

Perhaps Prescott wanted an explanation about

why Shaw was doing this. He didn't indulge.

Standish touched her copy of the folder. She continued: 'Another fact you need to know. The victim — her name's Elizabeth Chabelle — is seven and a half months pregnant.'

'Jesus!' from somebody. Gasps too. An obscenity.

'And one more thing: the unsub hid her on a ship. A sinking ship.'

Colter Shaw took over.

'It appears that the unsub is basing the crimes on a video game.'

Void reaction from the room.

'It's called *The Whispering Man*. That's the villain in the game. He hides his victims in an abandoned place. They have to escape — before other players, or the character himself, kill them.'

Someone in the back — an older male uniformed officer — called, 'That's pretty bizarre. You sure?'

'His kidnapping M.O. lines up with the gameplay. And he's left graffiti or printouts of the character at the scenes.'

'Photos are in the file,' Standish said.

Shaw: 'Any of you know how levels work in video games?'

Some nodded. Others shook their heads. The majority simply gazed at him the way they'd observe, with more or less interest, a lizard in a pet shop terrarium.

Shaw said, 'A video game's about meeting increasing challenges. You start out on the simple level, saving some settlers, trekking to a certain place, killing X number of aliens. If you're successful you move to a more difficult level. The Gamer's placed his victims in the first two levels of *The Whispering Man*.'

Standish added, 'The Abandoned Factory. That was Sophie Mulliner. Henry Thompson's was The Dark Forest. The third level is The Sinking Ship.'

The last level, the tenth, Shaw had learned, was hell itself — where the Whispering Man lives. No player in the history of the game had ever made it that far.

Prescott said slowly, 'An interesting theory.' Slowly and uncertainly.

There was enough corroboration that Shaw could *accept* theory over hypothesis in this case.

One officer, a uniform from Santa Clara, pointed to the whiteboard. 'That's why he's the Gamer?'

Shaw said, 'Correct.'

Prescott's partner said, 'Supervisor Cummings said you're profiling him as a sociopath.'

Standish cleared her throat. 'I said the likelihood of that diagnosis was about seventy percent.' She glanced at Shaw, who nodded.

'But no sado-sexual activity?' someone pointed out. 'Which you almost always see in the case of a male unsub.'

'No,' Standish said.

Shaw continued: 'We've been working with the company that publishes *The Whispering Man* — they're cooperating. The CEO is trying to track down suspects in the customer database. He'll call Detective Standish as soon as he finds some likely names.'

Standish said, 'All this is in the file.'

Prescott said, the fiber of doubt in his voice, 'If it *is* a ship, you know where?'

Shaw said he did not. Then added, 'He'll've left five objects she can use to save herself. One is food or water. Another will probably let her signal for help. Maybe a mirror or — '

One of the other suited agents said, 'We gotta lot of boats here. We don't have the resources to send drones and choppers over anything that floats.'

Ignoring the obvious, as usual, Shaw said, 'Or start a signal fire.'

Standish: 'We need to tell all the public safety offices to let us know if there're any fires or smoke on docks or boats themselves. It'll be a deserted place too.'

Prescott stepped forward. 'All right, Detective, Supervisor Cummings. We appreciate your work,' he said. 'We'll keep you posted on the developments.'

Two sentences that Shaw guessed were patently false.

Standish's face was emotionless, though her eyes settled. She was mad at the downgrading. But the CBI was state, the JMCTF was local. And if the FBI were here, they'd rule the roost. The way of the world.

While this ping-pong discussion had been going on, Shaw was wondering how much time Elizabeth Chabelle had until she perished from exposure. Or drowned.

Or until the Gamer, playing *The Whispering Man* with relish, returned to pursue her through the vessel or on the dock and shoot or stab her.

Prescott said, 'We'll consider what Detective Standish and her consultant have suggested. Somebody perverted by these video games.'

Which wasn't the theory at all.

The agent continued: 'Though, you ask me, I think anyone who plays them is a bit off.'

Shaw noted several of the officers staring at him without any reaction. The gamers in the room, he figured.

'We'll pursue that lead. We'll also follow standard protocol for an abduction. Get taps on all Ms. Chabelle's phones. She have a boyfriend, husband?'

Standish said, 'Boyfriend. George Hanover.'

'Taps on his too and her parents', if they're alive.'

'They are,' Shaw said. 'They live in Miami. All in the report.'

'Look at financial resources of the boyfriend and her parents to see if they might be ransom targets. Get a list of registered sex offenders in the area. See if she has any stalkers.' The Bureau of Investigation agent kept talking, but Shaw had stopped listening. He was watching a man in the corridor approach the glass-walled conference room.

It was Dan Wiley, now in a green uniform. The man still looked like a cop right out of a movie.

The detective — or whatever he was now that he'd been rotated to Liaison — was holding a large envelope. He knocked and, when nodded in by Prescott, spotted Detective Standish and walked over to her.

Prescott said, 'Officer, is that related to the Chabelle kidnappings?'

'Well, it's the ME's report on the latest vic. Henry Thompson.'

'I'll take it. BI's running the case.'

With a glance to Standish, Wiley handed the envelope to the tall agent and left.

Nearly to the door, he paused, looking back toward Shaw. A rueful smile crossed his face and, if Shaw's translation was correct, its meaning was that the cop was offering an apology.

Shaw nodded in return.

*Never waste time on anger.*

Prescott opened the envelope and read to himself. Then he announced to the room: 'Nothing new here. Henry Thompson died of a single gunshot, a nine-millimeter, determined to be from the same gun used in the Kyle Butler murder, a Glock 17. TOD was between ten p.m. and eleven p.m. Friday. He had also suffered blunt force trauma to the skull, resulting in a bone fracture and brain concussion. This was prior to the gunshot and prior to the fall from the cliff. He — '

Shaw asked, 'Where was the fracture?'

Prescott looked up, his head askew. 'I'm sorry?'

Standish asked, 'Where was the fracture?'

'Why?'

Standish added, 'We'd like to know.'

Prescott skimmed the report. 'Left sphenoid.' He glanced up. 'Anything else?'

Standish looked at Shaw, who shook his head.

She said, 'Nope. We're good.'

Prescott kept his eyes on her for a moment longer. He continued: 'He'd been injected with OxyContin suspended in water. Nonlethal, just enough to sedate him temporarily.' He handed the report to one of the two uniformed women officers. 'Make copies for the team, would you? Then transcribe it on the board. You probably have better handwriting than the boys.'

The officer took the report with a faint tightening of her lips.

Standish said to Shaw in a soft voice, 'So, why did I want to know where he got hit?'

'Can we leave?' Shaw whispered.

She looked over the room. 'Don't see why not. We're invisible anyway.'

As they walked to the door they happened to pass Cummings. He held up a hand. Standish and Shaw paused.

Was an issue looming?

Keeping his eyes on Prescott and the whiteboards, the supervisor whispered, 'I do not want to know what you two have in mind. But get to it. And get to it fast. Good luck.'

# 55

They were back in the Quick Byte.

Shaw was getting to recognize some of the regulars. Sitting nearby was the kid in the red-and-black-checked shirt whose potential romance with the beautiful young woman had been derailed either by her change of mind or as a cruel joke. He spotted a dozen others who seemed to treat the place as their home away from home. Some were talking to one another; some were on phones; most were communing with their laptops.

Shaw was browsing the internet, looking through medical sites, on his mobile. He showed Standish a diagram. A picture of the human skull, each of the bones composing it named. The sphenoid was just behind the eye socket.

'That's the bone?' She was silent for a moment. 'Okay. Next question: Is the Gamer right-handed?'

'That's *exactly* the next question. Because if he is, that means he hit Thompson from the front. And that's probably what happened because lefties make up only ten percent of the population.'

Standish's eyes swept slowly through the café. 'Let's think about this. Thompson's driving down the street, the Gamer's following. He passes Thompson, parks and waits, then pitches a rock into his windshield. Thompson gets out.

And up comes the Gamer, holding a gun on him. Thompson thinks it's a carjacking. Rule one: Give up the keys. You can always get another car.'

'But the Gamer slugs him with the gun, cracking his facial bone. Which means he didn't care if Thompson saw him or not. Even if he was wearing the mask, Thompson would get *some* description. So the Gamer meant all along to kill him.'

Standish said, 'The time of death in the report Dan Wiley brought Prescott. That's what tipped you.'

Shaw nodded. 'It was just an hour or so after Thompson was taken. The Gamer drove him to Redwoods Park, walked him out on the ledge and shot him right away. The Gamer's the one who set the fire to get our attention so we'd find the body — and the Whispering Man graffiti.'

'None of this is about playing a scary-ass game in real life.'

'No,' Shaw said. 'He was using the game to cover up murdering Thompson. That was my original idea. I thought that Tony Knight hired somebody to play a psycho to bring down Marty Avon. I got that wrong. That doesn't mean the hypothesis in general is wrong.'

'Sophie Mulliner was just part of the misdirection?' Standish asked.

'I'd think so.'

'And Elizabeth Chabelle?'

'Probably the same.'

'So she might be alive.'

Shaw: 'He'll want to make sure the game plays

out. So we'll assume she is.'

Standish: 'The big question: Who'd want to kill Henry Thompson?'

'He was a gay rights activist. Was he controversial?'

Standish said, 'Karen and I are involved in the community, I never heard of him. Gay in the Bay Area? Unless you're a cop, nobody cares.' She gave him a wry smile. 'What was he blogging about? Bet he stumbled on somebody's secret.'

Shaw found the notebook in which he'd recorded Brian Byrd's comments about his partner. He skimmed. 'Henry was working on three stories at the moment. Two of them don't seem very controversial — revenues in the software industry and the high price of real estate in Silicon Valley.'

'Tell me about it.' Standish puffed air from her mouth.

'But the third?' he said, reading. 'It's how gaming companies are illegally stealing gamers' data and selling it.'

Standish had not heard of this trend.

'There must be hundreds of gaming companies that collect data.'

'True. I have a place where we can start, though.'

'You going to put one of your fancy percentages on it?'

'Ten, I'd say.'

'That's ten percent better than anything else we've got. Let's hear it.'

'Hong-Sung Enterprises.'

Shaw explained about the goggles and how the

game turned your house and backyard into imaginary battlegrounds. 'Most companies data-mine information from things you do actively: fill out forms, answer questionnaires, click on products to buy. Hong-Sung collects data without your knowing it. The goggles have cameras. They upload everything you look at when you play.'

Standish was interested. 'Products in your house, the clothes you wear, how many kids you've got, a sick or elderly relative, if you've got pets — they sell that to data-mining companies? Smart. And Henry Thompson was going to write about it . . . Is that really a reason to kill somebody, Shaw? Conspiracy to mail me coupons for diapers for Gem? Or oil changes for that fancy camper of yours?'

'I think it's more than that. Maddie told me the company was giving the game and the goggles away to the U.S. military. When the soldiers or sailors play, they might look at something classified — maybe a weapon, an order for deployment, information about troop movements — and the goggles could capture and upload it.'

'Maybe audio recordings too?'

Shaw nodded. He replaced phone with laptop and looked up Hong-Sung. 'They've got links to the Chinese government. Anything the goggles scanned could go directly to the Chinese Ministry of Defense. Or whatever their military operation's called.'

Standish's phone pinged with a text. She sent one in reply. Shaw wondered if it had to do with the case. She put the phone away. 'Karen. We got good news. The last hurdle. We're adopting. Always wanted two.'

'Boy, girl?'

'Girl again. Sefina. She's four. I took her out of a hostage sit in EPA and got her into foster about eighteen months ago. Mother was brain-damaged from all the drugs and her boyfriend was warranted up his ass.'

'Sefina,' Shaw said. 'Pretty name.'

'Samoan.'

Shaw asked, 'We tell Prescott about Hong-Sung?'

'What would they do with it? Nothing. Remember, Shaw: simple. That's what they like. Ransom demands, bullets and drugs and lovers running amuck.' She frowned. 'Is there such a thing as 'running muck'? Is that what you run when everything's calm and good?'

Shaw was taking quite the liking to Detective LaDonna Standish. He powered down his laptop and slipped it and his notebook back into the bag. 'I'll try to find a way into Hong-Sung.'

'Could your friend Maddie help?'

'That's not going to happen. I'll see Marty Avon myself.'

Standish's tongue tsked. 'What happened to the *we?*'

'Got a question,' Shaw said.

'Which is?'

'Who's going to stay home with Sefina and Gem?'

'Karen. She writes her cooking blog from home. Why?'

'So you can't afford to lose this job, right?

357

That doesn't require an answer.'

Her lips pursed. 'Shaw, you — '

'I've been shot at, I've abseiled off a burning tree. I've decapitated a rattler halfway into his strike — '

'You did not.'

'Truth. And we can all agree that I can face down a mountain lion.'

'I'll give you that.'

'I can handle myself. If that's what you were going to say.'

'I was.'

'Anything I find pans out, I'll call you. You call SWAT.'

# 56

'The Astro Base.'

Marty Avon was speaking to Shaw but was gazing at an eighteen-inch toy on his desk. A red-and-white globe atop landing legs. His beloved gaze reminded Shaw of how his sister, Dorie, and her husband would look adoringly at their daughters.

'Nineteen sixty-one. Plastic, motors. See the astronaut.' A little blue guy, dangling from a crane, about to be lowered to the surface of Avon's desk. 'We didn't have space stations then. No matter. The toy companies were always a generation ahead. You could fire a ray gun. You could explore. Batteries required. Lasted about two weeks before the rush wore off. That's the nature of toys. And chewing gum. And cocaine. You just have to make sure there's a new supply available.

'I don't have much time,' Avon added, focusing on Shaw. 'I'm meeting with some people about Siliconville. We're getting some resistance from traditional real estate developers. Imagine that!' He gave a wink. 'Affordable housing, subsidized by employers — not popular!'

Like the company towns of the late-nineteenth and early-twentieth centuries, which Shaw knew about from his father's reading to the children about the Old West. Railroads and mines often built villages for their workers — who paid exorbitant prices for rent, food and necessities, often running up huge debts, which bound them forever to their employers.

He suspected Avon's apparent socialist bent would lead him to run Siliconville in a very different way.

'There's been another kidnapping. We think it's related. We need your help again.'

'Oh, no. Who?'

'A woman, thirty-two. Pregnant.'

'My God, no.'

Shaw had to give Avon credit that the first words out of his mouth weren't something to the effect of: more bad publicity for me and my game.

'We're doing everything we can with the proxies to find you a suspect. But it's taking more time than I'd hoped. We've cracked eleven. None of them are in the area.'

'Only eleven?'

A grimace. 'I know. It's slow. We don't have supercomputers. And some proxies are just so righteous you can't trace them back. That's why they exist in the first place, of course.'

Shaw said, 'Add these times too, when he wouldn't have been online.' He displayed his notebook and pointed to the hour Chabelle disappeared.

Avon typed fast and, with a flourish, hit RETURN. 'It's on its way.'

'I need something else. We have another hypothesis. Hong-Sung Entertainment.'

The CEO corrected, 'No, it's 'Enterprises.'

Hong Wei sets his sights high. Gaming's just a part of his businesses. Small part, actually.'

'You familiar with *Immersion*?'

Avon laughed, his expression saying, Who isn't?

'So you know how it works?'

The lanky man's fidget fingers maneuvered the cerulean astronaut back into the Astro Base. 'Here's where you might ask: Do I wish I'd thought the game up? No. Virtual reality and motion-based game engines sound good. The fact is, of the billion-plus gamers in the world, the vast majority sit on their asses in dark rooms and pound away on a keyboard or squeeze their console controller. Because they *want* to sit on their asses in dark rooms and pound away on keyboards. *Immersion's* a novelty. Hong-Sung's poured hundreds of millions into *Immersion*. Hong's less of a prick than some in Silicon Valley but he's still a prick. I don't have any problem with the game taking him to the cleaners when people get tired of hopping around like bunnies in their backyards. Which is going to happen. Why? Because it's not . . . ' His eyebrow rose.

'Fun?' Shaw said.

'*Exactement!*' Offered in a curious French accent.

And this grinning, goofy fellow had created one of the creepiest video games in history.

'What if *Immersion's* more than a game?'

Avon's squinting eyes moved from the space station back to Shaw, who explained his idea about the cameras on the goggles sucking up images from players' houses or apartments as they roamed their homes and uploading the data to Hong-Sung's servers for later sale.

Avon's eyes widened. 'Jesus. That is solid gold brilliant. Okay, now ask if I wish I'd thought *that* one up.'

'There's another what-if,' Shaw said. 'Hong-Sung's giving away goggles to U.S. military personnel. Presumably other government workers too.'

'To capture classified data, you're thinking?'

'Maybe.'

'My.' Avon considered this. 'You're talking a huge amount of data to process. Private companies couldn't handle it. You know what the Chinese government has? The TC-4. Thirty-five petaflops. Most powerful supercomputer in the world. They might be able to handle the load. But, I have to ask, how does this involve my game?'

Shaw: 'The second victim? Henry Thompson? He was writing a blog about how companies steal data from gamers. Maybe Hong-Sung — or some other game company — didn't want the story to appear and somebody mimicked a psycho gamer and killed him.'

'How can I help?'

'I need to talk to somebody who's got a connection to the company. Best if he works there. Can you make that happen?'

The implication being that since it was, after all, his game that was the hub of the crime, even if it wasn't Avon's fault, a little cooperation wouldn't be a bad idea.

'I don't know anybody there personally. Hong is secretive, to put it mildly. But it's a small world, SV is. I'll make some calls.'

# 57

Though he was inherently restless, Colter Shaw was not necessarily impatient. Now, however, with Elizabeth Chabelle missing and in grave danger and with the Gamer prepared to play out the final act in his *Whispering Man* game, he wanted Eddie Linn to show up.

Avon had made a half dozen calls and found a connection to Hong-Sung; a man named Trevor, whose further identity Avon didn't share, would put Shaw in touch with Linn, who was an employee of HSE. This cost Avon something significant; it was clear that he would license some software to Trevor, at a discount, in exchange for setting up a rendezvous between Shaw and Linn.

Shaw was presently in the appointed place at the appointed time: a park, carefully planned and maintained. Serpentine sidewalks of pebbled concrete, bordered by tall, wafting grasses and reeds, flower beds, trees. The grass as bright as an alien's skin in a C3 game. A tranquil pond was populated with sizable fish, red and black and white.

The grounds were balanced in color, laser-cut trim, perfectly symmetrical.

Setting Colter Shaw on edge. He liked his landscapes designed by the foliage and water and dirt and rocks themselves.

As he walked along the path he caught a small

glimpse of Hong-Sung Enterprises' U.S. head-quarters. The building was a glistening mirrored copper doughnut. To the side were four huge transmission antennas.

Presumably, just what was needed to beam stolen data into the ether.

Linn had told him to sit on a particular bench, in front of a weeping willow, or one nearby if this one was occupied. Shaw noted why: it was out of sight of the company's offices. The preferred bench was free. Behind it was a stand of thick boxwood, a plant that smelled of ammonia.

Now the impatience factor was cresting and Shaw, thinking of Elizabeth Chabelle on a sinking ship, was glancing at his phone for the time when he heard a man's tense, tenor voice. 'Mr. Shaw.'

Eddie Linn was a tall, narrow man of about thirty. Asian features. He wore a polo shirt with an HSE logo on the left chest and dark gray slacks that were slightly baggy.

He sat down next to Shaw, whom Trevor would have described to Linn. The man didn't offer his hand. Shaw had the ridiculous thought that Linn didn't want to transfer DNA, which might be used for evidentiary purposes.

'I just have a few minutes.' He frowned. 'I have to get back to my office. I'm only doing this because . . . ' His voice was fading.

Because Trevor had something on Linn. Extortion is a distasteful yet often very effective tool.

'Did you hear about the kidnappings?'

'Yeah, yeah, yeah. All over the news. Terrible.

And one victim killed.' Speaking high and quickly.

Shaw continued: 'That man was working on an article about stealing data from gamers. We're speculating that he was looking into *Immersion*.'

'Oh God. You don't think Mr. Hong had anything to do with it?'

'We don't know, but a woman's life's at risk. We're following up every lead. This is one of them.'

Linn fiddled with his collar. 'Who are you? Mr. Trevor said you were like a private eye.'

'I'm working with the police.'

He wasn't listening; he stiffened instantly as footsteps sounded, the faint grit of soles on sidewalk. Shaw had heard it only after Linn's reaction.

Linn put his hands on the seat of the bench and Shaw believed he was about to sprint away.

The threat, however, turned out to be two women, one pregnant and pushing a baby carriage that held a tiny sleeping child. They chatted and sipped iced-drink concoctions. The friend was younger and Shaw caught her glancing into the carriage with hints of envy in her eyes. The two women — one an accountant, he gathered, the other the mother — sat down on the neighboring bench and talked about how few hours of sleep they each got.

Linn, visibly calming, continued, though whispering now: 'Hong is a tough man. Ruthless. But killing someone?'

'You write code,' Shaw said. 'That's what Marty Avon told me.'

366

'Yes.'

'For *Immersion*?'

His eyes scanned the park. Seeing no threat, he leaned closer to Shaw and said, 'A while ago. For an expansion pack.'

'I want your impression of an idea we're looking at.'

Linn swallowed. Shaw realized he'd been doing that a lot since he sat down. 'Okay.'

He gave Linn his hypothesis about stealing data via the *Immersion* goggles. 'Could that be done?' Shaw asked.

Linn seemed stunned as he digested this. His first reaction was to shake his head. 'The cameras on the goggles are high-resolution. It would be too much data . . . unless . . . ' A near smile crescented his thin lips. 'Unless they didn't upload video, but screenshots, JPEGs, compressed some more into an RAR archive. Yes, yes, it could work! Then up it goes along with the other information to the mainframe here. It could then be processed and sold or used by the company itself. We have divisions that do advertising, marketing, consulting.'

'I think there's also a risk that Hong is stealing sensitive government information,' Shaw said. 'He's giving away thousands of copies of *Immersion* to soldiers.'

Alarmed, the HSE employee flicked his fingers together. He'd just fallen down the rabbit hole of government intrigue.

'What is it?' Shaw said. He'd noticed the man's eyes faintly squint.

After a moment: 'There's a facility in the

basement of the building. In the back. No regular employees are allowed in there. It's got a whole separate staff. Visitors show up by helicopter, go in, do whatever they do and leave. We heard it's called the Minerva Project. But no one knows what it's about.'

'I need you to help me,' Shaw said.

Before Linn could respond, though, Shaw was aware of a rustling sound behind them.

No, no, Shaw realized suddenly: a woman four, five months pregnant isn't going to have a newborn. She's pushing a doll in the carriage. He stood and gripped Linn's arm and said, 'Get out of here now!'

Linn gasped.

But it was too late.

The pregnant woman was pushing aside the carriage and rising. Her 'friend' was speaking into a microphone on her wrist and the source of the noise behind them turned out to be two minders, bursting from the boxwoods. The large Asian men's motions were perfectly choreographed. One held a Glock on Linn and Shaw and the other emptied their pockets.

Chill-eyed momma-to-be took the items. When she opened her Coach bag, Shaw saw that she too was armed. It was a Glock, nine-millimeter. The same brand of weapon that had killed Kyle Butler and, presumably, been used to pistol-whip and murder Henry Thompson.

A black SUV screeched to a stop on the wide sidewalk, feet away from them. One of the security men gripped Shaw by the arm and the other grabbed Linn. Both were shoved into the back, the middle-row seats, which were separated from the front by a Plexiglas divider. There were no door handles.

'Look, I can explain,' Linn cried. 'You don't understand!'

A second vehicle pulled up, a black sedan. The two women got inside, the one who was not pregnant held the door for the other, who, Shaw deduced, was the mastermind of the admittedly brilliant take-down operation.

The driver got out, folded up the baby carriage and placed it in the trunk, tossing the doll in afterward.

# 58

'Where are you taking me?' Eddie Linn asked, his voice vibrating like an off-balance washing machine. The SUV paused at an elaborate security gate, which then opened, and the vehicle sped through.

Shaw had two reactions to the question. First, the man's concern was solely about himself. Shaw supposed Linn would happily throw him to the wolves. Second, it was pointless to ask. Even if the guards in the front seat had been able to hear it through the Plexiglas, they wouldn't have answered.

When the Suburban stopped at the back door of Hong-Sung's futuristic headquarters, the guards nodded them out and directed them inside, where the group descended a flight of stairs. Shaw looked back, wondering if the pregnant woman's limo was behind them. It wasn't.

'Don't look around. Walk.' This from the bigger guard, who took Shaw's arm. Gripping tighter than even Tony Knight's men, who really knew how to grip.

'Don't push it,' Shaw said.

And was rewarded with a crushing squeeze.

Linn didn't need a jerk of the leash. He walked passively beside the smaller guard.

They were taking the prisoners down a lengthy, dim corridor. It might have been in the basement but it was spotless. The walls were bare. Somewhere, not far away, machinery hummed.

A two-minute trek took them to an elevator, in which they ascended to the fifth — and top — floor. It opened into a small, plain office. The receptionist, a woman of about forty, sitting at a wooden desk, nodded to the guards. Shaw and Linn were led through the wide double doors behind her. This room was larger yet just as austere as the receptionist's, hardly the place for the CEO of a multibillion-dollar conglomerate to work.

For that's who they were looking at: Hong Wei, whom Shaw recognized from the internet stories he'd downloaded. The dark-haired Asian was about fifty. He wore a suit, white shirt and blue shimmery tie. The jacket was buttoned. Shaw and Linn were deposited in chairs facing him. The guards stood a respectful distance back but also close enough to step forward and break necks in a fraction of a second.

The doors through which they'd entered opened again and the pregnant woman walked in. She carried a file folder and handed it to the man behind the desk. 'Mr. Hong.'

'Thank you, Ms. Towne.'

Shaw noted something odd. The man's desk contained no computer, other electronic device or telephone, either mobile or landline.

Hong opened the file and read studiously for a moment.

Linn was close to whimpering. Shaw had decided that while there might be consequences to his furtive meeting with Eddie Linn, dismemberment and being fed to the aquatic life in San Francisco Bay probably was not going to be one of them. Largely because it would have happened already.

Which meant his hypothesis of Hong's involvement shrank a few percentage points.

Hong read. Very slowly. And he seemed not to move a muscle. Shaw didn't even see him blink.

To Hong's right, lined up side by side like logs at the lumber camp where Shaw had worked summers during college, were a number of yellow wooden pencils and, to his left, a half dozen more. Those on the right had needle-sharp points. The ones on the left were duller. Did the CEO appreciate the dangers of digital communication so much that he relied on paper and carbon?

Hong read without any acknowledgment of the two men in front of him.

Linn took a breath to say something. Then apparently thought the better of it.

*Waste of time . . .*

Shaw waited. What else was there to do?

Finally Hong finished reading and looked at Shaw. 'Mr. Shaw, you are here because you were trespassing on private property. This park where you were sitting is owned by Hong-Sung Enterprises. There are signs.'

'Conveniently invisible.'

'You had a reasonable expectation that this was private property.'

'Because the landscaping outside the fence matches the landscaping inside?'

'Exactly.'

'That'd be a tough one for a jury to buy.'

'And since we were able to hear your conversation we had a reasonable expectation that Mr. Linn here was in the process of divulging trade secrets to you and — '

'My God, no, I wasn't!' The high voice rose even higher yet. 'I was just helping — '

'Which justified our taking you into custody, as if you were shop-lifters at a grocery store.'

Shaw glanced at Ms. Towne. Her face was calm and confident and he bet she'd be a loving and huggy mother when off the clock. She continued to stand, despite a nearby empty chair.

Hong tapped the folder. 'You make your living with these rewards, do you?'

'That's right.'

'What do you call yourselves? Rewardists?'

'I've heard that. I don't call myself anything.'

'And I understand you are not a private investigator; nor are you a bond enforcement agent. You assist in finding missing persons and escaped fugitives, and suspects who have not yet been identified or located, for rewards, traveling around the country from, say, Indiana to Berkeley, in your recreational vehicle.'

Shaw had some public presence but Hong had assembled that information in record time. And how the CEO knew that his most recent job was in Indianapolis and Muncie, and that he was at the university on his personal mission, was an utter mystery. 'That's all correct.'

Hong's face brightened, only just slightly.

'Then like PIs and like the police and like bounty hunters, which you would prefer not to be called, you solve puzzles for a living. You analyze situations and make decisions and to do this you must prioritize. And sometimes you need to do all of those at once and do them very quickly. Lives might be hanging in the balance.'

Shaw had no idea where this steamship of thought was bound for, though he was struck by the word *prioritize*, which was the reason his percentage technique existed. He said, 'True.'

'Mr. Shaw, do you play video games?'

Aside from once? Resulting in his stabbing death by a beautiful woman he would never see again? 'No.'

'I ask because playing games would enhance those very skills you need in your job.'

He reached into his desk.

Shaw didn't bother to tense. He wasn't fishing for a gun or knife.

Hong retrieved a magazine and set it before Shaw, *American Scientist*, a layperson monthly he was familiar with. Ashton, as an amateur physicist, had read it religiously. Hong opened it to the page marked with a Post-it note. He pushed it forward.

'No need to read it. I'll tell you. This article, from several years ago, was the inspiration for my Minerva Project.'

Shaw glanced down at the title: 'Can Video Games Be Good for You?'

Hong: 'It's a report from several prestigious universities about the physical and mental benefits of video gaming. Since we are about to

374

announce it to the world, there is no longer the need for secrecy regarding the Minerva Project. It's the code name for our Therapeutic Gaming Division.' He tapped the article. 'These studies show that video games can create vast improvement in patients with attention deficit disorder, autism, Asperger's and physiological conditions like vertigo and vision issues. Older patients in the trials report significantly improved memory and concentration.

'And even individuals with no disease can benefit. I'm thinking of your career, Mr. Shaw, as I said a moment ago. Game playing results in improved cognition, faster response times, the ability to switch between various tasks quickly, assess spatial relationships, visualization, many other skills.'

*Prioritizing* . . .

'That's the mysterious room, Mr. Linn. Minerva, the Roman Goddess of Wisdom. Or, I prefer to say, the Goddess of Cognitive Functioning. Now, I run a business and as the CEO I'm charged with making HSE money. The engine for Therapeutic Gaming, I decided, could easily be used for lucrative action-adventure and first-person shooter games. Hence, *Immersion*.

'Now, let me dispose of your concern — the reason you recruited Mr. Linn. About *Immersion*. Which I note that you've played, Mr. Shaw, despite what you told me earlier.'

Shaw tried not to register surprise. He would just assume, from now on, that Hong Wei knew everything about him.

'Yes, it is a goal to get young people around

the world off their behinds and exercise. I myself am a black belt in karate and tae kwon do and I practice Afro-Brazilian capoeira. I engage in those sports because I enjoy them. You cannot talk someone into exercising if they don't want to. But you can encourage them to pursue their passion. And if exercise is a necessary consequence, then they will exercise. That is *Immersion*.

'I have two recordings of conversations you've had about your concern we are stealing confidential data and giving it to the Chinese government. Military data in particular.'

Two? Shaw wondered.

'To address that concern, which is not unreasonable, considering you're trying to save the life of a young woman, let me say this: from the moment I envisioned *Immersion* and the forward-facing cameras we were developing, I knew that privacy would be a concern. I personally supervised the algorithms to make certain that every written word, every letter, every chart or graph, every photograph that the cameras scanned would be pixelated beyond recognition. The same with human figures in the slightest stage of undress. No toilets, no personal hygiene products. Dogs urinating, much less mating, would not make it into the *Immersion* system. Obscene language is filtered out.

'We've worked with law enforcement, military and government regulators around the country to guarantee that no one's privacy has been invaded. You can confirm this.' His eyes flicked to Ms. Towne. The glance was fast as a viper's bite. She stepped forward and gave Shaw a piece of paper with four names on it, along with their law enforcement affiliation and phone number. The first was FBI, the second Department of Defense.

Shaw folded the paper and put it away.

Hong turned to Eddie Linn. In a voice just as calm and flat as that with which he'd addressed Shaw, Hong said, 'Mr. Linn. At first, when Ms. Towne told me about your conversation with Mr. Trevor today, about insisting you meet with Mr. Shaw . . . Oh, no need to look confused. Your contract with us allows us to intercept all your communications.'

'I didn't know that.'

'You didn't *read* that. Which is on you. I was saying when Ms. Towne first told me about your disloyalty — '

'It wasn't — '

The marble gaze from Hong silenced him.

'I believed you would be doing what you'd done at Andrew Trevor's company: selling code you'd written based on his copyrights to third parties.'

So that was Trevor's leverage over Linn: this theft.

'It was nothing,' Linn said. 'Really. It was code that was just easier for me to write. Anybody could have done it.'

'But *anybody* didn't. You did. I've always been aware that you might be willing to sell me up the river.' Hong frowned. 'Is it 'up the river' or 'down the river'?'

'Down the river,' Shaw said. 'From the slave

377

trade. New Orleans. Up the river is something else.'

'Ah.' A look of satisfaction from learning a new fact. 'Today, your transgression wasn't theft of copyrighted material. But it was a betrayal. So your career with HSE is now terminated.'

'No!'

'Since there was the blush of good cause in this whole matter, I will not do what I first thought: to make certain you never work in the tech world again.'

Linn's eyes widened. Tears glistened. 'Will you give me a month? Just to give me a chance to find something new. Please?'

Hong's steadfast face registered a splinter of disbelief. He glanced at Ms. Towne, who had a hand on her burgeoning stomach. She nodded. Hong continued: 'Your office has already been cleaned out and your personal effects are in a van on the way to your house in Sunnyvale. They'll be left on your back porch, so you'll want to get there straightaway. After you leave my office, you'll be escorted to your car and shown off the grounds.'

'My mortgage . . . I'm already overdue.'

Shaw began to speak. Hong lowered his head and said, 'Please, Mr. Shaw. You knew this was a possibility, didn't you?'

He'd put it about twenty percent.

'Since this incident has had a happy ending and I have lost no secrets or been the victim of sabotage, I'm inclined to help you out, Mr. Shaw. Thinking that this Mr. Thompson, your blogger, was going to expose some secret in the data-mining world, a secret worth killing for? That's infinitely unlikely. Stealing one's data? Everyone these days soaks up your data as if using a sponge. The boy making your submarine sandwich at the local franchise, your car repair garage, your coffee shop, your pharmacy, your internet browser — and I'm not even up to credit rating companies, insurers and your doctors. Data is the new oxygen. It's everywhere. And what happens with an abundance of any product? Its value diminishes. No one would murder for it. You should look elsewhere for your kidnapper. Now, good day.'

He picked up a pencil, examined the tip with approval and pulled an overturned document toward him. He said to himself, 'Up the river, down the river.' Another nod.

Hong waited until Shaw and Linn were at the door and could not read the words before turning the sheet faceup.

# 59

Shaw and Standish were in Joint Major Crimes Task Force Annex No. 1.

The Quick Byte Café.

Standish hung up her phone. 'Hong. And the company. Clean as a whistle. Homeland Security, the Bureau, DoD.'

'The Santa Clara County Middle School Board of Supervisors too.'

'The . . . ' Frowning, Standish cast a quick glance. 'Oh. A joke. You don't joke much, Shaw. Well, no. You do. You just don't smile, so it's hard to tell.'

She tossed down her pen, with which she'd been recording the results of her calls — doodling, really. She toyed with the heart-shaped earring. 'I've got to say, we've struck out a few times here. Knight. Hong-Sung. You don't seem as upset as I thought you'd be.'

'Struck out?' Shaw was confused. 'Knight got us to Avon. Hong Wei gave us the idea that Thompson probably wasn't killed because of the data-mining story.'

Her phone hummed. And from the timbre of her voice when she spoke, he knew it was her partner, Karen.

Shaw pulled out his laptop, logged on and ran through the local news feeds once more. His notebook was ready. Of the stories he skimmed, none were relevant to Elizabeth Chabelle's kidnapping.

There is a little-discussed aspect of survivalism that some people call destiny and some call fate and some, the more earthbound, call coincidence. You're in a bad way. There is no solution to the crisis you face, one that seems certain to kill you or de-toe you, say, thanks to frostbite.

But then? You survive. With your ten little appendages intact.

Because someone or something intervenes.

Colter Shaw himself learned of this concept when he was on a survival run, alone, in December. Fourteen years old. His father had driven him to a remote corner of the Compound and let him out of the truck, to make his way back over the course of two days. He had everything he needed: food, matches, maps, compass, sleeping bag, weapon. The sky was blue, the weather cold yet above freezing, the trek that lay ahead unchallenging and through spectacular scenery.

An hour later, he was crossing a fast-moving stream on a fallen oak that would have been a solid bridge had it not been a host to termites and carpenter bees, who'd been dining on its insides for years. In he went.

Gasping from the cold, Colter scrabbled up the stream bank, shivering fiercely.

He didn't panic; he assessed. The matches, in a waterproof container, and the knife were on him. He'd had to jettison the backpack when it dragged deep below the surface. He gathered leaves and cut pine boughs and soon had a fire going. In forty minutes or so his core temperature was stable. But he was ten miles from the Compound, now without his compass or map or pistol, and by the time he was safely warm and his clothes and boots dry it would be too late to hike. He needed to spend the time until nightfall building a lean-to big enough to take the fire inside; the air smelled like rain.

This he did. And while it was still light enough to see, Colter watched squirrels as they searched for nuts they'd hoarded. He followed only the gray squirrels; the reds don't bury. He found several stashes in abandoned burrows and collected walnuts; acorns are edible yet too bitter to eat without boiling to remove the tannins. He drank stream water and ate and fell asleep confident the trails he'd spotted before the dunking would lead him in the general direction of the Compound.

He woke up about six hours later to the blizzard. Two feet of snow was on the ground.

Colter's head had sunk with despair. The snow covered the trails he'd noted yesterday. He had four walnuts left.

Would he die here?

As he surveyed the rolling white landscape, he noticed something beside the lean-to: a large orange backpack. He yanked it inside and, with trembling fingers, opened the zipper. It contained energy bars, a wire saw, extra matches, a map and a compass, a thermal sleeping bag. Also: a weapon — the Colt Python .357 that he carried still. The gun that was his father's pride.

Ashton Shaw had not returned to the cabin after dropping Colter off. He'd been following the boy all along.

*Intervention . . .*

Which is what happened now.

Shaw's phone hummed. It was the toy man, Marty Avon.

'We still have a way to go with the proxies. For what it's worth, one of the subscribers logged on a few hours ago without turning on his VPN — his proxy, you know. His real IP address popped up. He fit our criteria about being an obsessive player but had been offline when the crimes occurred. We traced him to a house in Mountain View.'

'May have something,' he told the detective. 'It's Marty.'

Standish disconnected her personal call and took the phone and had a brief conversation, at the conclusion of which she gave Avon her email address. It was only a moment after they disconnected that the detective's phone chimed. She read: 'I'll DMV him and see what our databases have to say.' She typed: 'Okay. Forwarded.'

They sat in silence for a moment. Shaw looked around the café, focusing on the computer history wall. Mario the plumber and Sonic the hedgehog. Hewlett and Packard. ENIAC, an ancient computer as big as a semitruck. Then his eyes took in the front door of the café and he recalled seeing Maddie Poole for the first time as she walked inside, twining her red hair around a finger.

*So. You're wondering, what's up with stalker chick . . .*

Standish's phone sang out once more.

The detective read quickly. 'His name is Brad Hendricks. No warrants, no arrests. He was detained frequently in high school. Bullying incidents. Don't know which end of it he was on. No charges filed. Here he is.'

He glanced down and must have stiffened.

'What is it, Shaw?'

'I've seen him.'

It was the boy in the red-and-black-checked shirt who'd been so harshly rejected by the pretty girl right here in the Quick Byte Café, two tables away from where Shaw and Standish now sat.

# 60

Brad Hendricks, nineteen, was attending community college part-time and lived with his parents in a lower-income area of Mountain View. He also worked in a computer repair shop about fifteen hours a week. In the high school fights Brad had been the one bullied and had then ambushed several of his tormenters. Bones had not been broken and noses were only slightly bloodied. All parties being in the wrong, the parents had chosen to let the matters go without police intervention. Brad played *The Whispering Man* and other Destiny Entertainment games forty or so hours a week — and presumably spent many hours at other companies' games too. He had minimal social media presence, apparently preferring gaming to posting on Facebook, Instagram or Twitter.

LaDonna Standish had started canvassing in the Quick Byte, displaying the picture of the young man, who'd been there earlier in the day and was not present at the moment.

Shaw was presently pursuing a related lead: browsing Santa Clara County and California State records — using Standish's secure log-in. What he learned — and it was quite interesting — he recorded in one of his case notebooks.

He sat back, staring at the now-blank screen.

'What?' Standish said as she joined him. 'You're looking like the cat that got the cream.'

Shaw asked, 'Doesn't the cat get the canary?'

'Cream sounds better than a dead bird. Brad hasn't been here since you saw him earlier.' She went on to explain that none of the patrons now in the café knew him. A few recalled seeing him have the fight with the young woman he claimed he'd met online but couldn't remember seeing him before that.

Standish was tucking something into her wallet. She said to Shaw, 'Took a liking to me 'cause I'm a cop.'

'Who?'

'Tiffany. I'm now a lifetime member of the QB Koffee Discount Klub. You're one too, aren't you?'

'Invite's in the mail, I guess.'

'Work it. She's sweet on you, you know.'

Shaw didn't reply.

Standish's face grew solemn. 'So. We're talking cream and cat . . . What'd you come up with, Shaw? There any chance to save Elizabeth?'

'Maybe.'

★　★　★

Shaw parked on a street of old houses, probably built not long after World War II.

Cinder block and wood frame. Solid. He wondered if that was because of earthquake danger. Then decided: No, there wouldn't have been that much forethought put into these children's toy blocks of homes. Plop 'em down and sell 'em. Move on.

This was a different Mountain View from

where the rich lived. Different from even Frank Mulliner's place. Not as dingy as East Palo Alto but plenty grim and shabby. The persistent hiss of the 101 filled the air, which was aromatic with exhaust.

The yards, which would be measured in feet, not acreage, were mostly untended. Weeds and patches of yellowing grass and sandy scabs. No gardens. Money for watering the landscape — always expensive in the state of California — had gone for necessities and the crushing taxes and mortgage payments.

He thought of Marty Avon and his dream, Siliconville, recalling what he'd just read online a half hour ago.

*For decades, Silicon Valley has always looked for the 'Next Big Thing' — the internet, http protocol, faster processors, larger storage, mobile phones, routers, browser search engines. That search goes on and always will. The message that everybody has missed in the Valley: Real Estate is the true Next Big Thing . . .*

The house Shaw focused on was typical of the bungalows here. Green paint touched up with a slightly different shade, stains descending from the roof along the siding like rusty tears, discarded boxes and pipes and plastic containers, rotting cardboard, a pile of newspaper mush.

An ancient half-ton pickup sat in the driveway, the color sun-faded red. It listed to the right from shocks that had long ago lost enthusiasm.

Shaw climbed out and was walking toward the door when it opened. A burly man, balding and in gray dungaree slacks and a white T-shirt, approached. Looking at Shaw ominously, he strode forward and stopped a few feet away. He was about six-two. Shaw could smell sweat and onion.

'Yeah?' the man snapped.

'Mr. Hendricks?'

'I asked what you wanted.'

'I'd just like a few minutes of your time.'

'If you're repo, that's bullshit. I'm only two months behind.' He nodded toward the junker.

'I'm not here to repossess your truck.'

The man processed, looking up and down the street. And at Shaw's car. 'I'm Minnetti. My wife's name was Hendricks.'

'Brad's your son?' Shaw asked.

'Stepson. What's he done now?'

'I'd like to talk to you about him.'

'Brad ain't here. Supposed t'be in school.'

'He is in school. I checked. I want to talk to you.'

The big man's eyes went squinty. 'You're not a cop. You'd've said so. They gotta do that; it's the law. So what's the little shit done now? He can't've fucked your little sister. Not unless she's a computer.' He grimaced. 'Over the line. About your sister. Sorry. He owe you money?'

'No.'

He sized Shaw up. 'He couldn'ta beat you up or anything. Not that boy.'

'I just have a few questions.'

'Why should I tell you anything about Brad?'

388

'I've got a proposition for you. Let's go inside.'

Shaw walked past Brad's stepfather toward the front door. There, Shaw paused, looking back. The man slowly walked toward him.

The air within the bungalow was heavy with the scent of mold and cat pee and pot. If Frank Mulliner's décor was a C, this was a grade below. All the furniture was shabby and couch and chairs indented with the impression of bodies sitting for long periods on the ratty cushions. Cups and plates encrusted with food sat stacked on the coffee and end tables. At the end of a corridor, Shaw believed he saw the fast passage of a heavyset woman in a yellow housedress. He guessed it was Brad Hendricks's mother, startled that her husband had let an unexpected visitor into the home.

'So? Proposition?'

No offer to sit.

Didn't matter. Shaw wouldn't be here very long. 'I want to see your son's room.'

'I don't know why I should help you. Whoever the fuck you are.'

The woman's face — a round pale moon — peered out. Below the double chin was the burning orange dot of a cigarette tip.

Shaw reached into his pocket and extracted five hundred dollars in twenties. He held it out to the man. He stared at the cash.

'He doesn't like anybody to go down there.'

This wasn't a time for bargaining. He glanced at the man, his meaning clear: take it or leave it.

Brad's stepfather looked into the hallway — the woman had disappeared again — and he snatched the bills from Shaw's hand and stuffed them into his pocket. He nodded to a door near the cluttered, grimy kitchen.

'Spends every minute down there. Fucking games're his whole life. I'd had three girlfriends, the time I was his age. I tried him on sports, wasn't interested. Suggested the Army. Ha! Figure how that went. You know what me and the wife call him? The Turtle. 'Cause every time he gets outside, he goes into this shell. Closes down. Fucking games did that. We took the washer and dryer and moved 'em to the garage. He wouldn't let Beth go down there for laundry. Sometimes I think it's booby-trapped. You be careful, mister.'

The unspoken adjunct to that sentence was: I don't want the inconvenience of having to call the police if you touch something that blows your hand off.

Shaw walked past him, opened the door and descended into the basement.

The room was dim and it seemed to be the source of the mold stench, which stung Shaw's eyes and nose. Also present was the scent of damp stone and of heating oil, unique among petrochemical products. Once smelled, never forgotten. The place was cluttered with boxes, piles of clothing, broken chairs and scuffed tables. And countless electronics. Shaw paused halfway down the creaky stairs.

The center of the room was a computer workstation, featuring a huge screen and keyboard and a complicated trackball. He recalled what Maddie had told him about those who had preferences for playing on computers, versus those who liked consoles, but Brad also had three Nintendo units, beside which were cartridges of Mario Brothers games.

Nintendo.

*A shrine to the chivalrous who protect the weak. I like that one better . . .*

Ah, Maddie . . .

A half dozen computer keyboards lay in the corner, many of the letters, numbers and symbols worn away, some keys missing altogether. Why didn't he throw them out?

Shaw continued down the uneasy stairs. Nails were needed in three, maybe four, places to keep the structure safe. Some boards sagged with rot. Shaw clocked in at about one hundred and eighty pounds. Brad's stepfather was clearly two hundred and fifty or more. He presumably didn't come down here much.

The cinder-block walls were unevenly painted and gray stone showed through the swaths of white and cream. Posters of video games were the only decorations. One was of *The Whispering Man*. The pale face, the black suit, the hat from a different era.

*You've been abandoned. Escape if you can. Or die with dignity.*

There was a flowchart on the wall — measuring three by four feet. In handwriting as small as Shaw's yet much more careless, Brad had detailed his progress through the levels of *The Whispering Man*, jotting hundreds of notes about tactics and workarounds and cheats. He'd gotten as far as Level 9. The top of the chart,

Level 10, Hell, was blank. The level no one had ever attained, in the history of the game, Shaw recalled.

A sagging mattress sat on the box spring, with no frame. The bed was unmade. Empty plates of food and cans and bottles of soft drinks sat near the pillow. A stack of music CDs rested beside a decades-old boom box. All the boy's disposable income went into gaming gear, it seemed.

Shaw sat in Brad's chair and watched the screen saver, a dragon flying in circles. He followed the hypnotic motion for a full three minutes. Then he pulled out his phone and made two calls. The first was to LaDonna Standish. The second was to Washington, D.C.

# 61

'I mean, people want to come here? For the fun of it?'

Colter Shaw and LaDonna Standish walked through the chaos of the C3 Conference. Shaw carried a backpack over his shoulder. A woman security guard at the entrance had examined the contents carefully, using what looked like large chopsticks to probe. Standish's gold shield had not exempted him.

The detective's head was swiveling, left to right, then back, then up, to take in the huge high-def screens.

'I got a headache already.'

As before, there were a hundred different blaring sounds: spaceship engines, alien cries, machine guns, ray blasters . . . and the never-ending electronic soundtracks with the ultra-bass pedal tones that seemed to exist unrelated to any game. It was as if the conference organizers were worried that a few seconds of silence might creep in like mice in a bakery.

Shaw shouted, 'We're not even in the loudest part.'

They dodged their way through the crowds of intense youngsters, passing by the Hong-Sung booth.

HSE PRESENTS

*IMMERSION*

THE NEW MOVEMENT IN VIDEO GAMING

Shaw glanced at the queue of excited attendees, goggles in hand.

He didn't see Maddie Poole.

Standish called, 'I'm going to tell you one thing, Shaw. Our daughters are not getting involved in this game shit.'

He wondered what games would be available when Gem and Sefina were old enough to play. Wondered too how on earth Standish and Karen would keep them from the console controller or the keyboard.

In a few minutes they came to the Knight Time Gaming booth, where Tony Knight's developer, Jimmy Foyle, greeted them at the entrance.

He shook Shaw's hand and, after introductions, Standish's.

'Let's go inside,' Foyle said, nodding them in.

They followed him into the working area of the booth, where Shaw had met with Knight and Foyle the day before. The three sat at the conference table. Foyle pushed aside promotional materials for the new installment of *Conundrum*. Three employees sat at the three computer stations. Shaw couldn't tell if they were the same ones as before; all Knight Gaming workers were oddly identical.

The detective said to Foyle, 'It was your idea how to find the subscriber to *The Whispering Man*, the one who's a suspect. We really appreciate it.'

'I had some thoughts, that's all,' Foyle said modestly. He was as shy as the other day. Shaw remembered the press described him as a 'backroom kind of guy.'

Shaw had called earlier and told him there'd been another kidnapping and that they had a suspect, could he help once again? He'd agreed.

Shaw now explained about Brad Hendricks.

Standish added, 'We think it's him but we're not sure. There's no grounds for a warrant . . . ' She looked to Shaw.

'Brad lives at home with his parents,' Shaw said. 'I went to see them — he's in class now. I . . . convinced his stepfather to help us.'

The game designer asked, 'Turning against his own stepson?'

'For five hundred dollars. Yes.'

Foyle's brow furrowed.

'He let me take all of this.' Shaw hefted the backpack onto the table. Foyle peered inside at the scores of external drives, disks, thumb drives, SD cards, CDs and DVDs, along with papers, Post-it notes, pencils and pens, rolls of candy. 'I just scooped up what was on the boy's desk.'

Standish said, 'We looked through some of it. The drives and cards we could figure out how to plug in. All we got was gibberish.'

'You need somebody to decrypt it,' Foyle said, 'and you can't go to your own Computer Crimes people because you can't get a warrant.'

'Exactly.'

'Because what you're doing is . . . '

'Irregular.' Standish leaned forward and said evenly, 'We'll lose the chance to present any evidence we recover in court. But I don't care about that. All that matters is saving the victim.'

Foyle asked, 'If he's following *The Whispering*

*Man* gameplay, what level would it be?'

'The Sinking Ship.'

Foyle winced. 'Around here? Hundreds of tankers and container-ships, a lot of them have to be abandoned. Fisherman's Wharf, Marin. Pleasure boats everywhere . . . '

Shaw said, 'Your *Conundrum*'s an ARG, alternate reality game. Marty Avon told us that it only works because your servers're super-computers.'

'That's right.'

'Can you use them to break the passcodes?'

'I can try.' The man peered into the backpack. 'SATA drives, three-and-a-halfers without enclosures, SDs . . . thumb drives. Some he's made on his own. I don't recognize them.' He looked up, his eyes eager at the idea of a challenge, it seemed. 'You know, I might find a symmetric back door. And if he uses first-gen DES, then anyone can crack that.'

Shaw and Standish regarded each other, exceptions to the 'anyone' rule.

'If that's the case, I could have readable text or graphics in hours. Minutes, maybe.'

Standish eyed her phone for the time. 'Brad Hendricks's going to be out of class soon. Colter and I are going to follow him. He might lead us to Elizabeth. If he's just left her to die, though, you're the only hope.'

# 62

A half hour later, LaDonna Standish was piloting her Nissan Altima along an increasingly deserted region of western Santa Clara County, keeping a safe distance behind the car they were following.

Shaw texted Jimmy Foyle:

Brad Hendricks is on the road — not going home. Colton and I are following. Maybe on way to kidnap site but can't tell. Success with encryption?

A moment later the game designer texted back.

First SATA drive, can't crack. He used 2-fish algorithm. Working on SD cards now.

Shaw read this to her.

Standish gave a wry laugh. 'Two-fish. Computer stuff. Who comes up with those names? Why Apple? Why Macintosh?'

'Google makes sense to me.'

A glance his way. 'You gotta smile sometime, Shaw. It's like a contest now. I'm going to make it happen.' She steered the Nissan around two more turns, then slowed at the top of a hill, keeping far enough back so they wouldn't be spotted in the rearview mirrors.

In the distance was the hazy blue of the Pacific Ocean. From here, it lived up to its name.

'And our backup?' Shaw asked.

A glance at her phone. 'Nothing yet.'

Both Shaw and Standish had understood they couldn't request tactical backup from the California Bureau of Investigation, given their 'renegade' investigation. They'd be closed down in an instant or would have to talk their way up through the ranks to find someone senior to support them. No time for that. Standish had sent some texts, to see if she might 'improvise' backup. Apparently with no success. She sent another message.

Shaw opened *The Whispering Man* gameplay booklet that Maddie Poole had bought for him. He was skimming to look for anything to help them when — if — they found where Elizabeth Chabelle had been abandoned.

### *Level 3: The Sinking Ship.*

*You've been abandoned on a Forrest Sherman-class destroyer, the USS Scorpion, which has been struck by an enemy torpedo and is sinking in shark-infested waters, a hundred miles from land. You're in a cabin with a bottle of water, a cotton handkerchief, a double-sided razor blade, an acetylene torch and a container of engine lubricant.*

*There are a number of crew members on the vessel and only one life raft remaining, hidden on board. You must find the raft before the ship goes under.*

*Gameplay clues:*

1. The more members of the crew who die, the more resources will be left for the others.

2. The ship is rumored to be haunted by the ghosts of the crew of a World War II destroyer, also named the Scorpion, that went down in 1945. A ghost can achieve his final rest by taking the life of a sailor on your vessel.

3. There is something large cruising nearby underwater. It might be a megashark — or might be a submarine, though whether it's friendly or enemy is not known. The radio gear on the Scorpion was destroyed by the torpedo strike.

You've been abandoned. Escape if you can. Or die with dignity.

Shaw read Maddie Poole's margin notes: In the chapter on Level 3, The Sinking Ship, she'd written: More stabbings on this level than the others. Knives, razors? Gasoline too. Look out for flares.

He spotted a passage in the front:

CS:

You game.
I game.
We both game . . .

# Xo,
# MP

Standish asked, 'Shaw?'

He set the booklet down.

She continued: 'Got a question. Your impression? Brad Hendricks's homelife? His parents?'

'Bad, *A* to *Z*. A stepfather happy to sell the boy out even before he knew the facts. Mom, all but comatose in an armchair, watching TV. Smell of pot in the air. The way she looked at her husband, you couldn't help seeing *bad choice* written in her eyes. Couldn't tell about physical abuse. Probably not. The house was a mess.'

'That's why he gets lost in the games. His social life is make-believe.'

*The Turtle* . . .

The route was taking them through increasingly deserted hills and forest. The road was serpentine, working to their advantage. They were hidden from view by trees and brush but were able to follow glints of chrome and glass ahead of them.

'You have your weapon?'

'I do.'

'Don't shoot him, okay?' Standish said. 'The paperwork for something like that . . . ' She clicked her tongue.

'You've got a sense of humor too.'

'I wasn't being funny.'

Ahead of them, the car turned onto a dirt road.

Standish braked and they consulted the GPS. The unnamed road ended about two miles ahead, at the ocean. There was no other exit. She drove on, remaining some distance behind now yet not too far. It was a balance. They couldn't take him too early; he had to lead them to Chabelle. They couldn't lag too much either, because he was here to kill the woman and they'd have to move in fast.

At ten miles per hour, they rocked along the unsteady road.

'I'm going to see about starting a new division.'

'In the Task Force?'

She nodded. 'It's a different kind of street in SV, different from EPA and Oakland. But it's still street. Look at Brad. I want to get to kids like him early. So they have a chance. I can do just what I did back in the 'hood. Talk to the parents, teachers. It puts a frame around the kids, people see them differently, for the first time.'

'Were you in a crew, Standish?' Shaw asked.

A smile on her face as she tugged on the heart earring. 'A mascot. I was a mascot.' A laugh. 'My daddy, badass. Frankie Williamson. You can look him up. Oh, Lord, that man was a tough one. At home, he was the best father you could want. All of us kids, he took care of us. I'll show you pictures sometime. His crew'd come around and bring us stuff.' She shook her head, nostalgic. 'In the den they'd do their business, exchange the envelopes — you know what I'm saying? With us, they brought us Legos and board games. Cabbage Patch dolls! I was thirteen and had a crush on Devon Brown you wouldn't believe and Daddy's crew was giving me dolls! They were all so proud, though, so of course I made a fuss.

Why, I've got pictures of me sitting on the knee of Dayan Cabel. The hitman? That boy'll never see the outside of San Quentin in twenty lifetimes.

'I'm going to start that program. It's in the works. Street Welfare Education and Excellence Program. SWEEP.'

'Like it.'

She watched the dust trail of the car ahead of them settle. 'This is weird crime, Shaw, fantasy crime. Like the Zodiac, Son of Sam. I don't want fantasy anymore. Helping kids stay alive. That's real. How about you, Shaw? You run with a crew? I could see you in a black leather jacket, smoking behind the gym.'

'Homeschooled with my brother and sister.'

'You're kidding.' She then nodded out the windshield. 'Road ends up there. We can't go any farther; he'll see us.' Standish steered into a stand of trees and cut the engine.

They climbed out and, without communicating, both left the doors open for the silence. They started forward on ground that Shaw pointed toward: pine needles. They moved about thirty feet into the dunes and crouched not far from the car they'd been pursuing.

A moment later the driver climbed out, the man Shaw and Standish had concluded two hours ago at the Quick Byte was the Gamer: not Brad Hendricks at all but the brilliant if shy game designer Jimmy Foyle.

# 63

Silhouetted against a haze-dulled sun, Foyle turned toward the ocean and stretched.

Shaw and Standish eased lower into the congregation of brush and yellow grass. The man would undoubtedly be armed with the Glock with which he'd killed Kyle Butler and Henry Thompson, though at the moment he held only his key fob in one hand and, in the other, a small bag. Inside the sack would be some of the items from the backpack Shaw had given him — the detritus from Brad's gaming station desk in the family's pungent, dank basement. Pens, batteries, Post-it notes.

Foyle had returned here, to the place where he'd stashed Elizabeth Chabelle, as Shaw had anticipated, to plant these things as evidence implicating the innocent boy; they'd have his fingerprints and DNA on them.

The kidnapper's next step, Shaw was sure, would be to head straight to the Hendrickses' house and hide the murder weapon in the backyard or garage. He'd then call in an anonymous tip as to where Elizabeth Chabelle was, giving a description of Brad, maybe a partial tag number of his car. The police would find her body and the evidence here, which would eventually lead to the family house.

This had been a gamble on Shaw's part but a rational one, a sixty or seventy percent one. He concluded that Brad Hendricks was innocent and that it was Jimmy Foyle who was the Gamer, so he'd set up the trap, pretending to enlist his help in the decryption, hoping he'd the take the bait: the contents of the backpack.

It was Foyle, whom Shaw and Standish had just been following, texting the man occasionally to make him believe they were elsewhere tailing Brad Hendricks.

And where was the sinking ship?

Foyle walked between two dunes and disappeared.

Shaw nodded in that direction and he and Standish rose and followed. At the crest of a dune they crouched, looking down at an old pier that jutted fifty feet into the choppy Pacific. Midway along it was an ancient fishing boat, half sunk.

'Your armor snug, Shaw?'
They were both in bulletproof vests. He nodded.

'You know how to cuff somebody?'

'I can. Better with restraints.'

Standish handed him two zip ties. 'I'll cover him. You get his weapon and get his hands.' She drew her Glock, rose and walked forward silently to the sand. Twenty feet from Foyle, she raised her weapon and aimed. 'Jimmy Foyle! Police. Don't move. Hands in the air.'

Foyle jerked to a stop, turning slowly.

'Drop the bag. Hands up.'

Shocked, he stared their way. Dismay flooded his face.

'Drop the bag!'

He did and lifted his hands as he looked from Shaw to Standish and back to Shaw, no doubt understanding how this had come together. The great computer game strategist had been outplayed. Bewilderment morphed to anger.

'Get on your knees. Knees! Now!'

Just then, from behind them, came the blaring sound of a car horn.

Shaw realized then that the key fob was still in Foyle's hand. He'd hit the panic button.

Instinctively, the detective started to turn at the sound.

'Standish, no!' Shaw shouted.

Foyle crouched and drew his Glock. A series of ragged flashes sprouted from his right hand. Standish gave a high yelp as slugs tore into her body.

# 64

Shaw dove for her, squinting against the sand spitting into the air from Foyle's gunshots.

He drew his own Glock, raising the weapon in both hands, steadying it, scanning for a target.

Foyle had circled to the left, sprinting flat out through the trees, and Shaw had no clear shot. Foyle's car started up and sped away.

Shaw returned to Standish, who was writhing in agony. 'Okay, they don't teach you this shit. Hurt, hurts.'

He assessed the damage: Two slugs had hit the vest. She'd taken one in the forearm, which had nicked the suicide vein, and one low in the belly.

Shaw slipped his gun into his jacket pocket and put pressure on the wounds, saying, 'Had to be sensitive, didn't you, Standish? Couldn't shoot a man armed with a BMW key fob?'

'Get to the boat, Shaw. If Elizabeth's still . . . Go!' A gasp.

'This's going to hurt.'

He put pressure on Standish's abdominal wound, pulled her locking knife from its holder and, gripping the blade, used the weight of the handle to flick it open, one-handed. He lifted his bloody palm away from the wound only long enough to cut a strip of his shirt-tail and tie a tourniquet. This went around her biceps. He used a branch to tighten the cloth. The fierce bleeding in Standish's shattered lower arm slowed. He closed the blade and slipped the knife into his pocket.

'Hurt, hurts . . . ' Standish repeated, gasping. 'Call it in, Shaw. Don't let him get too far.'

'I will. Almost there.'

There wasn't much to do with the gut shot, except pressure. He gathered some leaves and placed them on the wound and then found a rock that weighed about five pounds. He set this on top. Standish groaned in pain, arched her back.

'No. Stay still. I know it's tough, but you've got to stay still.'

He wiped his hands on his jacket and slacks so he could use his phone. He dialed.

'Police and fire emergency. What's — '

'Code 13. Officer shot,' Standish said weakly.

He repeated this, then looked at his GPS and gave the longitude and latitude.

'What's your name, sir?'

'Colter Shaw. Supervisor Cummings at the JMCTF'll know me. Armed suspect. Fleeing from location I gave you. Might be headed east in white late-model BMW, California plate, first numbers 9-7-8. Didn't get the rest. Suspect is Jimmy Foyle, employed by Knight Time Gaming. Wounded officer is Detective LaDonna Standish, also with the Task Force.'

The dispatcher was asking more questions. Shaw ignored her. He left the line open and set the iPhone next to Standish. Her eyes were dim, lids low.

Shaw released the tourniquet for a moment. Then tightened it again. He pulled a pen from

Standish's breast pocket and wrote on her wrist, slightly lighter than the ink, the time he'd twisted it tight. It would let the med techs know that it had been binding the arm for some time and that they should relax it to get blood circulating, to minimize the risk she'd lose the arm.

No words passed between them. There was nothing to say. He set the pistol next to the phone, though it was clear the woman would be unconscious in a few minutes.

And probably dead before help arrived. Yet leave her he had to.

He pulled off his jacket and vest and covered her with them, then stood. Then:

Sprinting toward the sea, Colter Shaw eyed the craft closely.

The forty-foot derelict fishing vessel, decades old, was going down by the stern, already three-fourths submerged.

Shaw saw no doors into the cabin; there would be only one and it was now underwater. In the aft part of the superstructure, still above sea level, was a window facing onto the bow. The opening was large enough to climb through but it appeared sealed. He'd dive for the door.

He paused, reflecting: Did he need to?

Shaw looked for the rope mooring the boat to the pier; maybe he could take up slack and keep the ship from going under.

There was no rope; the boat was anchored, which meant it was free to descend thirty feet to the floor of the Pacific Ocean.

And, if the woman was inside, take her with it to a cold, murky grave.

As he ran onto the slippery dock, avoiding the most rotten pieces, he stripped off his blood-stained shirt, then his shoes and socks.

A powerful swell struck the ship and it shuddered and sank a few more inches into the gray, indifferent water.

He shouted, 'Elizabeth?'

No response.

Shaw assessed: there was a sixty percent chance she was on board. Fifty percent chance she was alive after hours in the waterlogged cabin.

Whatever the percentages, there was no debate about what came next. He stuck an arm beneath the surface and judged the temperature to be about forty degrees. He'd have thirty minutes until he passed out from hypothermia.

Let's start the clock, he thought.

And plunged in.

# 65

'Please. Save yourself.'

Twenty minutes later Colter Shaw was inside the sinking ship's cabin, at the bulkhead door separating him from Elizabeth Chabelle. With the flowerpot shard, he continued to try to chip away the wood around the hinges.

'You with me, Elizabeth?' Shaw called.

The *Seas the Day* settled further. The water was now streaming in through the gap in the front of the cabin. Soon it would be cascading in.

'My baby . . . ' She was sobbing.

'Keep it together. Need you to. Okay?'

She nodded. 'You're nah . . . nah . . . not police?'

'No.'

'The . . . then . . . ?'

'Boy or girl?'

'Wha . . . what-t-t?'

'Baby. Boy or girl?'

'Girl.'

'You have a name for her?'

'Buh . . . Buh . . . Belinda.'

'Don't hear that much.

'You need to get as high as you can on the bunk.'

'And your . . . ?' Whispering. 'Name?'

'Colter.'

'Don't . . . Don't hear that much.' She smiled. Then began to cry again. 'You . . . you

'. . . you've done everything you . . . you can. Get
. . . out. You have a family. Get out. Thank you.
Bless you. Get out.'

'Farther, climb farther! Do it, Elizabeth.
George wants to see you. Your mom and dad in
Miami. Stone crabs, remember?'

Shaw squeezed her hand and she did as he'd
asked, paddling to the bunk and climbing it. He
tossed away the useless ceramic shard.

Time left on the hypothermia clock? It
would've run out. Of course.

'Go!' she called. 'Get out!'

Just then gray water, flecked with kelp, poured
into the forward cabin through the gap where the
window had been.

'Go! Puh . . . Please . . . '

*Die with dignity . . .*

Shaw scrabbled to the front window frame
and, with a look back toward Chabelle, vaulted
through and outside, into the ocean. Dizzy from
the cold, disoriented.

A wave hit the boat, the boat hit him, and
Shaw was shoved again toward a pylon. His foot
found a deck railing and he pushed himself out
of the way just before he was crushed.

He heard, he believed, Chabelle's sobs.

Hallucination?

Yes, no . . .

Shaw turned toward the submerged stern of
the boat and swam hard for it. He'd stopped
shivering, his body saying, That's it. No point in
trying to keep you warm.

With the forward window gone, the water
rushed inside as if flowing through a rent in a

411

broken dam. The ship was going down fast.

When the cabin was almost entirely underwater, Shaw took a deep breath and dove straight down.

At about eight feet below the surface, he held on to a railing and, remembering where the door handle was located, gripped it hard. Bracing his feet on the cabin wall, he slowly extended his legs.

The door resisted, as before. But then, at last, it slowly swung outward.

A gamble of his, paying off. With Sophie, the Gamer had left one door open. The rules of *The Whispering Man* stated there was always a way to escape if you could figure it out.

Here, the only way out was the cabin door. It wasn't sealed with screws; it was held fast by the unequal pressure: water outside, air within. Shaw had speculated that as soon as the water was the same height on the inside as on the outside, it could be wrestled open. And it could.

The transit of the door seemed to take forever. Finally there was enough of a gap for him to kick inside, grab the nearly unconscious Chabelle and pull her out. Together they floated free of the *Seas the Day*, which disappeared beneath them, rolling to the starboard as it sank. The suction following the ship pulled them after it, but only momentarily. Soon they broke again to the surface, both gasping hard.

Shaw, kicking, looked around, orienting himself.

They were still thirty feet from the shore. The pier was five feet above them yet featured no ladder. The pylons, slick and green, couldn't be climbed.

'You with me?' Shaw shouted.

Chabelle spat out water. A cough. A nod. She was very pale.

Kicking to keep them on the surface, Shaw used one hand to fend off the pylons as the indifferent waves shouldered them toward the pier.

The only way out was the shore . . . What he saw wasn't encouraging. The sharp-edged stone — fossil gray — was also covered in the green moss-like growth. There were places where he could get a grip, it seemed, but to get close meant being at the mercy of the ocean, which surged against the rocks. It would fling them against the rocks too, breaking them the way the water itself broke.

'Muh . . . my baby, baby . . . '

'Buh . . . Belinda's going to be just fine. Guh . . . got you out of the *Tuh . . . Titanic*, didn't I?'

'Baby . . . '

Okay. It had to be the rocks. No time left.

As he turned them both toward the shore, Elizabeth Chabelle screamed. 'He's back! He's come back!'

Shaw looked up and saw the silhouette of a figure running toward the pier.

However fast the 911 responders were, they couldn't possibly be here by now, unless via helicopter, and no helicopter was near. It would be Jimmy Foyle. He'd returned to take out witnesses.

Shaw kicked hard, fighting to turn toward the

pier. They'd hide under it and risk the rise and fall of the water, trying to avoid the spikes and nails and sharp barnacles on the pylons.

Once more the cold arms of the ocean didn't cooperate. They kept Shaw and Chabelle nice and centered, six feet away from the pier. A bull's-eye for Jimmy Foyle, who was, Shaw knew very well, a fine shot.

Shaw blinked water from his eyes and looked up . . . to see the figure dropping to his belly on the rotting pier and extending a hand.

Which held not a pistol but something . . . Yes, something cloth, a rope of bulky cloth . . .

'Come on, Shaw, grab it!' The figure was Detective Dan Wiley.

So their backup had made it after all. He was the one Standish had texted for assistance. Since they weren't on the case, they needed someone unofficially, and the only person Standish could think of was the Liaison officer.

After two tries, Shaw managed to grip what Wiley'd lowered.

Ah, clever. Wiley had bound Shaw's jacket and his own together. He'd tied his belt onto the end, like a rescue harness.

'Under her arms!' Wiley shouted. 'The belt.'

While the cop held his end firmly, Shaw worked the belt over Elizabeth Chabelle's head.

The big man pulled her upward. She disappeared onto the top of the dock. The improvised device was lowered again and Wiley tugged while Shaw's feet found some purchase on the pilings. A moment later he too scrabbled onto the pier.

# 66

*Never hesitate to improvise . . .*

Which was, of course, one of the rules in Ashton Shaw's voluminous *Book of Never*.

At the moment, his son Colter was thinking of a more specific variation:

*Never hesitate to use the efficient heater of a dinged-up gray sedan to warm the core temperature of a hypothermia victim.*

Shaw was reflecting that this was a pretty good rule as he sat in LaDonna Standish's Nissan Altima. Parked nearby were eight or nine police cars, representing various agencies, and the ambulance where Elizabeth Chabelle was being examined.

Shaw's shivering had lessened and he turned the heat down some. He was in a change of clothing provided by the Santa Clara Fire Department, a dark blue jumpsuit.

Shaw's bloodstained phone hummed with an email. It was from Mack, his private eye, and was in response to the call he'd made in Brad Hendricks's den just before he'd begun collecting drives and other tidbits from the desk with a tissue.

He read the email carefully.

Hypothesis became theory.

Shaw noted a medical technician stepping from the ambulance and, frowning into the glare, looking around. He spotted Shaw and approached. Shaw climbed out of the Nissan. The tech reported that Chabelle's multiple heartbeats — the one emanating from her chest, the other from her belly — were both strong. The medics had assured her that the amount of drug Foyle had used to sedate her would have no lasting effect on mother or child. Both would be fine.

For LaDonna Standish, however, the same could not be said.

Shaw had steeled himself to the fact that she had died from the terrible wounds. But no. The detective was alive, in critical condition, and had been medevacked to a hospital in Santa Clara, which had a trauma center specializing in gunshot wounds. She'd lost much blood, though Shaw's tourniquet and his jotting down the time had probably saved her life, at least temporarily. The technician told Shaw she was still in surgery.

Dan Wiley was standing near his car, speaking with Ron Cummings, the JMCTF supervisor. Prescott and the unnamed shorter agent from the CBI were present too, but Cummings now was in charge.

Because, Shaw guessed, it was his officer and not theirs who'd found the perp and rescued the victim.

With help from the concerned citizen.

Shaw could see another participant in the festivities. Thirty feet away, Jimmy Foyle sat in the backseat of a police cruiser, head down.

It was Dan Wiley who'd collared him. The detective had been on the narrow road to the beach where Standish had texted him they'd be, when he found Foyle's white BMW speeding toward him.

While the man may have been a lousy

detective, he'd proved he had a cool head under fire. With his unmarked car he'd played a game of chicken, driving Foyle into a ditch. When the game designer leapt out and began firing, blindly, Wiley had simply squatted behind his car, holding yet not firing his weapon until the man's magazine was empty, and then went after him. The tackle must have been a hard one. Foyle showed evidence of a bloody nose and his left hand was deformed by a thick beige elastic bandage. The protruding fingers were purple.

Cummings noted that Shaw had emerged from his hot lodge of a sedan and the supervisor walked his way. Prescott and the other agent started after him. Cummings uttered something and they stopped.

'You okay?' Cummings asked.

A brief nod.

The Task Force commander said, 'Foyle isn't talking. And I'm at sea.'

Some irony in the comment, considering that they were standing thirty yards from the Pacific Ocean, where Shaw and one extremely pregnant woman had nearly drowned.

The setting sun flared atop Cummings's shiny head. 'So?'

Shaw explained, 'Marty Avon told me he'd found someone who fit the perfect profile of the Gamer: Brad Hendricks had been spotted at the Quick Byte Café, he was obsessed with *The Whispering Man* and he was offline when the kidnappings occurred.'

'You thought he was too perfect.' Cummings would not have risen to be Joint Task Force

417

Senior Supervisor Cummings without being shrewd. 'Like he was being set up.'

'Exactly. His proxy was suddenly shut down and his name conveniently appeared. Oh, Brad was worth checking out as a suspect. And I did. I went to see his parents, went through his room. It was a pretty grim place. But I've searched for plenty of missing teenagers and a lot of their rooms are grim too. I noticed something he had on the wall. It was a chart of his progress through *The Whispering Man*. I realized it was the *game* Brad was obsessed with. Not the violence the game represented.

'That kid had absolutely no desire to get out into the real world — and, frankly, do much of anything, let alone go to the trouble to kidnap anybody.'

*The Turtle . . .*

'So I settled on the idea he was most likely innocent. Somebody wanted him to take the fall for killing Henry Thompson. Who? I looked at what Thompson was blogging. We'd already considered the data-mining blog. That turned out to be unlikely. I also considered his story about the high cost of property and rentals in Silicon Valley.'

A scowl. 'Real estate here? Tell me about it.'

'Marty Avon created a syndicate to buy up property and create low-cost housing for work-ers. Was the syndicate guilty of kickbacks or bribes? Was Thompson onto them? I used LaDon-na's account to get into the county and state databases. Avon's syndicate is nonprofit. None of the principals will make a penny on it. There was

418

nothing for Thompson to expose there. Maybe he'd come across another real estate scam but I didn't have any leads there.

'Then I stepped back. I thought about how we got onto Brad Hendricks in the first place. Jimmy Foyle. I remembered that Marty Avon — with Destiny Entertainment — told us that game companies' databases could be hacked easily. Foyle was a talented white hat hacker.'

Cummings shook his head and Shaw explained what the term meant.

'I guessed he hacked *The Whispering Man* server and changed Brad's log-in times to make it look like he was out when the crimes occurred. Brad was at the Quick Byte recently, which would link him to Sophie, but nobody'd seen him before. He'd gotten a text from a young woman who said she wanted to meet him there. I'm sure it was Foyle pretending to be her so people would spot Brad, associate him with the café. Then today, since he'd done what he needed to — kill Thompson — he shut off Brad's proxy and we got his address.'

'But why kill Thompson?'

'Because his blog about a new revenue source for software companies was going to expose what was really going on.'

'What was that?'

'Tony Knight and Jimmy Foyle were using their games to spread false news stories for profit.'

# 67

Shaw said to Cummings, 'Earlier, my private eye opened a subscription to the video game *Conundrum.*'

He explained that he'd asked Mack to go back and look over broadcasts that appeared in the few minutes before the game loaded. The PI found a number of stories in those broadcasts that were blatantly false, spreading rumors about businesspeople and politicians.

Shaw lifted his phone and paraphrased Mack's notes about several stories that he himself remembered from the past few days: 'Congressman Richard Boyd, suicide because of rumors of texting young gay prostitutes. No reports of such activity prior to the 'story' appearing in Knight's game. Boyd's wife had just died and he was reported by family members to be in unstable condition. His death may throw the balance of power in Congress up in the air.

'Arnold Farrow, CEO of Intelligraph Systems, Portland, was forced to step down after rumors he spoke favorably about interring Japanese American citizens during the Second World War. No reports of such incident prior to the story appearing in Knight's game.

'Thomas Stone, Green Party candidate for mayor of Los Angeles, rumored to have been affiliated with ecoterrorists and to have participated in arson and vandalism. He denies it and no charges were filed.

'Senator Herbert Stolt, Democrat-Utah, subject of hate mail campaign for proposing a tax on internet usage. First reported in Knight's game. Stolt denies any such proposal and no record of such a proposal exists.'

Shaw tucked his phone away. 'Tony Knight's offered his games and add-ons for free, provided you sat through news broadcasts and public service spots. And he didn't dare let Thompson find that out. For three or four years, the company's revenues had been declining. Their one big game — *Conundrum* — wasn't doing well; and Foyle, the designer, couldn't come up with any new ideas. Knight was desperate. He was sort of a player — in the traditional sense of the word. I'd guess he contacted lobbyists, politicians, political action committees, CEOs, floating the idea of offering a platform to broadcast whatever they wanted: lies, rumors, defamatory and phony news stories.'

'Video games as a way to get propaganda in front of an audience.' Cummings was both appalled and impressed, it seemed.

Shaw added, 'A young audience. An impressionable audience. And it goes a lot deeper.'

'How so?'

'You got game add-ons for registering to vote. And there were plenty of suggestions about who to vote for — some subtle, some not so subtle.'

He noticed Wiley walk to the car where Foyle was handcuffed in the backseat. He opened the door and bent down, spoke to him.

Cummings said, 'And all under the radar. It's

just an add-on to a video game. Who'd even think about it? No regulation. No FCC, no Federal Election Commission. All fake news and opinion. How big an audience?'

'Tens of millions of subscribers in the U.S. alone. Enough to sway a national election.'

'Jesus.'

Shaw and Cummings watched Dan Wiley close the back door of the car. He walked forward, the handsome, unflappable TV cop.

Cummings asked, 'He going to talk?'

Wiley: 'He looked at me like I was a bug. Then said he wanted a lawyer and that was that.'

# 68

Brad Hendricks was hunched forward, sitting in front of the high-definition computer screen in his basement lair.

The young man, motionless, ears enwrapped in large headphones, typed frantically, yet with dead eyes fixed on the Samsung screen. Nothing existed but the game, which was, Shaw noted without surprise, *The Whispering Man*.

Shaw continued to the basement but stopped at the foot of the stairs, peering at the computer screen.

A window reported that Brad now had eleven objects in his KEEP BAG.

A memory came to Shaw. Ashton had made him, Russell and Dorion prepare GTHO bags, near the back door — the door facing the mountains. The bags — intended, yes, for a get-the-hell-out situation — contained everything you would need to survive for a month or so under even the most extreme circumstances. (When older, Colter had learned the real acronym among survivalists was GTFO. Ashton Shaw would never have condoned such language in front of the children.)

Shaw approached, wide and slow.

*Never surprise an animal or a human . . . unless you need to surprise them for your own survival.*

Brad turned his head, saw Shaw and turned back to the game.

Subtitles appeared at the bottom of the screen.

THE HYDRAULIC PRESS WILL BE OPENING IN FIVE MINUTES. GET THROUGH IF YOU CAN. A REWARD AWAITS ON THE OTHER SIDE.

But, Shaw recalled, the Whispering Man himself was the coach. The master of the game sometimes helped you. Sometimes, he lied.

The boy turned his ruddy face to Shaw, pulling off the headphones and pausing the game. He brushed his straight, shiny hair from his eyes.

'Brad? Colter Shaw.'

He handed the young man the backpack, containing most of the items he'd taken to Jimmy Foyle.

Peering inside, Brad said, 'Never liked *Conundrum*.'

'Ads, infomercials.'

Brad gave a frown, as if at something so obvious it hardly needed stating. 'No, no. Jimmy Foyle's smart — *too* smart. We don't need a quadrillion planets. He used to be good but he forgot what gaming's all about. He made a game for himself, not for players.'

*Fun*, Shaw recalled Marty Avon telling him. A game has to be fun.

Brad pulled out the disks and drives and arranged them on the desk. He looked affectionately at one as if happy a dog that had wandered out of the yard had now returned.

He arranged them in some harmonious order. 'Do you know why silicon is used? Silicon? Used in computer chips?'

'I don't, no.'

'There are three types of materials. Conductors let electrons through all the time. Insulators don't let any through. Semiconductors . . . Well, you get it. That's what silicon is. They let electrons through sometimes and not others. Like gates. That's the reason computers work. Silicon's the most common. There's germanium. Gallium arsenide's better. This whole area could have been called Gallium Arsenide Valley.' He picked up the headphones. He wanted to get back to the game. The screen pulsed impatiently in its waiting state.

Before he could put them on, though, Shaw asked, 'You ever get outside?'

'No. Too much glare on the screen.'

Shaw, of course, had meant something else.

'Why don't you grind? On Twitch?'

If Brad was surprised that Shaw knew the term, he gave no indication. The boy offered a smile but a sad one. 'That's for the pretty people. In nice rooms. With fun things on the walls and made beds and clean windows. You're on webcam all the time. The subscribers expect that. They expect you to be cool and funny. And talk out your gameplay. I don't do that. It's instinct, the way I play. Only twenty-two people in the world have gotten to Level 9. I'm one of them. I'm going to get to 10. I'm going to kill the Whispering Man.'

'I want to give you something.'

No response.

'It's the name of somebody you might want to call.'

Still silence. Then the hands lowered the headphones.

'Marty Avon. The CEO of Destiny Entertainment.'

Now a flicker of emotion.

'You know him?'

'I do.'

'To talk to?'

Shaw found the number on his phone, lifted a pen from Brad's desk and wrote it on a Post-it. He placed the yellow square near an empty yogurt container and five books about *Minecraft* gameplay. 'Tell him I wanted you to call. If you're interested in a job, he'll talk to you.'

Brad glanced at the slip of paper quickly and his attention wavered to the screen.

Then the headphones were back on. The avatars were in motion. The knives were drawn. Laser guns powered up.

Shaw turned and walked up the stairs. In the living room he glanced at the parents, mother on a couch, stepfather in an armchair, both focused on a crime show on TV.

Without a word, Shaw passed them by and stepped outside. He fired up his dirt bike and rode far too fast through the damp evening.

# 69

'This's him.'

Helmet in hand, Colter Shaw was standing in the doorway of Santa Clara Memorial Hospital, the third word in the name ever curious to him in connection with a house of healing because it suggested the place had had its share of failures.

He nodded to the woman who'd just spoken, in a whisper worthy of the Whispering Man. LaDonna Standish.

From her elaborate bed, surrounded by elaborate machines, she continued: 'Colter, this is Karen.'

He recognized her from the picture on Standish's desk. She was a solid woman, tall and with a farm girl look about her. Her hair, which had appeared blond in the photo, was a vibrating tone of orange-red, two shades brighter than Maddie Poole's.

A pretty girl of about two studied him; she held a stuffed rabbit, made from the same material as her red gingham dress. She had her mother's blue eyes. This would be Gem.

'Hello,' Shaw said. He saved his smiles for moments like this — with his nieces, mostly.

The girl waved.

Karen rose and shook Shaw's hand firmly. 'Thank you.' Her eyes were wide and radiated gratitude.

Shaw sat. He noted flowers and cards and

candy and a balloon. He was not a bring-a-present kind of person. Not averse to the idea; he just tended not to think about it. If he came back, maybe he'd bring her a book. That seemed practical; you couldn't do much with balloons.

'What do they say?' He glanced at Standish's vastly bandaged arm and was surprised they'd been able to save the limb. The belly wound was hidden under functional blankets.

'Broken arm, nicked spleen — I'll probably get to keep it. You don't need a spleen, Shaw. You know that?'

He recalled something about that from his father's lectures on emergency medicine in the field.

'If they take it out, you can get infections. My doctor' — she floated away for a moment, the painkillers — 'he said the spleen is like a bush league pinch hitter. Not vital but better to have one. I can't believe I fell for that, Shaw. A car horn.' A faint smile. 'The doctor said you knew what you were doing. You treated gunshots before?'

'I have.'

It was one of the first lessons their father gave them in emergency first aid: pressure points, tourniquets, packing wounds. Other advice too:

*Never use a tampon in a bullet wound. People say you ought to. Don't. It'll expand and cause more damage.*

Ashton Shaw was a wealth of wisdom.

'When're you getting sprung?'

'Three, four days.'

Shaw asked, 'You heard the whole story?'

428

'Dan told me. It's about disinformation, propaganda, lies, getting the kids to vote . . . and vote certain ways. Starting rumors. Last thing in the world we need now. Destroy lives, careers . . . Lies about affairs, crimes. Bullshit.' Standish drifted away, then back. 'And Knight?'

'Vanished. They locked down his airplane and detained his minders — conspiracy. But no sign of him.'

Which is why a Task Force officer was stationed outside her door.

Karen handed a picture book to Gem, who was growing restless. She'd brought a bag filled with books and toys. Shaw's sister did the same and had taught him the art of distraction for the times he baby-sat. He didn't do so often but when he was called for duty, he made sure he was prepared.

He knew survivalism under all circumstances.

Then the tears appeared in Standish's eyes.

Karen leaned forward. 'Honey . . . '

Standish shook her head. She hesitated. 'I called Cummings,' she said.

Karen said, 'Looks like Donnie's going to administration.'

Standish said, 'He didn't want to tell me. Not now, when I'm laid up. But I had to know. He said my job's safe. Just no street work. It's policy. He said nobody wounded this bad's ever gone back in the field.'

Shaw thought of her plan to get onto the street, which would now apparently be permanently derailed.

Or not. The tears stopped and she roughly

wiped her face. There was something in her olive-dark eyes that suggested there would be future conversations with the JMCTF about the topic. His nod said *Good luck.*

Karen said to Shaw, 'When Donnie's back home, if you're still here, you'll come for dinner? Or will you be on the road?'

'She's a' — Standish whispered the adjective — 'cook.' Because her lips didn't move much when she spoke the censored syllables, Shaw assumed they were 'kick-ass.'

'I'd like that.'

Wondering where the stack of his father's documents would lead him in his search for the answer to the secret of October 5. Maybe he'd still be here. Maybe he'd be gone.

They talked for a bit longer and then a nurse came in to change dressings.

Shaw rose and Karen threw her arms around him and whispered once more, 'Thank you.'

Standish, bleary-eyed, just waved. 'I'd do that too. But I don't think . . . you'd appreciate the screaming.'

He stepped to the door. Standish whispered, 'Hold on, Shaw.' Then to her partner, she said, 'You bring it?'

'Oh. Yeah.' The woman dug into her purse. And handed him a small brown paper bag. He extracted a disk of cheap metal about four inches in diameter. In the center was a five-pointed star embossed with the words:

OFFICIAL
DEPUTY SHERIFF

# 70

You're a hero.'

This was from she's-sweet-on-you Tiffany.

'TV and everything. Channel 2 said they invited you in for an interview. You didn't respond.'

Shaw ordered a coffee and deflected the adoration. He did, however, say, 'Was a big help — the video. Thank you.'

'Glad for it.'

He looked around. The man he was going to meet hadn't yet arrived.

A pause. Tiffany napkin-wiped her hands, looking down. 'Just . . . I thought I'd put this out there. I'm off later. Around eleven. That's pretty late, I know. But, maybe, you want to get a bite of dinner?'

'I'm beat.'

The woman laughed. 'You look it.'

True. He *was* tired, to his soul. He'd taken a fast shower at the camper, changed clothes and then headed here. If he hadn't gotten the phone call, he'd be asleep by now.

'And I imagine you're headed out of town pretty soon.'

He nodded. Then glanced at the door.

Ronald Cummings pushed through it. He surprised Shaw by nodding with familiarity to Tiffany, who gave him a smile. 'Officer. The usual?'

Shaw raised an eyebrow.

The supervisor said to him, 'We people get out too ... Yes, please, the usual, Tiff. How's Madge?'

'Doing well. Still training. I tell her a half triathlon is as good as a whole. She's, like, no it isn't. Kids these days.'

She fixed him a latte, or some other frothy concoction, and both Cummings and Shaw sat. Not many free tables. Open laptops were scattered throughout the place like cherry blossoms in April.

Cummings sipped and diligently wiped away his white mustache. 'I have to tell you something and I wanted it to be in person.'

'I gathered.' Shaw drank a bit of his coffee.

Tiffany appeared with what seemed to be an oatmeal cookie. She set it before Cummings.

'You?' she asked Shaw.

'I'm not a sweet guy. Thanks anyway.'

A smile, more affectionate than flirtatious.

When she'd walked away, Shaw looked over at the supervisor.

'It's really good. Tiffany makes them herself.' He nodded at the cookie.

Shaw said nothing.

'Okay. There's a hold on the operation against Knight. This, by the way, I am absolutely *not* telling you.'

'Hold?'

'There's a warrant, but the feds're sitting on it.' Cummings looked around and leaned forward. 'It looks like one of Knight's clients — who hired him to break a fake-news story or two — was a lobbyist working for a certain politician. Maybe there's a link to this individual, maybe not. But if Knight's arrested and his name surfaces, then his future plans're derailed. I mean, plans for a trip to Washington. A trip that would last four or eight years.'

Shaw sighed. He now understood why the feds had not been at the Elizabeth Chabelle briefing.

Cummings chewed some cookie. 'And you're about to ask: What about us? The Task Force or the California B of I. Making a state case against Knight.'

'I was.'

'We have to stand down too. That word came from Sacramento. Only for twenty-four hours. Make it look like we're marshalling evidence or following up leads or some nonsense. Then we all — feds too — hit his last-known locations. Flashbangs, tanks, big splash.'

'By then he'll be on the beach in an extradition-free country.'

'Pretty much. We caught one plum — Foyle. And we've closed down his operation.'

'And the Whispering Man gets away.'

'The . . . Oh, the game. Standish told me you were . . . bothered about Kyle Butler. And Henry Thompson. You wanted Knight arrested.'

Or dead.

'You've called in all your favors?'

Cummings had lost interest in his heavy-duty baked good. The coffee too. 'Favors I didn't even have. And word is, we sit tight.'

'Twenty-four hours?'

The man nodded.

'And there's nothing you can do?'

'I'm sorry. The only way Knight's going to prison is if he strolls into the Task Force with his hands up, says, 'I'm sorry for everything,' and surrenders.' He gave a tired smile. 'LaDonna told me you do this percentage thing? Well, you and I both know the odds of that happening, now don't we?'

Shaw asked, 'You, or the feds, have any idea where Knight is?'

'No, we don't. And I wouldn't tell you if I did.' Cummings glanced into Shaw's eyes and must've seen something in them that was troubling. 'I know how you feel, but don't do anything stupid here.'

'Tell that to Kyle Butler and Henry Thompson.' Shaw rose and picked up his helmet and gloves. He nodded to Tiffany and headed for the door.

'Colter,' Cummings said. 'He's not worth it.'

The supervisor said something more but by then Shaw was outside into the cool evening and didn't hear a word.

# 71

Jimmy Foyle might've been expecting a visitor but he clearly wasn't expecting this one.

He blinked as Colter Shaw walked into the interview room at the Joint Major Crimes Task Force. Coincidentally, it was the room where Shaw and Cummings had had their get-together a day or so ago. To Shaw it felt like ages.

Foyle sat down across from him. While there were rings cemented into the floor, the man wasn't shackled. Maybe the turnkeys had assessed Shaw as being able to deflect an attack.

The designer muttered, 'I have nothing to say to you. This is a trick. They want to get a confession. I'm not saying anything.' The man's lips tightened.

Shaw had to admit he felt some sympathy for him. What would it have been like to throw your entire life into your art and then, at his young age, to realize that you'd lost your spark? The muse had deserted you?

'This is just for me. What you're going to tell me doesn't go anywhere else.'

'I'm not going to tell you anything. Go to hell.'

Calmly Shaw said, 'Jimmy, you know what I do for a living.'

He said uncertainly, 'You go after rewards . . . or something.'

'That's right. Sometimes it's finding a missing child or a grandfather with Alzheimer's. Mostly,

I track down fugitives and escapees. There's a fair number of people I've put into prison. People who're not very happy with me. Now, I checked your incarceration schedule. You'll be in San Quentin until your trial. I've put four prisoners in the Q. If you don't help me, I'm going to talk to a screw or two I know. Those're guards, by the way. You'll learn that soon enough. They'll spread the word that you're a friend of mine and — '

'What?' Foyle stiffened.

Shaw held his hand out, palm first. 'Calm, there . . . And I guarantee that word'll spread fast.'

'You son of a bitch.' He sighed, then leaned forward. 'If I say anything, they'll hear.' A nod at the ceiling, where presumably hidden microphones were hard at work.

'That's why I'm going to write down the questions and you're going to write down the answers.'

He removed from his bag one of his case notebooks and opened it, then he uncapped a pen. It was a cheap, flexible plastic one provided by the guards, who had explained that the Delta Titanio Galassia, with its sharp point, was not a wise implement to take into an interview with a suspected murderer.

436

# 72

It's easy to *not* die,' Ashton Shaw is saying to Colter, then fourteen. 'Surviving is hard.'

His son doesn't bother to ask what he means. The professor always gets to his point.

'Lying on a couch in front of a TV. Sitting in your office typing reports. Walking on the beach. You're avoiding dying . . . Say, hand me another piton.'

Even at that age Colter notes the irony in his father's comment about the ease of not dying since they are presently one hundred and twenty feet in the air, on Devil's Notch, a sheer rock face just across the boundary of the Compound.

Colter hands him the piton, and, using the tethered hammer, Ashton whacks the metal spike into a crack, tests it and hooks in the carabiner with a sharp click. Parallel on their course, father and son chalk their hands and move several feet higher. The summit is only ten feet away.

'Not dying isn't the same as being alive. You're only alive when you're surviving. And you only survive when there's a risk there's something you can lose. The more you risk losing, the more you're alive.'

Colter waits for this to be translated into a Never rule.

His father says nothing more.

And so this becomes Colter Shaw's favorite

advice from his father. Better than all the Never rules put together.

Ashton's words were in Shaw's mind now as he downshifted the Yamaha YZ450FX bike and pounded along a dirt road on the way to Scarpet Peak, between Silicon Valley and Half Moon Bay. As at Basin Redwoods Park, where Henry Thompson had been murdered, this might have been an old logging trail but was now apparently the means of transit for hikers. He hit fifty-five, caught air, then landed like waterfowl in autumn skimming down to the surface of a lake.

Minutes counted. He twisted the throttle higher.

Soon he came to the clearing. Ten acres of low grass, ringed by pine and leafy trees.

He steered the bike out of the woods and killed the engine. This model of dirt bike — the 499cc version — came with a kickstand, a necessity for a street-legal conversion since you could hardly rest it on its side when you went shopping. He propped the bike up and removed his helmet and gloves.

How crazy was this?

Shaw decided: Doesn't matter. It was inevitable.

*Not dying isn't the same as being alive . . .*

The clearing reminded him of the meadow behind the cabin on the Compound — the place where Mary Dove had presided over her husband's funeral. Ashton had anticipated — one might say overanticipated — his death and had made funeral arrangements long before the fact. His mind was sharp and clever then and

438

rich with a wicked sense of humor. In his instructions he'd written: *It's my wish that Ash's ashes be scattered over Crescent Lake.*

Shaw gazed across the clearing. On the far end of the moonlit expanse were two cat's eyes of windows, glowing yellow. Just dots from here. The illumination was radiating from a vacation cabin, whose location was the information that Shaw had wrung out of Jimmy Foyle.

The jog to the cabin took him no more than five minutes. Thirty yards away he paused, looking for security. There might be cameras, there might be motion sensors. Shaw was relying on speed to his target and the element of surprise.

Tony Knight wouldn't be expecting anyone to come a'calling. After all, he had immunity.

Shaw wondered who the client was, the politician who'd hired Knight's broadcast anchors to spread phony rumors about his opponent and destroy his chances in a forthcoming election. Some senator? A represen-tative?

He drew his Glock and — habit — eased the slide back against the tight spring to confirm a round was chambered, then reholstered the weapon. Crouching, he moved to the front of the rustic cabin, not unlike the one Shaw and his brother and sister had grown up in, though this one was much smaller. The rough-sided house, Nantucket gray, would have three or four bedrooms. There was a separate garage and Shaw could see an SUV and a Mercedes parked out front.

This told Shaw that there were at least two minders with Knight. The man would be departing via helicopter; an orange wind sock sat nearby in the clearing. Two men would remain behind to drive the cars back.

Smelling pine on the cool, damp air, Shaw crept closer to the cabin, lifted his head briefly and dropped back to cover.

The image he'd seen was of Tony Knight on his mobile, pacing, gesturing with his other hand.

The CEO was dressed in weekend casual. Tan slacks, a black shirt and a dark gray jacket. On his head was a black baseball cap with no logo or team designation. This suggested his departure was imminent. He wasn't alone. There were two minders nearby. They were the same ones who'd abducted him from the floor of the C3 Conference while all eyes were on the pyrotechnic announcement about *Conundrum VI* overhead. One was on his phone and the other watching a tablet, earbud plugged in. He laughed at something.

Shaw waited three long minutes and looked again.

The tableau had not changed.

He circled the building, planting his feet only on pine needles and bare earth, and checked what other rooms he could see into. It appeared that just the three men were inside.

He stepped to the front door and tried the knob. Locked. A window, then.

Except that he never got to a window.

A fourth man now joined the party, walking

from the garage with a backpack over his shoulder and a duffel bag in both hands; he was squat and bulky, with a crew cut and long arms. Stopping quickly, he shucked the backpack, dropped the bag and started to reach for his hip. Shaw lunged; the man gave up on the gun — he couldn't get to it in time — and drew back a fist. But he had no target; Shaw dropped his center of gravity, ducked low and executed a passable single-leg takedown, a classic college wrestling move.

The minder was heavy yet he went down hard, flat on his back, gasping, his face contorted. The wind had been knocked from his lungs. Shaw drew his own pistol and kept it pointed toward, but not at, the man.

He wasn't stupid. He nodded quickly. Shaw pocketed the pistol, also a Glock, and patted him down for other weapons. There were none. He powered off the man's phone and took a set of keys. Shaw moved his finger in a circle. The minder nodded again and rolled onto his belly.

Shaw zip-tied his wrists and ankles and turned back to the house.

Key in the lock. He turned it — silent — and, drawing his gun, he opened the door and stepped into the hallway, aromatic with the smells of cooking: onions and grease. A glance around the dim place. The bedrooms, to the left, were dark. He'd have to take a chance on the kitchen. To look inside would expose him — because of a pass-through bar — to the men in the living room. The odds that there were five men here?

Small.

So, with a two-handed grip on his gun, Shaw stepped fast into the room, where the trio was sitting and pacing.

Knight dropped his phone and the 'Jesus Christ!' he uttered was nearly a shout. The minders spun around, starting to stand.

'No. Down.'

They complied slowly.

Shaw had noted how each held his phone or tablet. 'You.' Nodding to one. 'Left hand, thumb and forefinger. Weapon out. Pitch it toward me.' The other was told to do the same with his right hand.

There was no opportunity here for heroics or clever tactics, only foolishness, and they did as instructed.

Shaw tossed zip ties to them.

'How do we . . . ' one began.

Shaw offered a wry glance. 'Just figure it out.'

Using their teeth to hold and tighten the plastic ties, they bound their own wrists.

Shaw spotted a light panel against the far wall and walked to it, then flipped the switches. The grounds were brilliantly illuminated. Then he stepped to a spot near the kitchen, where he could stand and have complete cover of the room and a view out to the yard.

'Is anyone else here, other than the one tied up outside?'

'Listen, Shaw — '

'Because if there is and he makes a move, he's going to get shot. And that means there might be other shots.'

442

Knight said, 'There sure is somebody. And you better . . . '

Shaw looked at one of the minders — the one who'd been enjoying his comedy on the tablet until the interruption. The man shook his head.

Knight growled, 'The fuck're you doing?' Odd how anger negates handsome.

'Lift up your jacket and shirt and turn around, then empty your pockets.'

After a defiant moment the CEO did. No weapons.

Shaw picked up the man's phone and disconnected the call.

'How'd you find me? Was it Foyle? That fucker. Well, so what? You can call all the cops you want but nobody's going to touch me. I'm out of the country in an hour. I've got a get-out-of-jail card.'

'Sit down, Knight.'

'I'm sorry that kid got killed. Kyle Butler. That wasn't supposed to happen.' The man's eyes were widening with fear as he looked from Shaw's weapon to his cold eyes.

'I don't care. He did get killed. And so did Henry Thompson. And Elizabeth Chabelle and her baby almost died too.'

'Foyle was an idiot to kidnap a pregnant woman.' The legendary temper flared and Shaw believed he actually shivered with rage. 'So, what is this? You can't turn me in to the cops. You going to shoot me? Just like that? Vengeance is mine — that kind of bullshit? They'll figure out it was you. You won't get away with it.'

'Shh,' Shaw said, tired of the sputtering. He

443

withdrew his cell phone, unlocked it, opened an email and set the cell on the coffee table. He stepped back, keeping his aim near Knight. 'Read that.'

Knight picked up the unit — his hands were none too steady — and read. He looked up. 'You've got to be kidding.'

# 73

As Shaw steered the dusty, streaked Yamaha into the entrance of the Westwinds RV Center in Los Altos Hills, Colter Shaw noticed a sign he hadn't been aware of earlier. It was some distance from the park, maybe two football fields' worth, but the stark black letters on a white billboard were easily read: MAKE YOUR NEW HOME SILICON-VILLE . . . VISIT OUR WEBSITE NOW!

To think he'd suspected the toy aficionado of being the Whispering Man . . .

He drove along Apple Road. Anywhere else in the world, the name would refer to the fruit. Here, of course, in SV, it meant only one thing and that bordered on the religious. It would be like Vatican Drive or Mecca Avenue. He turned right, on Google Way, toward his Winnebago and, arriving there, braked more harshly than he'd intended. He killed the engine. After a pause he removed his helmet and gloves.

He joined Maddie Poole, who was leaning against her car's front fender, drinking a Corona. Without a word, she reached into the car and picked up another bottle. She opened it with a church key and handed the beer to him.

They nodded bottlenecks each other's way and sipped.

'Damn. You saved somebody else, Colt. Heard the news.'

He glanced toward the camper and she nodded.

445

The night was chill. He unlocked the door and they walked inside. He hit the lights and got the heat going.

Maddie said, 'She was pregnant. She going to name the baby after you?'

'No.'

Maddie clicked her tongue. 'Hey, was that the bullet hole from the other night? By the door?'

Shaw tried to recall. 'No, that was a while ago. In better light you can see it's rusty.'

'Where'd it happen?'

You'd think someone takes a shot at you, you'd recall instantly where it was, along with the weather, the minute and hour and what you were wearing.

Probably that job in Arizona.

'Arizona.'

'Hmm.'

Maybe New Mexico. Shaw wasn't sure so he let the neighboring state stand.

She smoothed her dark purple T-shirt, on which only the letters AMA and, below, ALI were visible beneath a thin leather jacket. She wore pale blue sandals, shabby, and he noticed a ring on her right middle toe, a red-and-gold band. Had it been there the other night? That's right, he couldn't tell. The lights had been out.

She looked around the camper. With her attention on a map mounted to a wall near the bedroom — a portion of the Lewis and Clark Expedition — Shaw quickly slipped his Glock back into the spice cabinet resting place.

'I never asked, Colt. What's with the reward

thing? Funny way to make a living.' She turned back.

'Suits my nature.'

'The restless man. In body and mind. So, I got your message.' She took a long sip of her beer. There was silence, if you didn't count the whoosh of traffic, audible even here, inside. In Silicon Valley, always, always traffic. Shaw recalled the Compound on windless days. A thousand acres filled with a clinging silence, which could be every bit as unsettling as a mountain lion's growl. He noticed the fingers of Maddie's left hand — her free hand — were twitching. Then he realized, no, they were air-keyboarding. She didn't seem aware of it.

Shaw said, 'I drove by the house. You were gone.'

'Conference is over. All us gaming nomads, packing up our tents. I'm getting a head start on the drive south.' The hour was late, 11 p.m., but for grinders like Maddie Poole it was midafternoon. 'I'm not much of a phone person. Thought I'd come by in person.'

Shaw sipped. 'Wanted to apologize. That's all. Not worth much. It never is. Still . . . '

She was looking over another map.

Shaw said, 'I had a thought. About our organization.'

'Organization?'

'Renaming it,' he said. 'From the Never After Club to the On Rare Occasions Club. What do you think?'

She finished her beer.

'Trash is there,' he said, pointing.

She dropped the bottle in. 'Couple years ago a friend of mine, she told me she was breaking up with this guy. I knew him pretty well too. She told me he hit her and pushed her down a flight of stairs. She went all drama on me, sobbing. So, naturally, I drove over to his place and beat the crap out of him. I mean, what else was there to do?'

As good an answer as any.

'Only, it turned out, she lied to me. Can you believe it? He dumped her and she wasn't used to that. She was spreading rumors that he was abusive so it wouldn't look so bad for her.' A shake of her head. 'And you know what? If I'd thought about it, I'd've known in my heart that boy'd never do any such thing. I jumped too fast. After, I tried to patch it up but, uh-uh, didn't work.'

Shaw said, 'No reset button.'

'No reset.'

'Anyway, Colt, even if you hadn't called I was going to come by. I've got this rule. Life's short. Never miss a chance to say hello to somebody, never miss a chance to say good-bye . . . Hey, look at that. I finally got a smile out of you. Okay, better hit the road.'

They embraced, briefly, and then she walked out the door. He watched her through the window as she slid into her car. A moment later she left two black, wavy tread marks, accompanied by ghosts of blue smoke, as she fishtailed onto Google Way and vanished.

Shaw let the curtain fall back, thinking: Never did find out what the tattoo meant.

# 74

The story was already on the air.

Shaw had turned on the TV to a local station.

*Tony Knight, the cofounder of Knight Time Gaming, has turned himself in to the Joint Major Crimes Task Force headquarters in Santa Clara. Knight was wanted for questioning in connection with the kidnappings and murders that terrorized Silicon Valley this past weekend. James Foyle, the other cofounder of the company and its chief game designer, was arrested earlier tonight . . .*

Shaw shut down the feed. That was all he needed to know. He wondered what conversations were going on in the offices of law enforcers around the state and in Washington at the moment. He suspected heated words, high blood pressures and very worried hearts.

He could still hear Knight's voice in the cabin off the clearing as he stared at the screen of Shaw's phone.

'You've got to be kidding me.'

Shaw had nodded at the mobile. 'Tomorrow morning at six a.m. that gets uploaded to the web and sent to fifty newspapers and feeds around the world.'

## $1 MILLION REWARD

FOR INFORMATION LEADING TO THE
WHEREABOUTS OF ANTHONY ('TONY')
ALFRED KNIGHT, WANTED FOR MURDER,
KIDNAPPING, ASSAULT AND CONSPIRACY
IN CALIFORNIA.

Below were a number of pictures of Knight
— some Photoshopped to represent him with a
changed appearance — and other information
about him that might lead a reward seeker to him.
There were details too on how to claim the money.

'I don't . . . I don't understand. Who's offering
this? Not the police? They agreed . . . ' He fell
silent, probably deciding it best not to shine a
light on the deal he'd arranged.

'I'm offering it,' Shaw told him.

'You?'

He was personally funding the reward through
one of his LLCs. When he said he made his
living by seeking rewards, a more accurate way to
phrase it was that he made *some* of his living
with rewards. Colter Shaw had resources beyond
that.

'Let me explain something to you, Knight. As
soon as that hits the news, hundreds of people're
going to be making plans to track you down. All
over the world. Wherever you think you might
want to go. No extradition laws? That doesn't
mean a thing. A mercenary'll find you, smuggle
you back to the States and claim the money.

'I've crossed paths with a lot of these folks and
they aren't the nicest kids on the block. For that

kind of money, some'll be thinking: bounty. And even if the announcement doesn't say dead or alive, that's what they're reading. You'll spend every minute of every day for the rest of your life looking over your shoulder.'

The man glanced at his helpless minders in disgust.

Shaw said, 'Only I can stop that from being uploaded. If anything happens to me, six o'clock, off it goes to the world.'

'Fuck.'

'You've got your friends in high places, Tony. Your clients. If they can put a hiatus on the investigation, they can put in a recommendation for a sentence. Something less than life. Now, put the phone down.'

He read the announcement once more and set the iPhone on the table.

'Back up.'

When he had, Shaw retrieved and pocketed the unit.

'Six a.m., Knight. Your move.'

Shaw had backed out of the house, crouched to make sure the minder on the ground was all right — he was — and jogged back to the far side of the clearing to retrieve his bike.

He now stepped outside and secured the Yamaha to the rack on the rear of the camper, locked it in place and returned. Just as he walked inside his phone hummed and he glanced at the screen.

He'd been expecting a call from this number, though the caller was a surprise.

'Colter? Dan Wiley.'

451

'Dan.'

'Say, people ever call you Colt?'

'Some do.'

'You know Colt's a brand of gun.'

'So I've heard,' he said. Like the one sitting under his bed at the moment.

Shaw glanced out the window at the charcoal tread marks Maddie's feisty car had left on Google Way. Had an image of meeting her in the Quick Byte. He filed it away in the same room where he kept the images of Margot Keller. He closed the door.

'So. Have some news. It's about Tony Knight. Ron Cummings — you remember him?'

'I do.'

'He asked me to give you a call and tell you.'

'Go on.'

'Just thought you'd want to hear this. Well, we — at the Task Force — were kind of wrangling with the feds about an op to find Knight?'

'Were you?'

'Yes, we were. And nobody was getting anywhere. Then all of a sudden, who walks into our office and surrenders?'

'Knight?'

'That's right. We booked him in on homicide, kidnapping and, everybody's favorite, conspiracy. Nobody knows why the hell he gave it up.'

'Good news, then.' He wasn't surprised that Cummings had delegated to Wiley the task of calling Shaw. Joint Task Force Senior Supervisor Cummings would want to distance himself from all things Knight. He wondered if the meeting at the Quick Byte had been a way of suggesting that

452

Shaw might want to take matters into his own hands while decidedly warning him not to. This one clocked in at fifty-fifty.

Wiley said, 'Oh, a whole n'other thing. We're getting Crime Scene stuff in. And I was looking over ballistics. The slugs that killed Kyle and that hit LaDonna were from the same gun, that Glock we found on Foyle. But the bullets the metro CS team dug out of the wall and tree near your camper yesterday came from a Beretta, probably. A forty-cal. You find any other weapon Foyle might've had?'

The beer bottle stopped halfway to Shaw's mouth. 'No, Dan. Never did . . . I've got to go. I'll be in touch.'

He disconnected without hearing Wiley's farewell.

Because Shaw doubted very much that Foyle had another gun — and even if he did, why would he switch from one to the other and back again?

No, somebody else broke into the Winnebago last night.

Three steps across the camper and he was pulling open the spice cabinet door, thrusting his hand through the jars of sage, oregano and rosemary for his Glock.

Which was no longer there. It had been removed while he was outside affixing the Yamaha to the camper.

Shaw heard the door to his bedroom open. He turned, expecting to see exactly what he saw: the intruder stepping forward, holding the Beretta pistol in his hand.

What he hadn't been expecting to see, though, was that his visitor was the man from Oakland — Rodent, the one who'd been carting around a Molotov cocktail, apparently hell-bent on committing a hate crime, burning down the graffitied homage to early political resistance. Shaw now understood that his mission was a very different one.

# 75

Sit, Shaw. Make yourself comfy.'

The same voice. High. Amused. Confident. Clearly Minnesota or Dakota.

Shaw tried to make sense, then just gave up. He sat.

Rodent pointed to the table. 'Unlock that phone of yours and set it down. Thank'ee much.'

Shaw did.

The man picked it up, his hand encased in black cloth gloves, with light-colored finger pads, which he used to swipe his way through the iPhone. His eyes flicked from the screen to Shaw — up, down, fast.

Yes, Jimmy Foyle was the one following Shaw at San Miguel Park and who delivered the eerie stencil drawings of the Whispering Man. That didn't mean, of course, that someone else wasn't conducting surveillance too.

*Never focus too narrowly.*

Rodent asked, 'This last call, incoming. Who was it from?'

Easily discovered. 'Joint Major Crimes Task Force. Silicon Valley.'

'Well, some kettle of fish that is, don'tcha know.'

'Doesn't concern you. It was about the kidnapping case I was involved in.'

Rodent nodded. He flipped through the log, surely noting the time stamp, which indicated that Shaw disconnected before Rodent had shown up with his fine Italian gun. Rodent set the phone down.

'Where're my weapons?' Shaw asked.

'Snug in my pocket. That little tiny thing. And the Python too. Under the bed. That's smart. And a fine piece of gun making, that model is, as I'm sure you appreciate.'

Confused, yes. But one thing Shaw understood: the man wasn't here because he was pissed off Shaw had ruined his bonfire in Oakland. That attempted arson had been about creating a diversion so that Rodent could break into Shaw's Winnebago.

He probably *had* uttered the words, during the confrontation, 'Why'd you do that, Shaw?'

The further question — what did he want in the camper? — was not yet answerable.

In the light within the camper Shaw could see the man's pocked face more clearly than the other day. He noted too a scar on the side of his neck, in roughly the same position as the one on Shaw. Rodent's wound had been more serious and the scar looked like the twin disfigurement caused by a grazing bullet: troughing skin and burning with the slug's heat at the same time.

The man was too much of a professional to hold his own pistol out toward Shaw. A fast person might slap aside the gun with one hand and strike flesh with the other. Shaw had done so more than once. No, Rodent kept the glossy black weapon close to his side, the muzzle trained forward.

Shaw said, 'You broke in last night, dent puller

456

and crowbar. Sloppy. To make it look like it was some methhead. Tonight you were subtler.'

Rodent had picked the repaired locks with a deft touch. Shaw, who had occasion to break into secure locations, was impressed.

The first time, Rodent had looked for whatever it was he'd wanted — and hadn't found it. He had done reconnaissance, finding the lockbox — which would take heavy equipment to remove or open — and the location of the weapons. Then waited until tonight to return for a visit in person — hiding until Maddie Poole had left.

With his left hand, Rodent fished in a pocket and extracted jingling handcuffs. These he tossed to Shaw, who dropped them on the floor.

A pause.

'Lookie, got to establish a rule or two.'

Shaw said, 'No cuffs. I don't know karate. You have my only firearms. I do know how to throw knives but I only have Sabatiers for cooking in the camper and they're badly balanced.'

'Rules, don'tcha know. For your safety and my peace of mind. Now, yessir, yessir, I've killed a soul'r two, though mostly in self-defense. Death isn't helpful . . . What's that word? Death's counterproductive. It draws attention, makes my life complicated. And that, I don't need. So I'm going to kill you? Nope. Unless, naturally, something you do requires me to kill you.

'I do hurt people. I like hurting people. And I hurt in ways that change them. Forever. A man who loves art, blind him. A woman who loves music, her ears. You can see where this is going.

We know about you, Shaw. You wouldn't do very well hanging out in a wheelchair the rest of your life, don'tcha know.'

Shaw gazed at the wiry man and kept his face a mask, while his heart was slamming in his chest, his mouth dry as cotton.

*Never reveal fear to a predator . . .*

'This is a forty-caliber gun. That's a big old bullet. Which I'm guessing you're familiar with.'

Shaw was.

'Elbows, ankles, then knees. There'd be virtually nothing left to repair. And I've got this thing that'll make the sound like a cough. Another one over your mouth for the screams. So. Put the cuffs on. I do not need to worry about you, Shaw. Cuffs or elbow?' He took wads of black plasticized cloth from his pocket. Some kind of silencer?

Shaw retrieved the bracelets and put them on.

'Now, we'll do our business and I'll be on my way. Is the envelope in the lockbox in your bedroom?'

'The . . . ?'

Patiently: 'I know you're not being — what's that word? — coy. You're in the dark here. I want the envelope your father's friend Eugene Young hid in the School of Sociology archives at Berkeley. That you stole a couple days ago.'

Shaw tried but couldn't process the change in direction.

'No, no, don't wan'ta hear 'Don't know what you're talking about.' We know you called Young at home, not knowing he was dead. Now, there's a look for you, Shaw. You usually give the great

458

stone face. The answer to your question: we had a tap on his line.'

They'd been monitoring his father's colleague, and now his widow, for fifteen years? And this was accompanied by a queasy sense of invasion. They'd been monitoring him as well.

Why on earth?

Rodent said, 'You found out about the envelope. Looking through Daddy's old stuff, maybe. And it sent you to the Sociology archives, where you 'borrowed it.'' His face tightened into a rat smile. 'Sociology. My goodness. One of the few places — really few — we didn't look. Because why would we? A subject your daddy had no interest in.'

'I — '

'Remember, don'tcha know. None of that 'confused' stuff.'

How had Rodent found out about the theft at Berkeley? Shaw thought back. He'd told Young's widow that he was staying at an RV camp in Oakland. Would have been easy to trace him to Carole's. Rodent had followed Shaw to Berkeley. Shaw hadn't seen him tailing. Because it's a good rule when riding a motorcycle to look ahead and to the side, not behind, flashing lights being the exception.

However, such logistics faded from Shaw's thoughts. More important: the word *we*, mysterious documents and a fifteen-year-old wiretap. Shaw realized that his father had maybe not been as crazy or as paranoid as he seemed.

*Never dismiss conspiracies too quickly . . .*

Shaw thought back to the letter Eugene Young

459

had written to his father. He asked Rodent, 'So where's Braxton now?'

Touché. A wrinkle in the pasty flesh between Rodent's eyes. 'What do you know about her?'

Well, one thing more than he'd known a few seconds ago.

*Her* . . .

The man's mouth tightened slightly. He'd been gamed. He said nothing else about Ms. Braxton, whoever she might be.

'Lockbox. Let's look inside.'

'Just a trap. Empty.' Being cuffed defeated Shaw's tactic of disarming the intruder when he reached in and broke a finger. He thought of the irony, given his nickname for the intruder. The trap was a big one, meant for rats.

'I guessed. Could be a reverse trap. Not sure that makes sense but you get the idea.'

Shaw opened it.

Rodent'd already pulled out a small halogen flashlight, which he now used to peer into the safe. He seemed impressed with the booby trap.

Back into the kitchenette. 'Where's the envelope? Or we start with the pain. This is entirely up to you.'

'My wallet.'

'Wallet? . . . On the floor. Facedown.'

Shaw did as told and felt the man lay something soft against the back of his knee, then apply pressure.

'It's the weapon.'

Shaw had guessed. It must be some kind of truly magic cloth if it could dull the sound of a .40 caliber pistol.

The man extracted the wallet and rolled Shaw over and upright.

'Behind the driver's license.'

Rodent fished. 'A claim check for a FedEx store on Alameda?'

'That's it. They have the original of my father's documents and two copies.'

It was in the strip mall that also contained the Salvadoran restaurant of the other day, with the coffee from Potrero Grande. After he'd left, on his way to Frank Mulliner's, he'd taken the manuscript in to have the copies made. He'd decided to leave the job there for a few days just in case the police, at the behest of the Sociology Department, came a'calling. Plausible deniability.

'Any other copies?'

'None that I made.'

Eyes leaving Shaw for only a second at a time, Rodent extracted his phone and placed a call, explaining to whoever was on the other end about the FedEx store. He recited the claim number. He disconnected.

'It's closed now,' Shaw said.

Rodent smiled. Silence, as he sent a text, presumably to someone else. His eyes scanned Shaw as if, were he to look away for a whole second, his captive would strike like a snake.

Finally, Shaw could wait no longer. He said, 'October fifth. Fifteen years ago.'

Rodent paused, looking up from his phone, not a twitch of surprise in his eyes. His voice was no longer high as a taut violin string as he said, 'We didn't kill your father, Shaw.'

Shaw's heart was thudding for reasons that had nothing to do with the fact that he was looking down the barrel of a large pistol.

'This is all a big soup of a mystery to you, that's pretty clear. And it should stay that way. I'll tell you this: Ashton's death was a . . . problem . . . for us. Pissed us off as much as you . . . Well, okay. That's not fair . . . But you get my drift.'

Rodent texted some more.

Shaw was dismayed. His heart sank. Because this meant his nightmare had come true: his brother, Russell, was their father's killer. He closed his eyes briefly. He could hear his brother's voice as if the lanky man were in the room with them.

*He's taught us how to survive. Now we have to survive him . . .*

Russell had committed the murder to save his siblings — and his mother too. She and Ashton had been virtually inseparable ever since they met forty years ago in the Ansel Adams Wilderness on the Pacific Crest, a National Scenic Trail extending from the Mexican border to Canada. Yet as his mind dissolved, the year or so before his death, Ashton grew suspicious of his wife too, occasionally thinking she was part of the conspiracy, whatever that was.

And what if saving his siblings and mother wasn't the only motive? Shaw had long wondered too if there was a darker one. Had Russell's resentment finally boiled over? Dorie and Colter were very young when the family moved. Neither remembered much, if anything, about life in civilization. Russell was ten; he'd had time to experience the frenetic, marvelous San Francisco Bay Area. He'd made friends. Then, suddenly, he was banished to the wilderness.

Angry all those years, never saying anything, the resentment building.

*Russell was the reclusive one . . .*

Rodent lowered his phone. 'For what it's worth, it was an accident.'

Shaw focused.

'Your father. We wanted him alive, Braxton wanted him dead — but not yet, not till she had what she wanted. She sent somebody to, well, talk to him about the documents.'

Talk. Meaning: torture.

'Near as we can piece it together, your father knew Braxton's man was on his way to your Compound. Ashton tipped to him and led him off, was going to kill him somewhere in the woods. The ambush didn't work. They fought. Your father fell.

'That was the second time Braxton's man screwed up, so he's no longer among the living — if it's any consolation.' Then Rodent tilted his head and gave a faint smile. 'The first time was he got kicked off the property by some kid. A teenager. A kid who drew down on him, some old revolver . . . My goodness, would that've been you, Shaw?'

*You're kind of like a Deliverance family, aren't you?*

The hunter . . . That's what he had been doing there, gunning for his father. Ashton Shaw, who

463

— everybody believed — possessed a mind so troubled it invented spies and forces set against him.

Ashton Shaw, who had been right all along.

Oh, Russell . . .

Colter Shaw had never felt his brother's absence more than at this moment. Where are you?

And why have you vanished?

He said, 'You know a lot. What about my brother, Russell? Where is he?'

'Lost his trail years ago. Europe.'

Overseas . . . This surprised Shaw. Then he wondered why that should, since he'd had virtually no contact since the funeral. Paris was no more far-fetched than the Tenderloin in San Francisco or a tract house in Kansas City.

'What's this all about?'

Rodent answered, 'I told you. Not your concern, don'tcha know.'

'What *is* my concern is Braxton. Accident or not. She's responsible.'

'No, that's none of your concern either. And, believe me, you don't want it to be your concern.'

Shaw wondered where the facial pocks had come from. Youthful acne? An illness later in life? Rodent had the wiry build and staccato glances of a military man or soldier of fortune. Maybe a gas attack?

Rodent's phone hummed. Lifted it to his ear. 'Yes . . . Okay. Back at the place.'

The FedEx caper had apparently been successful.

He disconnected. 'Alrighty, then.' He put away the black silencing handkerchief and, moving back to the far side of the camper, slipped his Beretta away. 'I'll leave the cuff keys under your car, the Glock and the Colt in the trash can by the front entrance. Don't try to find us. For your own sake, don'tcha know.'

# 76

Fifteen minutes of contortions on unforgiving blacktop to fish the keys out from under the Malibu with his feet. The duration of the discomfort expanded because he needed to field questions from a ten-year-old boy.

'What'chu doing, mister? That's funny.'

'Got an itch on my back.'

'You do not.'

After freeing his wrists, it took another five minutes to find the Glock and Colt. He was particularly irritated that Rodent had dropped them in a trash can containing the remnants of a Slurpee. Shaw would have to strip both weapons and apply heavy dosages of Hoppe's cleaner to remove the cherry-flavored syrup.

Back in the camper, he prescribed a Sapporo beer to dull the pain from the pulled thigh and neck muscles. Then he transferred his contacts, photos and videos from his iPhone to his computer, checked them for viruses and placed the mobile in a plastic bag and took a hammer to it. He texted the new number to his mother at the Compound, his sister and Teddy and Velma.

He then dialed Mack's number in D.C.

'Hello?' the woman's sultry voice said.

'I'll be on burners till I get a new iPhone.'

''K.'

Charlotte McKenzie was six feet tall, with a pale complexion and long brown hair, her brows elegantly sculpted. During the day she wore a stylish but dull-colored suit, cut to conceal her weapon if she was wearing her weapon, and flats, though not because of her height; her job occasionally required her to run and when it did she had to run fast. Shaw had no clue what she'd be wearing now, presumably in bed. Maybe boxers and a T. Maybe a designer silk negligee.

Shaw loved the way she made lobbyists cry, the way she sheltered whistle-blowers, the way she found facts and figures that, to anyone else, were as invisible as cool spring air.

Those who knew both of them wondered, Shaw had heard, why they'd never gotten together. Shaw occasionally did too, though he knew that, like his heart, Mack's was accessed only by negotiating an exceedingly complex and difficult ascent, rather like Dawn Wall on El Capitan in Yosemite.

'Need some things,' he said.

'Ready.'

'There's a picture on its way. I need facial recognition. Probably a California connection but not certain.' From his computer he sent her an email containing an attachment of a screenshot of Rodent from the video he'd taken during the Molotov cocktail incident.

A moment later: 'Got it. On its way.' Mack would be sending it to a quarter million dollars' worth of facial recognition software running on a supercomputer.

'Be a minute or two.'

A pause, during which clicks intervened. Mack made and received her phone calls with headset and stalk mic so she could knit. She quilted too.

In anyone else these would jar with her other hobbies — of wreck scuba diving and extreme downhill skiing. With Mack, they were elegantly compatible.

'Something else. I'll need everything you have on a Braxton. Probably last name. Female, forties to sixties. She might've been behind my father's death.'

The only response was 'B-R-A-X-T-O-N?'

In the years he'd worked with her Mack had registered not a single breath of surprise at anything he asked her to do.

'That's it.' He thought back to the note that Eugene Young had written to his father:

*Braxton is alive!*

'May have been an attempted hit on her fifteen years ago.'

This introduced the unsettling thought that his father was a member of a murderous conspiracy too.

'Anything else?'

He thought about asking for the address of one Maddie Poole, a grinder girl who lived somewhere in or around Los Angeles.

'No. That'll do it.'

*Click, click, click.* Then silence and a different tap — that of a computer keyboard.

'Got him on facial recognition.'

'Go ahead.'

'Ebbitt Droon.' She spelled it for him.

Shaw said, '*That's* a name, for you.'

'I'm sending you a picture.'

468

Shaw reviewed the image on his screen. A twenty-something version of Rodent.

'That's him.'

*Droon?*

'His story?'

Mack said, 'Virtually no internet presence but enough fragments that tell me he — or, more likely, some IT security pro — scrubs his identity off the 'net regularly. He missed a pic I found in an old magazine article about vets. It was a JPEG of the page, not digitized, so a bot would miss it. Boyhood in upper Midwest, military — Army Rangers — then discharged. Honorable. Vanished from public records. I sent the one-twenty to someone. They'll keep looking.'

An enhanced facial recognition search — based on one hundred and twenty facial points, double the usual. That 'someone' would probably mean a security agency of some sort.

Mack said, 'Now. Second question. Braxton, female. Nothing. That wasn't much to go on. I can keep searching. I'll need people.'

'Do it. Take what you need from the business account.'

''K.'

They disconnected.

Colter Shaw stretched back on the banquette. Another sip of Sapporo.

*What's this all about?*

From a stack of old bills — in which he kept his important documents — he extracted the note Professor Eugene Young had sent his father. He'd hidden it in a resealed power company envelope.

*Ash:*

*I'm afraid I have to tell you Braxton is alive! Maybe headed north. Be CARE-FUL. I've explained to everybody that inside the envelope is the key to where you've hidden everything.*

*I put it in 22-R, 3rd Floor.*

*We'll make this work, Ash. God bless.*

*— Eugene*

The two Cal professors, his father and Eugene Young, were involved in something obviously dangerous, along with 'everybody,' whoever they might be. Rodent's side wanted Ashton alive; Braxton's people wanted him — presumably the others too — dead. But only after finding the envelope.

The stack of pages was the key to something that his father had hidden somewhere. He went back to his notebook and skimmed through the pages he'd jotted at the Salvadoran café. Precious little. He found only a notation of the pages whose corners had been turned down.

*37, 63, 118 and 255.*

He hadn't bothered at that time to jot their contents. He tried to recall: an article from the *Times*, one of his father's incoherent essays ... Wasn't one a map?

Staring at the numbers, trying to recall.

Then it struck him. There was something

familiar about the numbers. What was it?

Colter Shaw sat upright. Was it possible?

*37, 63, 118 and 255* . . .

He rose and found his map of the Compound, the one LaDonna Standish had been looking over, on which he'd pointed out the climb he had planned when he visited his mother.

Spreading the unfolded chart in front of him, he ran his finger down the left side, then along the top. Longitude and latitude.

The coordinates, 37.63N and 118.255W, were smack on the middle of the Compound.

In fact they delineated a portion of the caves and forest on Echo Ridge.

The man of few smiles smiled now.

His father had hidden something there, obviously something important — worth dying for. And he'd left the envelope as a key to its whereabouts. The caves of Echo Ridge.

*Bears in the big ones, snakes in the smaller . . .*

The coordinates didn't pinpoint a very specific place; without other degrees in the numbers, they defined an area about the size of a suburban neighborhood. Even if Rodent and his crew made the deduction as to what the numbers represented — quite unlikely — they would never find what Ashton had hidden. Shaw could. He'd know the man's habits, his trails. His cleverness.

On his burner, he took a picture of the coordinates, encrypted the image, sent Mack and his former FBI agent friend, Tom Pepper, a copy, telling each to keep it safe.

Then he ripped the sheet from his notebook

and soaked it in the sink until it turned to pulp.

What did you hide, Ashton? What is this all about?

With his Colt Python in his jacket pocket, he opened another beer and, holding it in one hand and a bag of peanuts in the other, walked outside. Not in the mood for conversation from neighbors curious about the recent O.K. Corral scene at his camper, he carried a lawn chair to the back, set it down and dropped into it.

The chair was his favorite, upholstered in the finest of brown-and-yellow plastic strips, unreasonably comfortable. This spot in the RV camp offered a pleasant view: waving grass and what might pass for a stream meandering by on its way through never-sleeps Silicon Valley. He kicked his shoes off. The grass was spongy, the sound of the water seductive and the air rich with eucalyptus scent. If a crazy man with the face of a rat and an impressive Italian gun hadn't just threatened life and limb, Shaw might very well have spent the night in his sleeping bag here. Clearing the senses by passing dusk to dawn this way in the forest. Or riding a dirt bike at top speed. Or roped onto a ledge five hundred feet up a cliff face. These were perhaps acts of madness. To Colter Shaw, they were an occasional necessity.

Half a beer and thirteen peanuts later, his phone hummed.

'Teddy,' Shaw said. 'What're you doing up at this hour?'

'Velma couldn't sleep. Algo spotted something you might be interested in.'

'Hey, Colter.'

Shaw said to the woman, 'Mulliner'll start sending the checks in the next month or so.'

'Plural?' Velma said. 'Did I hear plural checks? You didn't do installments again?'

'He's good for it.'

Teddy said, 'Made the news here, even. Saving that pregnant lady. And you caught the Gamer to boot. Don't you just love the media, coming up with names like that?'

Shaw didn't tell him that the moniker had been invented not by a news anchor but by a diminutive police detective whose married name was derived from a Pilgrim — and a famous one at that.

'What've you got?' Shaw asked. Now that he knew his father's documents were smoke and mirrors, there was no reason to remain in the Bay Area.

Teddy asked, 'You inclined to go to Washington State?'

'Maybe.'

Velma said, 'Hate crime. A coupla kids went on a spree and painted swastikas on a synagogue and a coupla black churches. Set one church on fire. It wasn't empty. A janitor and a lay preacher ran out and got themselves shot up. Preacher'll be okay, the janitor's in intensive care. Might not wake up. The boys took off in a truck and haven't been seen since.'

'Who's the offeror?'

'Well now, Colter, that's what makes it interesting. You've got yourself a choice of two rewards. One's for fifty thousand — that's joint

473

state police and the town. The other's for nine hundred.'

'Not nine hundred thousand, I'm assuming.'

'You're a card, Colt,' Velma offered.

Shaw sipped more beer. 'Nine hundred. That's what one of the boy's families scraped together?'

'They're sure he didn't do it. The whole town thinks otherwise but Mom and Dad and Sis are sure he was kidnapped or forced to drive the getaway car. They want somebody to find him before the police or some civilian with a gun does.'

'I'm hearing something else,' Shaw said.

Teddy replied, 'We heard Dalton Crowe's going after it — the fifty K reward, of course.'

Crowe was a dour, hard-edged man, in his forties. He had grown up in Missouri and, after a stint in the Army, had opened a security business on the East Coast. He found that he too was restless by nature and closed the operation. He now worked as a freelance security consultant and mercenary. And, from time to time, he too sought rewards. Shaw knew this about him because the men had had several conversations over the years. Their paths had crossed in other ways, Crowe being responsible for the scar on Shaw's leg.

Their philosophies about the profession differed significantly. Crowe rarely went after missing persons; he sought only wanted criminals and escapees. If you gun down a fugitive using a legal weapon and in self-defense, you still get the reward. This was Crowe's preferred business model.

'Where're we talking?'

'Little town, Gig Harbor, near Tacoma. I'll send you the particulars, you want.'

'Do that.' Shaw added that he'd think about it, thanked them and disconnected.

He tucked in the earbud and called up a playlist of tunes by the acoustic guitarist Tommy Emmanuel on his music app.

A sip of beer. A handful of peanuts.

He was thinking of the options: the nine-hundred-dollar reward in Tacoma, Washington, for tracking down perpetrators of a hate crime. No, he reminded himself.

*Never judge without the facts . . .*

Two suspects who'd allegedly defaced religious buildings and shot two men. Maybe supremacists, maybe a love triangle, maybe a dare, maybe an innocent boy taken hostage by a guilty one, maybe a murder for hire under the guise of a different crime.

We've certainly seen that lately, haven't we?

The other option: Echo Ridge, searching for the secret treasure.

So. Gig Harbor? Or Echo Ridge?

Shaw took a quarter from his pocket, a fine disk, with its profile of greatness and its regal bird.

He flipped it into the air and it glistened as it spun, a sphere in the blue glow of the streetlight lording over Google Way.

In his mind Shaw called it: Heads, Echo Ridge. Tails, Gig Harbor.

By the time the silver disk came to rest in the sandy soil beside his lawn chair, though, Colter

Shaw didn't bother to look. He picked up the coin and pocketed it. He knew where he was going. The only things to figure out were what time he would leave in the morning and what was the most efficient route to get him to his destination.

# Author's Note

Writing a novel is, for me at least, never a one-person operation. I'd like to thank the following for their vital assistance in shaping this book into what you have just read: Mark Tavani, Tony Davis, Danielle Dieterich, Julie Reece Deaver, Jennifer Dolan and Madelyn Warcholik; and, on the other side of the Pond, Julia Wisdom, Finn Cotton and Anne O'Brien. And my deepest gratitude, as always, to Deborah Schneider.

For those who would like to learn more about the fascinating world of video gaming, you might want to take a look at these works: *Replay: The History of Video Games*, Tristan Donovan; *The Ultimate Guide to Video Game Writing and Design*, Flint Dille and John Zuur Platten; *The Video Game Debate*, Rachel Kowert and Thorsten Quandt; *A Brief History of Video Games*, Richard Stanton; *Game On!: Video Game History from Pong and Pac-Man to Mario, Minecraft, and More*, Dustin Hansen; *Blood, Sweat, and Pixels: The Triumphant, Turbulent Stories Behind How Video Games Are Made*, Jason Schreier; *Console Wars: Sega, Nintendo, and the Battle That Defined a Generation*, Blake J. Harris. You might also enjoy a novel by William Gibson (who coined the term *cyberspace*) and Bruce Sterling: *The Difference Engine*, which mixes fact and fiction in a tale about building a steam-powered computer in 1855.

Oh, and while you're at it, take a look at a thriller called *Roadside Crosses*, in which video games also figure prominently. One of the investigators actually analyzes the body language of an avatar in the game to get insights into a possible murderer. The author is some guy named Deaver.

We do hope that you have enjoyed reading this large print book.

Did you know that all of our titles are available for purchase?

We publish a wide range of high quality large print books including:
**Romances, Mysteries, Classics**
**General Fiction**
**Non Fiction and Westerns**

Special interest titles available in large print are:
**The Little Oxford Dictionary**
**Music Book**
**Song Book**
**Hymn Book**
**Service Book**

Also available from us courtesy of Oxford University Press:
**Young Readers' Dictionary**
**(large print edition)**
**Young Readers' Thesaurus**
**(large print edition)**

For further information or a free brochure, please contact us at:
**Ulverscroft Large Print Books Ltd.,**
**The Green, Bradgate Road, Anstey,**
**Leicester, LE7 7FU, England.**
**Tel:** (00 44) 0116 236 4325
**Fax:** (00 44) 0116 234 0205

*Other titles published by Ulverscroft:*

## SOLITUDE CREEK

### Jeffery Deaver

At a small club on the Monterey Peninsula, news of a fire sends panicked people running for the doors — only to find they are blocked. Half a dozen people die and others are seriously injured. But it is the panic and the stampede that kill; there is no fire . . . Busted back to rookie after losing her gun in an interrogation gone bad, California Bureau of Investigation Agent Kathryn Dance finds herself making routine insurance checks after the fire. But when the evidence at the club points to something more than a tragic accident, she isn't going to let protocol stop her doing everything in her power to take down the perp. Someone out there is using the panic of crowds to kill, and Dance must find out who, before he strikes again . . .

# CARTE BLANCHE

## Jeffery Deaver

Fresh from Afghanistan, James Bond has been recruited to a new agency. Conceived in the post-9/11 world, it operates independent of Five, Six and the MoD, its very existence deniable. Its aim: to protect the Realm, by any means necessary. The Night Action alert calls Bond from dinner with a beautiful woman. GCHQ has decrypted an electronic whisper about an attack scheduled for later in the week: casualties estimated in the thousands, British interests adversely affected. And 007 has been given *Carte Blanche* to do whatever it takes to fulfil his mission.

# EDGE

## Jeffery Deaver

In Washington, D.C., when Henry Loving targets police detective Ryan Kessler, the investigator and his family are immediately put under government protection. Loving is a ruthless 'lifter', hired to extract information from his victims. And he uses whatever means necessary, including kidnapping, torturing or killing their family. Corte is assigned to guard the Kesslers; an uncompromising officer devoted to protecting his charges. A brilliant game strategist, he knows how brutal the lifter can be — six years earlier, Loving killed someone close to him. The situation escalates into a deadly battle of wits between protector and lifter. But as the lifter closes in on his prey, will Corte protect his charges, or expose them to a killer in the name of personal revenge . . . ?